AWAKENING

AWAKENING

BOOK ONE OF THE BERSERKER CHRONICLES

KEVIN D. MILLER

BIFROST BOOKS

AWAKENING

Book One of the Berserker Chronicles

Copyright © 2020 Kevin D. Miller

Cover Copyright © 2020 Kevin D. Miller

Cover Art by Ryan T. Bittner

Cover Design by Edits By Stacey

Editing and Formatting by Stacey Smekofske at EditsByStacey.com

Map "Yggdrasil" Created by Colin McCrory: Special permission granted to use in the printing of this book.

Published by Bifrost Books

Paperback ISBN 978-1-7357066-0-3

Digital Book ISBN: 978-1-73557066-1-0

To my Mother, a warrior of no equal. Who fought day and night against cancer to the very end. Though I miss her every day, I know she is at peace within the Halls of Valhalla.

THE NINE REALMS OF
YGGDRASIL

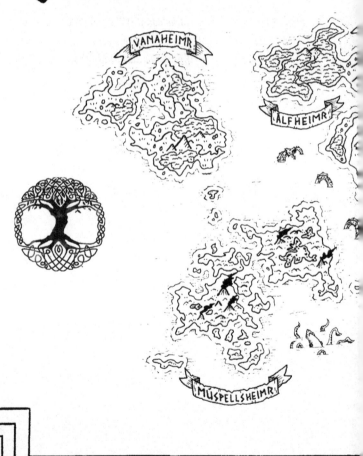

"Vincit qui se vincit"
    He who conquers, conquers himself.

— Publilius Syrus

PROLOGUE

Alexander never thought that he would live long enough to enjoy quiet nights like this. He noted it was a particularly cold night as he stepped onto his back porch. His breath sent out a little fog, and he marveled at how peaceful winter could be in the Icelandic forest. The freshly fallen snow sparkled as the Northern lights flashed through the night sky. Alexander never grew tired of watching their fiery dance. He only wished his wife, Helga, was still around to enjoy the peace and quiet. Sighing contentedly, Alexander reached down, grabbed a bundle of firewood, and turned to head back inside. Suddenly he froze. He felt it, a tingling he hadn't felt in a long time, danger. Scanning the surrounding forest, Alexander couldn't see anything out of place, but the feeling that something was out there, something that didn't belong, still pulled at him like the tide. Alexander stared into the darkness for a few more moments, but the forest remained silent, unwilling to give up its secrets. Alexander shrugged and went back into his house. For the first time in years, he locked the door behind him.

As Alexander sat by the fire, the warmth failed to chase away the feeling that someone or something was out there roaming his forest. A familiar howl rang out from deep within the forest, pulling Alexander out of his thoughts. A second later similar howls answered. Alexander could identify each individual wolf by their howl; he had known this pack for years. Settling back in his chair, he envisioned the wolves in full force. The howls continued to ring across the forest. In all his years living in the forest, Alexander had never heard so many wolves at once. They sounded agitated. *They must sense it too,* he thought. Alexander groaned as his knees popped and his old bones protested the sudden movement of getting to his feet. It was as if his body knew what he was planning to do and was voicing its discontent. It had been decades since he had been in a fight, but it seemed he was being called out one last time. *Hell,* Alexander thought, *I may see Helga sooner than I thought.*

Pulling on his thick wool parka, Alexander grabbed the double-bladed ax he used to chop wood. The weight felt comfortable in his hands. The ax had been his weapon of choice from the time he was strong enough to swing one. His mother had pushed him to branch out and learn to use other weapons, but it wasn't meant to be. The ax was the weapon of his ancestors, and he honored them by using it. The cold hit Alexander like a hammer, clearing his senses and waking him up to the world around him. The Berserker had laid dormant inside of him for decades now, but Alexander could feel the old battle lust stirring within. The forest had gone too quiet, the howls of the wolf pack had died down. Goosebumps speckled Alexander's body as the tension in the air thickened. Alexander knew why. A predator not of this realm stalked his forest.

Alexander silently crept through the forest. The snow crunched lightly beneath his weight; his senses screamed at him to turn back, but he ignored them and pressed on. It had been decades since he had felt the thrill of a fight, and he relished the feeling.

A bird pierced the silent forest with a loud squawk. He peered through the tangle of trees and branches; he could barely make out a blotch of darkness that seemed to be darker than the surrounding forest. As he moved closer, the air blew warm breaths on his face with each step. Alexander was within ten feet of the odd black blotch when he noticed that the snow had completely melted away. Steam rose from the freshly uncovered earth in a circle around the object. Thick drops of water splashed down from the tree branches above, puffing into steam upon hitting the forest floor.

Alexander continued to move slowly around the dark object but didn't see anyone or anything. Creeping ever closer, his feeling of unease intensified. As Alexander stepped around the inky darkness, the heat had him sweating through his clothes. He stopped dead in his tracks. His blood ran cold. From the back, the round black object drank in all the available light, but now that Alexander was in front of it, he could see it opened up to a world of fire and lava. Alexander knew what he was looking at; he just couldn't figure out why it was here. The dark blob was a bridge to another realm. However, it differed from any bridge he had used in his youth. This thing was more like a rip in the fabric of reality. Whoever did this was immensely powerful. Peering into the gateway, memories from a lifetime ago came flooding back to him. Muspelheim, the realm of fire and lava. The home to an unimaginable evil. It was a place he had hoped to never see again.

As if in answer to his thoughts, something rose out of the molten river that lay beyond the bridge. Alexander's stomach backflipped as he recognized the creature that was steadily stalking towards the bridge. *It's the beginning of the end*, Alexander thought. *Ragnarok is here.*

As the being stepped through the bridge and into Alexander's world, the frigid forest air hissed and steamed in protest to the fiery monster's trespass into Midgard. Alexander stared up at the molten giant and thought he looked even taller than he had appeared decades ago. Alexander backed up, making sure he was out of range of the monster's hulking sword. He knew a fight was inevitable. Alexander closed his eyes and freed the dormant Berserker, embracing the long-forgotten thrill of the fight. Icy fire burned along his veins as his muscles grew and strengthened. Alexander knew, even in his enhanced state, that he was no match for the force of nature that stood before him. He only hoped to fend the giant off long enough to create an opening and run for help. Hopefully, with luck, he could lose the creature in the forest.

Alexander opened his eyes, filling his old frame and flooding his veins with the familiar icy burn of the Berserker. Any thoughts of running vanished as a thin red haze of rage colored the edge of his vision. Fear and doubt evaporated and was replaced with excited determination at the chance to cross blades one last time with a worthy foe. *Who gives a damn that I'm well into my sixties?* Alexander thought.

"I am the last of an ancient and powerful Berserker clan, bestowed with the power of Thor, chosen to defend Midgard from invaders such as you. How dare you step into my realm, Surtr," Alexander growled. "You aren't welcome here. I will say this one time; return to Muspelheim or face my wrath."

Surtr's molten eyes studied Alexander. A voice Alexander had hoped to never hear again thundered in the clearing. The fire giant's voice washed over Alexander like an oncoming forest fire.

"You arrogant and foolish Midgardian. Do you have any idea who you are speaking to? Face your wrath? Don't think I don't remember you. You are one of the few beings who was lucky enough to escape me the first time we fought. You will not be so lucky this time. By Hel's will, I have been given a second chance to finish the fight you started many years ago."

"You think I'm afraid of you, giant?" Alexander boasted, "I have faced hundreds of enemies and killed them all. Last time we faced, we were in your realm, but now," Alexander gestured around. "You are far from Muspelheim. I have the advantage here."

Surtr laughed and pointed his massive sword at Alexander. "You truly don't know what I am, do you? I cannot be killed by the likes of you."

Surtr blurred, moving with a speed no normal human could track. But luckily for Alexander, he wasn't a normal human. This also wasn't his first fight. Alexander had been waiting for Surtr to make the first move and was ready for him. Surtr's burning blade slashed through the air mere centimeters from Alexander's face as he dodged out of range. A blast of scalding air washed over Alexander as Surtr's blade sliced through the air. Alexander rushed forward, relishing the speed his Berserker state granted him. Alexander hoped to throw Surtr off by attacking him head on. Slashing upward, Alexander attempted to split open Surtr's unarmored stomach. Before the ax hit, Surtr lashed out, kicking Alexander square in the chest, causing him to fly backward. He slammed into a tree trunk with a bone crunching crack. Alexander felt the ancient pine sway back and forth from the impact. Snow rained down from the branches above, pelting him in wet kisses. Alexander struggled to catch his breath. *Damn, that hurt. I can't afford to take too many hits like that,* Alexander thought. Struggling to his feet, Alexander felt every cell in his body struggle with the pain. He suspected a few of his ribs cracked, but nothing felt permanently damaged or out of place.

Luckily, years of training had taught Alexander to never let go of his weapon in a fight. Even in his old age, he still had the wherewithal to keep hold of it. Alexander used his ax as a crutch and looked up at Surtr. His enemy hadn't even bothered to follow up his attack; he just stood there studying Alexander.

"You've grown old, Berserker. You weren't a match for me decades ago. You certainly aren't one now."

Alexander eyed the giant, "Ha, I'm just warming up, Surtr. Before long I'll have you running back through that bridge, crying to whoever sent you here," Alexander boasted. However, deep down he knew he was finished. That kick had hurt him more than he cared to admit. His back was ablaze with pain and his legs felt like wet noodles. *I must have damaged my spine when I hit the tree*, Alexander thought. "This fight will be over before I get a chance to heal," Alexander grumbled.

Alexander eyed the fiery giant and quietly thanked the gods he had the foresight to leave a letter to his Berserker heir. He had wished he could have had more time with his daughter and grandson. He'd wanted to introduce them to the idea of realms, gods, and supernatural creatures slowly, but as with all great plans, it fell apart. Alexander could only hope they would find the journals.

There is no way this attack is random, Alexander thought. A being such as Surtr doesn't leave his realm unless provoked, and for a bridge to open right in his backyard, linking Muspelheim to Midgard–it was too much of a coincidence. The gods were moving against each other; he could feel it.

Wincing in pain, Alexander steeled himself.

Whispering reverently, Alexander breathed into the icy wind, "Odin, Allfather, my time on this mortal plain has come to an end. I, one of Thor's anointed, choose to die with an ax in hand, and can only hope to be welcomed into the halls of Valhalla." A raven cawed an answer to Alexander's prayer somewhere in the trees. Even though Surtr was far stronger than him, Alexander couldn't just roll over and die. That wasn't the Berserker way. Taking a deep breath, Alexander took a two-handed grip on his ax, feeling the smooth grip of the handle form perfectly to his weathered and calloused hands. He charged, bellowing a war cry. Surtr moved in as well, sensing the fight was coming to an end. Surtr brought down his massive sword in an attempt to split Alexander in two, but Alexander saw it coming and blocked the attack with his ax. Sparks flew in all directions as the two blades met. Alexander's ax blade chipped and bent along the edge where it met Surtr's sword, but that didn't faze Alexander.

Quick as lightning, Alexander swung for Surtr's outstretched forearm. Alexander thought he had scored a hit, but it merely bounced off Surtr's thick hide. Alexander, unwilling to relent, swung a horizontal slash meant to take the giant in the knee, but Surtr's burning blade materialized and Alexander's ax slammed edge first into the flat of Surtr's broadsword with a loud clang. The resulting tremor ran up Alexander's hand and arm, causing them to momentarily go numb. Dodging to the left, Alexander averted a savage punch aimed for his head.

Alexander ducked and dodged Surtr's onslaught. He never gave up, always looking for an opening to attack. Spinning the ax between attacks, Alexander continued to duck and dodge, waiting for the giant to make a mistake. Alexander knew he couldn't keep this up for much longer, but he couldn't waste his attack either.

Alexander backed away. Overconfident, Surtr grew bolder with each attack and was swinging wildly. Just as he had hoped, Alexander's opportunity came as he ducked under a slash meant to take his head off at the neck. Ducking under the smoldering blade, he stepped in as Surtr's blade slammed into an ancient pine tree. The force of Surtr's blow nearly cut the massive tree in half, but luckily for Alexander, the blade stopped three-fourths of the way through.

It only took him a second, but that was all the time Alexander needed. Alexander knew this was his only chance, and he swung with all his might. His blade hit Surtr in the stomach. Sparks fluttered to life as Alexander's ax impacted Surtr's hardened skin. A look of shock crept across Surtr's face; Alexander's blade carved out a shallow cut. Surtr blurred, attacking faster than Alexander thought possible. Not knowing where the attack was coming from, Alexander flung himself backward, but it wasn't fast enough. Surtr's blade buried itself deep into Alexander's right shoulder.

Alexander crumbled, falling to his knees as Surtr pulled the blade free in a spray of blood. Alexander's vision blurred. Through the pain, Alexander focused on a thin trickle of molten orange blood seeping out of the cut chiseled into Surtr. Surtr followed Alexander's gaze and looked down. He dabbed lightly at the bleeding wound.

In his grave voice, Surtr intoned, "You are the first to injure me in decades. Be proud as you go to your death." He heaved the sword above his head, "Give my regards to the Aesir. Their rule over the realms has ended. Ragnarok begins." Reverently, he brought his sword down for the killing blow.

Alexander, broken and bleeding, moved on reflex, brought up his ax in an overhead block, but it wasn't enough. Knowing that his time had finally come, Alexander hoped he had made his ancestors proud and that his family would be ready for what was to come. The Berserker mantle that he had held for so long would finally pass on.

A flutter of wings and a caw from the onlooking raven were the only sounds in the silent forest as Alexander slumped back, dead. Surtr took a long moment to stare down at his fallen foe before turning and disappearing through the bridge.

CHAPTER 1

"Can I have two shots of tequila and a Blue Moon?" a pretty girl yelled from across the packed bar. Her shoulder-length blonde hair set off her bright green eyes that gleamed through a pair of trendy glasses. She wore a low-cut blouse that increased her chances for attention. She batted her eyes a few times and leaned forward just enough to display an ample amount of cleavage. Leif was reminded of the many other struggling actors and actresses strewn across Los Angeles, out on the town, mingling with whoever they think can get them their next part in a T.V. show or movie. Leif just poured her drinks and moved on to the next thirsty customer. *It's sad really,* Leif thought. Not a night went by where the bar wasn't full of the young and hungry packed tight to drink away their Hollywood rejections.

Leif, on the other hand, didn't have dreams of making it big. Leif's sky-blue eyes complimented his six-one frame, but he wasn't into the Hollywood scene. Besides, Leif never had the ability to tan, so he was paler than the average Los Angeles resident. His pale Icelandic features and muscular build made him somewhat exotic in L.A. For the moment, he was content to tend the bar till the wee hours of the morning, meeting new and sometimes interesting people each night. Seeing them get smashed out of their minds was entertaining. The Slumbering Lion was the perfect place to do just that. Leif merely wanted to enjoy his twenties without worrying too much about a career, a mortgage, or having kids weigh him down. Leif had seen what high paying careers do to people. They suck the very life out of you, always demanding more. Leif's father was the perfect example. He had been an attorney to the core. Leif wondered whether his father cared about his job more than their family. His father would wake up early, come home late, and he always looked haggard. Leif didn't want any of that. So, he happily tended bar, night in, night out, making a good living off of wages and tips.

True to its name, The Slumbering Lion had a sleeping lion painted over its door with a few painted beer bottles scattered around it. The bar had a small patio area in the front to let smokers exhale their cares as they drank. Two red tinted windows flanked the front door. Edison lights dangled from black cords on the ceiling, giving off just enough light to see dark forms mingle across the bar. A large artificial palm tree lit the middle of the room with dim white lights curled around the trunk and branches. Low tables were spaced randomly around the room to give patrons the chance to get off their feet and chat with their friends. The bar rested against the far wall of the room, stationing Leif and Karina, his fellow barkeep and sometimes actress. Karina had moved to L.A. from London, and her accent drove the male customers wild.

As the night progressed, Leif got an odd prickly sensation at the base of his neck, like he was being watched. One might think that shouldn't be too odd. Leif was watched night after night by multiple people, all jockeying to be the next to be served. So, of course, people were watching Leif. But this felt different. Leif couldn't explain it. It was an itching sensation at the back of his neck. Every time he turned to grab a glass or drink from the illuminated shelf behind him, the sensation ran down his spine and gave him the shivers. In the nearly two years Leif had worked at the Slumbering Lion, he had experienced nothing like it.

The ding of the bell hanging near the bar signaled the last call, and the normal rush of customers moved in for their last drink orders. Leif made his way down the line, pouring shots, filling beers, and mixing cocktails. That's when a male customer caught his eye. Leif couldn't explain why he stopped to study the man. There wasn't anything particularly unusual about him. He was medium height, tan, well-muscled, and had black hair pulled back into a shoulder-length ponytail.

Leif could throw a penny in any direction in L.A. and it would probably bounce off someone that matched his description. The man's eyes made Leif pause. They were dark, almost black in the bar light. The stranger stood up and walked to the bar, sending a chill up Leif's spine. The man's movements were too precise, and his smile showed off too many teeth. An irrational urge to run welled up in Leif's stomach as he stared at the man. It was as if there was an aura of malevolence surrounding the stranger. As the man approached, he had said something, but Leif's mind went blank as he fought to suppress his fear. A vulpine grin split the man's face as if responding to Leif's uneasy feeling. "I'm sorry sir, what were you having again?" Leif asked, breaking the silence.

"I'll have an Old Fashioned," the man said, and even the sound of his voice set Leif's teeth on edge. When Leif turned to grab the whiskey, he again felt the strange prickling sensation. Leif made the mysterious man his drink and slid it over to him, all too happy to get away from him. "Thanks," the man said as he paid. Then he turned with his drink in hand and disappeared into the crowd. Leif couldn't pin down exactly what was off about the guy, but somehow, he knew deep down that he was dangerous. Trying to get the odd encounter out of his head, Leif turned back to the few remaining patrons waiting to get their drinks.

Leif chalked up the weird feeling and encounter with the stranger to be a combination of fatigue and the fact that there are just some downright weird people in LA. Leif closed up, did the usual chores with Karina, then locked the place up behind him.

Parking is difficult in LA, especially near the bars and nightclubs, so Leif usually called a cab or walked to work. It seemed like the perfect night for a walk. *After spending most of the night in a cramped bar, some fresh air would be nice,* Leif thought. It was a cool mid-March night with a light breeze. Leif popped in his headphones, turned up the volume, and lost himself in the rhythmic beats of "Our Time to Go" by State Champs.

After walking a few blocks, the joy from finishing a busy shift washed away and left Leif with a growing sense of exhaustion. Leif regretted not calling a cab, but he felt he had walked too far to call it quits. He was drained and just wanted to be home. He used a side alleyway shortcut he normally wouldn't take. Leif was by no means a small guy, but he still tried to avoid walking down dark alleyways at night. Anybody who watched crime dramas or horror movies knows to avoid them. Leif told himself to be a big boy and stop acting like a baby.

Halfway into the alleyway, Leif's vision suddenly tunneled, and a headache crept across his forehead. Leif had frequent headaches, so that wasn't unusual. He drank an excessive amount of caffeine to help him stay awake during his late-night shifts. That combined with a constant lack of sleep was a potent combination, so Leif didn't think much of the thumping pain. But after a few more steps the pain intensified, as if someone had reached into his brain and squeezed. Leif gasped and stumbled; the pain was almost too much to bear. Leif leaned against the wall and slid to the ground. A copper taste filled his mouth and a small dribble of something warm spread across his lips. With more effort than it should have taken, Leif reached up and dabbed at his mouth and nose. His fingers came away red with blood. The pain reached a crescendo and Leif passed out.

CHAPTER 2

Leif woke with a start to a sight so foreign he had to blink several times to believe it. He was looking at the back of a massive black furred wolf. It was sitting so close he could have reached out and touched it. Leif thought he was dreaming, but the pounding in his head told him otherwise. Leif closed his eyes and then opened them to confirm. Yes, there really was a wolf, an honest-to-god wolf in L.A., sitting not two feet from Leif, facing the street beyond the alleyway. Frozen with fear, he was at a loss what he should do. It was way bigger than any wolf he had seen at the zoo or on TV. He wanted to get up and run, but the image of him getting mauled kept him still. He hoped to not arouse the wolf's attention.

A low growl thundered from the wolf, and Leif painfully turned his head to look beyond the alleyway. Goosebumps erupted across Leif's body.

The strange man from the bar faced the alley from across the street. The fifty-foot distance didn't prevent Leif from feeling the man's black eyes bore into him. The wolf gave one more deep-throated growl that sounded more like a motorcycle revving its engine than a sound that came from a living creature. The threatening man took the hint and turned to leave, stuffing his hands into his pockets and whistling a tune Leif didn't recognize. Once the man was out of sight, the wolf turned and made eye contact with Leif for a brief second. Leif froze. He couldn't have moved if he wanted to. The wolf's yellow eyes locked onto his. It made a small chuffing noise, then stood up and disappeared down the alleyway. Leif, still rooted to the floor, let out a sigh of relief at not being eaten.

After a quick slap to check that he was actually alive, Leif used the wall to stand up. He stumbled a few feet as he felt all the blood rush to his head. Leif noticed two things immediately. First, his headache was gone. In fact, Leif felt surprisingly good. He felt like he could run a mile without breaking a sweat. Second, and by far one of the more shocking things he had seen tonight, the normal, black, starless sky above was replaced with a laser-like show that would put Las Vegas to shame. Green and yellow fire danced across the sky in an ever-changing pattern. After what could have been one minute or fifty, it dawned on Leif that he was staring at the aurora borealis. The northern lights were flashing above L.A.? "What the fuck?" Leif blew out. Whatever it was, Leif had a feeling it wasn't good. Tearing his gaze away from the lights above, Leif decided he should get home and behind a locked door before aliens came down from the sky or something else equally weird happened.

Running, he rounded the street corner to his apartment, sprinted the last hundred feet, and was up the stairs to the front door in a flash. He entered the code to the lobby of his apartment building, and a loud CAW-CCAAWW broke the silence, causing Leif to jump out of his skin. Quickly scanning the area, Leif spied two ravens perched on the telephone wire over his right shoulder. *Stupid ravens*, Leif thought as he struggled to reign in his out-of-control heartbeat.

After entering the code, Leif pulled the glass door open and stepped inside, double checking the front door to make sure it had closed all the way behind him. Leif walked over to the elevator and pushed the call button impatiently. Leif turned to look out the glass doors and could still see the two ravens perched on the wire outside, motionless. Leif got the distinct feeling the two birds were watching him. Suddenly, the elevator dinged, and Leif jumped in, not giving the ravens the chance to morph into a mutant of some kind. "I think I'm done with tonight," Leif said into the empty elevator.

Ten minutes later, Leif fell into bed. With his head propped up on a pillow, he stared out his bedroom window, watching the green and blue fire streak across the sky. Leif checked the news, Facebook, Instagram, and Twitter, but no one was talking about the sudden appearance of the aurora borealis. You would think when the sky suddenly lights up with vibrant waves of blues, greens, and yellows, the world would be abuzz with it. But no, not a single word. *Hell, maybe I hit my head when I passed out and now, I'm seeing things,* Leif thought. *Whatever is happening, it seems to be happening only to me.*

Leif laid in bed for a while, trying to sleep, but he was too amped from the nights' events. He jumped onto the internet and looked up giant wolves. Scrolling through the hits, Leif saw many scientific articles on wolf species, but nothing that seemed to match the beast he saw. Just when he was about to give up the search, he came across the reference to the Vargr on an obscure website. The site he was visiting was a conspiracy website, you know the type; forums on Bigfoot sightings or when the best time to visit Loch Ness is. One entry was about packs of massive wolves, or Vargr, killing hunters in a remote forest in Siberia. The author of the article was off his rocker, but the name Vargr sounded vaguely familiar. Leif had heard the name once before, a long time ago. If Leif remembered correctly, his Grandfather, Alexander, had mentioned them once when he was telling him stories as a kid.

There were hundreds of hits when Leif typed Vargr into Google. A lot of them were reference guides to tabletop games or characters in books. But after scrolling for a bit, Leif learned that Vargr were mentioned in Norse Mythology as being descendants of the Norse god, Fenrir. There wasn't much information on them, but what he found described them as larger than the average wolves with human-level intellect. They traveled between the realms hunting prey. Leif searched for a little while longer but wasn't able to learn anything more. Letting out a sigh, Leif finally felt the outer edges of exhaustion. He got up, brushed his teeth, washed his face with a warm washcloth, then laid down.

Leif's dreams were filled with giant wolves, snow packed forests, and Vikings battling supernatural creatures. In the throes of Leif's dream, a single figure stood out from the rest. He was always where the fighting was most savage. He towered above the rest, appearing to be a mountain of muscle, but he moved with the grace of a jungle cat. The man's eyes glowed, reminding Leif of two orbs of lightning. The battles were a savage melee of swords and axes, punctuated by fierce and sometimes inhuman battle cries and screams of pain. The dream felt as if he was in the thick of battle, fighting side by side and sometimes back to back with the brothers and sisters of his clan. During the skirmish, Leif suffered a knock to the head that caused him to wake with a start.

Drenched in sweat, Leif sat up, gasping. His sheets were twisted and soaked. He peeled himself out of bed and gulped down a few cups of water. "What the hell was that?" Leif asked the empty room. *I've always been an active dreamer*, Leif thought, *but it's never been like that*. Leif could still feel the icy air of the snowy forest, the worn leather grip of the twin axes in his hands, and the jarring impact each time he blocked or attacked. His entire body felt sore, like he had just worked out for three hours straight without taking a break. *What the hell is going on?* Sadly, the universe remained silent.

The clock above the stove told him it was 8:30 A.M. Leif knew there was no chance in hell he would get any more sleep. He pulled on workout pants and a running shirt and decided a long run could help clear his mind. Leif pulled the blinds open; the strange phenomenon in the sky was still present, though it was dimmed by the rising sun. Dancing greens, blues, and yellows traced through the sky. *Why am I the only one who can see it?* Leif wondered. Stepping outside, he took a deep breath to clear his mind. Putting in his wireless earphones, he turned the volume up and the electric beats of Deadmau5 filled Leif's psyche. Leif failed to notice the two ravens spread their wings and follow as he rounded the corner.

CHAPTER 3

Typically, Leif ran out of steam somewhere around forty-five minutes into his run, but today he felt great. He was light on his feet and didn't feel winded in the slightest. Back at his apartment, Leif took a long gulp of water from his insulated water bottle and headed toward the shower.

While walking to the shower, Leif unexpectedly stubbed his toe. The pain exploded across his foot and Leif's vision went red with rage. An icy fire shot through his veins, spreading throughout his body. Just as Leif felt he would lose it, the fiery wrath was gone. The pain in his little toe subsided and the blinding rage instantly vanished. Confused by what just happened, Leif looked down to examine his stubbed toe. But it was the sight of his dropped water bottle that caused Leif to stop in his tracks. The heavy metal bottle was crushed, as if it had been an aluminum Coke can. *How the hell did I manage that?* Leif thought. Goosebumps exploded across his body as his heart played the drum solo from Van Halen's "Hot for Teacher."

Something was happening to him, and Leif felt scared because he didn't know why he was changing. Not wanting to break anything else, Leif carefully set the crushed bottle on the nightstand and finished his trek to the shower. Waiting for the water to heat up, Leif ran his hands through his strawberry blonde hair; it was cut short and plastered to his head with sweat, sticking out at odd angles. Examining his muscular frame, Leif didn't appear any stronger than he was yesterday. Lifting his hands to his face, Leif flexed his fingers, open and closed. *How the hell did I crush that bottle? Adrenaline?* Leif was shaken but was also at a loss as to what to do. He hoped a warm shower and some coffee would clear his mind and make sense of what was happening.

LEIF HAD another closing shift at The Slumbering Lion. He changed into his work clothes and called a cab because he wasn't about to go walking around lest he stumble into another giant wolf. When he stepped out of his apartment's elevator and onto the street, Leif stopped in his tracks. The combination of the aurora borealis and the sunset was a breathtaking sight. The twisting cascade of reds, blues, and greens was mesmerizing. Leif pulled out his phone and snapped a picture, but when he looked at the photo all he could see was the orange light of sunset. Confused, Leif took another picture, but it was the same. Furrowing his brow, Leif reset his phone, then took another photo and still nothing. Now Leif was freaking out. *Why the hell can I see it, but it won't show up in a photo?* The impatient cabby's horn startled him from his trance. Shaking his head, Leif got into the cab and left for work.

Work was normal. Drinks were poured and people got drunk; it was a typical night at the Slumbering Lion. Leif received a call from an unknown number, but it was a busy night, so he screened the call and let it go to voicemail, then finished out the rest of his shift.

Back in his apartment, Leif changed his clothes and his stomach let out an earthquake of a rumble. *Damn!* Leif thought.

Dialing up a local pizza joint, he ordered a large meat lover's pie. When he hung up, Leif checked his voicemail. Remembering the missed call earlier and thinking it was a telemarketer, Leif came close to deleting the message without listening to it, but thought better of it and hit play.

"Hello, Mr. Auzoux. This is Officer Johnson from the Palm Desert Sheriff's Department. I regret to inform you that Shelby Auzoux was killed in the early hours of Saturday morning. What's more is we have received information that an Alexander Auzoux also passed early Saturday morning. I know this must…"

The phone made an audible cracking noise when it hit the floor. Suddenly feeling woozy, Leif tried to make it to his couch, but his legs gave out before he could make it and he ended up sprawled out in his tiny living room. His mind raced. *My mom and Grandpa, the only family I have left, are dead? No, this must be a mistake. They've got the wrong person. I just spoke to my mom earlier this week, and she was fine. She was planning on going to some knitting party or something like that with her friend Molly later this week. And Grandpa, he lives in Iceland. How the hell could they know he was dead?* Denial took hold of Leif as he recounted the impossibility of the situation. The continued denial brought strength back to his limbs and Leif grabbed his phone.

This just some sick joke, Leif thought. He dialed Officer Johnson's number. *I will get this cleared up, then give whoever's idea it was to mess with me a piece of my mind.* Leif tried to ignore the newly cracked screen as he pulled up the number. *Fuck, I'm going to make them pay for the repair*, he thought. Right before he hit the call button, Leif's intercom buzzed.

Leif vaguely remembered that he ordered a pizza. Pushing the receiver, Leif heard through the speaker, "Pizza man, can I come in?"

"Sure, come right up," Leif responded.

Leif pocketed his phone. The expected knock at his door came a few moments later. "Just a minute," Leif called out as he searched for his wallet and found it in his work pants. Leif was looking through his wallet for the right credit card when he stepped aside to allow the delivery guy in. He missed the wide grin on the man's face. Finally freeing the right card, Leif looked up and froze.

Leif took an involuntary step back as he stared into the hauntingly familiar black eyes of the strange man from the bar. The man brought his finger up to his lips and made a shushing sound as he closed and locked the door.

"What are you doing?" Leif demanded as he backed into his living room. The man's smile widened. In the full light, the man's eyes gleamed like polished obsidian. His canine teeth were a little too sharp to be human, but the real kicker was his ears. They poked out from under his hat and were pointier than a normal persons'. *Was it an elf? First wolves and now Elves? Maybe I am going crazy*, Leif thought. "Get the hell out of my apartment! If you don't leave right now, I'm going to call the cops," Leif blurted out.

"You don't need to involve the Midgardian law keepers. It would be unfortunate if you force me to kill more of your kind," the man purred.

Leif was pressed firmly against the kitchen bar that separated his living room from his kitchen. He had nowhere to go. "Who are you? Why are you following me, and what is a Midgardian?" Leif demanded.

The man placed the pizza box down on Leif's coffee table and opened it. The aroma filled the room, but instead of salivating, Leif's mouth went bone dry. The man reached down and took a slice.

"Grab a slice, Midgardian. There is no use for this to go to waste," he said, gesturing towards Leif with his free hand. His jacket opened ever so slightly, revealing the edge of the man's shirt. It was drenched in blood.

Leif's blood turned to ice.

The man noticed Leif's reaction, and he looked down, "Oops, yes. The delivery boy was disinclined to hand over the pizza and his jacket, so I was forced to show him the error of his ways." The man allowed a slight smile to grace his lips. He then reached into his jacket and unsheathed a curved knife that was easily eight to ten inches long. The blade gleamed in the light as he turned it this way and that. "It's really a shame when you think about it. Your kind really drew the cosmic short straw in almost every way. Your lives are short, your bodies are fragile, and the vast majority of your kind lacks the talent to manipulate the surrounding energies. In the grand scheme of things, it was probably best that the gods shut down the major bridges to this realm. Your kind would have most certainly been enslaved or killed off by your betters thousands of years ago. It's too bad that is all going to change."

"What?" Leif interjected.

"That isn't something you will need to worry about. I don't know what Hel has against you or your family, but she obviously sees you as a threat. So again, I say, sit down, enjoy a slice of pizza because pain and loneliness will be your only companion from here on out," the man said.

Leif was confused about absolutely everything the intruder had said. But once the man unsheathed his knife, a sudden rainstorm of sensations flooded Leif's mind. All of his anxiety drained away, and a white-hot rage filled the void left by his fear. A red fog began to form around the edges of his vision as an icy fire spread through his veins. His rage built, and hatred towards the man grew along with the fire in his veins. Leif felt as if he had downed a supernatural pre-workout energy drink. For lack of a better term, Leif felt invincible.

Leif instinctually pushed himself off the kitchen bar and sprinted towards the man. The intruder had just enough time to widen his eyes in surprise before Leif tackled him. Leif felt a sharp pain in his right shoulder but paid it no mind. The two rolled back and forth, struggling for control of the other and crashed into Leif's TV stand, causing the flat screen to topple onto the man's head. Caught by surprise, the man momentarily let go of Leif's arms, and Leif struck out, knocking the man and the fallen T.V. off of him and onto the couch behind them.

Leif stood and felt a twinge of pain in his shoulder. Looking down, he saw the handle of a knife had been jammed deep into his shoulder. Blood seeped from the wound, coating his shoulder in gore, and a small voice deep in Leif's conscious mind screamed in horror. A more primal and brutal part of Leif's mind howled in anger. Snarling, Leif effortlessly pulled the knife out. Knife in hand, Leif advanced on the intruder. The arrogant smile vanished as the man leaped up and desperately looked around for a weapon. Finding none, he bared his teeth and charged towards Leif. It was clear he was a skilled fighter, but Leif in his enraged state didn't care. The man was fast, and Leif was pummeled left and right. Leif managed to block one or two of the man's attacks, but most got past Leif's feeble defenses. Leif occasionally lashed out with the stolen knife, but it was no use. Growing frustrated, Leif threw the knife, but the man easily dodged to the side and rushed forward. The man attempted to kick Leif, but his leg bumped against the coffee table and threw him off balance. Leif's rage-fueled mind knew he was no match for the man, so he simply tackled his foe to the floor. The two crashed to the ground with Leif landing on top. The man's breath exploded as he grunted in pain. Leif followed up with hammer blows as he pinned the man to the ground. The pure ferocity of Leif's attack batted aside any attempts by the man to block or strike back. Leif's fist connected with the man's face time and time again, bouncing his head off of the hardwood floor in rhythm: thump, thump, thump, thump. Blood misted the walls with each of Leif's punches, coating the wall and staining the nearby couch red. The man's hands flung out wide, searching for anything to attack Leif with. The man's right hand bumped the handle of his lost knife.

If Leif hadn't been in such a fury, he would have seen the man grab the knife and plunge it into his side. Leif roared; the pain enraging him further. Ignoring the knife, Leif took a firm grip around his attacker's throat and squeezed. He continued to squeeze until he heard an audible pop in his attacker's neck. The man went limp.

Panting and bleeding, Leif fell back. The knife was still firmly planted in his side. His attacker was dead; the red fog of rage receded, and conscious thought took control again. Leif did not understand where the all-consuming rage had come from, but as it faded, the pain of his wounds took its place.

Leif's left eye was swollen shut, and he could barely see out of his right eye. The deep gash in his shoulder was bleeding profusely, and he could hardly feel his right arm. His knife-penetrated side burned like fire. He dared not touch it. A curtain of warm blood oozed down Leif's arms and torso. He struggled to reach for his phone, but his arms and body felt strangely heavy. A moment later Leif blacked out. He slumped to the floor beneath the hand-shaped cracks indented into his countertop.

CHAPTER 4

Leif woke to someone poking and prodding his shoulder. Everything that had happened in his apartment came rushing back to him in an instant, and he opened his eyes in a panic. It was clear he wasn't in his apartment, which caused even more panic.

"Wooh, ooh, there Mr. Auzoux. It's ok. You're safe now," a soft voice soothed.

The familiar sounds of a hospital beeped and hummed into his brain. Leif tried to sit up, but pain exploded in his side and he collapsed back down with a groan. Leif noticed a doctor studying him intently. She was short, not much taller than five feet. She had shoulder length raven black hair. Her hair framed her kind, dark chocolate eyes.

"It's probably best that you remain laying down Mr. Auzoux. Let me introduce myself. I'm Doctor Wong, and I run the trauma unit at St. Gabriel's Hospital. You were brought in unconscious and suffering from several grievous wounds last night. Luckily for you, none of them appeared to be life-threatening. I was actually just reviewing your charts, and incredibly, many of your wounds have already begun healing. It's something of a medical miracle if you ask me. Much of the bruising and swelling you had last night is already gone. The cuts to your shoulder and side were deep but missed vital organs. We had to stitch those areas, but even they appear to be healing at an exponential rate."

"To be quite honest, I have never seen anything like this before. If you don't mind me asking, have you always healed so fast? Are you taking any supplements that may aid in healing?" Doctor Wong asked with a twinkle of excitement in her eyes.

Leif felt a little groggy and was probably a little high from whatever pain medication they were pumping into him. He took a few seconds to respond, "Um, no. I don't think so. To be honest, a few days ago I blacked out, and ever since then, weird things have been around and happening to me," Leif confessed.

"Hmmm," Doctor Wong murmured as she wrote something down on her clipboard. "Ok, Mr. Auzoux, I want you to rest. There is an officer waiting outside who wants to speak with you. I had requested that he come back later so you could rest and recover, but he was insistent that he speak with you the moment you were conscious. If at any time you feel overwhelmed or need a break, please push the red button by your head, and I will come in and make him leave, got that?"

"Thanks, Doc," Leif mumbled nervously. Butterflies began playing the bongo in his stomach at the prospect of being interrogated by a police officer. Doctor Wong walked to the door, gestured to someone at the side and left.

An officer in the typical blue uniform walked in after her. He was of average height, had buzzed brown hair that was graying a little at the temples, and he looked to have a permanent scowl.

"Good evening. I'm Officer Behrens of the L.A.P.D.," he said. "I know you went through a lot in the last couple of days, but there are still a few details that we need to go over before we clear you, is that ok?" There was something in his tone that set Leif on edge.

"Um, sure. Am I under arrest or something? Because that psycho attacked me," Leif's voice rose a little with the possibility of being arrested and prosecuted for murder. The heart monitor to Leif's left beeped faster.

Officer Behrens glanced at the monitor and made a calming gesture with his hands. "Leif, may I call you Leif?" he asked.

"Sure," Leif said.

"Let me ease your mind a little. We reviewed surveillance camera in the alleyway just north of your apartment, and it captured the suspect attacking and killing the poor pizza delivery boy. It also captured the man as he donned his clothes. We just want to know why and what happened between his killing of the pizza boy and us getting to your apartment," The officer's voice trailed off slightly, which caused Leif to look up sharply.

"Is there something else?" Leif asked.

"Mr. Auzoux, if you don't mind, could we discuss your attack first? Also, as we talk, if you don't mind, I would like to record our interview. It helps me write my report later."

Leif noted the name change, but he was too tired to push it. Leif nodded, and the officer pulled out a small handheld recorder and set it on the table next to Leif's bed.

Leif went over the attack with the officer from opening the door, to what his attacker said and the fight that ultimately ended with Leif killing the man. Leif left out the Midgardian stuff, his attacker's weird inhuman appearance, and the blinding rage and invincible feeling that Leif experienced.

"Ok, Leif. It's a clear case of self-defense. Do you have any idea why this man was trying to kill you? The suspect came after you specifically. You said he mentioned someone by the name of Hel, I believe it was?" Officer Behrens said as he referenced his notes.

"Honestly, no. I don't know anyone by that name, but I had seen my attacker twice before," Leif said. The officer's head popped up from writing on his little notepad and he gestured for Leif to continue.

"Well, a couple nights ago, I think it was Friday night-God, it feels so long ago now. I was bartending at the Slumbering Lion when my attacker came up and ordered a drink around last call."

"Why did he stick out to you? You probably serve hundreds of people a night."

"There was just something off about him," Leif stated. "I wish I could say it better, but that's really it. Nothing out of the ordinary happened when he ordered. There was just something off about the encounter. I remember getting the chills while I spoke to him."

"Ok," Officer Behrens said. "That's perfectly understandable. So, you said you came across this man twice. When was the second time?" Officer Behrens asked.

"The second time was later that night, or early the next morning, really. I had decided to walk home and get some fresh air. When I got close to home, I took a shortcut through an alleyway near my apartment, and when I was about halfway into the alley, I felt sick and blacked out for a few moments. At least I think it was a few moments. When I came to, I saw the man was there across the street, staring right at me. When he saw that I noticed him, he turned and walked out of sight." *Well, there was also a massive fucking wolf there too. But there's no way in hell I'm telling the officer that,* Leif thought.

"And that's it," Leif continued. "I didn't see him again until he was in my apartment spouting nonsense and trying to kill me."

"Ok," the officer said. "And there isn't anyone you could think of that has a grudge against you or your family?"

"N…" Leif trailed off before finishing. There was something tugging at the edges of his morphine fogged mind. Something important that he was forgetting. Then it hit him like a steamroller. *My Mom and Grandfather had been killed. And then I was attacked!*

As the fog of the call from Deputy Johnson cleared, the heart rate monitor spiked, causing Officer Behrens to look up, then back towards Leif with an arched eyebrow. Leif's vision blurred, and a hollowness settled into his stomach. Tears began streaming down his cheeks as realization set in that the earlier call hadn't been a mistake. "I, um," Leif faltered, then took a breath and began again. "I don't know of anyone that has a grudge against my family, but um, right before my attack, I got a call from a Deputy from Palm Desert."

Gesturing towards a chair next to Leif's bed, the officer asked if he could take a seat, and Leif nodded. With a heavy sigh, Officer Behrens looked Leif right in the eye.

"Just before we answered the disturbance call at your apartment, I was speaking with a Deputy Johnson from the Palm Desert Sheriff's station. He told me he had been trying to get a hold of you, but you weren't calling him back. He contacted our department to have us do a wellness check. I was the lucky officer to be at my desk, so I took the call. Then out of nowhere, I hear dispatch say your name. Worrying it was all connected, I rushed over. But by the time I got there, you were already being loaded into the ambulance. Deputy Johnson confirmed to me that both your mother and grandfather were killed. I know it's difficult, but I need you to dig deep and try to think who could be behind this. All three of you live very far apart. Which means whoever is behind this has considerable resources at their disposal. I can't imagine they will give up on you just because you survived the first attempt."

As the words sank in, the world around Leif disappeared. He no longer heard the gentle beeping background noise of the busy hospital. Leif's mind went blank as the words echoed through his numb mind. Leif registered that the officer had continued to speak to him, but he wasn't up to talking anymore. His insides had been ripped open, then hollowed out. It was as if his mind had switched to autopilot, answering the officer's questions in simple yeses or nos. After twenty or so minutes, the officer left Leif to his grief. He rolled over and cried himself back to sleep.

LEIF LEFT the hospital a day later to the wide-eyed astonishment of Doctor Wong. He was completely healed. The knife wounds to his shoulder and stomach had disappeared and were replaced with angry red scars. Leif could tell Doctor Wong wanted him to stay longer, but according to the tests, Leif was as healthy as any person could be.

Hailing a taxi, Leif headed home. After another random bout of insufferable sadness and a crying spell, it dawned on him that it would be up to him to plan the funerals. He was the last Auzoux. Leif didn't have any cousins or relatives that he was aware of.

As much as Leif dreaded the funeral planning, he quickly learned that having something to do helped ease the ache in his heart. Leif called Deputy Johnson back and suffered the same round of questions he got from Officer Behrens.

It felt like deja vu. He wondered if all law enforcement worked off the same script when investigating similar crimes. After what felt like hours talking with the deputy, Leif hung up with promises that he would be down to make arrangement for the transportation of his mother's body.

Leif decided he would hold both funerals in Iceland. His mother had come to the states for college, then fell in love with his father and never left. However, she never lost her connection to her homeland, keeping in touch with many of her childhood friends there. It was also where her mother was buried. It made sense to bury her there.

The following weeks flew by in a blur. Leif had a few more episodes of blinding rage that he couldn't quite explain, but a bent steering wheel and a few holes in his apartment wall were the only consequences. Leif really couldn't explain where the anger and newfound strength was coming from. He had always been a pretty mellow person, but now, even small things made him see red.

Leif eventually chalked it up to grief and tried to get past it. Leif had arranged for his flight and the transportation of his mother's body. He had a church already set up for the funerals. After hearing what happened to him, the manager at the Slumbering Lion was extremely understanding, and he had even hired a few extra security guards to escort his employees to their cars after their shifts.

When the news of his attack and the death of his two other family members broke, Leif had been assaulted with phone calls. At first he felt grateful for the calls. It showed the tragedy that struck him, and his family didn't go unnoticed in the community, and that they wanted to solve the mystery of his family's murder just as much as he did. But after the first few interviews, it became clear to Leif that all the reporters wanted was the next big headline. When he couldn't provide the answers they wanted, they started to take large leaps in facts. One reporter insinuated that Leif killed them both for some unknown inheritance. When questioned about it, Leif's vision went red and he slammed his fists into the coffee table, shattering it into a million pieces. Before Leif's rage took completely over, the reporter fled the coffee shop. After that, Leif stopped accepting reporters' calls and emails. He even deleted his Facebook and Instagram accounts. He didn't need the distraction as he searched for answers.

Leif sat in traffic on the 405 thinking it will be good to get away from Los Angeles for a few days. He had been lucky with his flight, booking it at a time that bypassed the rush hour that plagued all Angelenos.

Once he got to LAX, he pulled his luggage from his car and was surprised to hear a caw-caw above. Two ravens stood at the edge of the departing terminal. *That's odd*, he thought. *You don't typically see birds near airports.* Death by propeller or jet engine is a pretty strong deterrent. Leif could swear the two birds were looking directly at him. More than a little unnerved, he closed the trunk as the birds cawed a few times at each other and flew out of Leif's view.

CHAPTER 5

BOOM BOOM! Leif lurched awake to the plane touching down in Reykjavik, Iceland's capital. *Thank God*, Leif thought. *I slept the entire flight.*

Leif disembarked, starving. He'd slept through the meal service, so he grabbed a quick bite at Mathús House of Food. While scarfing down a burger, he rushed to pick up his luggage at baggage claim. After the headache of renting the car, Leif pulled his jacket tight and stepped out into the Icelandic air where he stopped dead in his tracks. A large cloud of frost puffed out of his whispered "Wow," marveling at the beauty before him.

Over the past few weeks, Leif had gotten used to the strange light show flickering over the Los Angeles sky. But the dancing lights of green, blue and yellow Leif had watched in L.A. were intensified here. Beautiful felt like a poor description. Leif had spent hours researching strange lights in the sky on the internet but couldn't find any references to what he had been seeing and he feared if he brought it up to anyone, they would lock him up or want to run several tests to see what was wrong.

Forgetting the frigid weather, Leif gazed wide-eyed up at the sky as the colorful phenomenon flickered back and forth across the sky in mesmerizing patterns. Shaking himself out of the daze, he grabbed his luggage and walked through the rental agency's parking lot. Of course, his car was parked in the furthest spot.

Leif didn't understand a lick of Icelandic, but luckily, he didn't need to with G.P.S. It had been years since Leif had been in Iceland, and despite the unfortunate circumstances of his return, it still felt good to be back. Leif felt a little sluggish from jumping so many time zones at once, so he rolled down his windows, enjoying the fresh freezing air blowing across his face.

Leif loved living in L.A., but driving through a forest of ancient pine trees freed him. *I can almost forget all the worries of my life back in the states... almost,* Leif thought.

Leif didn't understand why the multi-colored aurora appeared to only him, but he truly wished he could show others the amazing spectacle. The blues and greens flashing across the backdrop of the dark and ancient forest mesmerized him. The fire dancing in the sky cast shadows, allowing Leif to glimpse figures moving through the forest. When the aurora flickered, they were gone. The shadows were much too big to be wolves. Leif suspected they were of the same species as the Vargr. The thought of wolves the size of horse keeping pace with his car caused Leif to drive a little faster. *God forbid I get lost or pop a tire. I doubt I could fend them off if it came down to a fight,* Leif thought.

Turning off the highway, Leif drove through the rocky side road that led to his grandfather's cabin. The narrow, tree-lined road made Leif feel as if the trees were pressing in on him, trapping him in this ancient forest with no way out. Leif swept his head from side to side and saw the ghostly green and blue flashes reflecting off the snow-covered road. After what felt like an eternity, he emerged from the forest into a familiar clearing that led to a lonely log cabin in a sea of trees. Images of his childhood flickered through his mind, just like the aurora above. Memories of running through the clearing flashed across his mind. He remembered pretending to be a warrior, fighting off hordes of rival Viking clans, playing hide and seek with his grandma, and snowshoeing through the forest with his grandpa as he related old Norse myths or taught Leif about the forest plants and animals. The place had always been warm and welcoming to Leif, but the cabin took on an air of sadness in its current state.

The exterior of the cabin reminded Leif of those iconic wood cabins you might see in Big Bear or Tahoe. It was two stories with two windows on the top floor, giving you a beautiful view of the forest and mountains surrounding the cabin. A wrap-around porch hugged the exterior. The table his grandpa had carved from a fallen tree sat lonely and blanketed in snow in one corner. Two rocking chairs, both missing their occupants, sat in the other. Three stairs led up to the big weather-worn crimson door where a bronzed wolf's head knocker hung in the center. When Leif was younger, he had thought the knocker was cool and had frequently asked his mom if they could get one for their front door back in the states, but she always refused.

Leif had always loved visiting his grandfather's house. The old, deep-red, burnished wood ran through the floors and walls, while a faded blue and red patterned carpet blanketed the living room and study. One of Leif's favorite attributes of the house was the myriad of paintings depicting Norse gods and battles. They were proudly displayed throughout the entire house. Leif's grandfather's baritone Icelandic accent echoed from beyond, retelling the Viking-age epics and myths, like "The Curse of Andvari's Ring" or Leif's personal favorite, "The Theft of Thor's Hammer." They would sit in his leather armchair, and his grandfather would read to Leif for hours.

Leif stood in the doorway and felt empty of those warm feelings. The cabin felt barren, as if the very life of the place had been extinguished with his grandfather's murder. He ghosted through the vacant house on silent feet, pausing at the doorway to his grandfather's small study. The door was open, but the darkness beyond veiled his favorite childhood hangout spot. "God," Leif exhaled. The room was a husk of what it used to be. Leif chose to leave his memory of the room intact a little longer and shut the door. He knew he would have to face the room in the coming days, but not today. *Let the memories rest for one more day*, Leif thought as he moved to the master bedroom.

Leif made his way up the stairs and listened to the memorable creak of the fifth step on the old wooden staircase. The familiar mixture of paintings and family photos lined the upstairs hallways. Leif passed the guest room and stepped into the master bedroom. With both his mother and grandfather gone, Leif found little reason why he shouldn't sleep here. The room smelled like the forest. Two massive windows looked out to the backyard and into the snowy forest beyond. A writing desk waited patiently for its owner with countless trinkets and writing utensils strewn across the wood surface. There were no paintings or photos in this room. Leif had always found the lack of wall decor odd and had meant to ask his grandfather about it.

Tears Leif didn't know he was holding back spilled down his cheeks at the thought. He wanted to rage at the unfairness of it all. To swear that whoever murdered his mother and grandfather would pay for what they had done, but Leif knew that it was useless. The police, Icelandic and American, had no leads, no prints, nothing. Moments when he brooded over the lack of evidence, the edges of his vision would take on the tinge of scarlet and then the anger would set in. It always ended in the same way. He would black out and then wake exhausted; everything around would be destroyed. Leif had chalked the episodes up to grief and had since vowed to keep his cool, lest he accidentally hurt someone else during one of these episodes.

Surrounded by items that reminded him of his mother and grandfather, Leif was awash in grief. *Why did I survive while they didn't?* Leif's mind fell into a tailspin of misery and survivor's remorse. His mental levee was broken; physical and mental exhaustion washed over him. All he could manage was a stumbling shuffle to the bed. He collapsed and was asleep before his head hit the pillow.

CHAPTER 6

Leif took in his surroundings and admired the frost that bloomed in the air. Battle cries and the screams of the dying echoed around him in the primeval forest. The battle ignored the dead and dying and raged on. Several of his clan's warriors surrounded Leif as they regrouped for another push. All of them were bloodied in one way or another, but none showed any sign of fear. Leif was proud. His clan was known for their ferocity, and after tonight, no one would doubt it. An inhuman bellow shook the forest in front of Leif, and his lips split into a wide grin.

"The gods smile upon us tonight. They have blessed us with a worthy foe." Raising his ax high in the air, Leif continued, "Let us show them that Midgardians are not to be fucked with! Whether in Valhalla or on Midgard, we shall toast to battles fought and enemies vanquished!" A cheer erupted amongst his clansman and Leif met it with his own. Lowering his arm, Leif banged his twin axes together, and his men quickly mirrored the gesture. The beat intensified as their bloodlust grew. Then, with a final shout, he and his men sprinted for the trees and their enemies beyond.

The darkness of the trees beyond cleared, and Leif ran to meet his waiting enemy. At the sight of his foe, his adrenaline spiked, washing away any remnant of battle fatigue. The monsters smiled and burst into motion, eager to meet the oncoming warriors. Leif's eyes were drawn to the giant directly in front of him. Its humanoid shape stood eight feet tall. His skin was tinged with a blue hue and was corded with muscle from head to toe. The giant's head was bald and had a long black beard that was split into three braids, hanging down from its chin. Over his broad, bare torso lay a single chest and shoulder plate made of a metal so black, it seemed to drink in the meager light around them. The giant's blood-red eyes glowed with a faint inner light that surveyed the battlefield around him and then locked onto Leif. Then, with one well-muscled arm, he reached back over its head and unlatched a double-bladed ax, taking it in a two-handed grip. The giant opened its mouth and bellowed a war cry so loud snow fell from the surrounding trees. A second later, similar war cries could be heard up and down the tree line as more giants stepped out of the darkness.

The creatures emerged carrying massive axes and swords. They too wore little to no armor. Some giants appeared to have twisted tattoos that ran up and down their muscled bodies while others were covered in ritualistic scars. Others stepped out from the shadows and glided into position. These beings looked more human than their companions. But they moved with a grace that no human could match. These newcomers were much shorter than their blue allies, closer to the size of a human, but Leif could tell even from where he ran that they were not human. Their eyes were jet black, and the tips of their ears were pointed. *Fucking great,* Leif thought. *Not only do we have to deal with these giants, but Dokkalfar as well. No matter,* Leif thought. Even if Hel, the goddess of the underworld, were to step out from the forest and join the invasion. It wouldn't make a difference. The clans would fight and die to protect Midgard.

Mere feet away, the giant was smiling and swinging its ax overhead. Leif was instantly on him, rolling to the left as the giant brought down its ax in a two-handed blow that was meant to split Leif in half. Snow and dirt exploded from where the ax hit the forest floor. Leif struck out with the ax in his left hand, aiming for the giant's muscular forearm and hoping to disable the thing before it could pick the ax back up. But the giant surprised him. It blurred, and a shower of sparks bloomed as Leif's ax collided with the handle of the giant's ax. A deep laugh escaped the giant's throat as it raised its hand and backhanded Leif in the chest. Leif flew backward, landing in a heap six feet away in the snow. Leif shook his head. His vision returned and was filled with the sight of a giant ax rushing towards him.

Not having time to roll away, Leif lifted and crossed his axes just in time to block the oncoming attack. The clang that rang out from the colliding blades nearly deafened him. The giant's red eyes widened in surprise. Leif's triceps screamed in protest as he pushed against the overwhelming strength of the giant. Knowing he had no chance of pushing the giant's blade away, but not wanting to give up, Leif dug deep. With his back pressed against the icy forest floor, he let out a roar of defiance. Leif pushed and rolled to his side. The giant's ax hit the ground with a thud a fraction of a second later. Leif scrambled to his feet, just in time to duck under a punch meant for his head. He struck out with his right arm and scored a long slice through the giant's muscled forearm. The giant bellowed in pain.

Putting some distance between the two, Leif noticed the giant studying him. *Yeah, that's right, asshole,* Leif thought. *I'm not some chump who you can run through. I will make you work for it.* The giant seemed to come to the same conclusion. It sashayed back to where his ax lay and picked it up; his eyes never left Leif's. It again took the ax in a two-handed grip, then nodded towards Leif. Leif twirled his twin axes once, speckling blue-black blood on the forest floor, then he nodded in return. After a brief breath passed between the two warriors, they moved. Metal flashed in the moonlight. Leif was ready for the giant this time. He did not commit too early or put too much power behind any one attack.

If he wanted to live through this fight, he would have to remain nimble and hope to catch the giant unaware. The two danced back and forth, trading blows as they moved around the battlefield. Nothing mattered except defeating the giant. Leif scored a cut across the giant's chest and thigh, but suffered several cuts in return; for now, none were life-threatening. Leif was in a groove, and he could feel the pattern of his opponent's attacks. His body instinctively moved with each sway and bob. A duck here, parry there, a step to the left to avoid losing his arm at the shoulder. Then time slowed as the moment he had been waiting for arrived.

The giant grew frustrated and over-committed on a strike. The giant stepped just a fraction of an inch too far and aimed to cut Leif's leg off at the thigh with a wildly overpowered slash. The miscalculation caused the giant to leave his right side open to attack for the briefest of moments. Leif kicked the giant in the overextended knee, causing him to fall off balance. There was no time to recover. The giant's blood-red eyes widened as he realized his mistake too late. Leif's left hand was already descending with ax in hand. He felt the sting of the impact as his ax struck true, shearing through muscle and bone of the giant's massive neck. Blood coated Leif as the giant dropped to the ground, headless. The sound of the battle raging around him returned, and Leif heard heavy footsteps. Before he could turn, he was tackled to the ground, hitting his head on a rock.

LEIF SHOT up in his bed with a start. He looked around wildly. *Where am I?* Leif thought. After a few panicked seconds, Leif remembered he was in his grandfather's house in Iceland. He wiped his forehead; it was slick with sweat. *What the hell was that?*

Leif thought as he struggled to slow his racing heart. His body ached all over. His legs burned with exhaustion, and a few spots on his arms felt tender to the touch, as if he had been punched repeatably. Knowing there was no chance of going back to sleep, Leif stood up and walked to the window. The sky was slowly brightening at the horizon. The ever-present aurora was streaking across the sky, snaking this way and that in the early dawn light. Leif felt reassured knowing that the mysterious sky fire would still be out there dancing across the blue sky, even when the sun dimmed the brilliance. Leif marveled at how accustomed he had become to the phenomenon. Leif leaned against the windowsill, and suddenly his whole back screamed in protest as pain flared across it.

"Fuck!" Leif yelled. "That shit hurts! Why do I feel this way? It was just a dream, wasn't it? There's no way I was actually fighting that blue giant, right?" A creak from the empty house was the only answer he got. "I really wish I knew what was happening to me," Leif said for what felt like the thousandth time.

Leif turned away from the window to head to the shower, but a wolf's howl pierced the silence, pulling him back. The howl went on unnaturally long and reached its crescendo; chills exploded across Leif's body. The silence that followed weighed heavily on Leif as he turned to go.

CHAPTER 7

Leif drank some coffee to clear his mind of that dream. He had planned to sleep off much of the jet lag during the day to be fresh for the funeral, but there was no way he would be able to fall back asleep.

Leif decided he would explore the house for a bit. A message from Helga, one of his grandfather's friends in town, let him know that all the arrangements for the double funeral were arranged, and that it scheduled for that night at 5 P.M. Leif felt an invisible weight lift from his shoulders. Knowing his mother and grandfather's funeral preparations were finalized was a tremendous relief. His grandfather's friends had been happy to take over once they learned of Leif's attack and subsequent hospitalization. They assured him all he would need to do was show up. Some of his mother's friends weren't too happy about the funeral taking place in Iceland; many couldn't make the trip, but Leif calmed them down by assuring them he would hold a wake for her once he was back in the states.

Leif walked through the silent halls of his grandfather's house, admiring the artwork until he found himself in front of the study. He opened the door and echoes of the countless hours spent in the room flashed through his mind. The sunlight drifted in from the open window against one wall, giving Leif a full view of the room. When he was a child, the room felt enormous, but now he felt his frame fill the room more fully.

A floor to ceiling bookshelf spanned two full walls. On one wall the shelves were packed full of books on Norwegian, Icelandic, Swedish, and Danish history. The other wall was filled with books on mythology and legends. Interspersed between the books on several of the shelves were photos of the family, an ornately carved hatchet, and a few Viking-age coins. A writing desk made of deep mahogany was nestled in one corner with a simple lamp that sat to one side. A framed tattered flag emblazoned with the family crest hung behind the desk. The crest included a midnight black wolf in mid-howl, crossed by two single bladed axes. Spanning the rest of the wall was a large oil painting depicting an epic battle. It had always been his favorite. The detail in the painting was truly amazing. Leif used to love picking out all the minor details in it. The large snow-covered pine trees towered over the forest floor, and if you looked close enough, you could spot an owl hidden amongst the trees, silently staring back at you. On the forest floor, Viking warriors covered in wolf and bear furs and leather armor could be seen interspersed between the trees, frozen in battle. Leif had spent hours as a kid imagining himself in the midst of that epic scene; as the haze slowly lifted from last night's dream, it felt eerily familiar.

Peeling himself away from the painting, Leif approached the neatly organized desk. The wooden chair creaked as Leif sat down. Everything in the house was essentially his now, so he didn't feel intrusive needling through the belongings, but he felt timid about it. He began slowly going through the drawers. Nothing stood out as important. The drawers were filled with pens, papers, and old bills. As Leif closed the top left drawer a slight thumbnail indent at the bottom caught his eye. Leif grabbed a pen and wedged it into the space. Two envelopes rested in the secret gap. One was addressed to his mom, and the other had Leif's name on it. Both were written in his grandfather's neat, angular writing. Leif opened the letter addressed to him.

Leif,

If you are reading this, then it means something has happened to both me and your mother. I had hoped it wouldn't come to this, but I fear what I have dreaded for so many decades is finally upon you.

First, you are not crazy. Second, I know the world you see around you has changed, significantly. Third, I need you to embrace the burning rage that has awoken inside of you. You need that rage in the fight to come.

The sky is full of light. That is a signal that the Berserker gene awoke within your blood. It is only awakened upon the death of the predecessor. The aurora that you can see is the veil surrounding our realm. The aurora connects our realm to the other nine realms ruled by the Aesir by way of the cosmic tree Yggdrasil. Due to the realms being connected by the aurora, powerful beings, such as the gods can move amongst the realms.

Your increased strength is due to the Berserker ability rising from the depths of your subconscious. It gives you inhuman strength and speed, but at a cost. Until you gain control over it, you will have little restraint of the rage and battle lust that accompanies this privilege. Even small annoyances that you encounter will be enough to trigger a fit. So, I caution you.

Upon my death, a letter will be sent to an old friend of mine, Arias. I have asked him to take you under his wing and help train you for the journey ahead. Arias is a good friend. He saved my life many years ago when I was arrogant and thought myself invincible. He is a Ljosalfar or Elf in English. He comes from Alfheim, a realm far different from ours. Trust Arias. He is a fierce warrior and will be of immense help as you learn to harness your power.

Many years ago, while exploring deep in the caverns of Myrkheim,

I stumbled upon a chamber that led me to the ancient beings known as the Norns. The Norns explained to me that the one to inherit the Berserker gene from me was destined to fight in Ragnarok.

You must master the Berserker and then seek out the Norns. I entrusted the location of the Bridge to the Norns to Arias. He will be your teacher and guide until you can get to the Norns. Seek Arias out. The last time we talked, he was running a small bookstore in Los Angeles.

There is a hidden panel on the lower shelves of the bookcase in my study. Open it and there you will find a trunk with vital information to help you.

I know you can do this. I will be watching from the halls of Valhalla.

— *Afi*

Leif sat motionless for a few minutes, trying to digest what he had just read. He read it again, and again, and again. After the fifth read, he let out a breath and leaned back. *I'm not crazy,* Leif thought. *I guess I am a Berserker now? Whatever that meant. If our family was in danger, why didn't Grandpa warn us about it?!* Leif felt his anger rise with an icy fire spreading through his veins. The realization that he was changing into the Berserker shocked him out of his anger.

With the episode over, Leif felt the need to know more. He moved towards the bookshelf, hoping the books and whatever else was in the secret trunk would have some answers. Leif pulled books out, hoping there was a false lever or something, but no luck. Next Leif attempted to pull on the shelves, hoping it would swing out, but that also didn't work. *Hmmm,* Leif thought. *No lever, the thing doesn't swing out. What the hell am I supposed to do?* "Would it have been so hard to explain just how the damn thing opens!"

Frustrated, Leif slammed his palm against the side of the shelf with more force than he had meant to and was rewarded with a soft click. He smiled. Leif noticed the bottom three shelves shifted backward two inches. He pulled the shelf to the left, revealing an alcove with a battered wooden chest nestled inside. Grunting with effort, he pulled the trunk out. Leif reached to unlatch the trunk, and the alarm on his phone went off. It was time for the funeral. "This will just have to wait till after," Leif sighed and pushed the trunk back into its hiding place. He then pulled the lower shelf back into place. He turned away from the family secrets and reluctantly went upstairs to change.

CHAPTER 8

Showered and clean-shaven, Leif fixed his tie in the mirror. Leif had never really had occasions to wear a suit and a tie, so it always felt a little uncomfortable when he was forced to wear one. He was still feeling jet lagged, so he brewed a quick cup of coffee and gulped it down. The funeral was being held at a church next to the ocean. His family had always loved the water. Leif thought it would be a perfect spot.

The forest-lined roads looked different during the day. The warm morning melted much of the snow from the treetops. It felt as if Leif was driving through a sea of green. The air was brisk and had a clean smell that only exists deep in the mountains away from the city. Leif inhaled deeply, feeling the chilly air sting his nose and lungs. It helped clear his mind.

His grandfather's letter weighed heavily on him, and he couldn't shake the words. It still didn't feel real, though the evidence of its truth was all around him. Something really had awakened inside of him. He felt stronger and healed faster—his brief time in the hospital was proof of that. It was easier to believe that portion of the letter. It was the other stuff that Leif struggled to wrap his mind around. The supernatural world was real—elves, gods, giant wolves, and who knows what else is out there?

Leif drove the rest of the way with the windows down, relishing the fresh air. As he pulled into the quaint little seaside town, he told himself to let go of the letter and its contents for now. He owed it to his mom and grandfather.

The church faced the formidable ocean. Much like a spiritual foe preventing the waves from seizing the faithless. The parking lot was nearly full. Leif unbuckled his seatbelt and stepped out of the car, gazing up at the church. The church was built mere feet from the lapping waves of the Atlantic. The single-story building had a single spire jutting up into the sky near the back of the building. The place didn't feel overly religious, which Leif was happy about, since neither he nor his family was very religious.

Leif proceeded inside and was greeted with two blown up photos of his mother and his grandfather. Leif felt his vision blur. "Ah, you must be Leif," a gentle but heavily accented voice approached. Wiping away the tears, Leif turned to an elderly man in a black suit. "You are the spitting image of Alexander, though you have your mother's blue eyes." The man stepped closer to Leif and held out his hand. "My name's Erik, I was a good friend of Alexander's. I am so happy that you could make it. Especially after the incident at your apartment."

Leif took the man's hand and was surprised at how firm his grip was despite his age. Though he guessed he shouldn't have been surprised since many of the people in this town still cut their own lumber and hunted for food. The Icelandic people are not a delicate people.

"I was saddened to hear about the passing of your mother. It's hard to believe all three of you were attacked and so close in time. It makes little sense; your family has always been so peaceful. Do the police have any leads on the attackers?" Erik asked.

"No, sir," Leif responded. "They seem to be as baffled as everyone else."

"Ah, well, that's enough of that, young Leif. Today is not the day to dwell on such sad thoughts. It's a day to remember and be happy for the time we had with Alexander and Shelby." Erik gestured towards the double doors leading into the chapel. Leif followed his lead.

The two-toned walls were split at head height. The top half was the same white color as the outside, with the other half being made of a polished dark brown wood. The pews were made of the same dark brown wood which made them disappear against the walls. Like most churches, the pews were separated down the middle, creating a long walkway leading to a raised podium. Flowers were hung from the side of each pew. Floor to ceiling windows provided an impressive view of the ocean. The church was almost full by the time the funeral started. As the last surviving member of his family, Leif felt it necessary to say a little about his mom and grandpa, even though he was not much of a public speaker. After Leif's eulogy, one of his mother's friends, Gabby Cane, elected to say some words, while Erik spoke about his grandfather.

Once the funeral was over, Leif walked past the podium and stared through the church's massive windows. Leif could feel the weight on his shoulders lifting. A good number of people had stayed after the funeral, and a low murmur from their hushed conversations wafted over him.

Leif scanned the mingled crowd, and he spotted a pair of softly glowing yellow eyes staring back at him. Leif blinked then and rubbed his eyes; the glowing orange eyes remained. Leif's blood went cold. The eyes belonged to a man of about thirty with high cheekbones, a sharp nose, and light blonde hair pulled back in a ponytail. Leif noticed the slight point to the man's ears. His glare was fixed on Leif. It wasn't the ears that unnerved Leif; it was the soft glow of his eyes. They stared back at Leif, unblinking, locking him in place. Leif wondered if this intense stare belonged to an elf. A hundred scenarios ran through Leif's head. *Is this Arias?*

If he was an enemy, Leif really didn't want to confront him in front of all of these people. If Leif was up against beings from another realm, they might not care what happens to other humans. The Elf must have sensed something was off because he locked eyes with Leif. He smiled, revealing unnaturally pearl white teeth with two canines that were far too long to belong to a human, and then nodded ever so slightly. A few people passed in front of Leif's field of vision, and the elf vanished.

Not wanting the Elf to return or trick him, Leif nervously slipped past the well-wishers and out of the church. He needed to be far away from here, lest he risked getting attacked. Leif was not up to listening to old stories at the wake in the local pub either. He wanted to get back to the trunk that waited for him at the cabin. Back in his car, Leif sped down the highway, breathing a sigh of relief as the comforting forest enveloped him.

Back at his grandfather's house, Leif meticulously checked each door and window to make sure everything was locked and no one or thing could get in. It was a great relief to change out of his suit and tie and head back to the study.

The sun had set by then, and the forest beyond the study had taken on a ghostly darkness. The soft colorful flashes of the veil whipped and snapped, giving off the only sliver of light in the room. Leif switched on the desk lamp and squatted in front of the bookshelf. He gently opened the hidden compartment and pulled out the trunk.

Leif took the time to inspect the old chest. It was made of a dark red wood with a steel band running the length of the rim. Two steel clasps locked the lid shut. Leif unlocked the clasps and slowly opened the lid. A cloud of dust and the smell of old books filled his nostrils as he peered inside.

The trunk was packed full of cloth-covered items. Leif rifled through the booty, comprising old books focused mainly on Norse mythology of one aspect or other, including The Aesir, The Hunt for Vanir, Mapping Midgard's Bridges, and Thor's Gift. Leif carefully unwrapped each book and gently set them aside. They looked ancient, and Leif feared they would crumble to dust with the slightest mistreatment. Leif found a few pieces of old rusted armor deeper in the chest. He was no expert, but he thought they were gauntlets and bracers. They were surprisingly heavy, and even though they hadn't been cleaned in a while, Leif could make out an intricate swirling pattern crisscrossing up and down the length of the set.

Setting those aside, Leif laid his eyes on two cloth wrapped items placed diagonally across the bottom of the trunk. Leif pulled the items out and grunted in surprise at their weight. He slowly unwrapped two beautiful single bladed axes. Their handles were about a foot and a half long and made of a deep brown polished wood. The heads of the axes were razor sharp, and the metal had a beautiful swirling pattern hammered into it. The metal gleamed in the low light of the study. The bottom of the ax blade ended in a wicked hook. Leif marveled at how well maintained the twin axes were, even though they had obviously been stowed away in the trunk for years. Carefully, Leif re-wrapped the axes, and he reverently set them next to the armor. He neatly returned the books to the trunk, filling it to the top.

Once everything was back in the trunk, Leif stretched and felt the joints in his elbow pop. Leif's mind was reeling from his grandfather's letter and what it meant for his future. He was at a loss as to what to do, but he also didn't want to stay still. Reading ancient books was certainly out, no matter how interesting or informative they were. He just couldn't fathom sitting down to read at the moment. Looking out the study window, seeing the flashing light of the veil dance through the trees, Leif knew he needed to be up moving in order to help organize his thoughts. Leif threw on his hoodie and changed into thick sweatpants before heading out for a walk through the surrounding forest.

CHAPTER 9

Flipping the porch lights on, Leif stepped out the back door. The small patio table and few chairs sat undisturbed. Leif filled his lungs with the frigid air, and he felt the tension in his shoulders ease. Beyond the large patch of grass that ran around the house, the Icelandic forest beckoned. Leif slowly walked farther away, and the light from the house faded. The moon and the dancing lights above were the only visible light. As Leif moved through the strangely silent forest, the veil caused the shadows to dance and shift around him. Though the fresh air helped, Leif still struggled to clear his mind of recent events. The truth of his grandfather's letter flashed above in shades of blue, green, and red. Leif knew he wasn't crazy, and he knew that someone had thrust him into a world he felt he didn't belong in.

Another thought sprang to life as Leif moved deeper into the forest. *If beings like Thor existed, are other gods of the ancient world out there? Is there some realm that accommodated Mount Olympus?* Leif let out a small laugh at the thought. "One earth-shattering mystery at a time," Leif whispered with a chuckle.

A caw-caw pierced the silence of the forest, causing Leif to jump in surprise. With his heart racing, Leif spotted two black shadows perched on a branch high in a tree. The cawing came again. Was it possible that Leif recognized the two ravens staring down at him? "What the hell are you two doing here?" Leif yelled. "Why are you following me?" They didn't answer him. One of them hopped back and forth on the branch, cocking its head from side to side; their eyes never leaving Leif's.

The hairs on the back of Leif's neck stood on end, and a chill ran down his spine. He turned slowly as he scanned the surrounding forest. Directly behind Leif, a pool of inky blackness unfurled between the trees. It continued to grow and undulate until a humanoid shape stepped out form the darkness and stood before him. The words from his grandfather's letter resounded, "Powerful beings can move between realms." The darkness of the pool receded, leaving a tall, heavily muscled blue-skinned giant in its wake. "Holy shit," Leif breathed. "This can't be happening. I'm not ready for this!"

As Leif watched the thing, he recognized what it was. The giant was one of those beasts he had been fighting in his strange dreams. The thing was mammoth, at least eight feet tall and thick with corded muscles. It wore dark leather pants, and a small chain of odd-looking animal skulls hung from a hook on its belt. He wore a single piece of steel-looking shoulder armor. Black tribal-like tattoos spread out from beneath the shoulder piece. He was bald with a large forehead, and a pair of close-set glowing red eyes framed a hooked nose and a long black beard. As the brute approached Leif, it smiled, showing off large, jagged teeth.

In one swift movement, the giant unhooked a massive two-handed battle ax from behind its back. Then it spoke. Its voice sent shivers down Leif's spine. "Young Berserker, didn't anyone tell you it's not safe to wander around the forest alone?" The voice was deep and spoke as if the words were heavy on its tongue. "I have long heard of the battle prowess of your kind. Your fate is sealed, but I hope you put up a good fight. It would sadden me if I had to report back to the dark goddess that you fell to me without a fight."

Leif froze as a terror so profound rooted him to the forest floor. His mind went blank with fear and uncertainty of what to do. Then suddenly, the fear evaporated and the familiar icy fire coursed through his veins. Leif's vision turned red. The Berserker waking up in response to the giant's threat, and Leif stoked the fire. *How dare this thing threaten me!* Leif thought. "You stepped into my backyard and have the balls to threaten me!" Leif growled, surprised at the venom in his voice.

His rage filled vision fogged, then crystallized. Everything around him snapped into focus. The fire in his veins cooled to a simmer, and Leif smiled. The giant watched Leif's demeanor change and smiled in return. Raising his war ax in a two-handed grip, the giant charged. Leif charged also; a primal war cry on his lips as he ran.

A mixture of adrenaline, rage, and a perceived feeling of invincibility suffused Leif. He covered the distance between them with ease. As Leif came within striking distance of the giant, it brought his ax down with tremendous force. But Leif sprang to the left just as the ax blade cut the air in front of him. Making a thumping sound as it sunk several inches into the hard-packed snow. Seeing an opportunity, Leif stepped in and punched the giant three times in quick succession in the ribs and muscled stomach. The giant grunted with each punch. Reeling back, Leif's fist throbbed as if he had punched a brick wall. Without missing a beat, the giant let go of his ax and backhanded Leif across the face. The blow sent Leif flying backward. Leif rolled and came to a painful and sudden stop against the trunk of a giant pine tree.

Fuck! That hurt, Leif thought as he spat blood on the snow. Reaching up, he felt a long shallow gash across his cheek. The red haze dissipated slightly as he lay there dazed. His head was swimming. The giant charged towards him, and Leif rolled to his feet. The ache in his head and back dissipated. Leif dove forward, rolling under a horizontal cut meant to take his head off. A loud crack rang through the forest as the giant's ax buried deep into the trunk of the tree. A small voice in the back of Leif's mind said, "There's no way you can beat this thing, you need to turn and run." But the voice was drowned out by a feral snarl. It took a moment to realize that the growl came from him. The Berserker wasn't finished yet.

Leif dodged again, barely missing the ax blade aimed at his stomach. Leif tried to go on the offensive by moving in close. He hoped to prevent the giant from using the ax, but just as Leif was in range for a punch, Leif felt a blinding pain in his stomach. Fearing the worst, he glanced down, and was relieved to see it wasn't the ax head but the haft. Leif felt his ribs crack from the impact, but the pain only fueled his anger. Leif attempted to wrench the ax away from the giant but failed miserably. The giant was unbelievably strong - stronger than Leif, even in his Berserker state.

The giant effortlessly lifted the ax high above his head with Leif still gripping the handle. With no other options, Leif let go, punching the giant in the face as he fell, landing awkwardly as he stumbled backward a few feet. A single line of blood oozed out from the side of the giant's mouth where Leif had slugged him. Leif was happy to see he had finally drawn blood.

In a flash, a single thought pierced the red haze of Leif's rage-filled mind, *RUN!* As he turned, Leif felt a flash of pain like a hot poker across his left thigh. Attempting to flee, his brain hadn't registered the source of the pain until it was too late. Leif put the full weight down on his left leg, and pain erupted. He collapsed to the ground in a heap. A massive gash ran from hip to knee, and blood was freely spilling out. Knowing he only had a few seconds before the giant was upon him, Leif pushed himself to his feet, using his good leg and the trunk of a tree to stand. He felt an itch in his leg that must have been a sign it was healing. Even though the pain was excruciating, it was manageable. Leif moved to run again, but he was too slow. This time the blade of the ax sliced cleanly through his shirt and hoodie into the soft meat of his arm. Fire erupted as the cold steel sliced through him. Leif screamed and fell to the side, clutching his arm, blood seeping through his fingers. It hurt like hell, but Leif could still move his fingers, so he took that as a good sign.

Battered, bleeding and exhausted, Leif scrambled backward. He fell against another tree trunk, and he knew that this was it. The giant seemed to know it. It slowly walked towards Leif with a smile planted on its ugly face. "You move well for one so young. It is a shame you will die here. You would have made a good warrior." It raised its ax over his head. Leif was terrified, but he couldn't look away.

Just as the giant's ax descended, a deep bestial growl rang out from behind the giant. The giant turned in response to the sound, giving Leif a view of two newcomers.

A massive wolf—no, a Vargr—and a cloaked figure stood about ten feet away. The cloaked figure reached up and pulled his hood back, revealing a set of glowing yellow eyes. His long black hair was pulled into a ponytail revealing a pair of pointy ears and a handsome youthful face. A single laugh escaped Leif's lips as he recognized the elf from his grandfather's funeral. The Vargr let out a low growl that Leif felt more than he heard. "Leave the Midgardian alone, Jontar," the elf said in a soft sing-song voice.

"You think I fear you, Ljosalfar? Ha, even with your overgrown pup over there, you are no match for me!" The giant said in its gravelly voice.

The giant stepped forward menacingly, swinging its ax a few times. The elf and Vargr separated without a word, forcing the giant to divide its attention between them. The Vargr snarled, revealing razor-sharp teeth, and the elf slipped out of his cloak. It unsheathed a long thin sword, which came free of the scabbard with a soft snick. Leif was transfixed. He was so focused on the fight that he hadn't noticed the pain in both his leg and arm decreased and the blood-flow slowed to a trickle.

The forest had gone deathly quiet as the three combatants squared off against each other. Then, as if choreographed, all three moved at once. The Vargr swiftly lunged for the giant's legs, attempting to hamstring the giant, but the giant was faster, lashing out with a kick that connected cleanly with the Vargr's jaw, sending it careening to the side. The giant simultaneously blocked a lunge by the elf meant to impale the giant through the ribs. The giant followed up by lashing out with a kick meant to take the elf square in the chest. The elf effortlessly dodged the giant's attack. The Vargr recovered from the blow to its head and slammed into the giant, causing the blue-aggressor to stagger. The elf danced in again, scoring a shallow gash across the giant's chest, drawing blood. The giant snarled and swung his ax horizontally, but the elf blocked the attack with his sword. The Vargr moved in again, this time lunging for the giant's massive arm, but the giant disengaged from the elf and rolled to his left, causing the Vargr to miss. The Vargr landed on silent paws and turned. A snarl escaped from its parted lips. The elf and the Vargr looked to press the attack, but the giant had other ideas.

The giant kept his ax held high; his blood-red eyes switched back and forth between the advancing pair. The giant stopped in a small clearing, and the same inky black pool that he had stepped through earlier formed behind him. Without hesitation, he stepped backward, disappearing into the darkness.

CHAPTER 10

The elf and Vargr turned their attention to Leif. Leif experimentally moved his injured leg and arm. It hurt, but minimally. Using the tree, Leif rose to his feet and squared off against the two. They may have saved him from the blue giant, but that doesn't make them allies. The elf must have sensed Leif's intention because he slowly and deliberately sheathed his sword and held his hands out. Leif still wasn't buying it. He was new to the supernatural world, and until he knew more about these beings, he would not take any chances.

The silence was finally broken when the elf took a step forward. The singsong voice rang softly in Leif's ears, "Leif, it's ok. My name is Arias. I was a friend of your grandfather's. You can trust me."

Leif relaxed. "You were at my grandfather's funeral! Why didn't you talk to me then?" Leif asked.

The elf chuckled, "You should have seen the look on your face when you turned around and saw me. I guessed you were still coming to terms with the supernatural, and I wasn't sure how you would react if I got too close. It wouldn't have been good for you to go berserk in the church with a bunch of Midgardians around. So, I decided I would stop by the house after the funeral and see if we could talk. When I arrived, I saw that the house was empty, and that's when I ran into Geri here." Arias gestured to the wolf who nodded its massive head slightly. "Geri and her pack had sensed something not of this realm entering their forest, and they had sent her to investigate. Fearing it involved you, we followed your trail and well...," he shrugged, "... you know the rest."

Leif stood up straight, nodding. "I'm freezing my ass off. So, if you don't mind, could we talk back at the cabin? Though I must say, I don't think Geri," gesturing at the massive Vargr, "will be able to fit through the back door."

The wolf eyed Leif intensely, and he could see the intelligence behind those eyes. Then, to Leif's surprise, the Vargr spoke. "I have no interest in what you and the Ljosalfar have to discuss," she said in a deep, gravelly voice. "My pack and I were only interested as a favor to Alexander. We shared the forest with him for many years. We felt we owed it to him to watch over his pup, and now we have." The Vargr nodded to Arias, turned and disappeared into the forest.

"Vargr," Arias said. "Such odd creatures. You never really know what they will do. One day they will fight to the death by your side, the next they are silently stalking you, keen on having you for dinner. Don't think the pack will be as friendly the next time you encounter one of its members. Now, as you said, it's cold and we have no idea if there are any other Jontar roaming the forest, so let us get moving."

Looking around, Leif realized in the fight he had gotten turned around and had no idea which way the house was. Arias must have seen Leif's confused look, "It's this way," Arias said, pointing behind him.

It was a silent twenty-minute walk before they arrived at Leif's grandfather's house. Leif sat across from the elf, silently watching as he calmly sipped his tea. Leif had been surprised at the elf's ability to navigate his grandfather's kitchen.

"As you have guessed, my grandfather kept me and the rest of the family completely in the dark about all of this," Leif said gesturing towards Arias, who merely raised his perfectly manicured eyebrow, but said nothing. "I am having a lot of trouble adjusting. I mean, I have been able to keep any outburst to a minimum, and the increased strength and healing is cool, especially since I seem to get attacked fairly regularly, but I really have no clue what is going on and why I keep getting attacked. My grandfather left me a letter, but it raises way more questions than it answered, even though I have read it a dozen times now. He mentioned you, and he also mentioned loads of other important stuff that I have no clue about. He said that you are supposed to take me to see something called the Norns." Arias's eyes widened slightly at the mention of the Norns. "You are obviously an elf, you fit the descriptions from stories and movies perfectly."

Arias chuckled slightly, "Yes, in your tongue I would be called an elf, but there are distinct types of elves that originated from my realm. My people are called Ljosalfar, which loosely translates to light elf," Arias said, taking a sip of his tea.

"What is this about the Norns?" Arias said, "And Alexander wants me to take you to them? That is no easy quest. No one outside of Alexander has seen them in thousands of years. Though, he did share the location of the bridge that leads to their realm. But that is a moot point right now." Arias said.

"Why is that?" Leif asked.

"Midgardians," Arias said, exacerbated. "In your current state, the smallest annoyance could trigger your Berserker. Until you can control your other side, I will not take you through the realms. Besides, I still don't know if I am willing to take you. It has been decades since I traveled the realms fighting Jontar and Dokkalfar. I have cut myself off from the other realms for a long time. The letter from Alexander came unexpectedly. The letter said much of the same things I'm guessing yours did about Ragnarok and wanting me to help you, but I am not entirely sure Ragnarok is actually here. It is such an old legend that many of my kind dismiss it as merely a tall tale meant to scare our young.

"So, I have a proposal. Come find me in L.A. in two weeks. That gives you time to finish up here and some time to gain control of the Berserker. We can revisit the question of Alexander's suicide mission then." Arias stood.

"But what the hell am I supposed to do in the meantime?" Leif flew out of his chair. Standing, Leif flushed at his outburst and took one long calming breath. "Sorry, I let my emotions get the better of me. I only meant, since the night of Grandpa and Mom's murder, I've been attacked twice by strange beings. I might add, the first attack put me in the hospital. I now apparently have an anger problem that if set off in the wrong place and time could cause me to go into a blind rage. And, oh yeah, I am supposed to stop a freaking mythological apocalypse, but I have no idea how. And you want me to just fly home and act like nothing's happened for the next two weeks?" Leif hadn't meant to, but he was practically yelling.

Arias smirked slightly as Leif finished, "I didn't say do nothing while you waited. Gods! Do Midgardians always need to have their hand held? That is why I liked Alexander so much. He always had a plan. I'm sure Alexander didn't just leave you a letter, right?" Arias asked.

"No, he left me several books, some armor, and two axes."

"Well, there you go," Arias pulled out a small business card and slid it across the table. "Here is my card, come find me in two weeks, and I should have an answer for you."

Arias put his cloak back on. Leif walked him out. At the door, Arias turned and held out his hand. Leif took it. Arias's hands were powerful and calloused. "Try not to die in the meantime,"

Arias said releasing Leif's hand. Arias turned and disappeared into the night.

Leif locked the door behind him. He pressed his back against the door and let out a frustrated burst of air while a wolf simultaneously howled in the distance.

CHAPTER 11

L eif's remaining two days in Iceland had the odd duel effect of flying by at a crawling pace... at least while he was stuck inside the house.

Though Leif was eager to read through his grandfather's old books, he was simply overwhelmed with the business of his mother and grandfather's estates. He would have loved a walk in the forest to clear his mind, but he knew that was an impossibility. One positive turn of events was that between the two estates, he now had enough money that he didn't have to immediately sell the house.

His final morning in Iceland, Leif woke up with a groan. The early morning was unwelcomed; especially with the prospect of a long flight home. It felt like he had just laid his head down and closed his eyes. He hated when that happened. Leif had been too lazy to pack the previous night, so he forced himself out of bed and began shoving clothes into his packing cubes. He brought his suitcase downstairs and loaded everything into the back of his rental car. Leif fastidiously packed up the trunk filled with all the Berserker information he needed to read up on. He called the airline, letting them know he would transport a chest filled with delicate items. Once everything was loaded, he locked the house up and left his grandfather's home.

Thankfully, the trip to the airport and the flight back home were uneventful. Leif smiled a little, thinking his new normal was hoping to not get attacked by a supernatural monster or get pulled into some life-altering event. *God-or is it gods? It's scary to think how quickly my life has changed in the past week.*

Leif landed in LAX around sunset. He was exhausted and was sick of traveling. He walked towards the baggage claim, and through the windows he glimpsed the splash of colors cascading across the sky. Leif wondered how those mystifying colors connected the other nine realms to each other. Does it connect to other realms or just the nine, if so, then why?

Sighing, Leif set out for his car in the long-term parking. Struggling to push the massive trunk full of books to his car, Leif felt an itch on the back of his neck. A week ago, he would have just brushed the feeling off and kept walking. After what he'd seen, he wouldn't be taking any chances. Typical of LAX, there were people everywhere, but no one stood out. After loading his luggage into

the trunk, he heard a familiar caw-caw. He looked up just in time to see two ravens launch into the sky. Leif quickly buckled up, cranked up the music, and jumped onto the dreaded 405.

Leif was exhausted and wanted to head straight home and go to bed. He was jet-lagged, cranky from being crammed into a too small plane seat, and he just wanted to pop a sleeping pill and go to bed. But he knew he needed to eat and at least skim through some of the books he had brought back with him. Leif thought about ordering a pizza, but memories of what happened the last time flashed through his mind and he quickly lost his craving. He jumped on Yelp and called for some Thai food takeout. Twenty minutes later, he was home scarfing down some delicious Pad See Ew and unloading his grandfather's trunk.

With the cache splayed out on his coffee table, Leif grabbed the closest book to him and opened it to the first chapter.

The creation of the Berserker clans dates back to an intra-realm invasion that had lasting ramifications not just to Midgard, but the other realms as well. What many historical scholars theorized was a mini ice age in 900 A.D. was in fact an invasion of Jontar and Dokkalfar. The Jontar and Dokkalfar, jealous of Midgard's lush world and resource rich environment, ripped a hole in the veil without the use of a bridge. This feat was previously believed to be solely the ability of the Aesir and Vanir. The invading forces stepped through and raided the surrounding Viking settlements. After weeks of bloodshed, a conclave was held, and a truce was forged between the Viking clans to unite and oppose the Jontar and Dokkalfar. Thus, a long and bloody war commenced. The clans were no match for the immense power of their foes and were outclassed in every aspect. The Jontar, giant humanoids from an icy realm known as Jotenheim, were naturally taller and stronger than the Viking warriors. While the Dokkalfar, a banished race of elves, were similar to Midgardians in stature, but far stronger and possessed elemental magic.

Though the Viking warriors were severely disadvantaged, they still valiantly fought against the invaders. After many bloody battles, the defending Viking clans broke. Many dishonored themselves and fled into the wilds, but a handful of warriors stayed, determine to fight to the end. These brave warriors banded together to make one last stand against the invaders. As expected, the losses were heavy, but when all was lost and the Jontar and Dokkalfar were close to victory, a thunderclap rang out over the battlefield. The sky darkened with clouds of the deepest black. The Jontar and Dokkalfar were undaunted by the storm and rallied together for their final charge, but a beam of lighting struck the center of the invaders' battle lines, vaporizing all who were caught within. In the blink of an eye, the lighting faded, and a mountain of a man stood in the very center of the lightning strike. He was heavily armored and carried a massive war-hammer in one hand. The imposing figure stared down the remaining Jontar and Dokkalfar, warning them they have broken the peace of the Aesir and that they must immediately return to their home realms or face destruction. It was said that many of the Jontar and Dokkalfar turned and ran for the tear in the veil, but some stayed and fought. This lone figure was the Aesir god, Thor, a powerful being known to be able to control lightning and the enforcer of the Aesir law. All who stood before him that day perished. Once the invaders had been defeated, he stepped up to the tear in the veil and with a wave of his hand, a flash of lightning sealed the rip in Midgard.

It was told that Thor was so impressed with the surviving warriors that he bestowed upon them a sliver of his power, creating the Berserker line. The Berserker gene was then passed down to the eldest of each generation upon the death of their progenitor.

Leif closed the book with a snap, causing dust to erupt into the air. He laid back against his couch, processing what he just read. *If what this book says is true, my ancestors fought in that battle and were given a portion of Thor's power! Berserkers literally have God-like power. This is insane!* Shaking his head in equal parts confusion and denial, Leif set aside his newfound godhood and pulled out the next book in the trunk.

This book appeared to be about a group of beings called the Aesir. The book explained that the Aesir were the ruling body of gods in the Norse Pantheon. The Aesir were made up of Odin, Thor, and Loki. These were all names Leif knew from his grandfather's stories, but it also included several other such as Heimdall, Sir, and Baldr, which Leif didn't really know much about. Diving deeper into the book, he found an extensive section devoted to the god Odin and started reading.

Odin, The Allfather, was the de facto king of the Norse gods.

He was thousands, if not millions of years old. There is little to no information on his origin. There are several documented instances of him going to battle with beings known as The Outsiders. It was through these battles that Odin grew in power and began his campaign to unite the realms near his designated throne world of Asgard. The great tree, Yggdrasil, sat at the center of the cosmos, connecting the nine realms along the winding limbs of the interstellar tree. Over the millennia, as Outsider attacks lessened, Odin slowly pulled away from taking an active role in the realms. Odin and many of the Aesir haven't been seen in thousands of years, and they have fallen to myth in many of the nine realms, especially amongst the short-lived races such as Midgardians.

To the Midgardians, more specifically the Viking culture, Odin was associated with war and death. In many of their depictions of him, he was an old wizened warrior, who wore an eye patch. No one knows how he lost the eye, but many Ljosalfar believe he lost it during his battles against the Outsiders. He was typically accompanied by two ravens, Hugin and Munin. They were said to travel the nine realms, keeping a silent watch and reporting any important news to Odin.

Two Ravens, huh? Leif thought. *Could they be Hugin and Munin? No way, for what reason would a literal god be following me? How weird would it be though if the most powerful god or being of Norse mythology has been following me, watching me? If it is, maybe he will have some information on who killed Mom and Grandpa! I will just have to ask him if I ever see him.*

The next section in the book was devoted to the god, Thor. Leif already had a basic knowledge of Thor through popular culture and the many stories his grandfather had regaled him with, but he figured it couldn't hurt to refresh his knowledge. *Who knows*, Leif thought, *I may just run into him someday.*

Unlike the sparse section on Odin, Thor's chapter was filled with stories and excerpts of his many exploits over eons. Within the section of Thor, a small chapter was devoted to the mythical hammer he carried with him, Mjolnir. Leif used to pretend he was Thor when he was a kid. He would run around his grandfather's house with a towel cape wrapped around his neck and a toy hammer in hand, doing battle against the forces of evil.

Thor was a one-man army. He was the enforcer of Aesir law. The book described the early years of the unification of the nine realms, and during that time it was Thor who would show up when a realm stepped out of line. There was even an excerpt about the invasion of Midgard by the Jontar and Dokkalfar and how he beat them back. It even mentioned the bestowing of the Berserker upon the surviving Vikings.

Leif flipped through a few more pages, skimming but not really reading until he came upon a faded but beautifully intricate drawing of Thor. Thor held a wide stance on a rock or hill, head raised to the sky, a shout escaping his lips, and Mjolnir raised to the sky. The inky sky was alive with lightning forking across the clouds and to the ground behind Thor. The armor was astonishing. A twisting pattern sculpted a path through the metal, interconnecting the channels into an intricate array, as if he was lightening incarnate. Leif admired the drawing for a few moments before a yawn escaped his lips.

Leif checked his phone; he hadn't realized how late it was. "This jet lag is going to be a bitch," he murmured. He closed the book, gently put them all back in the trunk, and closed the lid. Vowing not to be caught unarmed again, Leif picked up the twin axes and their belt and headed for the bedroom.

CHAPTER 12

L eif had a little less than two weeks to work on controlling his rage and understanding Norse mythology. Both were daunting tasks; anything Leif read while researching on the internet or at a local library was likely so far off from the actual truth that he struggled to pay attention to it. He felt that the only genuine sources of knowledge he had about the realms were the books his grandfather had given him, and many times he struggled to read them. All were handwritten. Apparently, only the Midgard realm had the printing press.

Besides the Aesir, there were several other beings that inhabited the nine realms. Leif struggled to pronounce their names. Alfheim, inhabited by the Ljosalfar, was a realm lush with forests. The book described the light elves as being tall in stature, with a teardrop-shaped face, pointed ears, and a slight slant to their softly glowing yellow eyes. It explained elves are one of the long-lived races, and if they don't die due to illness or injury, they have been known to live for a thousand years or more. Many among their kind were gifted with the ability to manipulate the latent energy that Alfheim is brimming with—Midgardians call it magic. Due to the generally calm nature of the Ljosalfar, the moderate climate of the forest realm, and its location on the great tree, Alfheim contains numerous bridges and has come to house an abundance of races.

Alfheim originally was home to two races of elf, the Ljosalfar and the Dokkalfar, known as Dark Elves. For eons, the two races lived in peace, sharing the beautiful land of Alfheim. But the peace was shattered when the Dokkalfar attacked, attempting to claim the entire realm for themselves. A long and bloody civil war followed, nearly engulfing the entire realm in fire and blood. Without the intervention of the Aesir, Alfheim would be a realm of dust and death. Due to the Dokkalfar starting the war and the many atrocities they committed, those that remained were banished from Alfheim and doomed to wander the realms, never having a home to return to. A majority of the remaining Dokkalfar settled on the surface of Myrkheim, the realm of the Svartalfar or Dwarf in your tongue.

The Svartalfar, the original inhabitants of Myrkheim, burrowed deep into the depths of the realm, excavating massive underground cities spanning the world. The Svartalfar are short in stature and long-lived, though not as long as the Ljosalfar and Dokkalfar. They prefer the company of their own kind over any other race. Many Svartalfar work in the great forges or in some type of craft involving their hands. The Svartalfar forges of Myrkheim were responsible for creating many of the legendary weapons wielded by the Aesir. There were many tales of spies from other realms or even rival clans attempting to steal the secrets from these famous smiths.

Midgardians were cut off from the rest of the nine realms by the Aesir. This isolation by the Aesir was because of several attempts by other realms to invade and dominate Midgard. Midgardians are short-lived, weak, and lack the ability to manipulate the energies of their world. They had become easy prey for the other races. Furthermore, the geological makeup of Midgard contains several unique minerals and elements, which are highly coveted among the other races, especially the

Svartalfar. The Svartalfar and Midgardians once freely traded, resulting in many legends popping up amongst the Midgardians. But when war broke out between the realms, the Aesir were forced to intervene. The Svarta-Midgardian war caused the Aesir to cut off many of the bridges connecting Midgard to the rest of the nine realms. Though a few fixed bridges still exist on Midgard, they require the use of magic to open, which less than one percent of their population can use. However, random bridges connecting Midgard to other realms still occur due to cosmic shifts amongst the limbs of Yggdrasil.

Leif closed the book with a sigh. He had been sitting on his couch for far too long and felt the urge to be out and moving. He would need to learn to fight and protect himself, so Leif researched martial arts classes and was close to signing up for a few uncommon types. However, he pictured himself going into a blind rage and fighting all who stood near him. With his enhanced strength, he would most likely kill someone, so he decided a punching bag would be much safer.

The gym was busy for it being the middle of the day. But hey, when you live in L.A., landing a part could very well depend on how good you look; there was no such thing as rest days. Luckily for Leif, there was an open bench rack. Leif started with an easy warm-up of 135 pounds. Leif lifted the bar and almost laughed; it felt like nothing to him. Leif re-racked the bar and put two more 45-pound plates on the bar. Laying back down, Leif calmed his breathing and lifted. Just like before, the bar moved effortlessly. *Holy shit*, Leif thought as he completed a rep as smoothly as before. Re-racking it, Leif sat up and laughed to himself. Leif wanted to push the bench further, but he didn't want to attract too much attention. I may be in good shape, but I think people would wonder how a guy who is only 180 pounds, is throwing up weight normally only seen with professional power lifters. So, he moved over to the squat rack and, not wanting to waste any time, started out at 225 pounds. Like the bench, he picked it up with ease and squatted down like it was nothing. Leif had always been into exercising, but he had always hated leg day and so he probably neglected his back squat more than he should. Before his change, he could squat 225 pounds, but only after warming up and not over four or five reps. But now, it was nothing. Leif added two more plates, making it 315 pounds, and though it wasn't as easy as before, it was still easier than it should have been. He moved as smoothly as an elevator. Leif re-racked the bar and blew out a breath. *Super strength: check,* Leif thought as he took a sip of his partially crushed water bottle.

Next, Leif stepped into the vacant side room that contained the gym's boxing equipment. Walking up to the punching bags, Leif shook out his arms to loosen them up as he bounced on his toes like a pro boxer. He didn't have any gloves, but he didn't expect to be here for too long. Even after lifting weights, Leif still felt on edge. He had been a mellow guy for most of his life, but the Berserker changed all that. There was a constant tightness in his chest that wasn't there before. *Hopefully, a few rounds with the bag will ease my mind,* Leif thought as he adopted a boxer's stance.

Leif took it easy for the first few rounds, not wanting to hurt his hands. He didn't know the extent of his newly found strength. He hit the bag at around fifty percent of his power, and it flew back with a resounding THWACK! He had never seen the bag move that much for anyone.

Smiling, Leif moved faster, dancing in and out of range of the bag in rhythm with the beat blasting out of the gym's speakers. Leif was really enjoying the sight of the bag being flung from side to side as he laid into it. Then without warning, Leif's mind fogged, and it was as if he was back in his apartment, dodging the flurry of attacks from the Dokkalfar. Just as quickly, he was falling back onto the icy ground of the Icelandic forest, freely bleeding from a cut to his leg and staring up at the Jontar as he swung his massive ax. A small portion of Leif's brain registered the icy fire racing through his veins signifying he was going Berserk, but

Leif's fear addled mind didn't care. Then it happened, like someone had flipped a switch in Leif's mind. He didn't want to be the victim anymore and so he attacked, dodging phantom punches and slashes from his Dokkalfar attacker. Seeing an opening as the Dokkalfar overreached, Leif stepped in and lashed out with as much strength as he could muster, punching the phantom directly in the jaw, launching him a good ten feet before crashing to the ground with a loud thump and the sound of broken glass.

Running on pure instinct, the berserked Leif looked around for his next opponent. With the perceived threat dealt with, Leif felt his rational mind slowly return and his eyes went wide with realization. Leif was still in the little side room of the gym, but it looked like a tornado had come blasting through the tiny room. Initially, there had been two punching bags hanging from thick metal chains near the far wall. Now, one bag lay slumped against the far mirrored wall. The mirror had shattered from the force of the bag; glass fragments spread out across the floor. The punctured bag bled a puddle of sand. The chain and a good portion of the ceiling lay draped over the battered bag. Turning away, Leif saw the other bag wasn't in much better shape. Though it was still attached to the ceiling, upon closer examination, Leif could see several enormous cracks radiating from the hanging hook and ceiling tiles. Leif bet one or two more hits and the thing would come free. Leif inspected the bag and saw the bag had a single massive hole around the middle where sand was spilling out, hemorrhaging across the floor.

Leif could hardly believe what he saw. What if someone had come in during this brief episode? What would have happened to them? And why did no one come to see what all the commotion was about? Thankfully, the music must have been too loud for anyone to hear him. He scanned the ceiling but didn't see any cameras. Leif felt bad for the damage he had caused, but he also didn't want to have to answer questions about how he could destroy a 200-pound punching bag with a single punch. *I will leave an envelope with an anonymous apology letter and some cash when I leave,* Leif thought. *I guess this happens when you get zapped with godlike steroids.* He was feeling excited on one hand, but also a little scared. *If I can get my other side under control, I could become unstoppable. With these powers I could become a real-life superhero, or if I lose control of the Berserker... a villain.*

CHAPTER 13

Back home, Leif showered and cleaned up. Night had fallen in L.A. and he wasn't really up to going out with friends. He didn't want to field question after question about his recent attack, nor did he feel like being asked about the funeral or hearing the same, "I'm sorry for your loss," clichés. He knew they meant well, but there is a finite number of times someone can hear the sentiment before it gets annoying. *Besides, I should probably limit my interactions with people until I get a grip on my anger problem,* Leif thought. He chuckled at his little joke. Leif faced his newfound fear of delivery men and decided to have some Indian food from a bomb place a few blocks over.

Leif idly walked through his apartment as he made the order, ending up in his bedroom. His eyes came to rest on the twin axes sitting silently on his nightstand. Leif could only imagine how many battles they had witnessed or how many lives the razor-sharp edges had taken. Leif had never considered what it meant to actually take a life. He remembered running through his parents' and grandfather's houses, fighting imaginary enemies, cutting them down without a second thought. But that was when Leif was young. As an adult, it was a whole different ball game. He killed the stranger with black eyes, the Dokkalfar, but that was in self-defense, acting solely on reflex. *Hell, I didn't want to kill him, but I mean… I had no choice. He would have killed me if I hadn't done what I did.*

Leif realized that he really had spent little time inspecting the axes and figured he should begin familiarizing himself with the weapons if he would need them in the future. They were identical in make and design, and though Leif didn't know much about axes or weapons in general, they looked to be finely crafted. He would expect to see them up on a wall at some eclectic collector's mansion, not here with Leif in his shitty L.A. apartment.

Leif picked up the weapons and walked around the room, feeling the axes out. Leif guessed they weighed anywhere from four to five pounds. The grips were smooth but were coarse enough that Leif wasn't worried that they would slip out of his sweaty hands. *I should still buy a pair of gloves just in case,* Leif thought. Leif squared up against an imaginary enemy like he had done many times as a kid and took some experimental swings. The axes sliced through the air like a hot knife through butter. Leif felt just like a real Viking gearing up for battle. He danced around the apartment, swinging at invisible foes, imagining blocking sword thrusts and attacking in ways that looked cool in practice, but would be disastrous in a proper fight.

The buzzer pulled Leif from his imaginary battle. Breathing heavy, Leif's forearms and shoulders burned a little, and he vowed to practice with the axes daily to get his muscles used to the unfamiliar weight and movements. Leif let the delivery man into the building. However, because of his current mistrust of strangers, he kept his axes within reach should he need them, but they were also out of sight so he wouldn't scare a poor human delivery boy. Leif hoped that he was getting better at picking out an elf or other beings not of Midgard. A knock came to his door a few moments later, and Leif was surprised at how nervous he was. *This is ridiculous,* Leif thought. I can't be afraid to answer the door for the rest of my life. Taking a deep breath, he opened the door. He was faced with a pimply teenager holding a takeout bag in one hand and a receipt in the other. Leif chuckled to himself as he signed for his food.

After dinner, Leif searched the internet for information on how to fight with axes. He had hundreds, if not thousands, of websites to choose from. Not feeling up to reading, Leif clicked on YouTube. Several videos popped up. At first, it was easy to filter through them, skipping anything anime or cartoon related.

They would be fun to watch but wouldn't provide Leif with much guidance. Some videos were cut from random movies. Figuring why not, Leif clicked auto-play and watched a flurry of bloody B movie fights involving ax fighting. It's a good thing Leif has a strong stomach because he may have lost his dinner during a few particularly bloody disembowelments or amputations. Mostly, the videos were nothing more than gory entertainment, but Leif at least got to see how one moves while using an ax in battle and some advantages and disadvantages against other weapons.

Leif spent the rest of the evening watching videos. Every once in a while, he would pick up one or both of the axes, attempting to recreate a move or two he saw in a video. By the end of the night, Leif had a few fresh holes in his wall and needed to replace one of his dining chairs, which was now missing one of its legs from a misplaced ax slice. Leif decided he had enough practice for the night and headed to bed for some much-needed sleep.

LEIF STROLLED through a cold and dark corridor that wouldn't look out-of-place in one of the medieval B-movies he had been watching earlier that night. Huge stone pillars were spaced out to each side of the dimly lit hallway. Small, ornate, metal lanterns hung high on each pillar, attempting to penetrate the darkness. Even with many lanterns, the shadows to each side were deep and dark. Curious, Leif stopped next to one pillar and inspected the odd-looking lantern. It was black with a single silver strip that wrapped around four posts. Clear glass was set in all four sides of the lamp. Leif was stunned when he noticed the flame within was tinged dark purple. Peering closer, Leif couldn't see the source of the flame; there was no candle or lightbulb within. The purple flame bounced back and forth, struggling to escape the confines of the lamp. *That's not normal. I am probably not on Midgard, but if I'm not on Midgard, where the hell am I?* He thought.

Leif watched the light flicker. It briefly illuminated the wall behind the pillars, revealing an enormous mural spanning the darkness on either side. Leif peered through the purplish haze. He could barely make out the outlines of a large painting spanning that same wall. *What's the point of having works of art if you can't see them?* Leif thought. Intrigued by the massive paintings, Leif stepped away from the pillar and stepped up to the mural. Leif wasn't particularly into art, but he could tell whoever painted this piece knew what they were doing. The mural was so big, he had to take a step back to truly appreciate it.

It was a picture of the cosmic tree Yggdrasil. There had been a drawing similar to the painting in one of the books Leif found in his grandfather's trunk. The roots of the tree twisted and turned in and out of the painting, while nine branches extended out from the trunk of the tree. The nine branches were all unique in shape and color.

The silence of the dark corridor was suddenly interrupted by a creaking noise that caused Leif to jump. He looked down both sides of the hallway, but he couldn't see anything. A chill ran down his spine as silence returned to the shadowed hallway. The stillness weighed heavily on his shoulders. He decided to move out from the shadows and get out of the flickering hallway. Stepping back into the purplish light, he looked down the corridor. All he could see in both directions was darkness broken up by the halos of dancing purplish light. Leif continued walking in the direction he thought was forward.

Leif increased his pace. He felt like he had been in the dark for hours. He could feel the dark hallway pushing in on him from all sides and he was eager to get out, but he felt the need to be cautious. In horror movies, Leif knew it was the overly scared or frantic people who died first. He knew that one misstep could set off an alarm or cause him to fall into some hidden pit.

Leif was struck right then at how weird his predicament was. *How did I get here?* It was as if the fog had been lifted from his mind. The last thing he remembered was being in his room back in L.A. He shook his head. *It doesn't matter how I got here now; I just need to figure out how to get out.*

After an exorbitant amount of time, the darkness of the hallway receded, revealing an imposing set of double doors. The huge doors were made of solid oak with a small detailed version of Yggdrasil carved into the wood. Peering closer, he saw two wolves sitting upside down on their haunches under the tree. Leif wanted to stay and examine the carving, but the better part of him told him to get out of the hallway. He played it safe and opened the door an inch or two and see what lay beyond the door before he went busting in unannounced.

The room beyond was spacious with a crackling fireplace to the left, and a set of chairs and low table a comfortable distance from the flames. Another large table took up much of the center of the room. Paper and books were strewn about the table, but Leif was too far away to read what they said. At the far end of the room, picture windows opened, leading to an expansive balcony. It appeared to be evening, but he realized he could be wrong. The sky was a mixture of dark brown and red. A soft greenish light filtered in from somewhere below the balcony. Leif remembered the etching on the door and wondered if he was upside down. *If I am in a different realm, maybe gravity works differently here,* Leif wondered.

Sudden movement lured Leif's eyes to a woman. She stood with her back to him, leaning against the wall of the balcony. She had shoulder-length, golden blonde hair that flowed down her back. She wore an open-backed, blood-red dress that exposed a well-muscled, feminine posterior. Leif could see the muscles under her sun-kissed skin shift when she changed positions. Leif had the feeling this wasn't someone he wanted to mess with. Unexpectedly, the woman spoke.

"Welcome to my humble abode, young Berserker," she purred with a voice made of silk and honey. Though she spoke English, she had a slight accent that Leif couldn't place. Leif was transfixed by the woman's soothing voice, but warning bells were ringing wildly through his brain. Leif remained glued to his spot.

"I had hoped to exterminate your kind in one fell swoop, but it seems the Norns have different plans."

An involuntary shiver ran down Leif's spine.

"You cannot understand the planning and maneuvering I have had to do over the eons to get to this point, only to hit a snag by you and your kind. But I am not unreasonable. And I will tell you this just once."

She turned and Leif's eyes went wide. Words could not describe her beauty. To describe her would be like describing a Hawaiian sunset to a blind man. She was nearly six feet tall. The red dress hugged her curves and left little to the imagination. Her golden hair fell to either side of her face, perfectly outlining it. She had red, lush lips and eyes that glowed the electric blue of a lightning strike. Her stare pierced Leif. A bright smile escaped her blood-red lips.

"I don't know what my uncle was thinking when he gave your kind such a powerful gift, but it is clear you Midgardians were too weak to control it. I don't know how the Norns hid your blood-line from my sight for so long, but I see you now. You have been lucky enough to survive two of my assassins, and so I shall grant you a boon. Stay out of my affairs and I will leave you alone, but if you take up the mantle unrightfully given to you by my fool of an uncle, I will destroy you."

She didn't raise her voice or change her disposition, but Leif felt the pressure of a heavy wind blowing against him. The woman held Leif's gaze for a moment more. The physical blow of her stare was enough to steal his breath away; he tried to inhale but couldn't. Then she turned, absently flexed her hand, and the pressure was gone. Leif gasped, trying to catch his breath. "Now go. Leave this place. Pray we never meet again."

CHAPTER 14

L eif bolted upright. The dreams left him feeling exhausted and drenched in sweat. Leif was happy to see he was back in his tiny apartment.

"It's not enough to continually be attacked, but now they are invading my dreams?" Leif mumbled into the darkness.

Collapsing back onto his bed, Leif let out a lengthy sigh. This dream was different than the others. The ones where he was fighting the blue giants left Leif feeling more like he was a spectator, but this time he was definitely in control. He wondered if the dream was an astral projection. *Who was that woman?* Leif thought. He picked through her words to try to gain some insight into her identity. It was clear she wasn't human, and he was sure she wasn't an elf. He recalled her saying, "My uncle gave you your gift," or something close to it. He assumed she referred to the Berserker. *And Thor was the one to gift my ancestors with the Berserker. Holy shit! If Thor is her uncle, then I most likely just met a god!*

A cold sweat broke out as a fear so profound seized hold of Leif that breathing was a struggle. *Grandpa! What have you gotten me into? This Arias better help me, or I will have to find the deepest darkest cave in America and hide there until all of this blows over.* Closing his eyes, Leif could still see the woman's burning blue-white eyes staring back at him. Leif knew he had little chance of sleep, knowing each time he closed his eyes, those lightening blue orbs were waiting for him.

According to his blindingly bright phone, it was 5:37 in the morning.

Ugh, Leif thought. *Can't I get attacked or threatened at a reasonable time?* Knowing it was pointless to stay in bed, he begrudgingly got up and figured he might as well go for a run. Maybe a little exercise and fresh air would clear his mind.

Closing the door behind him, Leif put on his earphones and started down the road. Leif was amazed at how much the Berserker had changed him, for better and worse. He came upon a long stretch of sidewalk free of stop signs or streetlights and launched into a full sprint. Faster and faster he went until the world around him blurred. When Leif neared the outer wall to a small park a few miles from his apartment, he tried something. Planting his feet, he vaulted the five-foot wall with ease and sprinted across the park without slowing down.

Leif ran towards the vacant baseball field and approached a tall chain-link fence behind home plate. Leif jumped, launching himself a good five feet into the air. Unfortunately, Leif's miscalculation caused him to smash into the chain-link fence with a bang. Leif had tried to grab hold, but pain exploded across his body as he collided with the fence. Crumbling to the grass in a heap, Leif let out a loud laugh. He got to his feet and brushed off the dirt and grass that clung to his body. He was surprised to see he was uninjured. Leif laughed again, *I could get used to this.* The few people strolling through the park or exercising hadn't noticed his fall, so he grinned and jumped again, soaring higher than an Olympic high jumper. With a huge smile on his face, Leif scrambled up over the fence. With a hint of trepidation, he jumped, coming down in a superhero landing. *This is amazing*, Leif thought. *I really am a modern superhuman!* He laughed at the thought of himself in brightly colored spandex.

Leif had been so engrossed in the freeing sensation of sprinting through the park, he failed to avoid a morning boot camp class. At the last second, Leif tried to stop, but he wasn't used to moving at such speeds, and he ended up tripping over his feet. He stumbled for a few feet and face-planted into the grass, nearly collided with the burly trainer and came to a rolling stop right in the center of the class. Still feeling the high from his adrenaline-fueled run, Leif got to his feet a second time and brushed off the dirt and grass before straightening and saying, "I'm sorry."

Before Leif could finish the apology, the muscle-bound trainer rushed forward and shoved Leif hard in the chest. The shove pushed Leif off balance, but wasn't enough to cause him to fall over. "Watch out, asshole!" The trainer growled, "You nearly ran me over! You could have hurt me or my clients! If you want to be stupid go, do it somewhere else!" The trainer moved in to shove Leif a second time; it was a mistake.

The icy fire of the Berserker flooded Leif's veins. Whatever control Leif had disappeared. Fire exploded through him. Leif's conscious mind was shoved aside as the Berserker took control. The trainer went from rightfully angry bystander to a threat. The trainer was pissed and when Leif failed to quail in fear, it caused the overconfident muscle-bound trainer to square up for a fight.

Leif attempted to suppress the rage within after the second push, but it was no use. When Leif saw the punch aimed for his head, there was nothing he could do but let go. Leif's fury-filled body moved on instinct as he caught the trainer's punch mid-swing. Quick as lightening, Leif punched the man in the stomach. The trainer doubled over; blood and vomit exploded out his mouth from the force of the punch. But the Berserker wasn't done. Leif let go of the trainer's arm and followed up with a vicious punch to his face, just below his ear. A loud crack resonated through the park as the trainer's jaw broke. He fell to the grass unconscious.

Leif assessed the man, and the red haze of rage receded as the threat was neutralized. A scream pulled Leif's attention away from the unconscious trainer. All the boot campers had their hands to their mouth, staring in wide-eyed horror at Leif. Several reached for their phones. Fear shot through Leif with the realization of what he had just done to the innocent man. *I've got to get out of here*, Leif thought. He turned and ran, using on all of his newly gained strength.

The sun hadn't fully risen yet. Leif hoped the bystanders wouldn't be able to get a good description of him. He reached the edge of the park but didn't slow. He wanted to be far from the park before the cops arrived. He moved onto the street, keeping his supernatural pace for a few more blocks. He then slowed, wanting to appear as a regular morning runner. By the time Leif had reached his apartment, he relaxed a little. He had run a ridiculous distance in minutes. Leif hoped no one would believe someone who lived so far could have traveled on foot from the park to Leif's apartment in such a short amount of time.

Leif let out a sigh of relief, but he suddenly was overcome with grief and sorrow. *Those people were terrified of me*, he thought. He wished that the trainer hadn't pushed him. He hoped that he hadn't permanently hurt him... or killed him. The thought chilled Leif. "Ok," Leif said to his empty apartment. "No more outbursts. I only have a few days left till I meet up with Arias, and I can't do that if I am in jail for beating the shit out of the first person who stubs my toe. It's time to hunker down and work on my control."

CHAPTER 15

The remaining days crawled by as Leif attempted to limit his time around people. His boss called him to ask if he was ready to come back. Leif thought it would be nice to get out and see his friends. But he decided it would be best for everyone if he stayed away, at least until he had the Berserker under control. "Sorry, Jerry, thank you for the offer, but I just don't think I am ready to come back just yet," Leif told his boss.

With his nights free, Leif spent a lot of time reading the books in the trunk or making a fool of himself as he practiced with the axes. After a day or two of his self-imposed exile, he decided he needed to get out or risk losing his mind to cabin fever.

He went to Santa Monica and watched the ocean for a bit, which helped soothe his mind. Leif was happy that his exile was soon ending ... hopefully. Though he hadn't had any more of those weird dreams, his encounter with the goddess had shaken him. She never outright said it, but her implications were clear. She sent the assassins to kill his grandfather and mother, and she attempted to murder him. The Berserker within him must pose a threat if a powerful being required assassins. Leif thought about his options, *I could either fight back, and hopefully kill that murderous bitch for killing my family or I can run.* He thought he could hide somewhere off the grid and hope whatever she has planned doesn't find its way to Midgard. He knew that was unlikely.

Whatever her plan is, Midgard will be affected. If I have the power to stop her, it is my duty to try. And besides, she murdered my family. For that alone, she deserved to pay.

Staring out over the crashing waves, tasting the salty mist as it washed over him, Leif realized he really didn't have a choice. He had to find the Norns. If there was a chance to stop the person behind his family's murder, goddess or no, he was going to stop her. With his mind made up, Leif headed to his car. It was time to go see an elf.

LEIF REREAD the creased and torn business card. He didn't need to; he had committed it to memory long ago. Bragi Books. He flipped the card over and typed the address into his map's app. Leif had considered showing up early to Arias's store demanding answers, but since he was his only ally and link to the other realms, he heeded Arias's words and waited the two weeks. It might have been a test to see if he could show control.

Leif found the store easy enough. It was nestled in one of those quaint little side streets, hidden from the average tourist. The street was filled with boutiques, coffee shops, restaurants, and vintage clothing stores. Leif was lucky enough to catch a car as it was just pulling out of a spot only a block away from the bookstore. Not minding a little walk, Leif grabbed his hoodie and zipped it up.

A minute later he found himself in front of Bragi Books. Leif took a deep breath. A chime rang as he stepped through the front door. The door closed quietly behind him as Leif took the place in. The store smelled of fresh flowers, cut grass, and a hint of old books. In the middle of the store, there were five equally spaced, double-sided bookracks that went from the floor to the ceiling.

They were packed to the brim with old, dusty books. At the outer edge of the store, a long table was covered with neatly organized boxes filled with vinyl records. Leif regarded the paintings on the wall. One depicted a lush green field with red and yellow flowers peeking out here and there. Another showed a green forest so thick with trees it blotted out the sky, and the final painting was of a beach with azure waves breaking upon the shore in a spray of white sea foam. The paintings were so lifelike, Leif felt like he could step through the frames and stroll around the trees and flowers.

"Ah, is it that time already?" The soft voice had a slight melody to it. Leif turned. Arias leaned against the doorframe at the back of the room. He was wearing dark blue jeans and a flannel button-up shirt with the sleeves rolled up. His exposed forearms were tanned and thick with corded muscle. His raven black hair fell to his shoulders, and his softly glowing eyes danced in the dim bookshop. Leif held Arias's gaze for a fraction of a second before looking away. He found it unnerving to stare into his eyes for too long. They glowed, which Leif had no idea how that was possible, and his pupils were slanted like a cat's eye. It was odd. Coupled with his pointed ears, it gave him a feline appearance.

"Well, don't just stand there. Come on back; we have much to discuss," Arias said, moving to the front of the store. He flipped over the open sign to say closed.

CHAPTER 16

Leif calmly sipped from a cup of tea as Arias reorganized a few items around the back room. Arias smiled when he noticed Leif staring at him. "So, Leif, how have the past few weeks been for you?" Arias asked.

"Really, that is the question you ask? Last time we met you saved me from being split in half by a blue giant."

"Jontar," Arias interjected.

"Jontar. Whatever. Then I essentially plead for your help right before you disappear, and the first thing you ask is 'how have you been?'" Leif almost growled the last statement as he felt the stirring of the Berserker. Leif stopped. He did not realize that he had half risen out of his chair. He took a deep breath and sat back down, attempting to let go of his anger at the asinine question. A small smile crossed Arias's lips as he took in Leif's outburst.

"Good, very good," he commented. "Leif, I am aware of your situation and also to some degree how hard this must be for you. I have only known one Berserker in my life: your grandfather. Though he showed exceptional control, he too would succumb to the monster inside once in a while. And that was after decades of training," Arias commented casually, but then continued. "These past few weeks, though frustrating, were a test to see if you could recognize the danger you pose to those around you should you let the Berserker out. What you just did, suppressing the urge, was a good start. It shows me you are strong of will, and trust me, you will need that. What you inherited is a gift but also a lifelong curse. Before we get to what I have learned, tell me how you have managed since your return from Iceland. You are here and not in some Midgardian prison, so I know you couldn't have caused too much trouble." Arias said.

The memory of Leif's encounter in the gym with the punching bag and the unconscious trainer in the park flashed through his mind and he shifted nervously in his chair.

Arias remained quiet for most of Leif's retelling of his self-imposed isolation. He occasionally asked a question, mostly about what it felt like before he berserked in the gym or why Leif didn't continue attacking the trainer.

When Leif finished, Arias smiled, "Well all things considered, you did well. You were smart to stop going to the gym after your outburst. As I understand it, the Berserker reacts to threats, and you imagining an enemy, combined with the flashback you experienced, must have triggered it." Arias frowned, "It was foolish for you to go into a crowded area like the park, and I hope you will refrain from doing that until you have the Berserker under control. He is lucky you didn't kill him. If he had stayed on his feet to fight back, he would probably be dead right now. Only two outbursts; that's admirable. From today on, you will train with me here, working on your control. But as I said, the Berserker is a part of you now, always lurking in the shadows of your mind, waiting to be unleashed. You must remain firm in your control. As you already know, one slip, one angry outburst in the wrong area, and innocent people will be hurt or killed. Did anything else happen?"

Leif almost said no, then the odd dreams he had been having crossed his mind. "Yes, actually," he said. "I had a few odd dreams. Only three actually, and to be honest, I don't even know if the last one counted as a dream."

Arias perked up. His glowing yellow eyes stared back at Leif intently. "Dreams, you say? The realm of dreams is a mysterious place, even for Ljosalfar. Please tell me what you saw, and spare no detail no matter how small," Arias encouraged.

Leif explained the two fighting dreams against the Jontar and Dokkalfar in the snow. Then, with a little apprehension, he explained his last dream with the goddess. Leif's description of their conversation caused Arias's eyes to widen.

"Your first two dreams could be just dreaming. Or possibly the awakening Berserker showed you past battles from one of your ancestors. However, the last one was no dream, Leif. Your conscious was called from your body, which is not a simple thing to do, not even for beings as powerful as the Aesir and Vanir. It takes an enormous amount of energy to call an unwilling mind from its body. I doubt it will happen again," Arias said.

"Ok, that's fine and good," Leif said, throwing his hands out wide in frustration. "But what does it mean? If it is so costly to do, why do it? And who was it that called me?"

"She is known as Hel, the goddess of death. As you may have guessed, she is behind the murder of Alexander and your mother. Since we last spoke, I reached out to a few of my contacts on Alfheim. And there are whispers of Jontar and Dokkalfar and even a few Orcs moving in the shadows, assassinating warriors and noblemen all in Hel's name. Anytime a being as powerful as Hel moves pieces on the cosmic board, it doesn't bode well for beings in the nine realms. If she spoke to you personally, then that means your kind, the Berserkers, poses a threat to her plans," Arias affirmed.

"What threat could I be?" Leif asked. "Yes, I am Berserker, but she is a god," Leif said in a desperate tone.

"By the gods," Arias said looking up. "Alexander must be smiling down from Valhalla, knowing he left this to me to deal with." Arias took a deep breath and pinched the bridge of his nose before continuing; it was a very Midgardian-like gesture, Leif noted. "I didn't want to scare you off too early, but I guess with Hel popping up in your dream, you should be fully informed before you take the next step. I will give you a choice. I need you to make this decision freely because if you train with me and continue on with what the Norns want of you, I will not always be around to protect you, especially if we are up against Hel." Arias stared at him. "I can see your mind is running like a Cyndqin runs from a hungry Tigrana. Speak your mind freely," Arias encouraged.

Leif took a deep breath, "I'm not running. Wait. What?" Leif said snapping him out of his thoughts and looking to Arias confused.

"Nothing," waving his statement away. Leif's knuckles popped as he clenched his fists in anger, "This bitch killed my family and tried to kill me! I'll admit the dream with her was pretty terrifying, but there's no way I can back down when she has made it personal."

Arias raised an eyebrow, "Good. You've got some fire in you. You need that in the coming months. Today we will go easy. There is much you need to learn. We will train here every day until I feel you are ready. Got that?"

"Yeah," Leif said.

"There is much I will tell you, but let's start with Hel. She is an old and powerful being on the scale of the Aesir and the Vanir. Odin The Allfather gifted her with rule over the underworld realm known as Helheim," Arias said.

"Underworld?" Leif asked.

"Yes, but not like the underworld that you Midgardians think of. Odin charged her to rule and maintain the realm where the souls of the cowardly and dishonorable are sent when they die. There is not much known about her outside of what has fallen into myths and legends. Like the other Aesir and Vanir, she was active in the early eons of the nine realms but has since retreated into her realm. She is the daughter of Loki and may have inherited some of his wickedness. She has one brother, Fenrir, who has never been seen by mortal eyes, but according to legend, he has the power to kill the Aesir. Fearing this power, the Aesir locked him away in a prison under Asgard.

"Many believe Odin banished Hel to the underworld realm to prevent her from freeing her brother. But of course, this is all speculation," Arias stood and reached for Leif's empty cup, "That's enough on Hel for now." Arias turned and disappeared through a side door.

When Arias returned, Leif still wanted to know more. He wanted to know why this was all happening. What could Hel's plan be, and if she was banished to the underworld, how could her plan be so bad as to affect the other realms? Leif held off asking those questions and instead asked, "What about the Norns? Who or what are they, and why is it so important that I find them?" Leif moved to the edge of his chair.

"The Norns. They too are old and very powerful, but they are something different. Apart from the Aesir and Vanir, no one knows exactly who or what they are. They were here before the great war between the Aesir and the Outsiders, and they took no side in the war. They are three sisters with the power to see and understand the river of fate that flows through the cosmos. There are stories of them appearing to those touched by fate, nudging them one way or the other. From the legends, they do not appear to be affiliated with any one group and are instead watchful guardians. The history of the realms is filled with beings searching for the Norns' home, the Well of Urn, but only a handful have been successful."

"But didn't you just say there are stories of people meeting the Norns?" Leif interjected.

"Yes, there are stories and legends of beings across the realms meeting the Norns, but it is always in some far-off cave or secluded meadow where some unsuspecting Ljosalfar or Svartalfar stumbles upon them. It is almost never at their home. It is said the Well of Urn is at the base of the great cosmic tree Yggdrasil. But as I said, very few have ever set foot in the Well of Urn. Alexander was one of them."

Leif's eyes went wide. But before Leif could ask anything, Arias cut him off.

"The short version of the story is the Norns foresaw a great battle and calamity to befall the nine realms. They believed the battle was inevitable, but the calamity that followed was more of a mystery. Whatever they saw flowed away from the destined path for the cosmos. They explained that at the center of the upcoming battle was a Berserker. That this Berserker was the fork in the river of fate. Depending on what he or she did, it would determine the flow of fate. Thus, the Norns instructed Alexander to return to Midgard and prepare for battle. Once your grandfather returned from the Well, he sought me out. We had been friends for many years by then, and he knew I would be interested in what he had learned. Alexander returned to Midgard. I remained in Alfheim for a few more years before deciding to come to Midgard. As the years passed with no signs of the battle to come, we went our separate ways. I enjoyed my time on Midgard and decided to travel the realm, learning as much as I could about your people. I settled down for a time here in Los Angeles. You were in luck; I have been here for many years, and as you have guessed, we Ljosalfar age very slowly compared to your kind. Thus, I figured I only had a year or two more before I should return to my home realm, lest some Midgardians become suspicious of me. But I digress. Long story short, the murder of your grandfather, the Jontar and Dokkalfar attacking you in the open, and now your conversation with Hel, must be the signs of the beginning of the war the Norns mentioned. The best bet we have right now is to train you to survive, travel across the realms, and locate the Norns."

"If my grandfather is on the short list of beings to have found the Well and he's dead, how are we expected to find it?" Leif asked.

"He told me where the bridge is. The proper question will be whether the bridge is still open. Some bridges are firmly set within the veil, connecting realms along the branches of the cosmic tree. Others come and go as they please, as if being blown across the realms. They connect realms at random for an unknown amount of time," Arias took a breath.

"Do not worry about the location of the bridge, your focus should be on harnessing the Berserker. Once you have proven yourself worthy of carrying the Berserker mantle, we can discuss the location of the bridge to the Norns."

Arias stood up, slapped Leif on the arm. "All right, enough talk. Let's see what you are made of." He gestured to an open area free of books and boxes. Leif hesitated, "Um, are you sure? I don't want to hurt you."

Arias laughed as he moved to the far side of the area and put up his arms in a guard position like a boxer. He even bounced around on the balls of his feet, taking a few experimental punches.

Leif shrugged, "Ok, but if I end up hurting or killing you, it's on you."

Arias grinned, flashing too many teeth. If he could ignore the glowing eyes, the smile alone would cause Leif to second guess his humanity.

Leif stepped up, copying Arias's stance and movements. They circled and weaved around each other, neither making the first move. Leif punched out a few times, but Arias danced away. Then it was Arias's turn. Leif was amazed at how easy it was to dodge Arias's punches. A minute or two into the fight, Leif felt more confident and went on the offensive. He took more risks, feeling his enhanced strength and speed would make up for any mistakes. Finally, Leif connected two solid punches, one to

Arias's gut, followed up with a right jab to his jaw that sent him stumbling. Leif smiled, thinking he might not have to train as long as he thought before he was ready.

Arias picked himself off the ground, wiped away a small dribble of blood from the corner of his mouth and came back with a different demeanor. He no longer adopted the boxer stances, but he took a more relaxed posture with his hands around chest height. His hands were no longer balled into fists but hung loose. Leif noticed the change but failed to understand what it meant. The overconfident Leif feinted a jab to Arias's right side, then followed up with a vicious punch to Arias's face. But in the last moment, Arias blurred, slapping Leif's punch away and pushing him off balance. Leif moved in, assuming Arias would dance away like he had done many times before, only he didn't. Staying rooted in place, Arias dodged a series of punches–high, low, high, high, low. Leif's fist met the air. Growing frustrated, Leif tried again, swinging faster and faster, hoping his enhanced speed could tip the scales. Leif didn't know how, but Arias continued to dodge. He moved a fraction of an inch each time, which infuriated Leif even more. As his anger grew, so did the icy burn of the Berserker. Leif inwardly smiled. *You've done it now. Once I let the Berserker out, you won't be dodging so easily*, Leif thought. Quicker than the eye could see, Arias stopped dodging, caught one of Leif's fists with a loud clapping sound and BAM, Leif was on the ground. Pain blossomed across his cheek.

The spreading pain across his face was extinguished as the icy burn took hold. His muscles strengthened with his increasing rage. Looking up, Leif now saw an enemy that needed to be crushed. Leif spit a glob of blood onto the ground and charged. The pretense of a friendly fight was gone. Leif attacked with fury, but Arias stood his ground with a wide grin on his face. Leif closed in and Arias stepped to the side. Leif flew past him. Books flew all over the place as he crashed headlong into a bookshelf. He was back up in a blur, moving faster and racing back towards

Arias. This time he came up short and swung at Arias with enough force to take his head off, but Arias ducked under the wild haymaker and punched Leif in his unguarded stomach. The pain and shock of the blow sent Leif to his knees, but the Berserker refused to cow down. A snarl escaped Leif's lips, and he stood back up and rushed back in. With a slight smile and a nod of approval, Arias quietly said, "Good."

The speed and power of Leif's punches continued to increase as his Berserker rage grew. Arias was being forced to dodge and dance away from Leif's enhanced punches. The two danced back and forth as they moved through the back room until Arias felt the exercise had gone on long enough. Once again, Leif feinted a punch meant for Arias's ribs, then quickly followed up with a right hook, but Arias wasn't fooled. He blocked the hook, taking the punch on his forearm, and he struck.

LEIF WOKE WITH A START. The first thing he noticed was he hurt all over. His head throbbed, his ribs felt bruised, and his legs and arms felt like they had their own painful heartbeats. The next thing Leif noticed was that he had landed on a box full of books and the edges of the hardback books were sticking into his back. Slowly getting to his feet, Leif attempted to pierce the fog that settled over his memories when he came out of a Berserk episode. He remembered taking the punch from Arias, knowing it was painful, but he could shrug it off. Then their exchanging blows, which Leif remembered his Berserker-self thinking he had Arias, and it was only a matter of time till Leif wore him out. Then darkness. A slurping sound pulled him out of his head. Arias sat in his chair, casually sipping his tea. Setting his teacup down, Arias asked, "So, tell me where it went wrong."

"Ugh," Leif grumbled. In truth, he was already feeling better. Many of the aches and pains from the brief fight had already faded, and the pulsing, mind-melting headache with which he had woken had dialed down to a minor annoyance.

Leif plopped down into the waiting chair across from Arias. "Well, I guess it started with me thinking I could take you," Leif said sheepishly. "Though I don't think you had to be so brutal about putting me down. If it had been any other Midgardian, you probably would have killed them with a punch like that," Leif finished.

"True," Arias said as he took another sip of his tea. "But you aren't a normal Midgardian, are you? You are much stronger and quicker than Alexander, even in his prime, which is good. That also makes you incredibly dangerous. I have seen all I needed to see for the day, so I ended the fight the quickest way I knew how: knocking you out. It had the added effect of teaching you an additional lesson," Arias said.

"That you're a bit of an asshole," Leif commented, as he rubbed his head. His head had stopped hurting. Leif felt like all of his injuries had healed up, but he was still a little annoyed with Arias.

Arias laughed. "No, true as that may be. You needed to learn the hard way that even though you are stronger and faster than you used to be, you are still only a Midgardian. You will always be at a disadvantage in a fight against beings of the other realms."

Leif hung his shoulders.

"But don't let that discourage you. You can use it. Because you are a Midgardian, many of your enemies will underestimate you. Not many beings of the nine realms have seen or even heard of one of your kind. I myself have only met one, and he was a master at using his enemies' preconceived notions against them. Until you Berserk and your eyes glow similar to an Aesir, most of your enemies won't give you a second glance."

"Wait!" Leif said, a look of confusion on his face. "My eyes glow when I Berserk? Like yours?"

"Yes, they glow, but not like mine. Your eyes change as you

release the power, signifying you are drawing on the small amount of power that Thor granted your kind. It signifies you have been blessed by Thor."

"This is awesome!" An enormous grin spread across Leif's face. "I've got to get a picture of it one of these days."

"Midgardians and their obsession with taking pictures," Arias shook his head. "Ahem" Arias, trying to change the subject, set his tea down with a clink and got to his feet. "You did well, but we still have a lot to do before you are ready." He held out his hand and Leif took it. "Come back tomorrow and we will begin your training in earnest."

CHAPTER 17

The next day, Leif drove back to Arias's store, excited to begin his training. Leif had been too amped to fall asleep the previous night. He put on Star Wars: Empire Strikes Back, which didn't help him fall asleep either. He had lain awake for most of the night imagining training with Arias. When Luke Skywalker was running with Master Yoda on his back, an image of Leif carrying Arias around in a similar fashion popped into his head, causing Leif to laugh for a good ten minutes. The thought then occurred to Leif he was living almost every person's childhood fantasy of training with some wise old sage in order to gain the strength to save the day. Leif thought it was cool.

The jingle of Arias's door brought Leif back to the present, and he closed the door behind him. The shop was empty once again and the door to the back room was wide open.

"Leif, is that you?" Arias called out from the room beyond.

"Yup, it's me. I'm here for round two and I promise you, this time I won't go down so easily," Leif said.

"Ha! I doubt that very much, Midgardian!" Arias retorted. "Change the sign to closed, lock the door, and come on back."

The back room was rearranged since yesterday's visit. The shelves of books were replaced with a heavy punching bag attached to the ceiling on a heavy-duty chain. *Smart*, Leif thought. *I don't think I'll be able to knock that one down*. A rack full of wooden weapons, staffs, swords, a double-bladed ax, and a couple sets of hatchets rested to the side of the practice space.

"What do you think?" Arias asked from somewhere behind Leif.

"Looks good; it kind of has a secret lair feel to it. I know! Can we name this place the Bat Cave? I'll be Batman and you can be some badass alternative version of Alfred who trains me to fight!" Leif turned around and found Arias standing in the center of a large ring taped off in the center of the storeroom. "You can start by teaching me how to sneak up on people like that," Leif said enthusiastically.

"You know," Arias said, "I like to think of myself more like Batman and you are my sidekick, who was that again? Robin. Yeah, you can be my Robin."

Leif rolled his eyes. "You will pay for that, old man," Leif said as he set his gym bag down and stepped into the ring to greet Arias. They shook hands, both smiling at their easy-going banter.

"You know, I may be old by Midgardian standards, but I am still quite young. My kind, barring injury or sickness, can live for hundreds of years. A few have even lived to be over a thousand years old," Arias boasted.

"Whatever, Legolas. What do you have in store for me today?" Leif asked.

Ignoring the jab, Arias said, "Today we will work on your hand-to-hand combat. We need to sharpen up your reflexes and work on your control. I want to push right up to the brink of you going Berserk, then have you shut it down. We will repeat that process until you can recognize when you are about to snap and shut it down. Once you have that covered, we will work on gaining some modicum of control when you let the monster out. That is where the pain will begin because just like last time, I will shut you down hard when I see you have lost control. We will then repeat the process until I feel you have some control over yourself. Right now, you are a raging bull--strong and deadly, but easy to dodge and predict. I want to turn you into a tiger, powerful and fearsome, but still in control."

"Makes sense," Leif said. "But um, when do I get to practice with the axes my grandpa left me?" Leif asked.

"When I feel you won't accidentally chop off your arm or mine," Arias said matter-of-factly.

"Oh, yeah, that makes sense," Leif agreed.

"Enough talk," Arias said. "We will fight like yesterday, but I want you to work on your control. When you feel the Berserker taking over, fight back. Try to hold on to your conscious mind for as long as you can," Arias instructed.

"But if I am so powerful when I'm fully berserked, why would I want to suppress it?" Leif asked as he stepped into the ring.

"Because I said so," Arias said. "You need to let go of your ego. Especially now that you will go up against beings far older and stronger than you. Now, come at me."

The two circled and tested each other. Leif would get impatient and move in. The two traded blows back and forth, getting Leif comfortable with the flow of the fight. Every once in a while, Arias would stop them, pointing out the myriad of openings Leif was showing. But more often, it was to explain how idiotic one of Leif's attacks was, pointing out missed opportunities or when he was overreaching.

"Keep your hands up; don't tense up; keep your knees bent," Arias coached before demonstrating the importance of the little tweaks. It wasn't long before all pretense of a fun training session evaporated. Sweat trickled down Leif's forehead as he tried to keep up with what Arias was telling him, while also trying to get in some good hits. Leif must have dropped his arm too low one too many times because Arias moved in fast, swatted Leif's feeble attempt to take Arias to the ground, and hammered Leif hard in the face.

Blood gushed from Leif's nose as his vision went black, then red. He had been doing a good job at keeping the howling Berserker at bay, but the hit caused Leif's attention to falter and the icy fire of his transformation grew. Leif welcomed it because with the blinding rage came the cooling of all of his aches and pains he had suffered from Arias's punishing strikes. The red haze filled his eyes. The rage and desire to rip Arias limb-from-limb was there, but there was something else... clarity. He knew if he charged in blindly, he would most likely end up on his ass. Leif still wanted to dash forward and tackle the smug elf to the ground, but he held back. He could see Arias was surprised by this, but he, too, held back, watching Leif warily. The two circled as the tension in the room grew with each step. Finally, Arias darted forward, ducked down, surprising Leif by smashing a hard kick into his thigh. Crying out in pain, Leif charged forward. All the thoughts of a controlled attack were smothered by a burning desire to crush the haute elf, but Arias was ready. Leif attacked. Arias grabbed his shirt, rolled backward, pulling Leif with him, and kicked up as Arias's back came in contact with the concrete floor. Leif was sent flying over Arias, out of the ring and into the wall with a thud. Arias continued his roll, getting to his feet in a single graceful movement. He casually walked to Leif, who was pushing himself onto his hands and knees. The rage was clear in his slightly glowing eyes, and Arias slugged him once, then twice, knocking the enraged fool unconscious.

Leif woke a few minutes later with throbbing pain to his jaw and shoulders. He was on the floor... again. Pushing himself up to a seated position, Leif nearly fell over as the pain magnified, thrumming through his body. He pushed through it. Arias was back in his seat, sipping tea again.

Frustration and annoyance crashed through Leif like a tidal wave. "Ah! You know there has got to be a better way for you to snap me out of my Berserker state," Leif moaned.

Arias took another sip of his tea. "Nope," he got up and moved back into the ring.

Leif narrowed his eyes. "Nope? That's all you've got to say? Hundreds of years on these realms and all you've got to say is 'nope?' Awesome!" Leif got to his feet.

Stretching a little to shake out the minor aches, Leif was eternally happy that he healed at an accelerated rate. The pain in his head and shoulders had already receded to a dull throb.

Arias motioned for Leif to step back into the ring. "You did well for a short time there, Leif. I could see you fighting to keep the Berserker back, but once you lost your focus, it came roaring out. Keep this up and in a few weeks, you may actually have some degree of control."

THE FOLLOWING month followed the same pattern. They would fight, Arias stopping every few minutes to correct Leif's guard stance, or to point out all the openings Leif was presenting him while Leif struggled to keep from letting the Berserker loose. As the two spared, Arias would kick it up a notch, pushing Leif to his limit, which would then force the Berserker out. Some days Leif showed exceptional control, keeping the rage at bay and actually using his head when he fought. Sometimes, all Leif would remember was waking up on the floor while Arias sipped tea. Leif was starting to hate tea.

Leif always had a flash of annoyance and sometimes even rage upon waking up day after day on the concrete floor of their makeshift training room. Even so, Leif had grown to like Arias. Though he was serious about their training, he still had a pleasant sense of humor, and it was easy to forget he wasn't human, let alone over three hundred years old.

After training two months straight with Arias, Leif marveled that he hadn't woken up sore or injured once. He was exhausted, though. A month into their training, Arias had given Leif the ok to return to work. Though Leif's control wasn't perfect, he had worked tirelessly at keeping the Berserker at bay. He could at least control it long enough to get to a spot where he could rage without fear of hurting anyone. His control was good, but it wasn't perfect. Leif ended up needing to replace his steering wheel twice. It seemed getting stuck in L.A. traffic was enough to break his control. Leif had kept those brief outbursts to himself. *Arias need not know every little detail of my life*, Leif thought.

A BUZZING SOUND and a sharp high voice called out, "Hey! Listen!" Leif grabbed his phone from the nightstand; the screen read "Link is calling." He inwardly laughed at his joke and answered the phone.

"Rise and shine," Arias said.

"Ugh, why are you calling me so early? Or have you decided that beating the shit out of me in the afternoon just isn't enough anymore?" Leif grumbled into the phone.

"You Midgardians," Arias sighed. "Always got something to say. No, you little ingrate. I was calling to say I think you have earned a break from your regularly beating and was wondering whether you wanted to go on a little field trip with me?" Arias asked.

"Field trip?" Leif repeated. "To where?"

"Well, I have been monitoring the veil lately, and it appears it is weaker than normal. Which makes it much easier to cross over to my home realm of Alfheim.

"I can open a bridge close to here which will drop us right outside the Ljosalfar capital city. I need to pick up a few supplies for our upcoming quest, and I figured we could kill two birds with one stone. I get to pick up my stuff, and you can get acquainted with being in a different realm filled with non-Midgardians. What do you say?" Arias asked.

"Hell yeah!" Leif yelled into the phone. "When can we go? Do I need to bring anything? Should I bring my axes?" Leif's mind was spinning. Though he loved his training sessions with Arias, he was getting bored.

"Meet me at the shop in an hour. It's a small hike and a bit of a swim. I will have a change of clothes to help you blend in while on Alfheim. Bring your axes. Hel's minions could be anywhere, but don't do anything stupid with them. I really don't want to see all my efforts in training you go down the drain by you getting killed or maimed while we are over there. Got it?" Arias had a serious tone.

"Yeah, yeah, I got you. I won't do anything stupid, I promise," Leif said.

"Good. Get dressed; we have a long day ahead of us," Arias hung up the phone.

CHAPTER 18

Leif showered and got dressed in a rush. He put on a pair of jeans, but then took them off, searching for his swimsuit, a t-shirt, and any random sweater he could find. Leif then wrapped the twin axes and belt in a towel and stuffed them in his backpack. Not sure how long it would take to get to the bridge or how long they would be on the other side, he filled up his semi-crushed Hydro Flask, grabbed some trail mix, and headed out the door.

The cool morning air helped to clear Leif's senses, but he felt like he was still moving a little sluggishly. He stopped by the small coffee shop down the street for an iced latte with an extra shot of espresso. Leif preferred cold coffee, even in the wintertime. After his first sip, he could feel the cobwebs clear. He grabbed an extra latte for Arias, hoping it would curb his natural grumpiness. Getting back on the road, Leif saw getting to the bookstore would take longer than he had hoped. "Stupid Los Angeles traffic," Leif moaned.

After what felt like hours, Leif parked in front of the dark bookstore. The sun had risen, helping burn away the brisk morning fog. Leif pulled his sweater closer to combat the chill. As Leif opened his trunk to grab his backpack, he felt a slight tingle at the back of his neck. Before he could react, he was pushed forward roughly, almost banging his head against the lid of the trunk. A snarl escaped Leif's lips as he prepared to fight off whoever had been foolish enough to attack him. He turned to face the target. Arias stood a few feet away with an arrogant smile on his face. Leif stood up straight, taking a few deep breaths to push back the Berserker. It took longer than he would have liked, but after a few minutes of deep breathing, Leif felt the last bits of icy rage recede, and he was his new normal angry self again.

"What the hell, man?" Leif growled once he had regained control. "Do you want me berserking out right here in the middle of the streets?" Leif threw his hands out to his side. Arias remained where he was, smiling the entire time.

"Man, you Midgardians can be such drama queens sometimes," Arias said. "I wanted to see how far you had progressed in your training. And I would say that's a C-. That's how you Midgardians grade your children, right? With letters?" Arias asked.

"C-," Leif said, flabbergasted. "C is barely passing! A few months ago, I would have berserked out and attacked you outright. Once I saw it was you, I could pull it back and control it. That was at least a B."

Arias looked unconvinced, "True, but I could sneak up on you. If I had been one of Hel's assassins, you would be dead right now. I will admit, your control of your inner Berserker has greatly improved. However, it still took you a few minutes to suppress it," Arias said. "You need to work on cutting that down. While we are out tracking down the Norns, we may need to cut and run in some situations, and I can't have you standing there, breathing heavily like some overweight dog out in the heat for a few minutes. You need to assess the situation, see you need not go Berserk, suppress the change, then move on. I stand by my grade. Now let's go. It took you forever to get here. What were you doing anyway?" Arias asked.

"It's L.A. man. It takes forever to get anywhere; besides, I brought a peace offering," Leif reached into the car and grabbed the extra latte he bought.

Arias smiled as he took a sip. "Ah, I think I was too quick to grade you. You now get a C+," Arias chuckled.

Leif shook his head, muttering, "I don't know why I bother."

"Quit your whining," Arias motioned for Leif to follow. Arias walked up to a four-door Tundra and unlocked it, "Hop in. The cave with the bridge in it will only be accessible for a few more hours, so let's get a move on it."

Leif comfortably sat in the front seat of the Tundra as Arias headed west on the I-10. It wasn't long before he turned onto Pacific Coast Highway and headed into Malibu. Leif enjoyed the ride; the winding road of PCH combined with the beautiful ocean view helped to ease his nerves. It wasn't long until Arias pulled off PCH onto a small dirt path and parked. A sheer cliff walled the side toward Malibu. Across the highway, thick trees obscured Leif's view of the ocean beyond. Arias and Leif got out, put on their respective backpacks and headed to the truck bed. Arias unlocked the tailgate and pulled out two longboards. He handed one to Leif, "I hope you can swim."

He walked up to the highway, looked both ways, then ran across the street, disappearing into the trees beyond. He must have realized Leif wasn't following him because a moment later he emerged from the tree line yelling out, "Come on! Let's go!" Snapping out of his confusion, Leif ran across the street and followed Arias into the thicket of trees.

It was hard going. Leif had to watch both his feet to prevent himself from tripping over fallen branches and roots, and he also had to watch his longboard. He had accidentally rammed it into Arias's back a couple times, which earned him a few angry glares. Leif knew he would get chastised once they went back to training. After twenty minutes of careful walking, they emerged from the trees and descended to a small sandy beach.

The beauty of this hidden beach absolutely mesmerized Leif. The thick trees obscured the beach from the road, and since they were high on a cliff, the small switch-back path down to the beach was completely hidden.

Leif guessed that not even the locals knew about this area. The little beach couldn't be more than thirty feet long and was only about ten feet wide. The cove was only twenty feet across before opening up to the ocean. "This is amazing," Leif commented to Arias. "Have you ever come across anyone down here?"

"Nope. This tiny stretch of beach is only accessible a few times a month. Most of the time, the tide rises and hides it from prying eyes. It is lucky for us because outside of renting a boat, this is the only way to reach the small cave mouth where the bridge is located. Let's keep moving. I don't enjoy sitting around in this area. The longer we stay here, the more likely a passing boat or those damn new drones may sneak up on us, and our little hiding spot will be spoiled."

Arias took off his shoes and put them in his backpack, and Leif followed suit. Arias rolled up his jeans, waded into the water, dropped his longboard in front of him, slid onto it, and slowly paddled out into the cove. Leif shrugged and stepped into the water. A shiver ran up his spine when his toes touched the frigid water. Leif dropped his board in front of him and jumped on. Leif was careful not to tip over as he paddled after Arias. Arias was already out of the cove, slipping out of sight. Not wanting to get left behind, Leif paddled faster.

By the time Leif made it out of the inlet, his hands had gone numb from the icy water. As Leif cleared the cove, he was happy to see Arias was about thirty feet away and up against the cliff wall. When Leif moved closer, he could see a small hole cut into the cliff face just large enough to fit a person if they crouched down. The surrounding area had several rocks protruding out of the water, preventing anyone from noticing the hole unless they were directly in front of it. With an air of annoyance, Arias looked back at Leif who was being battered back and forth by the waves. When Leif got closer, he moved nearer to the hole. He timed the waves for a few moments, then slipped into the hole as a wave brought him up against the cliff.

Once in the cave, Leif watched as Arias quickly turned around and grabbed the board before it could be pulled away on the ocean current. *Looks easy enough*, Leif thought. It was not. It took Leif several tries to get the timing of the waves right. Once Leif finally pulled himself into the tiny cave mouth, he was so excited to be out of the chilly ocean water that he almost forgot to grab his longboard.

With both longboards safely stowed against the cave wall, the two turned and half crouched, half walked deeper into the cave. Arias commented, "You are lucky I was here to remind you to grab your longboard because I sure as hell would not let you borrow mine on our way out of here. It would have been a long cold swim back to the shore for you."

"Yes, thank you, almighty Arias. I am eternally in your debt," Leif said sarcastically.

"You bet your Midgardian ass you are. Hmmm, Almighty Arias… that has a nice ring to it," Arias mused. The cave opened up enough to allow Leif and Arias to stand and walk side by side as they continued further into the cave.

The tunnel angled to the right, cutting off the sunlight flooding in from the cave mouth. When they moved far enough away from the light, a soft glow emanated from the walls and ceiling. It wasn't bright, but it provided just enough light to see where they were going. Leif stopped mid-step when he noticed there were several large glyphs carved into the rock walls and ceilings.

Arias saw that Leif had stopped following him. He stepped beside Leif and admired the glyphs as well.

"What are these?" Leif asked

Arias didn't respond right away. He continued staring at the markings for a long moment. Finally, he said in a voice filled with wonder, "These carvings help maintain the bridge between the realms. The great cosmic tree, Yggdrasil, powers these glyphs. By harnessing the power, we can open a bridge between realms."

Leif looked on in open-mouth astonishment at the myriad of runes that ran along the walls. Leif followed the flowing carvings along the wall to the end of the cave. The carvings ran all the way up to and along the back wall of the cave.

"Whoever created these bridges between realms, has power on a scale with the Aesir. The bridges exist in every realm, strategically placed in areas where the veil is weakened," Arias said.

"How are people able to find these bridges?" Leif asked.

"Many of them have been mapped through the eons, though occasionally a new one pops up. Even without a map, someone who is attuned to the magical flow of the cosmos can find them. These bridges radiate power. They are constantly drawing power from the limbs of Yggdrasill. Without trying, I can feel the magical energy pulsing through this room. It's overwhelming. A normal Midgardian wouldn't be able to feel a thing if they were to stumble onto this cave. You, however, with the awakening of the Berserker should be able to feel it if you focus hard enough. Close your eyes and still your mind," Arias instructed.

"This is an excellent starting point for your introduction to magic," Arias continued. "With practice, you will be able to feel the flow of magical energies around you, but it is highly unlikely that you will be able to harness and manipulate those energies. Don't ask me why. I don't know, but it seems that Midgardians got the short end of the stick magically speaking. There is only a small, and I mean small, percentage of your people who can actually manipulate magical energy to their own ends. But that's not the case with many of the other beings of the nine realms. For example, take Ljosalfar and Dokkalfar. We can all use magic of one sort or another. Close your eyes and see if you can feel anything. In the future, you may need to recognize if powerful magics are being used around you. You have been very lucky so far. You must be smart, quick, and have an agile mind like your grandfather. Now hurry up. I am getting a headache from the magic pulsing through this cave."

Closing his eyes, Leif strained to feel something-anything. As hard as he tried, there was nothing but the soft ocean breeze passing through the cave. The longer it went on, the more foolish Leif felt. WACK. Leif felt a sharp pain to his arm.

"Relax," Arias said, "You're trying too hard. It looks like you are about to have an aneurysm. You can't force the feeling; you have to clear your mind to feel it."

Leif took a deep breath, held it, then let it out in an explosive sigh. He let his muscles uncoil as the breath escaped. He did this a few more times, and his mind slowly emptied. It was only then that he felt an odd pulsing sensation in the back of his mind. It felt like a car slowly revving its engine. Then, just as quickly, the feeling slipped away.

"Good," Arias said, clapping him on his back. "Though you will never have the ability to wield magic, it is important that you continue to hone that feeling until you can recognize it on the fly. Once we are done with your training here on Midgard and begin our journey to find the Norns, we will work on picking up on the magic around you," Arias said over his shoulder, "Let's go; we are wasting time."

Arias stepped up to the cave wall, placed his right hand against it, and said a few words in a language Leif didn't recognize. With each word spoken, the sound hung in the air for longer than it should have. The symbols along the wall glowed with a soft red light, then there was a bright flash that caused Leif to shield his eyes.

CHAPTER 19

Leif stepped from the cave into a lush green forest. Massive pine trees spread out in all directions. Leif looked back at the cave they had just come from. When he widened his gaze, he could see the bridge mouth on this side was nothing more than a massive boulder covered in the same style of glyphs found in the cave on Midgard. Arias stepped up to the still open bridge and placed his hands on the side of the boulder. He again muttered a few words in the strange language. There was another flash, and the bridge closed. All that was left was the intact boulder, covered in symbols. *Amazing*, Leif thought. *If Arias is right and I can't use magic, I better not get lost because he is my only ticket home.*

Arias unslung his backpack and motioned for Leif to do the same.

Looking up through the sunlit canopy, Arias started, "Alright. It's close to mid-day here, so the streets of Karcoa will be busy. Our goal for this trip is to get you acquainted with Alfheim and to be around people from other realms. It is a short hike from here to the main roads that lead to Alfheim's capital city. That being said, try to not talk to anyone or bring too much attention to yourself. Midgardians are rare within the other realms. I don't want word to reach Hel or any of her minions that you were seen roaming around. It might tip her off that you are still working against her. Strap on your axes, then put this on," Arias reached into his bag and pulled out a long forest green cloak. Leif took the cloak and flung it over his shoulders. "Pull up the hood. With the hood obscuring your ears and eyes, no one will look too closely." He then pointed back towards the glyph covered boulder. "We will hide our bags behind the boulder. They would stand out too much here, so we can't bring them with us. Also, if we get separated, meet back here at sunset, ok?" Arias instructed.

"Don't draw attention to myself and if we get lost, meet back here at sunset. Got it," Leif said.

As they moved through the forest, Leif was in awe at the beauty of the place. The air smelled clean and free of the pollution he had gotten used to back home in LA. Birds of various colors and hues chirped and sang as they fluttered amongst the branches. As they searched for the road, the pair came upon a meadow full of bright yellow and orange flowers. Leif paused for a moment, enjoying the view of the flowers as they swayed in the forest breeze. He felt like he could have stayed there for hours watching the colorful flowers. Arias silently materialized next to Leif.

"Though I have traveled much of the nine realms, I still find my home on Alfheim the most beautiful. My entire realm is covered in forests and lakes. Now come on; you have seen nothing yet. Wait till we get to Karcoa."

They walked in silence for the better part of an hour. Leif wasn't sure how Arias could tell where they were going. Except for the occasional break in the trees, or stream, it all looked the same to Leif: trees, trees, and more trees. They eventually came upon a small cobblestone path cutting straight through the forest. As they turned onto the path, Leif asked, "Is this the way to the wizard?"

"Quiet, fool. We are trying to keep a low profile, remember?"

Arias hissed, trying to be serious. He did let a grin slip onto his face.

"So, tell me a little about Alfheim and your people, the Ljosalfar, right? My grandfather's book had little on your kind. It said you're a long-lived race, that your kind typically stays to themselves, and that there was a civil war a long, long time ago between the Ljosalfar and the Dokkalfar who shared this realm. It said that the Dokkalfar lost, and they were nearly wiped out because of it. The surviving Dokkalfar were banished after the war, right?"

"That's a good start. Well first, unlike Midgard, Alfheim is a world suffused by magic. It is all around us; the trees, the air, the water, the dirt we are walking on, and my people... magic runs through it all. The Ljosalfar can connect to it all. Because of this connection, we weave magic into much of what we do. As we get closer to Karoca, you will understand just how much we do with it."

A mile or two later, small lights could be seen hanging down from the trees along the path. Arias smiled and said, "This is a perfect example of how the Ljosalfar weave magic into the world around them," Arias pointed toward the lights above and said, "Take a closer look and tell me what you see."

Leif stared in wonder at the hanging lanterns. Each of the lanterns was crafted in a teardrop shape and made out of the same material as the trees. A clear membrane-like material let the light pass through it. Leif guessed that if he were to touch the clear substance, it would feel similar to the leaves.

"Are they growing out of the trees?" Leif asked.

"That's right. Long ago, some unknown Ljosalfar while traveling to Karcoa at night grew tired of carrying his torch, and he had the forest around him light the way instead. He cast a spell on the trees lining the path to grow lanterns to light the way for all who travel the road. He must have been a clever one because the spell he wove had the tree siphon off energy from the sun and moon and use it to power the lanterns, thus not harming the tree. The people of Karcoa, upon learning of the lantern trees, fell in love with the idea and searched the elf down to have him repeat the spell upon all the trees lining the paths to the city. They had hoped to line all the paths connecting Karcoa to many other cities on Alfheim, but manipulating the shape of that many trees proved far more taxing than expected. So now, the lantern trees are only used within the last few miles leading to Karcoa."

It was a little after mid-day, but the trees were so thick that they blocked much of the sunlight. The lanterns illuminated the path with a soft golden glow. Arias added, "So many Ljosalfar fell in love with the lantern trees, that in some areas whole swaths of these trees were created. The unknown elf could even get a few trees to produce different color lights. It is truly an amazing sight to behold, especially at night. If we are lucky and survive this little ordeal Alexander has gotten us into, one day I will take you to an area of the city filled with lantern trees where each tree is a distinct color. It is an amazing place."

Leif couldn't pull his eyes away from the hanging lanterns; they were amazing.

After another hour of walking, the peaceful quiet of the forest changed to a background hum of people walking and talking. The two travelers finally crested a tall hill, and Leif got his first view of Karcoa. As the cobblestone path rolled down the hill, it gradually widened to accommodate more foot traffic. The forest abruptly ended at the bottom of the hill and was replaced by a stone walkway running perpendicular to the path Leif and Arias was on. This new path spread out to thirty feet and was jam-packed with different beings.

At first, Leif thought many of them were human, but upon closer inspection, Leif spotted the slightly pointed ears sticking out from their flowing gold or raven black hair. Leif spotted what he thought might be one or two humans moving among the Ljosalfar, but he could have been wrong. Other beings could be seen moving through the throngs of Ljosalfar as well. Some were small and squat, with powerfully built arms and beards hanging down to their knees. Leif thought they must be Svartalfar. Leif also spied a few dark green skinned beings that he guessed were Orcs. They were taller than the average Ljosalfar and built like Olympic power lifters. Leif didn't overlook the two small tusks sticking out from their lower lips or the massive broadswords slung over their backs. Even though they were a good thirty feet from the moving crowd, Leif's hand subconsciously went to his axes hanging from his belt. Leif relaxed when he realized that many of the beings in the crowd were similarly armed. Many of the Ljosalfar had thin rapier-like blades hanging from their hips, while the few Svartalfar had war axes or hammers slung over their shoulders.

Leif leaned in and quietly spoke to Arias, "It's like out of some fantasy story I read as a kid. Elves, Dwarfs, Orcs. They are all here and fit pretty well into the descriptions out of Lord of the Rings. How is that possible?" Leif asked.

"I had been wondering when you would ask me that," Arias commented. "You know the bridge we crossed a few hours ago?" Leif nodded, "Well, that is a hard point bridge, meaning it's a fixed connection. Somehow, whoever connected the bridges between the realms created certain hard points throughout the realms that are permanently fixed and can be opened and closed by anyone who is magically strong enough. Some are random based on swaying cosmic connections. Many of your kind have unknowingly crossed over into this realm or one of the others. A few Midgardian authors crossed over into friendly territories and were able to return with great stories to tell, while others, who may have crossed over into Jotenheim, Muspelheim or Niflheim, most likely met untimely ends. There are even those who crossed over only to learn the bridge had closed up and then were stuck in whichever realm they crossed into. It is because many of those authors weren't making it up; they were merely retelling what they saw."

"Huh," Leif said, "That's pretty crazy. So, do you mean to say a battle for middle earth actually took place?"

SMACK.

"Ow," Leif rubbed the back of his head where Arias had smacked him.

"No, you fool. There was no battle for middle earth here; that part was made up. There have been many battles throughout Alfheim's history, that story most likely came from the great war between the Ljosalfar and Dokkalfar. As I read and watched the movies, there a few instances that seemed familiar to me."

"Cool," Leif responded, "You must tell me about it someday."

"Someday," Arias responded.

Leif gaped at the city beyond the moving crowd. What Leif had taken as just more forest beyond was actually the outer fringes of Karcoa. The trees were on a completely different scale. Each tree was as big around as a house and shot hundreds of feet into the sky. Leif fell into step behind Arias, as they approached the crowded walkway, but Leif was too transfixed by the trees to see where they were going. Leif could see that doors, windows, and balconies were cut into the trees. Small hanging bridges ran between the trees, connecting them like a suspended highway. Just like the forest, the canopy of the trees was so large that they almost blocked out the sky above, so hundreds of lanterns hung from the many twisting branches that spread out through the forest city. Some branches were so large that they had been converted into walkways. Leif could see Ljosalfar and Svartalfar walking on the branches and walkways, going here and there. Arias caught Leif staring and clapped him on the back. "Amazing, isn't it? I never get tired of seeing it. The whole city is built into the forest. As you go deeper into the city, the trees get older and bigger. The trees closest to the center put these monsters to shame," Arias said as he slapped one of the massive tree trunks. "And if you were to travel to the center of the city, you would see the crowning jewel of this great city; the Monarch. The Monarch is the oldest tree on Alfheim. It's said that its roots extend across all of Alfheim, connecting itself with each of the great forests covering the surface of this realm. The Monarch is also home to the Ljosalfar court, where the Eternal Queen sits on her throne. Hell, if we actually survive this little quest, we may be lucky enough to stand before her."

A light breeze wafted past them, bringing with it an intoxicating aroma of barbecue. Leif's stomach growled loudly. Arias raised an eyebrow in question.

"What!" Leif said defensively, "I skipped breakfast this morning."

Smiling, Arias said, "Come on, let's see if we can snag something quick to eat then." Leading the way, the two stepped out of the press of beings of the outer walkway and moved into the sea of trees.

Hanging lanterns were strung back and forth between the branches and balconies on each floor, providing just enough light to see. As they moved amongst the cobblestoned streets, cart welding vendors, selling gods-knows-what, called out to anyone who came within reach. Leif wasn't interested unless it was edible. A few streets over, Leif finally spotted the source of the mouth-watering aroma.

A little restaurant was cut into the base of one of the massive trees. Unlike many of the shops they had passed where the inside of the tree had been hollowed out at the base, they cut deep into the tree, leaving it open to all who walked by. It looked like one half of the base of the tree was cut away. There were no doors or walls. Leif glanced warily at the restaurant, afraid that the tree may split in half at any moment, but when Leif asked Arias about it, he shrugged it off, saying he was underestimating the strength of Karcoa's trees. It still made Leif anxious.

Shaking his head, he tried to focus on the elderly Ljosalfar that was grilling several thin slices of what looked like steak on a small wood fire grill. This was the first Ljosalfar that Leif had seen that appeared elderly. He was a little shorter than Leif, with slightly wrinkled skin, snow white hair pulled back in a shoulder-length ponytail, and his eyes had a softer glow than Arias's and were a shade darker too. Leif wondered just how old a Ljosalfar had to be to be considered elderly. *Arias is somewhere around 300 years old. This guy must be well into the thousands to look like that.* But despite his old age, he still moved with the same smooth feline grace as all the other Ljosalfar. As the elderly Ljosalfar turned, he smiled, displaying pearly white teeth, and asked Arias something in their singsong language. Arias pointed in response. The Ljosalfar nodded and pulled out four sharp sticks. He then deftly skewered several pieces of meat, sprinkled some spicy smelling powder on the skewers and handed them to Arias. Arias reached into his cloak, pulled out four silver coins, and handed them to the man. Handing Leif three of the skewers, Arias pointed to a small table and Leif took a seat. Leif eyed the skewers carefully.

"Looks like steak," Leif commented as he took a bite. "Mmmhmm, taste like steak too!" Arias chuckled as he took a bite from his skewer and chewed.

"Well, that's because it is steak," Arias commented, taking another bite.

"Hold the phone," Leif said, "You guys have cows over here too? I assumed it would be from some weird-looking creature called a grislac or something."

"Nope," Arias said as he chewed the last bite of his skewer. "Remember when I said there are some bridges that open unpredictably?" Leif nodded and continued scarfing down his skewers. "Well, that's also true for wildlife. Over the many eons, bridges have popped up at random times and cows, bulls and a whole host of other creatures have crossed through. And it wasn't a one-way thing. Many of your kind's myths and legends surrounding strange beasts were caused by things from the other realms crossing over and getting stuck, such as the Vargr, the loch ness monster, Bigfoot, Yetis and many others. They were all just creatures stumbling through bridges."

Leif swallowed his next bite in a hurry. "You mean to tell me Yetis are real!" he exclaimed.

Chuckling, Arias said, "Oh yes, they are very real. They are creatures from the icy realm of Jotenheim. Many Jontar clans require their young to travel into the frozen wastelands alone and unarmed to hunt down the Yeti and kill one before they can be trained as warriors. It's quite a dangerous rite of passage; many perish in the pursuit. During one of my excursions into Jotenheim, I was privileged enough to witness one of the rites."

"Sounds awesome," Leif commented as he finished his last skewer. "There is so much to see and learn. I hope I get the chance to travel the realms like you and my grandfather did."

All finished, Arias led Leif away from the restaurant. Now that his stomach was full, Leif was free to finally take in all the strange sights and sounds of Karcoa. As they turned down another cobblestone street, Leif wondered how Arias was able to navigate the forest streets. There were no street signs or other markings to show where they were going, but Arias never wavered or hesitated, so Leif guessed he knew where he was going.

The street they had just turned onto was fairly crowded. Leif could barely keep his hood down, keep an eye on Arias and also look at all the odds and ends being sold around him, but somehow, he managed it. On this particular street, many of the shops had a similar build to the restaurant they ate at. One whole portion of the tree was completely cut out, and a door was cut into the back wall which Leif guessed was used as a storeroom. However, these shops kept the two side walls of the tree standing, and several of the items they were selling hung from the walls or were placed on shelves built into the walls. One merchant they passed was selling a multitude of cloaks, pants, and other articles of clothing. The next shop was run by a squat, angry-looking Svartalfar that was selling all kinds of shields. Leif could hardly believe how many types of shields there were. He really wanted to stop and check them out, but Arias was steadily moving away from him. *Next time,* Leif thought as he turned and jogged after Arias.

The shops got more interesting from there on. Leif passed one shop filled with small glass orbs that were filled with several colored liquids, and another shop housed a single female elf, stirring a pot that glowed a soft blue and had mist slowly cascading down from the edges to obscure the wood floor. With each shop they passed, the urge to stop and investigate grew, but Leif knew he needed to keep a low profile, and he wasn't even sure they understood English. *I should have asked Arias that before we left*, Leif thought.

Turning away from another odd shop, Leif saw Arias had mercifully stopped walking and was talking with a Svartalfar. His shop was devoted entirely to swords. The walls were filled with a myriad of different styles and sizes of swords, including straight swords taller than Leif, curved blades that looked suspiciously like katanas, short Roman gladiolus, and others that looked similar to the blade Arias wore—a thin double-blade, similar to a rapier but sturdier. Arias unhooked his sword and handed it to the Svartalfar. He then unsheathed the blade and scrutinized the handle and blade before grunting and re-sheathing it. The Svartalfar then said something in a harsh guttural language and withdrew to his shop, disappearing into the back room.

"Gutir here is a master sword smith, especially with Ljosalfar blades. Your training has progressed lately, so I figured it was time to bring it in for repairs." Arias finished just as Gutir returned from the back room with a small metal token that had odd-looking scratches on it. He held the token out to Arias, who took it and nodded. He said something in the guttural language, and Gutir grunted and turned back to his shop.

"Come on," Arias said, "Let's buy you some travel clothes that won't have you standing out so much. Then we should get back to Midgard. I think we've been here long enough. The streets are crowded, and I don't want to risk someone seeing what you really are, especially now that I am weaponless."

Leif followed Arias as he backtracked through the forest streets. *I really need to ask him how he knows which way to go,* Leif thought. Leif suddenly heard a commotion from up the street and lifted his hood a little higher to see what was going on. Ahead he spotted a small pocket of space with a lone female figure walking down the street. The street was packed, but everyone was giving the woman a wide birth as she moved down the street. It reminded Leif of those videos he loved to watch on the discovery channel of a hungry shark swimming through a school of fish. As the lone figure got closer, he saw the distinct pitch-black eyes of a Dokkalfar. She moved with a predatory grace that screamed danger to anyone with eyes to see her. She was strikingly beautiful with raven black hair tied into a tight braid that fell down her back. The Dokkalfar had a teardrop face, with angular eyebrows and a small, sharp nose. Two crossed short swords were slung over her back. She was dressed in all black. Her black cloak had its hood pulled back and head held high. As she moved through the street, all eyes turned towards her, many showing open contempt. But she either didn't notice or didn't care. Arias grabbed Leif roughly by the arm and pulled him deeper into the clothing shop. He turned Leif around, hiding his hooded face from the crowded street. Arias covertly kept his eye on the street and didn't relax until the Dokkalfar had passed.

A few minutes later, he released Leif's arm. "What's wrong?" Leif asked, "I know I was attacked by a Dokkalfar and they are universally hated here, but we can't expect them all to be working for Hel, can we?"

"No, I seriously doubt that, but I know that Dokkalfar. She is a dangerous bounty hunter, and it wouldn't surprise me if Hel has an open bounty on any Midgardian sightings in Alfheim. That is most likely why the Dokkalfar is here prowling the streets. We need to get moving. Grab some clothes and let's go."

Leif hurriedly picked out the first few items he could see, including a green tunic with tan pants and dark brown riding boots. Despite the fear he felt at the sight of the Dokkalfar, he couldn't help but smile. He figured as long as he looked the part of traveling Ljosalfar, he might as well try to look like Link. Handing Arias the clothes Leif asked, "Hey Arias, do you know if any Dwarf's sell Hyrulian swords and shields?" The sight of a Dokkalfar in Karcoa had wiped away any sense of humor Arias had. He took the clothes and quickly paid for them without comment. Arias then stuffed the clothes into his travel pack and checked the street. With Leif in tow, they slipped into the flow of foot traffic.

A few tense minutes later, they were out of the packed cobblestone streets and back into the forest surrounding the city. Arias visibly relaxed after entering the forest and let out a sigh of relief as they made it back to the bridge with no incident. Leif could tell Arias wasn't in the mood to linger because he moved right up to the boulder, chanted the spell and was pushing Leif through the bridge the moment it connected. Back in the cave, Leif took off his cloak and handed it back to Arias.

"Well that got tense, don't you think?" Leif asked.

"You do not understand," Arias said in a somber voice. "Mere moments after I hand off my sword, a Dokkalfar just strolls down the street we were walking on. That's way too weird to be a coincidence, I'm just glad we got out of there with no one seeing us. Now let's get out of this cave."

Thirty minutes later, they were back on the PCH. Leif had the heater on full blast. He had mis-timed his jump out of the cave, fell right into the water, and was shivering so hard he thought his teeth might fall out. "I've been meaning to ask you," Leif's body shook with uncontrollable shivers, "Do any of the other beings in the nine realms also speak English?"

"Yes, actually," Arias said. "What you call English originated as a trade language between the nine realms many thousands of years ago, back when travel amongst the realms was much more common. A group of enterprising Svartalfar and Ljosalfar originally developed it. That is how it transferred over to your realm. A Ljosalfar traveled through one of the temporary bridges and got stuck. When he stumbled upon a group of Midgardians, he taught them the language. From there, it flourished into the language you speak now. The version you speak, and the version spoken on each realm deviated over the years, but enough survives to allow you to communicate if you needed to."

"Good to know," Leif said. "So, what other languages do you speak?"

"Given how widely I have traveled, I can speak a few more languages than the average Ljosalfar. English and Ljosa, the elvish language. But I also speak Svata, Jonta and a bit of Orcish. There are many other races amongst the nine realms, but by speaking those four languages, I can usually get my meaning across no matter where I am."

"Four languages, huh? And I thought I was special for passing high-school Spanish. Looks like I've got some studying to do once this is all over," Leif chattered through his teeth.

They drove in relative silence for the rest of the trip back to the shop. That was fine with Leif. He was still processing much of what he saw on Alfheim, specifically the odd items he had seen in the many shops in Karcoa. Leif really hoped Arias would take him back sometime soon so he could explore more of the elvish city.

CHAPTER 20

After the trip to Karcoa, Leif and Arias returned to their normal training schedule. In the mornings, Leif studied the books his grandfather gave him. In the afternoons, he drove to the shop where they would spar until sunset. Then Leif would rush home, change, and head to work. Leif's control of the Berserker continued to grow along with his hand to hand combat skills. Leif had only accidentally berserked one or two times a session, and half the time he retained at least a moderate amount of control. Arias still felt it necessary to knock Leif unconscious each time, which Leif felt was annoying. This continued for the better part of the next two weeks.

One early afternoon as Leif stepped through the back door leading to Arias's back room for another day of hand to hand training, he was abruptly struck in the face by something hard. Leif instantly dropped his gym bag. His hands flew to his face as pain exploded across his nose and eyes. Whatever struck Leif fell to the floor with a soft crash. "Ow! What the fuck was that!" Leif yelled as he dabbed at his split lip.

"For a warrior-in-training, you are easy to surprise," Arias commented from somewhere in the storeroom.

"Well, to be perfectly honest, I wasn't expecting to get

attacked here in your store, so yeah, I had my guard down," Leif said bitterly as he reached down to pick up the object Arias threw at him.

"That's your first mistake." Arias said stepping into the ring holding a wooden sword. "Whatever Hel is up to, she has already thrown an exorbitant amount of resources at you and your family, and just because you haven't been attacked lately doesn't mean she doesn't have some assassin waiting for the perfect time to strike. Think about it. You come here almost every day like clockwork. The shop is a perfect spot to be attacked, so you need to get your shit together and be ready at all times. Or am I just wasting my time? Your family dragged me into this fight, I don't want to spend all this time training you to have you killed by some two-bit assassin who catches you unaware."

"Alright, alright, I get it," Leif held up his hands. "I will be on guard, I promise. So that aside, what's with the sword?" Leif asked, gesturing with the wooden ax Arias had hit him with. "You finally tired of me beating your ass at hand to hand?" Leif teased.

Doubling over in mock laughter, Arias said, "Ha! you wish, Midgardian. The day you beat me in a fight is the day I hang it all up and retire somewhere peacefully. No, I have decided we need to speed things up. I'm hearing troubling whispers of Dokkalfar and Jontar moving along the periphery of Alfheim and other realms. More troubling is that there has been an increase of incursions by the Outsiders, which I cannot help but think is all connected to whatever Hel is planning. I think it's time we move to the final stage of your training." Arias gestured towards the wooden ax Leif was holding. "It's time you learn how to use those axes Alexander gave you."

"Hell yeah," Leif said as he walked over to the weapons rack and retrieved the other wooden ax.

Stepping into their makeshift fighting ring, Leif twirled the axes a few times, barely keeping his excitement under control.

Arias began, "As before, your goal should be to feel the Berserker within, but keep it at bay, releasing it only when you are in dire need of its strength. Now begin!"

CRACK! Arias smacked Leif on the right arm with a lightening quick lashing. Pain exploded across his arm; then it went numb. Before Leif recovered, Arias smacked Leif on the top of the head. Stars burst across his vision as he staggered back from Arias's two hits. Immediately, Leif felt the icy fire of the Berserker, but he gritted his teeth and held it at bay. *No, not yet,* Leif thought, *I can fight him without its help.*

Shaking his head to clear the Berserker, Leif took up a fighting stance. With the ax blades held out, he slowly inched back into the ring; he was ready for Arias this time. As he came within sword distance, Arias feinted a strike to Leif's arm again, but at the last moment, he changed directions, catching Leif on the other arm. Grunting through the pain, Leif jumped back, narrowly dodging Arias's second attack on Leif's head. Leif immediately followed up by closing the distance to Arias. Arias brought his sword down again, aiming for Leif's head, but Leif brought his left arm up. The two wood weapons came together with a crack, and Leif's fingers went numb from the impact.

"Good!" Arias exclaimed. "Your axes need to become an extension of you. Your attacks and defense need to flow together. You must move without thought because the moment you stop to think you have already lost." Arias punctuated his statement by stepping to the side and slamming his blade into Leif's stomach.

Leif gasped, falling to his knees as all the air exploded from his lungs.

Leif let the Berserker flood his mind and body. Recovering faster than a normal human, Leif shot to his feet. He swung his axes at Arias in a wild and unpredictable pattern. Arias for his part showed no reaction. He gave ground, dodging easily between Leif's enraged swings. This only infuriated Leif more. Snarling like a beast, Leif moved faster. All Leif saw was red. The two combatants blurred as they moved, never really staying in one spot for more than a fraction of a second. As Arias moved back and forth between Leif's wild strikes, his foot touched the edge of the practice ring. It was then that Arias stopped dodging and started blocking. CRACK, CRACK, CRACK. The sound of Arias's sword blocks was deafening, but he didn't let up. Without moving another step, Arias's blade was a whirling wall of wood as he blocked Leif's attacks.

As Arias continued to block Leif's attacks, he slipped in small attacks of his own. Unlike Leif, who in his berserked state chose only to attack, all of Arias's hits landed with resounding force. But no matter how hard he hit, Leif shrugged it off and continued to attack. Step-by-step, Arias regained ground while slipping in strikes to Leif's wrist, thighs, and side, pummeling his body. Berserked, he either didn't care or didn't feel them. Back in the center of the ring, Leif struck out with both axes in an overhead strike. Arias brought up his blade to block but misjudged the force Leif could bring to bear while berserked. Arias's sword cracked, then shattered from the superhuman attack. But before Leif could bring both axes down on Arias's head, Arias, quick as a striking cobra, caught both of Leif's wrists. The force of Leif's attack drove Arias to one knee. Leif and Arias stared each other down as both struggled to overpower the other. Then, slowly, Arias pressed up, getting back to his feet. Face to face, Arias flung his arms wide, throwing Leif's arms wide with his. Arias punched Leif in the stomach. The force of the blow doubled Leif over. Arias finished him with an uppercut that knocked Leif out cold.

Leif awoke on the floor... again. Staring up at the ceiling Leif exclaimed, "Gods, I am getting sick of waking up like this. And let me guess, you're sitting over there, sipping your tea like a jackass." Without waiting for a response, Leif rolled over. Arias was sitting at his table calmly sipping tea and reading something. "You know, sometimes I really hate you," Leif said as he tried to get up. Excruciating pain thrummed through his body and he fell back, gasping.

Arias nonchalantly uttered, "Oh, yeah, I wouldn't get up. Not yet at least."

"What the fuck did you do to me?" Leif half cried.

"I taught you a valuable lesson... again," standing up, Arias walked to Leif and squatted down onto his haunches. "You see, fighting with swords and axes is not like fighting with your fists. Your control and critical thinking while berserked during your last attack was that of an enraged toddler. You just keep swinging, hoping one will land. It's a foolish and idiotic way of thinking, and the reason many of your kind died out not long after receiving the Berserker gift. Your kin's fighting style was all brawn and no brains. In a fight, it makes you an easy target. You must work on your control. You have familiarized yourself with the transformation and how you think while berserked. We will now include forced meditation into your training."

"Meditation? Why?" Leif asked.

"I want you to bring out the Berserker as you meditate and focus solely on retaining your thoughts and reasoning. Trust me. Once you have mastered that, your mind should be able to retain some control as you let the Berserker out, making you a more deadly foe. You also need to learn to pay attention to pain. During your fierce but useless attacks, you left several openings, and I capitalized on them, hitting you non-stop. But did you stop or even feel it?" Arias asked.

Leif attempted to pierce through the red fog of his memory. "Yes, I remember getting hit, but I didn't feel any pain. I don't even think I would care if they hurt. All that mattered was smearing the floor with you."

"And now look at you," Arias gestured. "Even with your advanced healing, you struggle to move. Pain is important, especially in a fight. It's no use if you win a fight only to bleed out a few minutes later."

"Yes, I see your point," Leif felt a little sheepish. "It's just the moment I release the Berserker, all other thoughts disappear. It's like there is a whole other person living inside me. Most of the time he is sleeping, but when he wakes up, my thoughts get pushed aside for his. It's almost like Doctor Jekyll and Mr. Hyde, or Bruce Banner and the Hulk. The Berserker feels like a completely different person."

"That... is precisely the opposite of how you should think," Arias commented. "The Berserker isn't some unique personality lying in wait somewhere below your conscious mind. It's a tool-a power. And with any power, either you conquer it, or it will conquer you."

"I get it," Leif responded, "But putting it into action is something different."

"That is something you will have to figure out for yourself, Leif. I cannot walk the path you are on; I am merely your guide. But remember, you and the Berserker are one and the same. If you continue to separate yourself from it, then you will become like Doctor Jekyll and Mr. Hyde, but if you embrace your other side, then you will control it."

CHAPTER 21

J ust like the training in hand to hand combat, Leif and Arias got into a groove of training with ax and sword. However, with introducing the wooden weapons, Leif found that even with his faster-than-normal healing, the wounds and bruises inflicted by Arias's damn sword would stick around much longer than Leif had hoped.

Training with weapons was like learning to walk all over again. Distance, timing, blocking and attacking all changed drastically, especially with the use of axes. They were shorter weapons, so much of the training focused on blocks and counters. Arias had explained that many of the beings Leif would be facing would be expert fighters, and so Leif should focus on defense and then strike when his opponent slipped up. This seemed perfectly reasonable to Leif; the only problem was that the moment Leif slipped up and released the Berserker, he automatically switched to attack. It typically resulted in Leif unconscious on the floor.

Recently, Leif had started meditating. But this wasn't like your typical soft flowing music, scented candles, and yoga mats meditation. Leif started locking himself in his room. While there, he would clear away anything of value or fragile and then visualize himself in a fight, slowly releasing the Berserker. The moment Leif felt his grip on his conscious mind slip, he would dial it back. He would do this for hours, keeping his mind and body at the brink, then slowly pulling back. At first, Leif failed miserably, and when he came to, there were several holes in his wall. One time he even managed to rip his mattress in half! But he kept at it, and slowly the Berserker felt like an extension of himself—not some separate entity. Once, all that he saw and felt was a red-hot rage. The rage wasn't gone, but it was more controlled and focused. He no longer moved on pure instinct.

The fruits of Leif's mental training showed during his weapons training. Leif had developed his own style of fighting. He had taken Arias's warning to heart and focused much of his training on defense and small counter moves, but with his control of the Berserker growing, he added a new layer to his style.

The familiar thwack of wood-on-wood reverberated through the storeroom as Leif blocked Arias's sword thrusts. Pushing off with one of his axes, Leif struck out with his other ax, aiming for Arias's right shoulder, but the Ljosalfar quickly pulled his sword back at an angle, blocking Leif's attack. Leif followed up with a swing with his left arm, aiming low, but Arias merely stepped back, giving him the space he needed for a quick overhead strike. Crossing his axes, Leif took the hit on the shafts, hearing the wood crack slightly as they took the force of the strike. Leif took one small step then kicked out, landing a solid blow to Arias's solar plexus. Arias fell backward, but he turned, rolled, and came to his feet with a smile all in one graceful move. Arias charged in a blur. His sword flicked out—high, low, high, high. Leif blocked them all... just barely. It seemed Arias had turned it up a notch. All Leif could do was block and move. On the defense, Leif attempted to catch Arias's blade between his axes and pull him off balance. Arias expected the move and as Leif pulled, Arias moved with the maneuver and punched Leif twice in the stomach and once in the face before dancing away to avoid an ax thrust meant for his neck. Before Leif could react, Arias lashed out again, snaking his wooden blade around Leif's ax. Then he flicked his arm to the side, dragging Leif's arm with him, leaving Leif wide open.

As Arias flicked Leif's right hand out, leaving Leif's right side undefended, Arias followed up with two rapid punishing blows, one to his ribs, which sent pain racing across his side, then one to Leif's right temple. A sharp crack sounded as the wooden blade rebounded off Leif's skull. Leif stumbled back. His hands went to his head momentarily. Though the pain was excruciating, it was also exactly what he was waiting for. Using the pain, Leif opened himself to the Berserker, letting the power flood through his veins, cleansing the pain. As the pain receded, Leif felt stronger, faster, and more importantly, he was in control. His nightly meditations had paid off. Though he could feel the power wanting to take over and consume him, he fought it down.

Leif pulled his hand away from his temple, stood up straight, and stared Arias down. "You're going to regret that," Leif said as he twirled his wooden axes. Arias's eyes widened slightly. Then he settled back into a guard position, feet spread shoulder width apart, blade held in a two-handed grip at an angle to protect his upper body. Leif grinned, then moved. Leif was faster than the average Midgardian, but now, drawing on the Berserker, he was almost on par with the Ljosalfar. He crossed the distance in a fraction of a second, but before he got too close, he slowed and brought up his ax to block Arias's blade as Arias swung forward, hoping to catch Leif unprepared. The wooden weapons came together with a loud thwack. Apparently, Arias was taking Leif seriously, because he wasn't holding back. He moved with feline grace as he glided between attack and defense. Arias was testing Leif's defenses, poking and prodding.

Leif for his part hungered for the attack, but he held it at bay, waiting for his moment. He was holding his own against Arias, always keeping his twin axes in motion. Block, strike, block high, block low, counter strike. Arias was a force of nature, pushing

Leif even as he drew on the Berserker to strengthen his muscles and speed up his reactions. But the more Leif pushed, the harder it was to contain the rage. Then, as if the universe came into alignment for one perfect moment, Arias brought down his blade in an overhead strike. Leif leaned back, and he raised his axes, forming an X as he caught Arias's blade. All at once, Leif released the restraints he had on the Berserker in one explosive movement. As he did, he pulled back with both axes with all his strength, shattering both his axes and Arias's blade in one swift movement.

Leif had been waiting for this moment. He reacted immediately. Arias stood stunned for half a second too long, and he paid for it. Leif dropped the broken axes the moment they shattered and closed in with Arias to take him down, hand to hand style. With a one-two combo, Leif pummeled Arias in the ribs then face causing him stumbled to the side. Leif didn't stop there. The Berserker raged for him to keep fighting until Arias was down and out. Leif moved with Arias as he stumbled, landing two more punches to the left side of Arias's face, then a quick dropkick to Arias's chest, which sent him flying. Arias fell hard on his back, but he recovered quickly, rolling then scrambling to his feet. Leif knew he should stop, but he had let too much of the Berserker out at this point and was struggling to regain control. When Leif moved in with Arias, Arias deftly took control of the fight once again.

Leif woke up a few minutes later, but to his surprise, Arias wasn't in his normal chair sipping tea and silently judging Leif. The surprised student watched his mentor use a washcloth to wipe away the blood from the cuts to his face. Getting to his feet with a groan, Leif slowly limped over to his chair and sat down. "Damn, I almost had you there. If I had held on for just a little longer, you would have been toast," Leif said.

"Ha, keep dreaming Midgardian. You got in a few lucky punches, but I had it all under control. After all, I wasn't the one drooling on my floor from being knocked unconscious," Arias boasted.

"Touché," Leif laughed.

Arias held out his fist for a bump. Smiling, Leif obliged him. "You did well. I am proud of you. When I saw you draw on the Berserker, I was ready to knock you out, but you came in smart, defending and pushing for openings. You still have years, maybe decades till you have perfect control of the Berserker, but we just don't have that much time. You are as ready as I can make you for the journey to the Norns. Get your things in order, we will leave the day after tomorrow."

Leif was in shock. Had he just heard what he thought he heard? He quickly stood, knocking over his chair. Leif caught Arias on his shoulder. "Wait, wait, wait. We are leaving? Just like that? I show a small bit of control and now we are off? What if I freak out in Alfheim, or gods know what other realms?" Leif panicked.

A sad smile crossed Arias's face for the briefest of seconds. "That is a risk we will have to take. We have postponed this for long enough. My goal was to get you acquainted with the Berserker, then push you to keep control of your thoughts and actions, even if only for a short time as you drew on that power. And as you just demonstrated, you have achieved that, and so there isn't much more I can teach you. The rest of your training must be done in here." Arias poked Leif in the temple, "And here," he poked his chest. "And of course, who knows what the Norns will have in store for you. You can look forward to that. Also, I met with an old friend the other day. He had just returned from Alfheim with troubling news. It's not just Hel's minions that are on the move. An Outsider pushed past the Aesir's defenses and was actually seen on Myrkheim. It ended up killing several Svartalfar warriors and Dokkalfar before Thor himself showed up and fought it. From what my friend says, the damage caused by the battle was immense, but Thor foght the Outsider to a stalemate and it retreated into the void, outside of Aesir controlled space. I cannot help but think somehow the appearance of an Outsider is connected to Hel and whatever she is planning."

"Um, who or what exactly is an Outsider? And why are they so dangerous?" Leif asked. Arias blew out a long breath and settled down in his chair, signaling Leif to follow. "I'll tell you, but no questions. Trust me, we will have plenty of time to talk during our journey to the Norns, and we have much to prepare before we leave. I know it will be hard, but just hold on to your questions till later, deal?" Arias asked.

"Deal," Leif responded immediately.

"The Outsiders," Arias began, "are the brothers and sisters of the King of the Aesir and ruler of the nine realms, Odin Allfather. However, the Outsiders, unlike the Aesir, did not agree with Odin nor his rule, so they rebelled against him. They are ancient beings that existed before the unification of the nine realms under the Aesir. You probably know more about the Outsiders than you think. The Outsiders visited Midgard at one point or another and were worshiped as deities. Many of the gods of your ancient history were Outsiders. Greek, Egyptian, Mayan, Aztec, Indian Pantheons and many more were all Outsiders." Leif opened his mouth to ask a question, but Arias quickly shushed him. "Thousands of years ago, war broke out between the Outsiders and the Aesir for control of the nine realms. The battle was so great that many realms outside the nine realms were destroyed.

"Eventually, Odin and his forces banished the Outsiders and gained dominion over the nine realms with it. Ever since, the Outsiders have been testing the physical and magical defense placed around the nine realms. Odin and the Aesir have successfully kept the Outsiders away from the nine realms for thousands of years. Until now. The fact that one could get through the Aesir's defenses around the same time Hel is planning something troubles me. It cannot be a coincidence."

Arias took a deep breath, "Ok, that's enough for now. Get going. Meet me back here at sunrise the day after tomorrow." Arias stood up and motioned Leif towards the door.

"But, where did the Outsiders and Odin come from? Where did they go when Odin banished them from the nine realms?" Leif asked as Arias continued to push him out the door.

"No more questions; we will be here all day and night if I stop to answer. I will answer what I can in time. Now out!" Arias shoved Leif out the front door of his shop and quickly closed the door behind him.

Leif peered through the glass door and saw Arias's mouth, "Go." He pointed down the street to where Leif had parked his car.

"Fine!" Leif scoffed, "You're no fun, anyway." He turned and stalked off towards his car.

CHAPTER 22

Once Leif got home, he showered off the grime and blood from the training session then called his boss. Derek, the general manager at the Sleeping Lion, was sad to see Leif go, but after Leif explained to him he had found himself after his mother and grandfather's deaths, he seemed to understand. Leif explained this wasn't permanent, that he would be back, and Derek gave a noncommittal answer before they hung up.

Leif wrote a letter to his landlord explaining he would be away for a while, and he included a check to cover rent for the next few months. Next, he called a friend and asked if they could check in on his place. He also canceled his mail delivery. "Boom," Leif said as he hung up his phone. "Ok, now time to pack," Leif said to himself. "But what should I bring? I doubt REI has an Alfheim section in their store."

Leif rummaged through his closet, pulling out the set of travel clothes he had bought on his previous trip to Alfheim, a few spare shirts, pants, and a pair of heavy hiking boots. He then wrapped and packed his axes. His backpack was full, but he realized that once they crossed the bridge, he would switch to his travel clothes and hang the axes on his belt, so that would free up some much-needed space.

The next morning, Leif slept late, reasoning that it may be a long time before he would get to enjoy the comforts of sleeping in a bed. After lounging longer than necessary, Leif lazily got up, ate a full breakfast, then headed out to buy some more supplies at Camping World.

Leif browsed the store until he narrowed down the list of things he felt he would need. At the checkout line, he cringed each time the checker beeped another item, and the total increased. *Thank god Grandpa and Mom had money stashed away, or there's no way in hell I would have been able to afford all of this,* Leif thought. Leif walked out with a bigger hiking backpack, a water purifier (because who knows what weird supernatural bacteria may be lurking in the water), five boxes of matches (because you know... fire and *Cast Away*), and a folding knife (figuring he shouldn't rely on his axes for mundane things because it might dull the blades). He also ended up with a crank flashlight since he didn't think there would be a supermarket or Costco to pick up replacement batteries. *The Boy Scouts got it right,* Leif thought as he mumbled, "Be prepared."

As each hour ticked by, he got more and more nervous and so he figured some fresh ocean air would do him some good. He also didn't want to be cooped up in his apartment on potentially his last day on Midgard. Leif went to Santa Monica. He would grab some food on the way home and at least attempt to sleep.

THE COLD WINTER breeze blew in on the waves and washed over Leif, chilling him slightly. He smiled as he savored the salty ocean air and smooth as silk sand between his fingers. The soft crash of the waves soothed Leif's racing mind at the prospect of what was to come. For a moment, he could be just a normal person again, enjoying the peaceful sunset. Leif marveled at the flickering colors of the veil flashing across the sky. He had gotten so used to the veil in the past few months that he hardly noticed it anymore. The veil competed with the last fleeting rays of sunshine. The two meshed into a sight so beautiful Leif wished he could paint it. The reds, oranges, and pinks of the sun snaked between the flashing blue and greens of the veil to create a scene that had the power to bring tears to Leif's eyes. *It truly is a shame that so few get the chance to see what I see*, Leif thought.

Once the sun set and the veil dominated the night sky, Leif dusted the sand off his pants and walked up to the promenade. As usual, the promenade and ocean street were packed with tourists and locals. Not wanting to fight for a table, Leif picked the first restaurant that had an opening and sat down to eat. After ordering a few rounds of beer to help relax him, Leif left a generous tip, then began the long walk back to his car.

As Leif moved away from the busier streets, he got the feeling he was being followed. Not wanting to give anything away, he slowed a bit, closed his eyes and focused on his hearing. After a few moments, Leif picked out two distinct footsteps moving towards him. Not wanting to lead them back to his car, Leif turned down a street at random and continued his slow stroll. *Had Hel figured out I was planning on continuing my search for the Norns? Did her spies catch wind of my traveling with Arias to Alfheim?* Either way, Leif was ready this time. He was unarmed, but he felt confident after training with Arias that he could hold his own, even against Dokkalfar.

The two would-be attackers closed in on Leif. If they were indeed Hel's men, Leif didn't want a fight to go down in the middle of the street, so he turned down the closest alleyway. Leif's adrenaline must have spiked because his heart was racing, and the icy cool of the Berserker prickled across his skin, but he held it at bay.

"Hey," his stalker called out from behind Leif. "Wait up, I

think we're lost, could you help us out?"

Lost, Leif thought. In this day and age, where every cellphone had GPS, not likely, but Leif turned anyway. Placing a smile on his face, he turned and let out a sigh of relief. They were regular Midgardians. They were common thugs, and both wore jeans, thick sweaters and looked to be in their mid-to-late twenties. The man on the left had shaved sandy blond hair, a hooked nose, and dark green eyes. A gap between his teeth was proudly displayed within his sinister grin. The second man had slick dark brown hair, blue eyes, and a sharp nose. He was the type of guy who would tell you his name and you would forget it immediately. His only distinguishing feature was a small diamond stud in his right ear. He almost looked bored. Leif's newly honed instincts told him that this guy was confident that whatever they had planned to do, Diamond stud wasn't worried.

Boy, did they pick the wrong person to fuck with, Leif thought. He waived and said, "Sure, how can I help you?" Gapped-tooth was only a few feet away from Leif when he dropped his friendly smile. He flicked open a folding knife and said, "If you don't want to get hurt, hand over your keys and wallet."

Leif raised both hands, palms open, "Hey, listen, I don't have any money and my car broke down the other day, so trust me you don't want my keys. Why don't we all just go our separate ways and I will forget this ever happened, ok?"

They didn't like Leif's solution. Stud pulled out a knife of his own, and pointed it menacingly at Leif. "Hey dumbass, don't play stupid. If you don't want to gain a few extra holes, empty your pockets!"

Laughing, Leif mumbled, "Well, I tried."

"Hey, what's so funny?" Gapped-tooth asked.

"It's nothing really, I was just laughing at how the universe works sometimes," Leif said honestly.

Stud promptly stepped forward and slugged Leif in the face.

The force of it rocked Leif back on his heels, causing him to take a small step backward. *Good punch*, Leif thought.

Laughing, Gapped-tooth yelled, "That's right, asshole. Keys, wallet, and phone or we start cutting."

Leif tasted blood on his lips, "Really guys, you will have to try much harder than that." Leif let a little of the Berserker out.

Something in Leif's demeanor must have tipped the two muggers off that Leif was no normal human. Gapped-tooth lunged forward with his knife hand, aiming for Leif's stomach. Leif's training with Arias must have sped his reflexes; it surprised him at how slowly his muggers were moving. Leif watched as the knife moved with glacial slowness towards his stomach. Leif sidestepped Gapped-tooth, who had over-committed his attack and stumbled past him. Stud moved in, hoping to catch Leif off guard. He swiped left, then right, attempting to cut Leif and put him off balance. However, his movements were too obvious. Leif could see where the knife was going almost before the mugger moved.

As Leif ducked under a wild sideways stab meant to disembowel him, he saw Gapped-tooth sneaking up behind him. Not wanting to take them both on at the same time, Leif struck out with a vicious jab to Stud's kidney. The attacker's breath exploded out as he stumbled backward, coughing and struggling to regain breath. With Stud out of the way, Leif dodged away from Gapped-tooth's slash aimed for Leif's throat. Not wanting to get cornered against the alleyway's wall, Leif squared up against Gapped-tooth.

"What's your problem, bro?" Gapped tooth said breathlessly.

Leif laughed, "Did you really just call me bro? You two idiots couldn't hit the side of a barn with those wild swings, let alone stab me with that butter knife you're holding."

That seemed to strike a nerve because Gapped-tooth let out a snarl-like sound and lunged forward again. Leif fought the urge to yawn. "Did you really just snarl? What are you? Part stray dog?" Leif teased.

Leif had been enjoying his taunts a little too much because he failed to notice Stud charge at Leif from the side. He wrapped Leif in a big bear hug. Gapped-tooth took advantage of the blitz and scored a shallow gash across Leif's left ribs. Leif yelped more in surprise than in pain as the knife finished blazing an iron hot trail across his side. Gapped-tooth laughed in triumph.

"There you go, dumbass," Stud said into Leif's ear. "You see, we weren't playing around earlier. We are going to cut you up good for disrespecting us."

Leif, more annoyed than worried, decided that playtime was over. Looking directly into Gapped-tooth's eyes, Leif whispered, "My turn." Using the pain in his side to fuel the Berserker, Leif released the mental hold and felt the rush of power course through him.

While he was still held in a bear hug, Leif clamped down on Stud's arms and slowly pulled his arms away from Leif's body. Leif wanted him to feel just how powerless he was. Stud fought back, straining against Leif's iron grip. Leif threw his head back, smashing it into his attacker's face, half hearing, half feeling Stud's nose break with an audible crunch. Only then did he release his arms. Leif whipped around and kicked Stud in the stomach. The force of Leif's berserked kick sent the mugger flying sideways ten feet before he crashed through a set of trashcans and bounced off the back wall of the alleyway. Leif could have sworn he felt Stud's ribs crack when he kicked him, but Leif was beyond caring at this point.

Leif turned to face the wide-eyed Gapped-tooth. He had gone a bit pale in the face. But Leif had to give it to his attackers, they had guts. Leif just kicked his friend ten feet into the air and Gapped-tooth was still standing his ground.

"You're—you will pay for that," the attacker stammered out. He again lunged wildly at Leif. Leif nonchalantly caught Gapped-tooth's wrist and squeezed. Leif smiled as he felt his attacker's wrist snap. The man bellowed in pain, but Leif wasn't done. He wanted to teach these two a lesson. He pulled the man's arm out, locking his elbow, then brought down his other arm against Gapped-tooth's elbow. It snapped with a loud crack. The noise snapped Leif out of his bloodlust. Gapped-tooth sucked in a breath at the sudden and intense pain, but before he could scream, Leif punched him in the stomach, causing him to crumble to the street.

Clutching his now broken wrist and arm, he looked up at Leif with terror in his eyes. Leif suppressed the Berserker's lust to continue with these idiots' lesson. Leif merely said, "I gave you ample opportunity to walk away." He turned his back on the failed muggers and casually walked towards the opening of the alleyway.

He could feel the Berserker's desire to run back and finish off the weaklings, and he was hard pressed not to give in. But he would not let the Berserker control him. Leif knew if he gave in to the Berserker's bloodlust, he would either end up killing a bunch of people or end up in jail. Leaning against a fence, Leif let out a breath. He closed his eyes and focused on controlling his racing heart. After a minute of deep breathing and reassuring himself that no one would attack him, he finally felt the urges to rip and rend everything around him subside, and he could think clearly again.

The trembling was gone, and Leif felt safe enough to get back to his car. Just then, a loud CA-CAW rang out, piercing the quiet calm of the cool winter night. Leif looked up and spotted two black ravens perched on a roof. The pair sat staring at him with an unnatural stillness. Leif flipped them off, turned away, and muttered under his breath, "Yeah, yeah, I'm still here. Your mythical warrior hasn't cracked."

CHAPTER 23

L eif woke with a groan as his alarm shrieked at him. Rubbing his eyes, Leif cursed Arias for wanting to start their adventure so damn early. Leif savored what was likely the last shower he would take for a while. He dressed, picked up his bag, and walked out, locking the door behind him.

Leif parked in one spot designated for the bookstore and spotted Arias closing the back door of his shop. He carried a heavy looking travel backpack and a cloth-wrapped package that Leif guessed was Arias's sword. *He must have picked it up from the Svartalfar blacksmith,* Leif thought. Leif unloaded his travel bag from his car and put it into the back seat of Arias's truck. Leif got into the front seat and buckled his seat belt.

The click of the seatbelt buckle triggered a click in his mind. He was really doing this. He was crossing over into another realm. With an elf. Who he has known for less than a year. To hunt down three mythical women. Leif's stomach knotted as he nervously bounced his leg, waiting for Arias to finish locking up. Once Arias finished, he got into the driver seat and took a double-take at Leif.

"You all right?" Arias asked. "You've gone pale."

"I'm all right," Leif breathed. "It's just all hitting me right now. You know what we're doing. I mean, it sounds crazy, right?" Leif asked.

"Oh," Arias said, "From a Midgardian perspective, it sounds insane. Like something out of one of your books or movies, but to me, it's par for the course. I used that phrase properly, right?" Arias asked. "The Ljosalfar are an inquisitive race, and many of my kind in their early years spend a few decades exploring, visiting the realms before settling down. As for me, I never stopped. Alexander and I used to disappear for years, exploring the unknown regions of the nine realms. It feels good to be going off again into the unknown, not knowing what we will find. You know?" Arias mused.

"No, not really." Leif retorted. Taking a few deep breaths, Leif focused on calming his mind and the hurricane of butterflies bouncing around in his stomach.

They made it to the turnout on PCH in no time. Arias pulled much farther off the road before putting the truck in park. "I really hope some idiot doesn't impound my truck. If they do, it will be a long walk when we get back." Arias turned when Leif didn't respond and saw he was still pale as the moon.

"You need to relax, Leif. Nothing has even happened yet," Arias clapped Leif on the shoulder, "We are still on Midgard. You're still up for this, right? I didn't just waste the past few months, training you for you to go belly up on me, right?"

Leif shook his head. "I'm fine. I'm fine. Let's just get going. I will be better once we are on the move," Leif emphasized his need to keep moving. He unbuckled his seatbelt and got out of the truck. A few minutes later they were down in the cove, paddling through the frigid water.

This time Leif went first, and he made the jump into the tiny cave on the first try. After pulling his paddle board in, he watched as Arias smoothly entered the cave. Not wanting the boards to wash away during high tide, they lugged the cumbersome boards deeper into the cave than before. Arias signaled for them to change into their travel clothes. After a few awkward minutes of changing, Leif was decked out in his travel cloak, green tunic, and brown pants with his twin axes hanging on each hip. Leif realized he had done little walking with the axes on his belt, so he would have to get used to them bouncing around as he walked.

A few moments later, they found themselves at the end of the cave and Arias was once again muttering in the Ljosalfar sing-song language. Leif had tried to make out the individual words, but it all meshed together seamlessly as Arias's spell opened the bridge. Leif focused on picking up the subtle throbbing in the back of his mind, signifying the flow of magic. He was happy that it came much easier this time. The gentle thrumming of the magic intensified as Arias's spell pulled the bridge open, linking Alfheim and Midgard together. Once again, bright light streamed into the cave as the cave wall disappeared.

CHAPTER 24

Shading his eyes, Leif cinched up his backpack and left Midgard, his home, for what possibly could be the last time. Once he was through, a soft breeze and the crisp air of the forest replaced the damp salty air of the cave. The distant slapping of the waves died away and was replaced by the gentle rustling of the leaves and the occasional bird call from somewhere high in the treetops. After stepping clear of the bridge, Leif turned and watched as Arias muttered a few words to close the gate behind him. Smiling, Arias turned and said, "There's no turning back now."

"True enough," Leif said, "So what's the plan? How do we go about finding the Norns, especially if no one besides my grandpa has seen them in thousands of years?"

"Good question, Padawan," Arias said. "The Norns are ancient and powerful beings. The fact that they haven't just appeared in front of you or pulled you into their realm is troubling. It means they are being careful. When beings that can see and control the flow of fate remain hidden, it shows just how serious this threat to the realms is. Alexander told me the location of the bridge to their realm. The only problem is it is located under the capital city on the Svartalfar realm of

Myrkheim. The Svartalfar jealously guard the bridges to their realm, so we must first secure passage. Lucky for us, I have met many Svartalfar during my travels, and a few even owe me a favor or two. So, our plan is to head into Karcoa and speak with one. Hopefully, he will reveal the location of the bridge and help get us across it."

"Did you just call me Padawan?"

"What? It seemed appropriate. In my lengthy stay on Midgard, I watched many movies to help blend in with your kind. I particularly liked the Star Wars franchise, and it seems fitting. I am the handsome yet powerful Qui-Gon Jinn, and you are the young Anakin, coming to me to train and harness the power within." Leif stopped in his tracks.

"I want to argue with you, but it kind of makes sense. But you know Qui-Gon dies in battle, right?"

"Of course, I do," Arias said with a scoff. "It is every warrior's dream to die in battle and ascend to Valhalla. Besides, I have no plans to die on this quest, Midgardian. I am on my home turf. I know these lands and its people. The real dangerous part of this quest will happen long after I leave you with the Norns. I am merely a currier, ferrying you to the Norns."

Though Arias was talking big, Leif could see in the way Arias ghosted through the forest. He was on edge. His eyes were always moving. He talked a big game, but he was showing signs that he was a little nervous about their mission to the Norns.

"I have another question then, oh mighty master," Leif said, with a hint of sarcasm. "Why aren't we just crossing directly over to Myrkheim?"

"Oh, you think it's that easy to cross between realms, do you? That the bridges are akin to a cell phone? One just dials up the realm they want to go to, cast a little spell and bing-o-bongo, we are crossing into Myrkheim?" Arias asked, exacerbated.

"I don't know, Arias. This shit is all new to me. How the hell am I supposed to know how inter-realm travel works? I mean, I don't even know if I am in the same galaxy or universe anymore," Leif complained.

Arias stopped in his tracks, "Of course we are in the same universe and galaxy, the realm is just another way of saying planet. I thought you knew this. All the realms are scattered throughout the galaxy and are connected through the cosmic tree. Did you pay attention to anything I said over the past months?" Arias threw up his hands and started walking again.

"Wait," Leif yelled out. "If that's true, then that would make you an alien! Holy shit! I've been hanging out with an alien all this time, and I didn't even realize it!" Leif laughed and jogged back up to Arias.

"Actually," Arias said, "At the moment, you're the alien here, Midgardian."

"Holy shit!" Leif exclaimed, a big smile spread across his face, "You're right, this is awesome! But back to my main question. If we are heading to Myrkheim, why didn't we just find a bridge that leads directly there?" Leif asked.

"That's because they don't exist anymore. The Aesir destroyed them all. In fact, they destroyed most of the bridges that led to Midgard. Your kind was deemed too weak, so they cut you off from the rest of the nine realms in what they thought was an act of protection, but they missed some bridges. They burned many of the records that contained the locations of the bridges. In fact, the bridge we crossed over is a closely guarded secret amongst a select few of Ljosalfar. If the Aesir were to learn of it, no doubt Odin would send one of the Asgardians down to find it and destroy its connection. So, we need to keep any word of you being here as quiet as possible."

The natural lanterns couldn't distract Leif this time. "Wow! That was a lot of information, without explaining anything. Why were the bridges to Midgard closed? Just think of how different my world would be if the Aesir hadn't closed off Midgard." Leif said.

"You will not drop this, so I will explain a little," Arias said. "Long ago, back when the bridges were still intact, many other beings of the realms saw that you Midgardians lacked the ability to control magic and were, in fact, quite weak. They began preying on your kind, sending raiding parties through the bridges, killing and stealing resources. At first, these attacks were slight, not really gaining the attention of the peacekeeping Aesir. But the offenders grew bolder and bolder. Then some enterprising Jontar and Dokkalfar joined forces and sent in an entire invasion force. Thousands of your people died. I think your history books called it a mini ice age. Word got back to the Aesir. The Allfather sent Thor and a few others to deal with the problem personally. The Berserkers were endowed with Thor's gift, and together with Thor, they dealt with the problem. When Thor returned to Asgard, Odin decided enough was enough, and he had the bridges destroyed. The other races didn't take the news well. Especially the Svartalfar. The Aesir are gods, so everyone just put their heads down and went on with their business."

When Leif and Arias reached Karcoa, it was mid to late afternoon. Arias had Leif pull his hood up to prevent anyone seeing he was Midgardian, and they plunged into the narrow streets of the forest city. Leif once again wanted to stop and explore the shops and examine the weird curios the vendors were selling, but Arias wasn't having it. Arias weaved through the crowd like wind through the trees, while Leif struggled to keep up. Arias eventually stopped at a cart to buy some meat on a stick. Handing a few sticks to Leif, he turned and once again ghosted through the crowd.

They moved deeper into the forest city. The trees that made up the shops, restaurants, and homes grew larger and larger until they were so big that their leaves and branches were densely intertwined, blotting out the sunlight above. The branches were lined with the living lanterns, while the shops and restaurants hung lanterns above their doors and windows. Still, the streets were filled with deep pools of darkness. The deeper they went, the once heavily trafficked streets slowly emptied.

Leif felt with the dwindling crowd it was okay to pull off his hood, but Arias caught his wrist. "Don't," he said with a warning in his voice. "We have entered the Svartalfar quarter, which isn't the nicest area in the city to outsiders. It wouldn't help our cause right now if they discovered you were Midgardian. Keep the hood up until I tell you."

"But it's so dark, I can barely see. Those lamps don't work for shit," Leif complained.

"The Svartalfar like it that way. Back on their home realm, they all live underground, so they have little love for sunlight. That's why they chose this part of the city. The trees grow so close together that the sunlight never makes it down to the ground level."

Rolling his eyes, Leif dropped his hand, resting it on the head of his ax, and continued to follow Arias in silence.

After a mind-numbing number of twists and turns, Arias stopped in front of an old and gnarled looking tree with a single shop cut into the ancient tree trunk. A sign hung above the door, but it was written in a language Leif didn't understand.

"Hey, what does that say?" Leif said pointing to the sign.

"The Drunken Hammer, in Svata," Arias responded, not missing a beat.

The door to the shop was propped open by a massive war hammer, and Leif could hear a clanging sound reverberating from somewhere deep inside the shop.

Arias looked up and down the street and stepped in with Leif right behind him. Leif's senses were assaulted by a combination of tobacco smoke and the rhythmic clang of metal on metal. The walls were packed with shelves displaying swords, shields and other weapons of war that Leif wasn't as familiar with. Arias headed into the back while Leif looked around the store.

Leif eyed a round shield made of black metal with an inlay of gold creating a circular pattern. It was beautiful; truly a work of art. Leif had no doubt it cost a small fortune. Looking at the other items in the shop, they all looked both functional and beautiful at the same time. Leif doubted any of these swords or shields were simply meant to be hung above a fireplace or on a mantel. They were meant to cleave and rend. Abruptly, the rhythmic beat of metal on metal stopped, pulling Leif out of his veneration. In the newfound silence of the shop, Leif heard a gruff, guttural sound coming from the back of the shop and Leif guessed Arias had found his friend. A few seconds later, Arias called for Leif to join them.

Leif opened the door to the back room, and a rush of dry, blistering air rushed over him. Leif immediately broke out in a sweat. A short squat Svartalfar stood next to a forge that glowed bright orange. After taking a few scalding breaths, Leif stepped into the room, moving next to Arias. The two continued to converse in Svata while Leif silently melted in his travel cloak. Leif had never been this close to a Svartalfar before. Surprisingly, they closely matched the fantasy literature and movie depictions. The Svartalfar was somewhere between three and four feet tall, had long brown hair tied back in a ponytail and a beard that hung down to the middle of his chest. His beard was tied near the bottom with a silver chain, probably to prevent any strays from getting burned off by the forge. The Svartalfar's eyes were sunken and deep brown, like the earth beneath their feet.

Arias said something in Svata and gestured to Leif. The Svartalfar turned to Leif and looked him up and down. Leif could have sworn he was scowling. Arias motioned for Leif to take his hood off, so he did. Upon seeing Leif's face, the Svartalfar pushed himself away from the forge and ambled up to him. Once he was within a few feet, quick as a snake, the Svartalfar struck out with a solid punch to Leif's gut. Leif was caught completely by surprise, and he doubled over from the force of the punch. The Svartalfar tried to follow up with a solid right hook to Leif's jaw, but his instincts kicked in as he used the pain of the punch to fuel his strength. Gritting his teeth against the pulsing pain in his stomach, Leif sidestepped the Svartalfar's punch and followed up with a left hook of his own, connecting directly with the Svartalfar's left eye socket. Leif was unsure of the reason for the sudden attack, and he held nothing back. The Svartalfar flew sideways and crashed into a workbench. Tools and half-finished weapons shot out in all directions. The Svartalfar sat stunned for a few seconds before slowly getting to his feet. *The little bastard is tough*, Leif thought. Leif prepared himself, feeling the Berserker raging within to be let out and teach the tiny fool a lesson, but he repressed it. The Svartalfar suddenly let out a hearty belly laugh that would have put Santa to shame. The little man walked up to Leif, arms out to the side, palms up, and clapped Leif on the arm. He then turned to Arias and laughed out something in his guttural language. Arias laughed and said to Leif that, "Bargog had heard stories that all Midgardian's are whiny weaklings, but he said that you've got some balls on you."

"What the hell, Arias?" Leif yelled.

Arias was trembling with suppressed laughter. He squeaked out, "Svartalfar respect strength, and well, they really don't like Midgardians. If you had backed down or shown fear, it's very likely Bargog would have beaten the shit out of you. Then he would have refused to help us. So, good job." Arias gave a thumbs up.

"Good job," Leif said accusingly. "Screw you, how about next time you warn me about something like that?"

Arias chuckled, "Sure, but if you couldn't take on one Svartalfar, then we are going to be in big trouble." During the exchange between Leif and Arias, Bargog stood calmly, watching them bicker.

Once they were done talking, Bargog walked over to a table festooned with different-sized hammers, chisels, and other tools. He took off his heavy working gloves and apron and set them on the table. Bargog's exposed barrel chest was heavily muscled, featuring a tattoo of a crossed war hammer and ax. Bargog picked up a white shirt and put it on. He turned back to Arias and said something in Svata. Arias laughed and nodded, clapping Leif on the back. "Bargog has agreed to help us."

"Awesome!" Leif said sarcastically. "So now what? Do we head for the bridge?"

"Nope, we grab a drink."

"Huh? Didn't you say we need to keep a low profile while in the city? I don't think a pub crawl is exactly low profile," Leif said reproachingly.

"Your new friend over there wants to celebrate his first fight with a Midgardian by having a drink, and since he is the key to finding the bridge to Myrkheim, I figure we should indulge him. The Svartalfar love to drink. It won't hurt to have a few pints, get him to tell us the location of the bridge, then sneak out of the city."

Shrugging, Leif acquiesced and headed back towards the storeroom. Bargog picked up a massive war hammer as tall as himself and hooked it to something on his back. Leif guessed the war hammer had to weigh close to one hundred pounds, but the Svartalfar lifted the hammer like it weighed nothing. *I'm glad he didn't hit me with that*, Leif thought.

They followed Bargog down the street to a strangely carved tree trunk. Leif guessed the sign above the door read, "Bar," in Svata because Bargog opened the wood door and gestured for them to follow. Pale orangish light and a sweet-smelling tobacco smoke escaped out into the open air. Leif was met with hostile stares from every Svartalfar in the room. A short Svartalfar with rubies hanging from his beard hopped off a tiny stool and approached Leif. Leif guessed from the Svartalfar's puffed out chest he was trying to look intimidating, but Leif paid him no mind.

Before the angry little guy got too close, Bargog rushed

through the door and interposed himself between Leif and the angry Svartalfar. The newcomer said something in Svata, pointed at Leif then to the door, but Bargog wasn't having it. Bargog responded by placing a hand on his war hammer, and Arias placed his hand on the hilt of his sword. This seemed to subdue the Svartalfar a bit. With a loud huff, the angry Svartalfar turned and stalked back to his stool. Leif saw him whisper to a few other Svartalfar around him, but that was it. Bargog pointed to an open table at the back of the room and the trio had a seat.

The smoke grew thicker the deeper they went into the bar. Leif had to cover his mouth and nose so he wouldn't start coughing. He felt light-headed. *Hmm, maybe I should try to snag some stuff and try it. I do enjoy the occasional cigar.* Leif thought. He leaned over to ask Arias, but as if he read his mind, Arias shook his head. "Nope. It's not for Midgardians, Svartalfar begin to smoke at an early age; it is a part of their society. This stuff will knock you on your heels for a week. We can't afford that right now. But if we survive this, I'll buy a little for you and you can smoke till you can't see straight."

Leif shrugged, "Deal." Leif silently prayed the tiny wooden chair that held him wouldn't break. He asked Arias what was the deal with the angry stares and the ruby-bearded Svartalfar at the bar.

"That angry little guy, as you say, is from a gem clan. They have a strong hatred for Midgardians. Many of the Svartalfar present are from branch clans to his, so that's why they all uniformly hate you."

"Whoa, back up," Leif said. "Why does his clan hate Midgardians?"

"Remember when I told you about the Aesir shutting down the bridges leading to Midgard?" Arias asked.

Leif nodded.

"Well, long before the invasion, the Svartalfar and Midgardians had a mutual agreement for the export of the precious metals and stones found on Midgard to the Svartalfar home realm of Myrkheim. Svartalfar love gold and precious stones and they have mined their realm dry of these valuable items. While Midgard is brimming with these precious stones and metals. Long ago, an enterprising Svartalfar clan crossed over and struck a deal with many Midgardian clans. For a time, that agreement worked out great. The Midgardians were supplied with Svartalfar-made weapons in return for all the precious metals and stones they could mine. It was a prosperous deal for both parties. However, once the invasions began, the deal fell apart. The attacks weren't just from Jontar and Dokkalfar looking for a fight or new lands. Svartalfar clans not included in the agreement crossed over, striking deals or attacking rival traders. Then Odin closed the bridges. The Svartalfar saw the failure of Midgardians to repel the attacks as a weakness that cost them their valuable source of metal, stones, and gems, and they have held a grudge against Midgard ever since. The Svartalfar over there," Arias jerked his head towards the Svartalfar who was glancing in their direction every few minutes, "Is most likely connected to one clan who got rich off their Midgard mines only to have it run dry when the bridges were closed. My recommendation is to keep your head down, don't stare too much, and just maybe we will get out of here without a bar fight."

"Jesus. That's an awful long time to hold a grudge over some stones and gold, don't you think?" Leif asked.

"Not to them," Arias responded. "The Svartalfar love those precious stones and metal. As you have seen for yourself, they have a gift for building items with their hands, be it weapons, construction, works of art, you name it. They are masters of the art, and those stones and metal were invaluable to them. Whether it was for the stone's special properties, ability to hold a magical charge or purely for aesthetic purposes, those items were essential and when the shipments stopped, many went out of business or got involved in trade wars that turned bloody. So, you see, it just wasn't a few diamonds and gold, but almost the entire Svartalfar economy. Myrkheim relied on the trade with Midgard, and when it stopped, everything crashed. It's understandable that they are furious with your kind."

Leif grumbled something about them being crybabies as he sat back and pretended not to notice as all the Svartalfar periodically shooting him scowls on their tiny, pinched faces.

A heavy set Svartalfar brought over three tankers of an amber liquid that Leif guessed was beer. The bartender left without uttering a sound or looking in Leif's direction. Leif picked up the mug, admiring the craftsmanship. It appeared to be made out of some type of horn. He tentatively took a sip. It had a strong berry flavor with smooth hints of honey on the back end. *Damn*, Leif thought, *not bad*. As Leif took another sip, he relished the flavor. That was when Leif noticed Bargog staring at him. Turning to Arias, Leif asked, "What's Bargog's deal? Why is he staring at me? Am I going to have to fight him again?"

Arias translated. Leif hoped without the fighting part, and Bargog responded. "He's never met a Midgardian before and was wondering if all of them are as strong as you? I explained that you were a fabled Berserker, and that made you stronger. Though I think this only made him want to fight you even more." Arias explained as he smiled and shook his head.

Arias conversed in Svata with Bargog. Quickly getting bored, Leif's eyes wandered around the room, trying his best not to make eye contact with any of the steely-eyed Svartalfar. Leif noticed various war hammers hung sporadically along the walls. Each hammer differed greatly from each other and had a little Svata inscription underneath. One had a shorter handgrip that was made of dark polished wood with a flowing pattern etched into the haft. The handle was well worn and smooth, with little grooves cut into the grip for better control. The head of the hammer was made of dark steel, one side square and the other with a wicked point. Leif felt sorry for any poor fool who got hit with either side of that monster.

A clap to Leif's shoulder made him jump. Drawing himself back to Arias and Bargog, Leif saw they had both finished their drinks. "Got what we needed?" Leif asked.

"Yes. Bargog has laid out where the bridge to Myrkheim is and will be sending word ahead to the village that he vouches for us. He also gave me this." Arias opened his palm to show a small gold medallion with a hammer on one side and a giant tree on the other.

"Cool, what is it?" Leif asked, reaching for it. Arias snatched his hand away before Leif even got close. "It's a token saying that we can be trusted. The Svartalfar are a secluded bunch, but with his word and the medallion, it should be enough to secure passage through the bridge. Bargog explained the bridge will bring us to Svartalfheim. That is the city Alexander was in when he found the passage to the Norns, which will save us time. Hopefully, the tunnels and passages Alexander explored are still there because I am unaware of any other way to reach the bridge." Arias said.

"Why don't you ask Bargog?" Leif asked.

"He hasn't been back in decades, so he wouldn't know. It's no matter," Arias sighed. "I know the area Alexander was exploring, and with this," he held up the coin, "We can cross over and explore the city unmolested, which is all we can hope for. Now come on, I think we have pushed our welcome as long as we can; let's leave before one of these guys gets just a little too drunk and takes out their frustration on you." Arias reached into his traveler's cloak and pulled out a few gold coins and slapped them down on the table.

As they navigated between the crowded tables, Leif could feel the Svartalfar's gaze boring into him. A few Svartalfar dropped their hands to the hafts of their hammers or axes, but luckily none of them drew their weapons. Stepping out into the night air,

Leif let out a sigh of relief. "Damn! That got tense," Leif said, clapping Arias on the shoulder. "Now what? Start heading towards the bridge?" Leif asked. As he followed Arias and Bargog down the darkened road.

"We are going back to Bargog's shop. I'll pick up a few last-minute supplies from him, and then we will leave the city. I got a bad feeling back in the pub, so I want to put some distance between us and Karcoa. I think it was a mistake to reveal ourselves so publicly. Hopefully, we can get into the forest before word can get back to Hel's people. It is an old forest; deep magic runs through those trees. It will be hard to track us once we enter."

Leif inspected the scantly lit cobblestone street and realized he couldn't tell what time it was. It didn't feel that late, nor did he think they had spent too much time in the bar. *So why the hell are all the shops closed?* Leif wondered. A funny feeling ran down his spine. Looking over, Leif could see that Arias and Bargog were deep in a lively Svata conversation, causing Leif to second guess his paranoia, but he couldn't shake the feeling that something was wrong.

Turning down another street, Leif spotted four figures blocking their path. A whoosh of air brushed past Leif's ear. A loud thwacking sound split the silence of the street somewhere behind him. Leif involuntarily jerked to the side a moment before Arias bellowed, "DOWN!" and unceremoniously tackled him to the ground. Leif felt the wind get knocked out of him, leaving him gasping for air and answers. Arias used his forward momentum to roll onto his feet. Arias's thin Elven blade made a satisfying snick as it came free of its scabbard. Leif remained flat on the cobblestones, gasping for breath.

After a few hurried breaths, Leif rolled to the side, finding shelter behind a protruding root of a nearby shop tree. A loud thwack reverberated through the root seconds later. Two arrowheads pierced the root inches from his head. "Holy shit,"

Leif yelled. "This dude can shoot through the tree?" Two more arrowheads materialized with a thwack, mere inches from the first two. Leif yelped and jerked back. *Fuck this,* Leif thought, *I gotta get out of here before one goes straight through and hits me.*

Bargog hunkered down behind a tree root across the street. He held his war hammer ready; his eyes were mere slits as he scanned the street for enemies. His furrowed eyebrows gave him a ferociousness usually reserved for gargoyles. Meanwhile, Leif tried to control the torrent of fear and panic rising from his stomach.

He spotted Arias a root or two ahead of him, and Arias called out, "Four attackers, only one archer. There isn't much we can do about them hiding all the way back here!" Arrows continued to burst from the root. Leif felt the Berserker take hold. Risking a glance over the root, Leif spied a lone figure standing back, while two ax-carrying Svartalfar and a Dokkalfar armed with a curved sword advanced. Another arrow sailed past Leif's ear, nearly cutting it off. Terrified, Leif gave in to the Berserker. He was almost relieved to feel rage replace his fear. As the familiar red haze pooled at the edge of his vision, Leif unhooked his twin axes and readied himself. A vicious war cry preceded Leif's entrance from behind his hiding spot, drawing all eyes to him.

In one smooth movement, Leif threw the ax in his right hand with as much force as he could manage at the Dokkalfar archer. The ax flew end over end. The dull end smashed the Dokkalfar in the center of his chest, knocking him off his feet. Using the distraction to their advantage, both Arias and Bargog burst from their cover and engaged the advancing enemies.

Leif went for the Svartalfar closest to him, who wielded a massive two-handed ax. Wanting to catch the Svartalfar by surprise, Leif kicked out, hoping to drop-kick his attacker, but the Svartalfar was faster than Leif thought. The Svartalfar dodged, putting his nose to Leif's belly, which prevented him from swinging his massive ax. The Svartalfar struck out with the haft of the ax, hitting Leif in the meaty part of his right bicep. The force of the hit spun Leif back. The Svartalfar immediately reversed his grip on the ax and swung horizontally in an attempt to slice Leif's belly wide open. Leif blocked the thrust with his remaining ax, grunting from the impact. With Leif's free hand, he punched the Svartalfar twice, momentarily stunning him.

Shock and outrage flashed across the Svartalfar's face. The pressure against Leif's ax arm let up for just a moment as he recovered from the punches. Using the momentary reprieve to his advantage, Leif pulled down and back with his ax hand, causing the curved edge of his ax to lock over the haft of the Svartalfar's two-handed ax. Leif delighted in the certainty the Svartalfar had in his own strength. The Svartalfar refused to back down or let go of the ax. Leif used the Svartalfar's arrogance against him and pulled with all his strength, locking his ax against his attacker's. To his attacker's surprise, he was pulled off balance. Leif stepped forward as the Svartalfar struggled, and he kneed the Svartalfar in the face. Blood erupted from the Svartalfar's nose as he fell backward.

Leif had fully given himself over to the Berserker. All the control he had practiced with Arias had fled. He moved towards the defeated Svartalfar, letting out a growl of victory over his foe. From somewhere deep in the red fog, a voice called out that the Svartalfar was no longer a threat. The Berserker paused for a moment as Leif struggled to reign in the bestial rage. He picked up the Svartalfar's ax and approached the bleeding Svartalfar. Sounds of battle rang out around him as Arias and Bargog continued to fight. The Midgardian paid them no heed. All that mattered was the enemy in front of him. The Svartalfar's eyes were wide with fear, and he tried to scramble backward, but the Berserker kicked out one of his arms. The Svartalfar fell to the ground with a cry of pain. The Berserker raised the stolen ax over his head. He looked down at the disarmed Svartalfar and paused. Leif pushed the Berserker aside just long enough to give his fallen enemy some mercy and allow him to flee, but the Svartalfar didn't. The Svartalfar seized the opportunity to pull a dagger from his boot, and throw it. Leif flinched as the blade flew past, drawing a thin cut along the left side of his face.

Surprise and fear flashed through Leif, allowing the rage to reassert itself. One-handed, Leif brought the ax head down with all his might. With a loud thunk, the ax blade bit deep into the crown of the Svartalfar's head as the Berserker roared in triumph over his defeated enemy.

Riding the frenzy that comes from battle, Leif turned to the dueling Arias and Dokkalfar. Both elves dodged and weaved back and forth, moving with deadly grace and fluidity. Their Elven blades flashed and clashed in the low light of the street almost too fast to see. Bargog disarmed the remaining Svartalfar by stabbing his opponent in the arm with a small knife hidden in the handgrip of his hammer. THUMP. CRACK! He then finished the surprised Svartalfar off with a hammer blow to the chest, cracking all of his bones in his torso and shredding his internal organs.

The Berserker looked for the remaining attacker. Without warning, a familiar ax flew past Leif, mere inches from his face. It was the recovered archer. A sickening smack came from behind Leif. He turned, realizing the Dokkalfar hadn't been aiming for him. Leif's ax was deeply embedded into Bargog's chest. Blood poured from the corners of his mouth as he sank to his knees and collapsed. Time seemed to slow. Leif screamed, "NO!" The sun that had burned like a scorching summer afternoon went supernova. The blinding rage suffused him with power. Tearing away from Bargog, Leif locked eyes with the offending Dokkalfar. A cruel smile spread across his lips, exposing sharp, pointed canines. Leif pulled his ax free of Bargog's chest and sprinted towards the archer.

Still smiling, the Dokkalfar unsheathed his sword as Leif approached. This relaxed and haughty behavior only infused

Leif's anger. "All right, fucker," Leif breathed, "you thinking just because I'm human I am weak, but you have no fucking clue who I am. I will enjoy wiping that grin off your face." Just then, a cry of pain sounded. Leif's quick glance was rewarded with Arias's thin Elven blade protruding three feet from his opponent's back. The dying Dokkalfar tried to reach towards Arias, but he pulled his blade out in a quick motion and stepped away. The bleeding Dokkalfar stumbled once, then crumpled to the cobblestone street. Blood pouring from his wounds.

Leif turned back to the lone assassin. His stupid smile was gone and replaced by a frown. These idiots obviously thought they would be more than a match for Leif's group. Now outnumbered, the Dokkalfar slid his hand behind his lower back and produced three throwing knives. In one sinuous movement, he whip-cracked his arm forward. Instinct alone saved Leif's life. He dove to the side, avoiding the projectile. Arias simply blocked the incoming knives with his sword. As he scrambled to his feet, Leif watched the assassin turn and sprint down the street. A beastly snarl escaped from Leif's lips at the prospect of the sniper getting away. "Oh, hell no, you don't," Leif yelled. Before he could pursue the fleeing Dokkalfar, a hand locked onto his forearm like a vice and pulled him to a stop. White hot anger flashed as he watched the Dokkalfar disappear into the shadowy gloom of Karcoa's empty street.

Running on instinct, the berserked Leif swung at Arias, but Arias easily batted Leif's attack away. "Let go!" Leif bellowed and swung again, but just like before Arias batted his attack away.

"No," Arias responded. "We need to get the hell out of the city before he reports back to his superiors. We can't afford another fight. We need to run."

Leif wasn't having it. The Berserker howled inside Leif's mind. But the fight was over. Leif reached through the frenzy toward the sanity of Arias's words. He fought to regain control of his mind.

"We got lucky this time," Arias continued. "The fact that they brought such a small group was folly. But they won't underestimate us again. We got what we came for. We need to be deep into the forest before they realize we left the city."

"Lucky!" Leif still struggled with Arias. "That fucker killed Bargog with my own ax!" Leif halfheartedly tried to hit Arias again, but to no avail.

"Listen to me!" Arias yelled, shaking Leif a little. "I know. I'm furious as well. Bargog was a friend, but there is nothing you or I can do for him now. He died fighting, which is how he would have wanted to go. We must continue and finish what we started. There will be many more fights along the way. One day when you finally meet your match, you will meet Bargog again in the halls of Valhalla, but not this day. You have a mission to complete and dying on some fool's quest of revenge won't accomplish anything. We will get our revenge for my dead friend when Hel and her ilk are destroyed. Got it?"

The promise of revenge seemed to pierce the Berserker haze, letting Leif back in. "Ok," Leif said, breathing heavily, "But with Bargog dead, how will we gain passage to the bridge?" Leif asked. "Wasn't he supposed to send word ahead of us?"

"He was," Arias said as he reached into his bag, "But we also have this," producing the gold medallion. "With this and my proficiency in Svata, it shouldn't be a problem. But we have to go, NOW!"

The fight fled from Leif's eyes, so Arias let go of his arm. He wiped the blood from his sword, then sheathed it over his back. Together, Arias and Leif reverently approached Bargog's body. Arias checked Bargog's pockets, finding a few gold coins. He pocketed them and turned to leave.

"Hey, what the hell are you doing?" Leif protested.

Arias snarled, "Get your head out of your ass! It's no use to Bargog now, but we can use it to further our cause. Quit acting like a child. We are no longer in your world, Midgardian."

Leif was shocked. No one in the surrounding shops, pubs, or upper story houses had come out to stop the fight or even see what the commotion was. Leif guessed it really was kill or be killed. Snapping himself out of his thoughts, Leif quickly cleaned his axes on one dead Svartalfar's tunic, then ran after Arias.

CHAPTER 25

Exhausted, bleeding, and an emotional wreck, Leif followed Arias through the maze of winding streets. After making it back to Bargog's shop without being followed or attacked, they hurriedly snatched up their gear and were out the door in record time. As they approached the outer edge of Karcoa, the streets slowly filled with pedestrians, forcing Arias and Leif to slow to a hurried walk. The press of so many Ljosalfars, Svartalfar, and other beings had Leif on edge.

Night was in full swing on Alfheim as Arias and Leif stepped free of Karcoa's trees and onto the massive walkway along the outskirts of the city. Before proceeding, Arias stopped and surveyed the area.

He turned to Leif, "Looks clear. According to Bargog, to find the Svartalfar village and the bridge, we will have to follow one of the main routes leading from Karcoa for a little over a day. The main road will branch off. One will lead towards the Ljosalfar city of Aegir on the coast, while the other smaller road will lead us to the Svartalfar village."

He took an assessment of Leif, "You look exhausted. There is only so much one can handle, even as a Berserker, but we need to push on, at least for a little longer. The more distance we put between us and Karcoa tonight, the better. We can camp in the forest, but we will have to be a suitable distance from the major road to make sure our campfire isn't spotted."

Leif was in a full adrenaline crash, and he barely mustered a nod before Arias turned and led them away from Karcoa.

Once in the forest, Leif breathed a sigh of relief. It was short lived because Arias set off at a jog. Cursing under his breath, Leif followed. Every once in a while, a break in the trees would give Leif a stunning view of the night sky above. Unlike the green fire that danced in the sky above Midgard, the veil on Alfheim was a dazzling electric blue. It was mesmerizing to watch as the blue shifted to teal, then cobalt, then to sea foam. Leif, exhausted and distracted by the veil, tripped several times during their run. A few agonizing miles into their flight, Leif struggled to keep up with Arias, but Arias never wavered or slowed.

Finally, Arias abruptly stopped. A few moments later Leif caught up to him and nearly fell over. His feet and legs felt numb and his mind was a jumbled mess. "We should be safe for now," Arias said while looking up and down the road. He pointed into the forest. "Let's scout out a good spot to rest for the night. I'll take the first watch."

Leif was too tired to respond, so he merely nodded.

He guessed they had trekked close to a mile through the forest, looking for a suitable spot to stop for the night. Each step he took was a minor victory. After an eternal ten minutes, Arias thankfully ended their grueling hike. Leif unceremoniously plopped to the forest floor and let out a moan of equal parts pleasure and exhaustion.

Setting his pack aside, Arias chastised Leif. "Get up, lazy ass. We aren't done yet. Go collect some firewood so I can get our dinner started."

Groaning, Lief got to his feet, "Shit, this sucks. Is it going to be like this every day?" Leif asked.

Arias scowled. Leif got the point, and he turned and trudged off into the forest.

Leif scoured the forest floor for twigs and fallen branches. Unexpectedly, a light flickered in the corner of his right eye, then quickly died out. Leif spun in the light's direction, dropping the wood he had gathered. His hands instinctively gripped his axes. By the time he turned, the light had already vanished. Leif peered through the darkness but could see only the silhouettes of the trees. Feeling guarded, Leif reluctantly took his hands off his axes. He reached down to pick up the bundle of wood he had dropped, but the flash came again, this time somewhere to his left. Leif spun again, but he still wasn't fast enough to catch the source of the light.

Then there was a bright flash directly in front of him. Pausing, Leif peered into the darkness and spotted what looked like a firefly. The bug flitted between the trees, pulsing in a myriad of distinct colors. Leif watched the lone bug as it moved through the forest, but then as if on cue, the forest exploded into color.

Leif stood mesmerized as a rainbow of color flashed and danced around him. The fireflies seemed to dance and sway in rhythm to some unknown beat. Leif silently wondered if anything ever mirrored the marvel at home. With a loud growl, Leif's stomach spasmed. He had been so exhausted from the fight and subsequent flight that he hadn't realized how hungry he was. Tearing his eyes away from the fireflies, Leif picked up the twigs, branches, and small logs that he had dropped, and walked back towards their camp.

Leif returned to the camp where Arias had cleared a compact space and laid out a ring of rocks. Arias gestured for Leif to set a few of the logs and branches in the fire ring. Arias used flint to get a small fire going. The night air had grown chilly, and Leif wanted to stoke the fire to help warm him, but was shut down. Arias said it had to be small in order to keep their position hidden. Leif ached all over, so he begrudgingly flopped down next to the tiny fire, hoping to bring some warmth back to his limbs. His leg muscles burned and pulsed to their own rhythm, constantly reminding him of how overworked they were. His forearms and back burned from the fight in Karcoa, and every time Leif reached for something, his hands shook with exhaustion.

Arias thankfully had thought ahead and packed a bunch of food. He provided several thin slices of salted meat wrapped in a cloth bundle. Arias placed the meat on a broad flat rock he had placed in the fire. As the meat sizzled and popped, Leif felt his mouth water.

Turning the meat with his belt knife, Arias sprinkled herbs onto the thin strips. "We will have to eat it all because I doubt the meat will keep for another day. Unless things have changed since the last time I trekked through Alfheim, there won't be any supermarkets along the way."

"No problem here," Leif said as he tried to contain his hunger. Thankfully, the meat didn't have to cook long.

Leif pulled out a small travel plate and fork and he sat back on a log, digging into the juicy steak strips, small red potatoes, and carrots.

Leif delighted in the taste of food on his tongue and the resulting full belly. He felt a deep exhaustion wash over him. Before he knew it, he was struggling to keep his eyes open. Suppressing a yawn, Leif said, "I don't know how much longer I can last. I'm beat tired."

Arias sighed, "You know, I had planned on regaling you with the story of how the Aesir became the rulers of the nine realms, but I will save it for another time. I think you've had enough excitement for one night. Get some rest, I will stand watch tonight."

It didn't take long for Leif to fall fast asleep.

CHAPTER 26

The fiery landscape beyond the bridge was clear. The bridge led to Surtr's home realm of Muspelheim. They had been hunting Surtr back on Alfheim for several days. They followed his path of destruction from Ljosalfar village to village and were always an hour or two behind the Fire Giant. Alexander had lost count of the dead and dying he had come across as their party pushed to catch up to the seemly unstoppable monster. The bloody path eventually led them back to the temporary bridge the fire giant had originally used to cross over to Alfheim. It was there that the group had paused, unsure of what to do. The harsh realm of molten fire was not welcoming to outsiders; only a being such as Surtr could survive the hell-like landscape.

"We can't go on," Glorgan said as he joined Alexander at the edge of the bridge. The glow of the fires beyond danced across Glorgan's face. Alexander turned to stare in disbelief at the Ljosalfar. *He's afraid,* Alexander thought. *I can see it in his eyes.*

"We can't stop now," Alexander said. He turned to the rest of the group. "We have come too far to stop now. That monster has murdered his way across the countryside over the past few weeks and we are so close. You want to turn and run? We owe it to the dead to get their revenge."

"Are you mad, Midgardian?" Glorgan yelled. "None who have crossed into Muspelheim and faced Surtr have returned."

Alexander scoffed, "It's always impossible until someone does it." Clapping Glorgan on the shoulder, he continued, "My friends, we can do this. If we can avoid a one-on-one fight and attack as a team, we can be the group that finally brings that bastard to his knees."

"Aye," Dracus said. "I agree with the Berserker. We have come too far to turn back now."

"Aye," the two Svartalfar, Bracus and Kalec said in unison. Elina was as silent as ever and merely nodded.

"Agreed," Alana echoed. "Glorgan, if you're too afraid," she said, turning to the Ljosalfar, "you can run home with your tail between your legs, but know when we vanquish the fiery beast, you will forever go down in history as a coward."

Glorgan's knuckles popped as his hand tightened over his sword hilt. "I am no coward, Alana! Aye, then! Let's get on with it. We will lose his trail if we wait any longer."

With a smile on his face and the excitement of the hunt filling his soul, Alexander stepped through the bridge, with the others close behind him.

Slow and steady breathing and the crunch of gravel under their boots was all that the group could hear as they stalked down the old lava tube. Dracus and Alana were the best trackers, so they were in the lead. The temperature in the lava tube was unbearable and sweat poured from their faces as they moved at a glacial pace, stalking their prey.

As the hunting party rounded another corner, Surtr stepped from behind an outcropping of rocks and with one great swing of his molten sword, he cut through armor and bone like it was paper. Before the bodies of Dracus and Alana hit the floor, Surtr was moving with glowing sword and eyes alight in an unnatural fury. He stepped past Glorgan's guard and rammed his sword through his gut. Glorgan let out his last breath.

Bracus and Kalec recovered first, bellowing a Svata battle cry. They raised their war hammers and attacked. Striking high and low in perfect unison, they forced Surtr back. When Surtr engaged Bracus, Kalec would press in harder and vice versa. For a time, Surtr was on the defense, blocking one then the other as they continued their attack, pushing him off balance. The Svartalfars' offensive had given Alexander time to recover. Shaking off the shock of his friends' deaths, Alexander released the Berserker. He took in the battleground with enhanced senses. The speed and ferocity of Bracus and Kalec was astounding, but when Alexander looked closer, he could see their hits would bounce harmlessly off the fire giant's thick armor-like hide.

Using the two Svartalfar as a distraction, Alexander advanced towards Surtr's unguarded side and waited for the right time to attack. Elina silently positioned herself opposite Alexander, catching his eye as she glided into place. They knew they didn't have much chance of killing Surtr in a direct fight. He was too powerful. They waited, hoping the Svartalfar were skilled enough to keep Surtr distracted long enough to find an opening.

Surtr's skirmish with the Svartalfar forced him to strike lower than he was accustomed to, causing him to overstep. Kalec drew in close, slamming his hammer hard against Surtr's right flank. The powerful blow caused Surtr to step off balance. Even so, Surtr lunged, taking Bracus's head off at the neck with a flick of his molten blade.

Time was running out. Alexander and Elina rushed in.

They both seemed to have the same idea. Nothing appeared to be strong enough to pierce Surtr's armor, so the pair focused on the small cracks and fissures crisscrossing his body. The heat emanating from the giant's body burned Alexander's face and hands, but he endured. Alexander slammed his ax deep into a long crack on Surtr's left flank. Simultaneously, Elina drove her thin Elven sword into a similar opening on Surtr's right flank, just below his ribs. Elina's blade smoothly slid halfway up the hilt. Surtr reacted immediately, bellowing in pain as a thick orange fluid burst from his mouth. He held his ground, even with both blades buried deep into his midsection. Surtr paused for the briefest of seconds, making eye contact with both Alexander and Elina. Alexander knew if he survived the fight, that sweltering glare would haunt him until the end of his days. Then Surtr dropped his sword and struck out with both hands, hitting Alexander and Elina simultaneously. The force of the punch sent Alexander flying back down the tunnel they had come from.

Struggling to his feet, Alexander saw that Elina wasn't so lucky as he had been. She had been flung back into the rock wall five feet from where she had stood. She now lay unmoving at the base of the wall. Alexander could see blood streaming from Elina's eyes and mouth, and he knew she was lost.

Kalec was the last of the hunting party on his feet. He let out a roar of defiance and barreled straight in, but it was no use. Alexander could not yell for Kalec to retreat; he hadn't fully recovered from the hit he had taken. Alexander watched as Surtr kicked Kalec with his burning foot square in his chest. Kalec's bones crunched upon impact, flipping him end over end down the opposite side of the tunnel.

Surtr victoriously turned his back to Alexander and stalked Kalec. With a sword and ax still buried deep into his sides, Surtr picked up his burning sword. Then in a voice like boulders crashing against each other he said, "You foolish mortals. You mean to destroy me, but you fail to grasp what I truly am. A being from beyond the realms cannot be killed by pitiful things such as yourself. I was born of fire and chaos. I was here when your pitiful Aesir claimed these realms, and I will be here when the Outsiders rip control of the realms from them." He triumphantly brought down his molten blade.

Surtr released his grip on his sword, and with a pained look he pulled the ax from his side. The wound oozed orange molten blood. Next, he pulled Elina's blade out with a grimace. He inspected the sword before throwing it to the ground.

Alexander knew he had no chance of defeating Surtr on his own, so he forced the Berserker to his subconscious. Alexander spotted a small outcropping sticking out from the wall to his left. His best chance of survival was to sneak away while Surtr was distracted, and he slowly got to his feet. He was careful to make as little noise as possible as he crept to his hiding place. Once Alexander was behind the rocks, he peeked out and saw Surtr's back was still turned. He seized the moment and ran as fast as he could. Alexander made it ten feet before the pain of his injuries overcame him, and his legs buckled. He gasped in pain, falling to one knee. In the silent tunnel, his utterance was as loud as a shout. A long second later, Surtr bellowed and sprinted after Alexander.

Knowing Surtr was mere moments from lopping his head off, Alexander shoved the pain back to the recesses of his mind and ran. Alexander relied on his enhanced speed and gained some distance from the fire giant. When Alexander rounded what he hoped was the final bend in the infernal lava tube, he smashed into something and was promptly knocked out.

CHAPTER 27

L eif bolted awake to being poked in the ribs. Still hazy from the recent dream or vision, Leif reached for his axes, ready to fend off an incoming fire giant. He rolled to his feet and prepared to release the mental dam that held the Berserker at bay, but at the last second, he stopped himself. Blinking in confusion, Leif took in the surrounding forest. The cool woodland air was a sharp contrast to the scalding hot air of Muspelheim that he was expecting. There was a slight tinge of sulfuric air that burned the back of his throat, but the wet grass and morning dew extinguished the remnants of his dream.

Arias stood with a long stick in his hand. He had a giant grin on his face, but the mirth in his eyes flickered and died when he saw Leif's confusion. Alarmed, Arias asked, "What's wrong?"

Leif faltered, then shook his head as if to clear it, "I had another one of those weird dreams. Only this time, I think I was seeing my grandfather's past."

"What did you see?" curiosity coating Arias's question.

Leif closed his eyes, reliving the dream. It felt so real, he could still feel the oppressive heat of the realm on his face, the smooth warm haft of the battle ax clutched in his hand, and the bone deep grief of fallen comrades. Leif lived it all as if it had happened to him. And those molten eyes, so full of hate and malice. Leif knew it would stay with him to his dying days.

"I watched a group of Ljosalfar and Svartalfar. They were hunting a fire giant named Surtr. They had pursued him all the way to his home realm but were ambushed."

"Unbelievable," Arias said, shaking his head. "This has to be the work of the Norns, showing you past battles that your Berserker ancestors fought in."

"How do you figure that?" Leif asked, sitting down near the fire.

"Because, I only know of three people who survived that fight. Alexander was one and is dead. The other two are Surtr and myself. Tell me Leif, what is the last thing you witnessed before I woke you?"

Reaching through the misty veil that exists between reality and dreams, Leif said, "Well, Grandpa was sneaking away, but Surtr heard him and was chasing him. Grandpa had just rounded a bend, and that's when I woke up."

"I see."

"What?" Leif asked.

"When Alexander rounded that last bend, he crashed headlong into me. He must have hit his head because he was knocked unconscious. I had tracked his party hoping to witness them slaying that vile beast. Instead, I ended up running for my life with Alexander slung over my shoulder. After I saved his life, we became close friends. During his time away from Midgard, we would often meet up and explore the realms together."

"But why would the Norns show me these dreams?" Leif asked.

"I don't know. Maybe because you don't have a fellow Berserker to train you. Maybe they hope for you to learn how to control your Berserker by reliving significant events in past Berserkers lives."

"He was so strong, my grandpa. Just from the brief glimpse I got, I could feel his power radiating from him. And his control over the Berserker was incredible. He had such mastery over it. He called it forth and shut it away with such ease. I am a pale shadow of what he was."

"It's true. Alexander was a fearsome warrior. But I can say with certainty that you are far stronger than he ever was. And you are still young, just coming into your powers. If you survive this quest and continue your training, there is no telling how powerful you could become. You must also remember that the vision you saw of Alexander happened after he had been living and training as a Berserker for several years. It was only through countless hours that he gained that mastery over the Berserker. Even then, I could amuse you with many stories. Some are comical regarding Alexander losing control of his Berserker. Do not despair in the difference between your powers but use it as motivation to match and surpass Alexander."

Leif felt a fresh sense of pride. He was proud to be Alexander's grandson. He also felt a determination to make him proud by surpassing him. "You are right, I will learn to push the Berserker to its limits. Then, hopefully, I can become strong enough to even scare the Aesir into leaving Midgard alone."

"Ha!" Arias laughed, "That's a tall order for a mortal. Tall order is the right saying for this situation, right?"

"Yes, yes, it is," Leif affirmed, but he was a little annoyed at being written off so easily.

Arias reached into his packed bag and threw Leif a bag of dried meat from the previous night. "Eat up. We leave the moment you are packed."

Leif opened the bag. His stomach betrayed how hungry he was by grumbling loudly.

An hour later, they were back on the road. It was a bright sunny day with few high-flying clouds blowing on the high Alfheim winds. Leif absently thought about how these long walks, cold nights, and boredom are never mentioned in epic novels or tales of knights and heroes in history. A hero is always given a quest. He then rides out with his faithful knights or sidekick, then fast forward to approaching the evil lair. No long hours of mind-numbing walking through a forest that very well could be a massive loop.

The sun rose high in the noonday sky, and the duo continued their uneventful walk, when abruptly Arias raised his arm, signaling them to stop. Tilting his head to the side, Arias looked like a dog that had just heard a strange sound. "Move!" Arias hissed, pushing Leif roughly in the shoulder, "Get off the road." Arias pointed to a spot off the road where five or six trees had all fallen in on each other. The two sprinted and jumped behind the fallen trees. Leif clumsily skinned his palms and added fresh bruises to his knees and shins as he came down hard behind the fallen trees. Arias followed right behind him, moving amongst the underbrush like a jungle cat, landing softly as he ducked down and hid next to Leif. From their hiding spot, many cracks and gaps between the trees permitted them to peer through with little fear of being seen.

They crouched for ten minutes, but nothing happened. Leif's racing heart calmed, and he strained to hear what Arias heard, but all he could hear was the sounds of the surrounding forest. Leif moved to ask if the coast was clear, but Arias raised his finger to his lips, shutting Leif down. Leaning forward, Leif went back to peering through their hideout. A few more tense minutes passed, but Arias remained motionless, so Leif refrained from saying anything and merely tried to stay still and quiet. To Leif's surprise, a rhythmic clop, clop, clop, slowly rose above the din of bird songs and rustling leaves.

Three horsemen galloped past their location. It was hard to tell who or what the riders were because they were covered head to toe in a black gunmetal armor. Each rider carried a large curved blade at their hip and a silver bow slung over their shoulder. They were surveying the area, looking for something.

Each rider wore a helmet that looked like it came straight out of a medieval movie. With his visor pulled up, one looked in Leif's direction. The soft yellow glow of the rider's eyes told Leif they were Ljosalfar.

Leif and Arias stayed behind the fallen trees well past the time that the riders had galloped by just in case a second group was trailing the first. Time passed until it became clear there was just the one search party on the road. At Arias's signal, the two stepped out from their hiding place and discussed what to do next. "They must have figured out we left the city," Leif commented.

"It's a good thing there are several roads leading out from Karcoa or we would most likely be dealing with a much bigger search party," Arias said. "We lost more light waiting them out, but I still think we should push on. We are close to the fork and once we turn off the main road, it will be hell for any pursuers to follow us. I don't think we should return to the road, we got lucky this time, but I don't want to push that luck. Let's push a little deeper and we'll just parallel the road for now."

The two turned their back on the road and moved deeper into the forest. The thickness of the brush prevented them from moving swiftly. Arias would stop them frequently, listening before motioning them on. They had to keep stopping to make sure they were still moving parallel with the road. Leif quickly learned that moving through a forest is arduous. No matter how careful he tried to be, twigs and branches cracked and snapped. He lost count of the number of times he tripped over a stray root. One time, he nearly fell into a small pit. Every once in a while, he would admire Arias, ghosting through the forest, not making a sound or leaving the slightest trail. Leif would have to ask him how he did that once they have time to relax. A few agonizing hours later, the two came upon a small dirt track that cut across their path.

"I think this is it," Arias said. "Wait here for a second. I will track this trail back and see if this is the one we want." Arias disappeared into the forest.

Leif sat down, took a swig from his water, and massaged his sore muscles. Leif marveled at how anyone could navigate a forest without a map; it all looked the same to him.

While Leif waited for Arias to return, a soft musical sound wafted through the still forest, drawing Leif's attention. At first, Leif thought he was just imagining it, but then he heard it again.

Intrigued, he got up to investigate. It sounded like it was coming from up the trail. His ears strained, and the music grew louder and clearer with each step. About fifty yards up the path, the sound resolved into a soft melody that was foreign but strangely familiar. Following the music, Leif came to a small fork in the path, but he still couldn't see the source of the melody. Closing his eyes, Leif focused, tuning out the soft rustle of the leaves and the melodic chirping of the birds. He endeavored to determine which direction the music was coming from, but then hesitated. He knew that he should go back and wait for Arias, but the music had such a powerful pull. With each step, the melody grew stronger and clearer and more alluring.

The forest thinned out and Leif stepped out into a clearing at the exact moment a soft voice joined the music, accenting the melody. The lyrics were in a musical language Leif had never heard before. Even though he couldn't understand the song, it sounded beautiful to his ears. He swayed slightly to the melody, feeling the exhaustion from the day's hike slowly melt away. He was left with a tranquil feeling that matched the picturesque meadow and pond before him.

The sun had fallen behind the mountains to the west, creating a brilliant light show as the setting sun gave the clouds a pink and reddish tint. The fiery clouds swept over the soft blue glow of the veil, creating a backdrop that photographers and painters could only dream of. Tearing his eyes away from the sky, Leif searched for the source of the song. A few fish leaped out of the pond, creating a soft ripple through the water. Leif continued to drink in the meadow, and his eyes finally fell on the source of the music that had so enthralled him.

Sitting on an enormous boulder that partially sat in the water were two of the most beautiful woman Leif had ever seen. One lay perched on the edge of the stone, feet absently swaying in the water. She plucked a small stringed instrument that looked similar to a harp. The woman appeared to be six feet tall, and her skin color was a deep shade of royal blue. The woman was clad in black leather clothing that barely covered her chest and thighs. The harp-like instrument sat on her well-muscled thighs as she plucked the strings. Her straight raven-black hair cascaded down each side of her heart-shaped face. With a look of deep contentment, her eyes remained closed as Leif watched her play. The other woman sat to her right and was dressed almost identically. She was equally beautiful, but her skin was a deep forest green, and her clothes were dark brown. She too had her eyes closed as she sang in the strange language. The pair swayed to the mesmerizing melody, and Leif subconsciously swayed with them.

Without thinking, Leif stepped out from the tree line and into the clearing. Simultaneously, the women opened their eyes and stared directly at Leif. Their eyes glowed with a soft green light. Transfixed, Leif walked around the pond towards them. Never slowing or stopping their song, the two women tracked Leif as he moved closer. A small smile crept onto their beautiful faces. Once Leif had come within twenty feet of the pair, the melody increased in pace, causing Leif's heart to race. The two women shifted slightly in Leif's direction, drawing themselves closer to Leif as he came within ten feet. Inching closer, the green-skinned woman stood and opened her arms wide, inviting Leif into her embrace. Leif opened his arms, but before he could touch the beautiful maid, Arias burst out of the forest and tackled Leif to the ground. Leif went down hard, gasping for breath.

"What the hell?" Leif wheezed.

Arias also seemed to be out of breath, "I had to break you free of their enchantment, you fool! Look around you!" Arias yelled. "Do you think two beautiful women just hang out in the middle of the forest!"

The women had stopped their song and were staring intently at Arias.

"They are water and forest nymphs!" Arias got to his feet and began dragging the still gasping Leif away from the women. They looked longingly at Leif. Their hurt looks on their beautiful faces struck Leif. Then, out of the blue, the pair played once again, only this time the melody had changed. The song had a sharper edge, and Leif no longer felt the pull that had called him.

After Arias dragged Leif from the outcropping, Leif slapped Arias's hand away. Arias stopped pulling him. Leif looked back at the pair of women, and the blue-skinned woman playing the harp smiled, revealing a pair of dagger sharp fangs that gleamed in the waning light. "Holy shit!" Leif exclaimed. She was no less beautiful, Leif thought, but now her face seemed to transform. It had a more predatory look to it, like a panther as it slowly stalked its prey. The music abruptly stopped, causing a deafening silence. The two women looked directly at Arias and spoke. It was barely more than a whisper, but somehow, it sounded like they were standing right next to them. "Well met Ljosalfar. Next time your little Midgardian may not be so lucky." The blue-skinned woman slipped down into the water, disappearing beneath the surface of the pond. The green-skinned woman turned and disappeared into the forest.

Arias let out an explosive breath and clapped Leif on the shoulder. "Boy, you don't know how lucky you are. They would have torn you limb from limb. Now come on. I found the trail and the perfect spot for us to camp for the night."

CHAPTER 28

The forest had reclaimed the long-forgotten castle. The roof had crumbled many years ago and large trees grew out of many of the rooms. Several moss-covered statues of Ljosalfar knights stood guard in the courtyard that led into what must have been the throne room. Arias and Leif moved deeper into the ruins. The next room they entered had an entire section of its back wall missing, giving Leif and Arias an unobstructed view of the untamed forest.

The pair explored the ruins for the better part of an hour before they chose an inner chamber that seemed to have the least number of trees growing in it. They decided it would be an agreeable place to camp.

Once they settled down and got their fire going, Leif couldn't hold it in any longer, "OK, Arias, spill it, what were those things?"

"They are Nymphs. They are powerful beings, connected to the land itself. They are seen as harbingers of danger and hard times ahead. They are similar to the sirens of Greek mythology. However, their beauty isn't a mask like the sirens, but rather a predatory evolution. Their unmistakable beauty combined with their bewitching music is the perfect weapon against lone and unsuspecting warriors. And once you are caught in their magical web, there is no escape—unless you have someone like me to snap you out of it. You are lucky I had dealt with their kind before, or we both could have ended up on that stone, bleeding out. They sacrifice unsuspecting travelers to the land to help strengthen the forest and water guardians in anticipation of coming disasters."

Leif sat there wide-eyed, listening to Arias casually explain how he was almost flayed by those beautiful creatures.

"Well shit, I'm glad you got there when you did. Next question, what is a forest guardian, and why did I have to be sacrificed to it?" Leif asked.

Arias leaned back and looked up through the forest canopy at the few stars that could be seen and spoke as if his mind was a million miles away. "The guardians are an ancient race of beings that felt it was their life's purpose to protect the surrounding realm. They were connected to the land and water in a way that no other being is. Due to this deep connection, the guardians cut ties with the other beings of the realms and went into hiding, only returning to protect their beloved forests, rivers, mountains, and oceans from those that would threaten them. The last time anyone saw a guardian was thousands of years ago when the realms were engulfed in war. With two nymphs working together, it can't be good. Whatever Hel is planning must be really bad if the nymphs are working together to prepare the way for the guardians."

"Super," Leif said sarcastically, "Is it possible to go a day without something trying to kill me? I am just a regular guy from Earth! I mean, come on man, what could I possibly do against these things? I'm only one man! Not too long ago, I didn't even believe in any of this shit. Now I've had so much of it I could be sick!"

Arias sighed, "Calm down. I really don't get it either. But for some unknown reason, Hel is damned determined to either kill or capture you. Which means you have a part to play. That's why we are pushing so hard to get to the Norns. If anyone can answer your questions, they can. Maybe you picked the cosmic short straw. It's not for mortals to understand the flow of fate."

Just then a horn blew in the distance, shattering the calm of the forest. A second blast sounded off, only this one was much closer. Arias was on his feet in an instant. He held his slender blade in hand as he scanned the area. Leif had his twin axes at the ready, but he wasn't sure for what. The forest had gone deathly silent again, as if it was holding its breath. Then, another even closer horn blast broke the silence. It sounded as if it were right outside the ruin. Arias turned to Leif and made a shushing motion, then turned and lightly tiptoed into the courtyard connected to their little campsite. Leif followed, clumsily attempting to move as stealthily as Arias.

Stepping into the room, Leif whispered, "What's wron..." But he was cut off as he collided with something. In the gloom a shadowy figure dressed all in black materialized before them. The moonlight broke through the cloudy night and pale light illuminated the courtyard beyond. Six cloaked figures detached themselves from the shadows of the courtyard, moving with the silent grace of a pack of wolves trapping their prey. The wraiths reached up and pulled back their hoods, letting their cloaks fall to the cracked and aged stone floor. The six beings had dark green skin, braided raven-black hair, high flat foreheads, and faintly glowing, deep-set red eyes. A large upturned nose hung above the creatures' mouth, which had two large tusks sticking out from their lower lips. They wore black trousers and shirts, but each had various skulls, pouches, and other unknown objects hanging from belts or sashes.

"Orcs," Arias hissed to Leif. The lead Orc's eyes snapped to Arias's, and it grinned, showing teeth that reminded Leif of a great white shark. The lead Orc made a flicking gesture with his left hand and short swords materialized in each of the assassins' right hands.

Another horn blast surged through the tension, and suddenly Arias smiled. He whispered to Leif, "We may be saved just yet. I thought they were hunting us, but I was wrong. We just have to hold out until the Skogur Borg arrive."

"The who?" Leif asked.

"Don't hold back," Arias said, "Orcs are notoriously skillful fighters." Leif's stomach was a cyclone of trepidation as he stared at the silent assassins arrayed before him. Catching Leif's eye, Arias nodded, then charged the assassins with a battle cry on his lips. The fear that had taken hold of Leif vanished as he watched his friend charge their enemies. Bolstered by Arias's battle cry, Leif released the Berserker with a snarl and followed.

The six orcs moved with an eerie silence that sent a warning through Leif's rage filled mind. There was no word, signal or crunch of gravel as the six Orcs broke into two groups, encircling and separating Leif and Arias. The once quiet courtyard was filled with the clash of steel on steel. Leif danced back and forth amongst his silent opponents, but was forced to remain on the defense, ducking and dodging. None of his training had prepared him for fighting multiple opponents at once, or how to work as a team in a fight. Leif was at a loss of what to do. Sparing a glance at Arias, Leif saw that he had managed to kill one Orc and was for the moment fending off his remaining two. Leif knew he would be more of a match for one or possibly even two of the Orc assassins, but whenever he engaged one, one or both of the other Orcs would jump in, forcing Leif to abandon his attack or risk getting skewered by their short swords.

Again, without so much as a word, the assassins maneuvered Leif and Arias further away from each other, boxing them in at opposite corners of the courtyard. Leif had suffered several minor cuts to his arms and legs during the fight, but nothing that wouldn't heal up if he survived. Leif had even gotten lucky a few times and landed a solid cut to one of his attackers' chests, drawing a long line of purplish blood. Leif rolled under a slash meant to cut open his stomach. Coming to his feet in a flash, Leif lashed out again, scoring a slash to the thigh of the Orc to his left. Leif had hoped to slow the assassin by going for his legs, but the Orc paid the wound no mind.

Berserked and feeling no fear, Leif had been confident he could fight his way free of the silent assassins, but that confidence came crashing down as Leif's back bumped into the outer courtyard wall, effectively pinning him in place. Still, the Orcs showed no emotion. They merely continued with their never-ending onslaught of cuts, slashes, and punches, keeping Leif on the defensive. Refusing to lie down and die, Leif dug down deep, nearly losing himself completely to the Berserker. He used the rage to move faster and hit harder, but it was no use. The three Orcs moved seamlessly.

A sudden spike of fear pierced the red haze of Leif's mind. Could his journey end this way? Knowing he had no other option, Leif opened himself fully to the Berserker. He didn't care if he lost his mind in the process, as long as he survived. Before the levy broke, a horn blasted just behind the courtyard wall. A moment later, the four figures in gleaming black armor that they had seen on the road earlier appeared in the mists of the courtyard. The figures split into two groups without making a sound. There was no thump of a footfall or clink of armor. Leif suspected magic played a role in these beings' silent movements.

The orcs faced the additional threat. Arias used the momentary distraction to dispatch one Orc with a sword thrust to its stomach. Two of Leif's attackers split off to face the black-armored knights, leaving just one Orc to face off against Leif. Pushing off from the wall, Leif renewed his attack against the Orc, finally going on the offensive. Sparks flew as Leif's twin axes flashed in the pale moonlight.

Leif smiled as the Orc tried and failed to maneuver Leif back into the courtyard corner. In what Leif believed was a sign of desperation, his attacker thrust its short sword at Leif's midsection, but Leif pulled on his enhanced speed, sidestepped the thrust, then hooked the Orc's outstretched arm with the curve of his ax. He pulled the Orc slightly off balance. Leif's other hand flashed, lopping off the Orc's sword arm at the elbow. Even with the loss of its limb, the Orc refused to utter a sound. Not giving the Orc a chance to escape or produce another weapon, Leif took two quick steps, and slammed the ax in his left hand into the Orc's neck, releasing a spray of purplish blood. Leif produced a berserked victory howl over his fallen foe and turned to face the next threat.

Surveying the blood-soaked courtyard, Leif's eyes fell on the four armored knights. They had come to their aid, but Leif knew nothing about them. They still had their weapons in hand, causing the Berserker to see them as a threat. Beside the knights, a battered and bleeding Arias panted in an attempt to catch his breath.

The red haze of the Berserker fueled Leif's rage, and he advanced on the black knight. With wide and fearful eyes, Arias spread his arms wide and sprinted in front of Leif, screaming, "No!" The knights spread out in a loose semi-circle around Leif and Arias. Leif perceived the move as a challenge. The Berserker howled in Leif's mind, and Leif struggled to maintain the little control he had. *These newcomers had come to our aid, but that doesn't make them our allies.* The Berserker agreed with this sentiment as it continued to flood Leif's mind. Leif struggled to maintain conscious thought. They hadn't attacked Arias, and Arias stopped Leif just now. But who were they? The Berserker didn't care about the who. It merely saw them as a threat that needed to be eliminated. Arias must have seen the internal struggle in Leif's eyes because he took a step closer, careful to keep his hands away from his sword hilt and explained in a soft tone. "They are members of the Skogur Borg, and if you attack them, they will tear you apart. Now restrain the Berserker!" Smack! The slap turned Leif's vision redder, but the paltry amount of consciousness Leif had worked hard to keep Arias's warning registered and sought to quiet the howling within his mind. With clenched fists and a deep breath, Leif took hold of the hateful hurricane and shoved it back down into the recesses of his mind.

CHAPTER 29

Arias spoke a brief phrase in elvish, then bowed slightly
to the black knights. Leif hadn't followed suit, and
Arias quickly slapped Leif on the arm, motioning for
him to follow. The four knights nodded to Arias and Leif. Arias
straightened and Leif could see him visibly relax.

Bloody and exhausted, Leif wanted to lie down, but he knew it
would be a while before they would get a wink of rest. Leif had
many questions running through his head, but for once he kept
his mouth shut and merely listened. Arias conversed with the
knight that Leif assumed was their leader. He was the only one of
the four who had any insignia on their dark armor. It was a
crossed horn and sword in blood red embossed over his heart.

Arias and the knight paused in their conversation, and the
lead knight made a cutting gesture. Then all four of the knights
synchronously unclasped their helmets and hooked them onto
their belt at their hip. As Leif surmised, they were all Ljosalfar.
Two of the riders were male while the other two were female.
Their luminescent yellow eyes flicked to Leif, causing him to shift
from foot to foot. Thankfully, Arias broke the silence by asking a
question in Elvish. He gestured to Leif, and all four turned their
piercing gaze back to Leif. All four were supernaturally beautiful.

Their leader had long obsidian hair tightly pulled back into a bun. The three other Ljosalfar had hair so gold it almost glowed in the moonlight. One female knight had her hair cut short, similar to a crew cut. Unlike the others, she also had an intricate tattoo running down the right side of her face. It reminded Leif of a Maori warrior's facial tattoos. The tattoo coupled with her glowing eyes gave off a wild Amazon warrior vibe.

Arias looked to the confused Leif and promptly switched to English, asking the group if they spoke English. "We do," their leader responded with a heavy accent. "My name is Jaeger, Kaftein of the Skogur Borg, these are my fellow huntsmen. This is Jol, Selga, and Foste." Each armored Ljosalfar nodded in turn.

"Kaftein, I feel that I must ask. Were you hunting the Orcs or someone else?" Arias asked.

Leif stiffened, but held still. He was more than happy to remain a bystander.

"The Orcs," The Kaftein said in a clipped tone. "A Ljosalfar historian was killed and a member of the royal counsel was taken from her chambers just the other day. It was believed to be an act perpetrated by these very assassins. Our unit had been tasked with hunting them down."

"But how did you track them all the way out here?" Arias inquired.

"Few are skilled enough to escape us when the hunt has been called," Selga, the tattooed Ljosalfar interjected in an arrogant tone.

"Of course, honored huntsmen. I meant no disrespect, and I am very grateful for your help."

"After the kidnapping of the Nobleman, we tracked the assassins to Karcoa. While within the forest city our scouts caught word that the Orc's leader, Caster, met with a Dokkalfar by the name of Nip. It was then a simple matter of tracking this Nip down and questioning him, and that led us here. It appears we caught up just in time. It is a pity we couldn't take any of them alive, though. No matter. We will take the bodies and return to our headquarters and see if we can figure out their motives."

"We already know what they were after," Leif interrupted, but he immediately regretted it. Four sets of eyes locked onto Leif. He immediately wanted to shrink away from their intensity.

"And what might that be?" The Kaftein asked. With a sign of annoyance.

Arias pinched the bridge of his nose. "Well, we can't say for sure about the killing and abduction, but the Orcs were more than likely hired by Hel to either kill or capture him." Arias hooked a thumb at Leif.

"Hel, you say," The other female Ljosalfar said, skeptical. "And why would one of the Aesir be interested in a lowly Midgardian?"

"We think it's because I'm a Ber—," Before Leif finished, Arias interrupted.

"We don't know why Hel is after him," Arias said, with a sidelong glare aimed at Leif. "I owed this Midgardian's family a life debt when he saved me after I inadvertently crossed a bridge to Midgard. His family took me in, and now I am repaying the debt by taking him into hiding."

The Kaftein narrowed his eyes at Arias's lackluster explanation, but he didn't push it. Looking up to the moon, he announced, "The night grows late. We need to report back our findings." He turned to his companions and barked something in Elvish. The three knights replaced the helmets on their heads and began collecting the dead Orcs.

The Kaftein locked eyes with Arias and Leif before slipping his helmet back into place. In a slightly muffled voice he said, "I do not have the time to fully question either of you, so I will take your word on the matter of the goddess and her desire for you. But I will give you this one warning, do not return to Karcoa while the dark goddess hunts you. She has no qualms with killing those who impede her goal, and I will not have the innocent citizens of Karcoa killed for your feud. If I learn you have returned, I will personally hunt you down." The Kaftein raised his hand in farewell and turned and disappeared into the gloom. His three companions following close behind.

After a few silent moments, Leif turned to Arias, "Why'd you stop me from saying I was a Berserker?"

"Even though they helped us with the assassins, that doesn't mean they weren't spies for Hel, trying to discern where we are going. Or even if they weren't spies, who's saying that they won't tell someone else who may be a spy. The fewer people that know of us, or where we are going, the better."

Leif hadn't really thought about it like that, but he knew that Arias's reasoning was sound. Clapping Leif on the shoulder, Arias said, "Come on, there's been enough excitement for one night. Let's head back to our camp."

The fire had died down to embers, so Arias sent Leif to forage for wood. Leif grumbled at first, but in truth, he was happy to be on his own; it gave him time to think.

The adrenaline from the fight had worn off, and Leif began to shake uncontrollably. *I still don't understand why Hel has chosen to fixate on me. I am only human. Ok, yes, I have some weird Berserker power bestowed by Thor, but I don't see how that could be any use against a freaking god. Hell, if I'm no match for the Skogur Borg or Orc assassins, how am I supposed to stand up to Hel?*

Leif was so frustrated he wanted to scream, but he settled for kicking a fallen pinecone. "Gods, what am I doing here?" Leif said. "I shouldn't have come; I should have taken Hel's offer to disappear." Leif felt pretty confident when he left Midgard, but now his confidence had been shattered by the recent battles. He felt that his insignificance couldn't possibly tip fate's scales. He toyed with the idea of running back to Karcoa and begging someone to open the bridge. He had gotten cocky in the fight back in Karcoa. *I should have known it was too easy. If beings like the Orcs are out here hunting me down, I'm just fucked.*

Leif felt his pulse race as his thoughts spiraled. He felt his mind fall into a full-blown panic attack. He dropped the wood and sat down, gasping for breath. A cold sweat extended across his forehead. *I must be an idiot,* he thought. *I will die out here and no one will know about it.* Spots popped and flashed across his vision as he struggled to breathe. Leif leaned against the wall and slid slowly down to the floor. Leif stayed there for what felt like an eternity, struggling to pull himself out of this sudden and intense depression. It could have been a minute or an hour, but his breath eventually returned as Leif wound down to a numb state. He was too tired and distraught to do anything but stare into the distance.

A whisper of movement caught his attention, and he woke from his addlebrained stupor to find Arias standing next to him. His slender sword was in his hand, and he stared down at Leif with a confused expression on his face.

"Are you hurt?" asked Arias as he surveyed the area. "Were there more Orcs?"

Leif shook his head.

"Okay. So, do you want to tell me what's going on?" Arias asked as he smoothly sheathed his sword and sat down cross-legged next to Leif.

"I can't do this, Arias. I just can't. We were mere seconds away from being sliced to ribbons by those silent freaks. They effortlessly separated us and nearly killed us both! If it wasn't for the luck of the gods, we would be heads on a platter, served up to Hel. If I was up against a Midgardian, some drug cartel, or gangsters, it would be another story, but I'm not. I'm set to take on a freaking god, and to get to her we have to fight through Dokkalfar snipers, Orc assassins, and whatever the hell else is lurking out there. These people have been doing this for hundreds if not thousands of years. I've been doing it for what? For a few months? Half a year? I am nowhere close to being ready for this. I will die out here. What if the Skogur Borg hadn't shown up?" Not giving Arias a chance to respond, Leif continued, "If they hadn't of shown up, we would be dead, Arias. Dead! I just can't keep doing this. It feels like at every turn there is some danger and I only survive because of luck or outside intervention. How long can that last? The Norns and the gods can just settle their grievances without me because I am done. Tomorrow morning I'm turning back, I'll follow the road back, sneak into Karcoa and beg some Ljosalfar to open the bridge back to my world and disappear. I'm scared, and just done. I'm done," Leif finished, shaking his head. Lief stared past the collapsed wall into the dark forest.

Arias followed Leif's gaze, "Listen, Leif. I understand how you feel. I feel a little of it myself. I've been around for a very long time--longer than you can believe--and I don't even understand why Hel is so fixated on you. If I were in your shoes, I would be scared as well. Half a year ago, you did not know of the wider realms. Then you were attacked, and miraculously, you survived! Not only have you survived, but you thrived, harnessing your powers. It is ok to be scared! Gods know, I understand. Those who spit in the face of their fear and fight on can be called courageous, heroes even. Leif, you are wrapped up in something that not only involves you, but it involves all the realms. Hel has shown she can find you wherever you go. She has underestimated you so far, I doubt she will do it again. I don't think we have had much time to talk to you about Hel, have we?" Arias asked.

Leif shook his head.

"She is the god of death and is not someone to be trifled with. If she deems you a threat to her plan- which I can reasonably say from everything so far, she obviously does- she will not let you go. She will send her assassins across all the nine realms to find you if she has to. And if she doesn't find you, you can bet your axes that she will send her people after your friends until you have no one left."

Leif's head whipped up sharply.

"What then, Leif? All that you will have accomplished is delaying the inevitable. Hel isn't someone you can just wait out. She is practically immortal and has been planning this for millennia or two." Patting Leif on the shoulder, Arias added, "I will not force you to continue, but take the night and really think this through. Remember why we are doing this: Hel killed your mother and Alexander. The Norns are the only beings who can shed light on what's going on. If you run now, you lose all hope of ever getting their help. But in the end, it is your decision. I can't make it for you." Arias stood, picked up the fallen wood Leif had dropped, and walked back to camp.

Leif sat rooted to the spot for most of the night, mulling over what Arias had said. It drove him crazy that Arias was right, but a small part of him continued to scream, "Run!" But no matter how he looked at it, he would have to see it to the end and either succeed or die trying. *Everyone always wants to be the hero, but no one ever thinks about the pain you have to endure to become one.*

As the early morning light trickled through the trees, Leif had decided. There really wasn't anything to consider. *Hel attacked my family, and she tried to kill me. I am a Berserker. I will avenge my family and make my ancestors proud.*

The Berserker flashed in the recesses of Leif's mind. Leif's words stoked the fire within. Leif's knuckles popped as he gripped the handles of his axes.

A feeling of strength warmed Leif, and he felt fueled by an inner force that previously hadn't been his to claim. The Berserker and Leif for the first time meshed into one seamless person. Their purpose was synonymous. Leif growled, "She will pay for what she has taken from me."

Mind made up, Leif released his white-knuckled grip on his axes and stood. His knees and elbows popped as he stretched out the night's sitting session. A guttural growl pulled Leif out of his thoughts, and he realized with a start that he was starving. The hiking, fighting, and constant state of stress had taken its toll on his body. He needed fuel for his toned physique. Gone was the stringy bartender body he had once carried. Leif looked like a fighter, sinewy and rugged. It was just what he needed to be if he had any hope of surviving this journey. The aroma of Arias preparing breakfast pulled the reinvigorated Midgardian from his morose state. Leif brushed off all the dirt and dried leaves, and walked back to their camp.

CHAPTER 30

"We are almost to the Svartalfar village," Arias said. "Judging from what Bargog said, we should be there by the end of the day." Arias and Leif sat around their campfire, protected from the early morning chill seeping from the forest. Arias knew that Leif would choose to stay. Leif sat down without saying a word and hungrily dug in.

It wasn't until after they had finished their breakfasts that Leif broke the silence. "Listen. I'm sorry about last night. The fight in Karcoa, the Nymphs and the Orcs... I freaked out and panicked."

"Think nothing of it," Arias said. "I was born to this world and all the things your people call supernatural. I can't imagine what it would be like to one day wake up and have the veil pulled from your eyes. You Midgardians have been isolated from the realms for so long. It's not surprising that you would go through moments of self-doubt. No one will fault you for doubting yourself or wanting to turn back, as long as you don't act on it. Have your moment of doubt, then shake it off because like it or not you are interwoven into the gods' plans, and sadly there is no way to cut yourself free."

Leif stared out over the slowly brightening forest. The mist that had fallen that morning was slowly dissipating, and birds sang their morning songs. Leif had to admit that even though he had been in constant danger since his Grandpa's and Mother's deaths, the awakening of his Berserker had also opened up entirely new worlds to him. He was still scared- Leif doubted he would ever stop being scared- but he wasn't alone. He had Arias. He would get vengeance for his family. His grandfather was a trained warrior and didn't go down without a fight. *But my mother, she was harmless! I can't turn my back on them or their sacrifice.* Leif said, "All right then, let's get moving. It would be nice to get to the village before nightfall and sleep in an actual bed, in a house, with four functioning walls."

Arias looked around in mock hurt, "What? Does the princeling not like his castle! Trust me. If this village is anything like the Svartalfar villages I've been to before, you won't be as thrilled about staying there as you might think." He stood and gathered his belongings.

"What do you mean?" Leif asked, but Arias wouldn't answer. He smiled and shook his head.

CHAPTER 31

They traveled for much of the day in silence, the events of the night before hung heavy on them. Finally, Leif broke the silence. Did my grandfather ever tell you anything about what the Norns said to him when they met?" Leif asked.

"I had been wondering if you would ever ask me about that," Arias responded as he tucked a stray strand of hair back behind his pointed ear.

"My mind has been a bit preoccupied as of late. I've been mainly moving and reacting on reflex. But it seems these walks through the forest are helping to clear the fog away," Leif retorted as he kicked a small pebble, watching it sail into the forest and disappear into the underbrush.

"I can still remember the day like it was yesterday," Arias mused. "I was sitting on the porch of my tree house in Karcoa, enjoying a fresh pint of Svartalfar red ale, when out of nowhere Alexander burst from a side street calling my name. Alexander was out of breath, covered in dried dirt, and his eyes had a slight haunted look to them. He entered my home and washed up, then met me at my dinner table." With a far off look in his eye, Arias explained that Alexander had found the bridge to the Norns in a catacomb on Myrkheim and that they foresaw his bloodline being vital in the ultimate battle, Ragnarok. Arias pressed him for more, but besides the location of the bridge, Alex wouldn't reveal more. Alex then swore Arias to secrecy, asking him not to reveal the location to anyone unless Alex allowed it. Arias replied to him with questions for much of that day, but no matter how many drinks Arias supplied to him, Alex refused to divulge what had been revealed to him.

"At first, I was angry, but I noticed it scared my friend. Whatever the Norns had told him, it had shaken him. I let up, and I promised him I wouldn't tell a soul. Alexander's shoulder's sagged in relief, and he thanked me. The next day, he returned to Midgard and never left the realm again."

"What do you think they told him?" Leif asked. "What could have scared my grandfather so much that he retreated to Midgard?"

"I honestly don't know. I thought on it many times over the years. It was even one of the reasons I came to Midgard, many years after Alexander had left. I had hoped the passing of years would loosen him up, but when I confronted him, he still refused to tell me. He simply asked me if I remembered the location of the bridge, and when I said yes, he breathed a sigh of relief and changed the topic."

"It's so odd," Leif commented.

"I agree. And so, you can understand my confusion when I got his letter asking me to train the one to inherit the Berserker gene, and then bring him to the very location he had sworn me to secrecy. Gods, I hope once we finally get there, the Norns can shed some light on all this."

Leif was about to respond when Arias held up his hand. "Wait, do you smell that?" Caught up in his conversation with Arias, he had failed to notice the heavy smoke smell wafting on the wind. It was coming from the direction they were walking. Arias held up his hand, signaling Leif to stop. Arias then brought his finger to his lips, making a shushing sound. The smoke slid past them as they stood, listening.

Leif strained to hear any signs of danger. At first, he had trouble placing what he was hearing, then it hit him. It was screaming and crying. He turned to Arias. He must have come to the same conclusion. Without another word, they both set off running.

As they ran, the cries grew louder. Besides the screaming and crying, Leif picked out an unfamiliar sound, a deep, guttural noise that he couldn't place. They continued to run, shrugging off their bags and other items that would be useless in a fight. Unburdened by their packs, they picked up their pace.

The trail curved and the trees slowly thinned to either side. Leif had to shade his eyes briefly when they exited the forest into the clearing. As his eyes adjusted, Leif gasped at the horror before him.

A tiny Svartalfar village ran against a mountain range. The forest had been cut back on one side of the village to allow space for farming and livestock. The village itself was simple; all the houses appeared to be made out of the trees from the forest. It looked like there had been thirty or so buildings in the tiny village before the attack. Almost all the structures were burning. Everywhere Leif looked, Svartalfar bodies lay scattered throughout the streets, bloodied and unmoving. He still hadn't seen who or what caused the massacre.

A scream broke through the silence, snapping Leif and Arias out of their trance, and they resumed their run toward the burning village. Arias signaled for them to stop once they reached the outskirts of the village. The two took a few moments to catch their breath as Arias slowly scanned the streets. Had they been too late, Leif wondered? A prone figure lay mere feet from them. Leaning down, Arias checked the Svartalfar's vitals, but it was obviously too late. Arias rolled the Svartalfar over to reveal a gaping wound in its chest.

Leif struggled to tell Svartalfar apart from one another, so he had no idea how old the Svartalfar was, but judging from the homespun pants and shirt he had been wearing, he was no warrior. A leather belt around the Svartalfar's waist was filled with all manner of tools. "Who do you think did this?" Leif asked as Arias continued to study the chest wound.

"I have no idea, but that," Arias said pointing to the wound, "is obviously a sword wound. It wasn't a Svartalfar who did it. The cut is too long. Keep your eyes peeled and stay with me. If I had to guess, I would say whoever did this is still lurking somewhere within the village. It's too early to say whether this was a random raid or connected to us somehow." Arias scanned the street.

"Random raid?" Leif asked. "It would be quite a coincidence if it was. The village we are heading to just happens to get attacked the day we arrive? This has to be connected."

"Don't assume," Arias berated. "You are still new to this realm. Raids such as this happen all the time. It is very much survival of the fittest here. You will live much longer if you don't make any snap judgments. Draw your axes and let's move." Arias rolled the Svartalfar back over, stood and slowly drew his sword. The blade exited the sheath with the smallest of whispers. Leif unhooked his axes and held them ready as they moved into the burning village.

Smoke hung heavy in the narrow streets, making it hard to see. Just as they had seen from the forest edge, corpses lay throughout the streets. The only signs of life had been the screams they heard when they entered the village, but they had heard nothing since. Leif understood what Arias said earlier about not assuming, but this just didn't feel right. His intuition was screaming at him. He wished to release the Berserker and challenge whoever did this. But at the moment, stealth was their best hope of figuring out what was going on. Leif didn't want to end up killing some innocent Svartalfar who accidentally startled him. So, he buckled down and fought the urge to release his more ruthless side.

Coughing and teary-eyed, they stumbled into what must have been the village center. Leif blinked a few times to clear his eyes. In the center of the square, five Svartalfar bodies were pinned to the ground with large knives stabbed through their hands and feet. Arias moved closer and inspected the weapons. For Leif, the brutality of the scene became too much for him. He turned away, leaning on a nearby tree, and threw up what was left of his lunch. The cruelty of this attack finally sent him over the edge.

"What the fuck is going on?" he yelled to Arias.

Arias held up his hand to silence Leif.

Leif wasn't having it; he wanted answers. Leif was ready to explode at the Ljosalfar, but Arias's face was frozen in fear, and it stopped Leif cold.

"We need to move now!" Arias hissed as he stood up and quickly moved towards the way they had come.

"What about the bridge? I thought we couldn't find the way without the help of someone from this village?" Leif asked in an inaudible whisper.

"We will find another way," Arias said. He was almost frantic, "We have to get as far from this place as possible, and fast."

Leif turned to follow Arias, but they both stopped dead in their tracks.

CHAPTER 32

A hulking figure blocked their way out of the village square. The massive creature took up almost the entire street. Leif searched for other exits, but similar figures blocked each of the four paths leading away from the village center. The figures moved as one, closing in on Leif and Arias. Each figure was over eight feet tall, heavily muscled, vaguely human in stature with dark blue skin. The blue giants were all bare-chested with intricate tattoos crisscrossing their upper bodies. A few held massive broadswords, one had a war hammer, while the one directly in front of Leif carried a large double-bladed ax.

Leif thought back to his fight with the Jontar in Iceland and shuddered. He had only survived that attack with sheer luck, and the intervention of Arias and the Vargr. Here, surrounded by five of them, Leif held no such hope. The Jontar stopped their advance, holding their ground as if waiting for something or someone. Leif whispered to Arias, "What do we do? We've got to get out of here."

Arias whispered back, "They stopped. Maybe they were told to hold us here? But I sure as hell don't want to wait around to see who for. We can't take them all at once, I might be a match for one of them, but with five, we won't last the hour. However," Arias let a smile creep across his face. "Whoever sent them made a mistake. Look how big they are."

"Yeah, I've noticed," Leif said sarcastically.

"No," Arias said impatiently. "Look around us, where are we?"

"A Svartalfar village," Leif responded.

"Exactly," Arias said. "They are too big. We can force them to bottleneck in the narrow streets of this village."

A savage grin spread across Leif's face as he understood.

"I'll forge a path. You just make sure you get to the street beyond. Oh, and make sure I don't get stabbed in the back in the meantime, ok?"

Leif nodded, and a chorus of nervous energy shot through him. Those pre-battle jitters disappeared in a furnace of fury as Leif released the mental dam holding back the Berserker. Taking a deep breath, Leif focused inward, reinforcing the mental bonds as he let a trickle of the Berserker's power out. The wave of icy fire that washed over his body came as a relief. Simultaneously, his fears and apprehensions dissolved and were replaced by an animal fury. Leif felt a feral smile spread across his face as he tightened his grip on his axes.

Sword in hand, Arias squared up to the nearest Jontar. He was about ten feet away, blocking the street beyond.

Leif focused on the other Jontar. They had moved closer but were still far enough to block the other avenues of escape. In a blink, Arias produced a thin, razor-sharp blade the length of Leif's hand and in one smooth whip-crack movement sent the blade careening toward the Jontar's face. Instead of waiting to see if the blade struck home, Arias blurred forward, following close behind the speeding knife. The Jontar twisted to the side, moving far faster than something so big should have been able to. Nonplused, Arias took two more quick steps and leaped forward. His sword flew from his scabbard in a spray of gleaming steel.

Unconcerned with the threat, the Jontar attempted to swat Arias out of the air like a pesky fly, but Arias flung out his hand, spraying a white powder that smacked the Jontar in the face. "ARRRGGG," the Jontar let out a bellow that echoed off the mountains above. Arias still in mid-jump stabbed out with his sword, but the giant, though blind, kept his cool and slapped Arias out of the air.

Leif moved in, running purely on warrior instinct. He ducked under the punch that sent Arias flying, and he slammed one of his axes into the unarmed stomach of the Jontar. Blue-black blood gushed out of the wound as Leif pulled the ax free, but the Jontar didn't flinch. Leif dodged to the side as the Jontar reached out blindly, barely staying out of his reach. However, a second Jontar materialized to Leif's side. Leif was hit so hard that he was sent flying down the vacant street, coming to a stop against the wooden wall of one of the burning buildings. Shaking his head, Leif spat out a wad of blood and stood back up. Arias sprinted to his side, blood running from his nose and ears. From the look he gave Leif, he must have known Leif was already deep in the berserked state, so he merely turned and squared up to fight the oncoming Jontar.

As Arias had guessed, the Jontar were too big to maneuver properly inside the tiny streets. Leif was fully enveloped in the Berserkers power, and his focus was solely on the fight.

Leif continued to attack, ducking and dodging the powerful attacks of the Jontar. Arias watched Leif take a pounding, but each time he got back up and launched himself back at the Jontar. The Jontar weren't particularly smart, but they would eventually split their ranks to pin them down

They were free of the trap, but Leif had unleashed the full Berserker. Leif took a hit to the chest that sent him flying into the wall next to Arias. Blood gushed from Leif's mouth as he crumbled to the street, just conscious enough to hear the battle rage on.

The Jontar reached back to free his massive broadsword.

Arias abruptly jumped back. The space he had just vacated was filled with the Jontar's blade. As the sword sailed past, Arias rushed in, but the Jontar moved faster. The Jontar quickly pulled back and brought the blade down in an overhanded strike that Arias met head-on. Sparks flew as the edges met. Jontar and Ljosalfar stared each other down, struggling for control. Arias grinned back as he held his own.

The Jontar redoubled his efforts, and Arias sidestepped, pulling his blade down. He caused the overconfident Jontar to fall forward slightly as the pressure holding him back disappeared. The Jontar took a small step to maintain his balance, and Arias lashed out, scoring a deep cut across the Jontar's chest before jumping back out of the range of the Jontar's sword. The Jontar paid no heed to the grievous wound oozing blood. However, the sting caused the Jontar to approach more carefully, poking and testing Arias for potential openings.

Sparing a quick look over his shoulder, Arias eyed Leif slumped against the wall. Leif wasn't moving. A pair of Jontar had flanked them in the meantime. The Jontar noticed Arias's momentary distraction and swung with all of his might, and Arias's sword was ripped from his hands.

The giant whipped his sword back, slicing Arias from shoulder to hip. He gasped in pain as the blade bit deep. Arias looked down as a massive boot pressed against his chest. With a loud crack, Arias smashed against the wooden house. Having lost all vestiges of strength, Arias crumpled to the dirt street mere feet from Leif. Struggling to remain conscious, Leif and Arias watched the pack of Jontar slowly approach their fallen foes. Smiles of satisfaction were planted on their faces.

Suddenly, a loud crack sounded close to their heads. Leif felt small but strong hands grip the back of his shirt and pull him backward. The Jontar's smiles vanished as their prey slipped from their grasp.

CHAPTER 33

Leif woke with a gasp. Pain radiated from his entire body. He looked around wildly, expecting to see one of those blue freaks rushing towards him. Confusion fogged Leif's mind when he realized that he was no longer outside in a burning village surrounded by blue monsters, but in a dark, dank and chilly room. It reminded Leif of an old fallout shelter, which made Leif wonder if he was underground somewhere. He attempted to stand up, but pain shot through his chest and he fell back against the bed.

Leif turned his head looking for Arias, but he couldn't see him anywhere. He was in a dimly lit room, alone. He reached out and his hand touched the smooth, icy stone walls. The room was a little small for a human, but Leif could still stand without bumping his head on the ceiling. There were two beds in the room, but the other was unoccupied. Looking to the empty bed, Leif noticed a lot of dried blood. It was unnerving. *Have I been taken prisoner? But then where is Arias?* Leif wondered.

The room was lit by two lanterns on opposite walls. The little fire bobbed and weaved inside the lantern. Leif stepped up to the lantern to get a better look. He had seen these lanterns before.

There was no candle, just a little flame bouncing back and forth. *So, I'm obviously not on Midgard. That narrows it down to potentially eight other realms…*

A knock came at the door, and it was then that Leif noticed he had been stripped down to his boxers and was covered in bandages. "Just a moment," Leif said. He looked around for his clothes and axes, but he couldn't find them anywhere. Without another word, the door swung open. Leif took a fighting stance.

An older Svartalfar stood in the doorway. Both his beard and hair were a gloomy gray. The newcomer's beard fell down to his knees and was tied with small jewels. He wore heavy leather boots, tan pants, and a dark green tunic with a single breastplate that covered the left side of his chest. On his back, he had mounted a double-bladed war ax as long as he was. The Svartalfar stepped into the room.

"You bedder?" The Svartalfar asked in barely understandable English. As the he spoke, he pointed a stubby finger towards Leif.

Relaxing a little, Leif shrugged and said, "Eh, I'll live." He could tell he had taken a beating fighting the Jontar, but luckily he could already feel his enhanced healing taking effect. By the end of the day, most if not all of his bruises would likely be gone.

The Svartalfar let out a laugh and stepped closer. He reached up and clapped Leif on the back. The force of it caused him to take an involuntary step forward. The Svartalfar continued, "Good, ye fighting spirit strong," pulling both arms in and squeezed his hands into a fist for emphasis. "Kalldrec no used to seeing Midgardians strong spirit."

"Um, thanks. If you don't mind, could I have my clothes back? And where is my friend, the Lojsalfar?"

Kalldrec stared at Leif as he talked, and he felt like the Svartalfar didn't understand a word he said. Leif made to ask again, but Kalldrec lifted his hand's palm out and said, "Follow," then turned on his heels and left the room. Leif looked down at his semi-naked body and shrugged. If they don't mind, I guess I don't either. He hurried out the door.

Leif could feel all the tiny bruises and cuts he had earned during the fight flaring. Individually they weren't bad, but as they pulsed and throbbed in time with each other, he fought to keep from gasping with each step he took. It amazed Leif at what he saw. Every ten feet the corridor branched off, leading down one direction or another. These corridors, as well as the one Leif and Kalldrec were walking down, opened up into rooms filled with wounded Svartalfar. Many Leif saw were covered in bandages or missing limbs. A few looked like makeshift operating rooms, with Svartalfar cutting and sewing furiously. Other rooms were filled with families consoling their young.

Leif guessed the Svartalfar had built this bunker under the village. After he had been knocked out, they had escaped down into the under city. Leif still didn't know exactly how that was possible with the Jontar hot on their heels.

He also noticed the distinct lack of any warriors patrolling the halls, present company excluded. "Hey. Where are we going? Where is my friend?" Leif asked.

Either Kalldrec wasn't paying attention or he didn't understand.

They turned down another corridor, and Leif expected the same bland dark color and flickering light, but this one opened up into an enormous chamber. Three marble pillars were set to either side of the room, leading to a massive bronze door. The same lanterns covered the walls on all sides, with three others hung from each of the pillars.

Leif spied two Svartalfar warriors standing guard on each side of the bronze door. They held long spears with a small red flag hanging just below the sharpened tip. Shadows crisscrossed the chamber as Leif approached the bronze door. Leif could just make out a hammer crossed with an ax carved into the door.

Kalldrec walked straight up to the guards and said something in their guttural language. Both warriors turned, staring daggers at Leif as they pulled open the doors. Kalldrec hurried inside, tugging on Leif's arm roughly to get him to follow.

The moment Leif stepped into the chamber, the doors closed behind him, barely making a sound. The chamber differed greatly from the dark and bleak hall he had just been in. It was as if he had stepped through a portal to a different realm. The room was lit by large gold braziers positioned at the four corners of the room. There were six similar pillars dividing the room. Lanterns spiraled up the pillars spaced every foot. Sparkling gemstones were inlaid into the pillars, causing them to glitter in the firelight. Leif pulled his eyes away from the sparkling pillars, taking in the four stone steps that led up to a heavy granite throne. A high-backed chair conveyed a sense of grandeur. A beardless Svartalfar sat on the throne, rolling what looked like a gold coin between thick knobby fingers. The figure had long brunette hair that flowed past their shoulders. They wore no helmet but were clad in a dark metallic suit of armor that was tailored to fit perfectly. The Svartalfar leader was in hushed conversation with another armor-clad warrior. He had a typical beard that stretched down to his knees.

Leif approached, and the seated Svartalfar waved the other off. It finally struck Leif that the armor-clad warrior was female. Her features were more angular, with a broad nose and the same dark brown eyes common to her race. She stared at Leif with open contempt in her eyes and a silent snarl on her lips. A massive war hammer rested on the ground; the haft leaned against the stone throne. Leif noted she kept her hand close to the grip as if at any moment she would snatch it up and put some serious hurt on whoever angered her.

The Svartalfar leader said something in her gravelly language. When Leif failed to respond, she switched to Ljosa. When Leif failed to answer again, she sighed and switched to English. "Would this tongue be better suited?" Her voice was heavily accented, but Leif could still understand.

"Yes, where is my friend?" Leif asked.

"Silence!" She barked back. "I am Vestri, ruler of this clan. I will only ask this once. Who are you, and why have you brought the attention of the dark queen to my lands?" The leader was obviously angry and the angrier she got, the stronger her accent got. Leif had to really focus to understand.

"Please, if you can show me to my friend, he will explain much better than me. I, just like your village, am an innocent bystander in something much bigger than you or me."

The Svartalfar leader waived a hand and said, "We have already spoken with your Ljosalfar friend. He showed me this." Holding up the gold coin that Bargog gave Arias. "It is hard to trust someone who showed up the same day Jontar appear, slaughtering my people, even if they carry one of our bridge medallions. Thus, I wish to hear your explanation. The Ljosalfar speaks of many grave and terrible things. We hope it to be a falsehood, nothing more than a treasure seeker's gambit to gain access to the secrets of the mountain. So, speak Midgardian or we will throw you out and let the Jontar have you."

Leif really didn't have any other option, so he told her everything. Not wanting to leave anything out, he started from the very beginning. He told of the night his mother and grandfather died, the attack at his apartment, and in the forest outside his grandfather's house. He talked about finding Arias and everything else up to waking up half naked all bandaged up. It had been quite a long story, and it felt good to lay it all out.

The Svartalfar sat as still as the granite throne she sat on while Leif retold his tale. Once Leif had finished, the leader said something in Svata. It sounded strikingly similar to a curse.

"So, the rumblings are true then," Vestri said. "We feared this was coming, but still had hoped it wasn't time yet. We will give you your things back. We will take you to your friend and give you safe passage to Myrkheim. Though I must warn you, I do not know if the Ljosalfar can make the trip. He has suffered a grave wound. Our healer has been attending to him." Vestri stood and snapped her fingers.

A warrior arrived, metal armor clinking as he came. She said something in Svata and the guard disappeared through a door in the side of the chamber. He returned in moments carrying Leif's gear. The guard unceremoniously dumped Leif's gear at his feet, then went back to his silent vigil. Vestri nodded once, then turned to leave through a large orange door to the left of the throne.

But before Vestri made it too far, Leif yelled out, "What do you mean you hoped it wasn't time yet?"

Vestri met Leif's eyes and said a single word, "Ragnorok." She then turned and disappeared through a doorway.

Kalldrec came down from the spot he had been standing and gestured for him to follow. Leif couldn't be sure, but the Svartalfar seemed a little more on edge this time. He kept glancing from side to side, scanning the obviously clear area for unseen threats. Leif guessed that even the mention of the word Ragnorok was enough to set the warrior on edge.

Leif passed through the door behind the throne room and into another hallway. The hallway beyond was much brighter than the few he had seen earlier. Leif looked up at the lanterns that contained the same dancing firelight, but the fire within these lanterns was much bigger and shone brighter than their smaller cousins in the other hallway. Between the doors and hallways, carvings ran along the corridor on both sides. The carvings depicted Svartalfar deep down in caves, excavating precious stones or swinging great war hammers and axes as they struggled against strange and terrible beasts.

They escorted Leif to a nondescript door where two warriors stood guard. The two warriors, with axes in hand, observed as they approached. One guard turned to Kalldrec and said something, but it must have been inconsequential because Kalldrec waved him off and pushed open the door to the guarded room.

CHAPTER 34

Leif barely recognized Arias. He was covered from head to toe in purple and blue bruises, and his head was wrapped in bandages. A ragged wound ran from Arias's shoulder to hip. Leif wanted to look away, but he forced himself to see the consequences of allowing the Berserker complete control. The wound was foul. It looked like the Jontar's blade had cut through Arias's ribs, but Leif couldn't see any of his organs, and he hoped that was a good sign.

The two healers were a blur of motion, cutting, stitching, and waving odd stones back and forth. While one healer waved a stone up and down Arias's body, her words hung in the air longer than they should have, causing Leif's senses to fuzz. Leif recognized the feeling from the cave; it was magic. He stood there watching until a healer turned to grab something and ran into him. Leif immediately apologized, but the healer ignored him. She turned to Kalldrec, who had fallen asleep in a chair in the corner. She kicked him awake, angrily pointed and said something before turning back to her work. Kalldrec got up and pulled Leif over to where he had been sitting and pointed at the chair next to him, saying, "Sit." He then pointed back to the healers and said,

"No bother," before sitting back in his own chair and promptly going back to sleep.

The healers continued their work for a few more hours. By the time they were done, they both looked ragged and exhausted. They had managed to close Arias's major wounds, but Leif did not understand what else they had done. While the healers cleaned up, Kalldrec woke up. One healer spoke to Kalldrec, occasionally gesturing to Arias. She finally finished with a shake of her head, which Leif suspected was a bad sign. Leif turned to Kalldrec, who looked like he wanted to say something, but he merely shook his head and patted Leif on the shoulder.

Shit, Leif thought.

As the gravity of the situation set in, Leif began to hyperventilate, which blossomed into panic.

A violent bout of coughing from the unconscious Arias brought Leif back to the present. Arias slowly opened his eyes as his coughing fit continued. A trickle of blood slipped from the corner of his mouth. Arias attempted to raise his arm, but a spasm of pain caused him to stop. Leif saw Arias look around; his eyes were wide with panic. Finally, he focused on Leif, and he visibly calmed. Arias smiled weakly, revealing his blood-stained teeth.

Leif's heart fell as he watched his friend struggle to turn his way before pain forced him to roll back onto his back. Leif had hoped once Arias woke up, he could recover, but upon seeing his condition, he didn't need to understand Svata to know what the healer meant.

Kalldrec stepped up to Arias and his eyes focused on the little warrior. They conversed for a while in Svata before the warrior patted Arias on the shoulder and walked out. Meeting Leif's eyes for the briefest of moments, Kalldrec closed the door behind him.

"Leif," Arias croaked, "There is much I still need to tell you." Leif grabbed the chair sitting in the corner and pulled it up next to Arias's cot. Up close, Arias looked ashen and winced with each breath. "You don't speak Svata, but I bet you've guessed my prognosis," Arias said. "That damn Jontar sword got me good. They closed up everything they could. But even so, it isn't enough to save me. Kalldrec suspects there was some type of poison on the blade."

Leif sat, dumbfounded. He knew this was coming, but hearing it felt like a physical blow.

Leif felt his shoulders slump, and he lowered his head, ashamed. "I'm so sorry, Arias," Leif said. "If I hadn't lost control, we would have been able to escape, instead I gave in to the Berserker and fought instead of cutting and running once we had gotten passed the Jontar. It's my fault you got wounded." The tears fell freely as Leif struggled to express his guilt. "Hell, if it wasn't for me you wouldn't even be in this godforsaken bunker. But no, I had to recruit you on this crazy quest, and we don't even know if we will find the Norns. I am so sorry." The silence after his confession made his sorrow even worse.

Finally, Leif noticed Arias staring directly into his eyes. "What?" Leif asked, "Why are you looking at me like that?"

"Don't despair for my passing, I have lived a long, long life full of both happiness and tragedy. You humans always focus on the end of one's journey as a time of sadness, and I have always struggled to understand that. This may be an ending, but it is also a beginning. Soon I will dine in Valhalla with Alexander. This is not the end. The brave and courageous will be called upon once again. On that day we will see each other again and will fight side by side as warriors do. Now I need you to listen. I have little time left."

Leif rubbed his eyes, took a swig from the water skin Kalldrec had given him, and sat back to listen.

Arias must have seen the determination in Leif's eyes because he leaned back down, winced and said, "Good. You still have a hard road in front of you."

CHAPTER 35

Taking a wet, gasping breath, Arias grimaced before starting. "Alexander explained to me that to find the Norns you will need to travel into the catacombs beneath Svartalfheim. There, in the tunnels, Alexander marked the entrance to the bridge with a small hammer. Leif, this won't be easy, but you must travel there and search out the entrance to the bridge. Beyond, I know not what the Norns have guarding the entrance."

Arias grimaced as he shifted on his cot, and Leif could clearly see he was in pain. Leif furrowed his brow. "That's all he told you? I have to find a carving on the wall in the middle of some catacombs? That could take months if it's still even there at all. And besides, you told me the Svartalfar hate Midgardians. I won't make it five steps in their realm."

Arias coughed, "I never said this quest would be easy, Leif. Speak with Vestri. Make her listen to you. Don't reveal too much; we don't know who's side she is on or if there are spies here, but you must make her lend you a guide. With a guide helping, you should be able to locate the catacombs. You can take it from there."

Shaking his head, Leif whispered, "I can't do this without you, Arias. There is so much more I need to learn."

Arias smiled and slowly shook his head. "I'm sorry Leif, this is where my path ends. Get to the catacombs. Find the Norns. Stop Hel." As Arias spoke, he grew paler and paler, and he had broken out in a sweat even though it was cool in the underground room.

Arias was struggling to breathe, and Leif knew it wouldn't be much longer. Leif's eyes watered as he sat watching his friend slip away. A small drop of blood trickled from Arias's nose as he spoke, and he reached out, grabbing Leif's forearm with a surprising amount of strength. Locking eyes, Arias said, "Listen to me, Leif. I know you don't think you are ready or worthy to defend the nine realms, but you are. I've seen you grow into a powerful warrior over the past year. You can do this. At the right place and time, one man can hold back the tides of darkness." Arias inhaled and smiled, "I will be sure to tell Alexander about you when I see him in Valhalla." The soft glow of Aria's eyes slowly dimmed, then winked out.

Leif sat there staring at his friend's body. He knew he was gone. Leif had spent so much time with Arias in the past year that he couldn't process that Arias wouldn't be continuing his adventure with him. It was easy for him to think Arias was merely sleeping. Leif shook his head, trying to dispel that thought. He had to accept his friend was gone. Tears blurred his vision and rolled down his cheeks. "I'm sorry," Leif whispered. Taking a deep breath, Leif reached out and put a hand on Arias's arm, "I am sorry, my friend. I promise I will find Hel and make her pay for what she has done."

CHAPTER 36

No one bothered Leif while he mourned. He stayed in Arias's room, staring at his fallen friend, going over everything that had happened. Even now, underground in an alien village, he found his circumstances hard to believe. Arias was his bridge between his new life and the dull, boring world back on Midgard. Now he was gone, leaving Leif to stumble around with the weight of the nine realms resting on his shoulders.

Leif wanted to be mad. He wanted to rage and curse Arias and his grandfather for cursing him with this fate, but in the end, he knew it wouldn't do him any good. From everything Leif had learned, it seemed this had been his destiny for a while. If he wanted to be mad at someone, it should have been Hel for trying to upset the balance of the realms. This thought seemed to calm Leif down and bring focus back to his sad and troubled mind. *The true villains of this story are the Outsiders and Hel,* Leif thought. These were the beings that Leif knew he needed to hunt down and make pay for all the pain they had caused him. With his priorities back in line, Leif sat for a little longer, trying to still his racing heart. He took in the last few moments he had with Arias. Leif wasn't sure how long he sat there, trying to clear his mind, but he stood up, hooked his axes onto his belt, and exited the room without a backward glance.

Outside Arias's hospital room, the two guards stood at rigid attention. As he exited, one of them stepped forward and Leif said in a commanding voice, "Take me to Vestri." The guard nodded and walked down the hall. The second guard gestured for Leif to follow, then fell in line behind him as they walked back to the throne room.

Vestri and Kalldrec stood over a table with hand-drawn maps spread across the table. Kalldrec saw Leif first and tapped Vestri on the arm, pointing towards Leif. She made eye contact and her shoulders dropped ever so slightly. "I see the Ljosalfar warrior has gone to the great halls. I am truly sorry to hear that. We will need every able warrior in the years to come if your story proves true. We have sent scouts to the town above, and it appears the Jontar have left the area. You will be free to go your own way." The Svartalfar leader turned back to her maps again, dismissing Leif with her silence.

Steeling himself, Leif took a step closer to the raised dais they stood on, causing both guards to shout a warning. Leif stated boldly, "I have no intention of returning to the forest above. Arias and I travelled all the way here to gain passage to Myrkheim, and that is exactly what I intend to do."

Vestri let out a small sigh and turned back to Leif, arching her small eyebrow. "Foolish Midgardian, you still smell of your world. What makes you think you alone have what it takes to continue on with this plan? Even if I were to grant you passage, what makes you think you are equipped to survive on Myrkheim? Our realm is nothing like the lavish forest world the Ljosalfar are so fond of. Without your friend, you would stumble around and most likely get lost down some abandoned tunnel, or get your throat cut by a passerby. Go home. You failed. Run and hide and pray Hel believes you to be dead." Again, Vestri turned her back on Leif to study her maps.

Leif could feel his temper growing and he feared if she continued to dismiss him and treat him with such disrespect, his Berserker may break through and Leif knew he wouldn't get anywhere if he accidentally killed everyone in the room.

He grit his teeth and let out a calming breath, "You must listen to me! You yourself mentioned the dangers to come. Yes, my friend and guide is dead, but before he passed, he told me where I must go to complete my journey. And trust me, you want me to get to where I am going. It may be the key to stopping the coming war. So, I ask again, will you help me?" This time, when the leader turned back to face Leif, her face changed rapidly, and she showed a hint of fear. She took an involuntary step back and bumped into the table, knocking over several items. This caused Kalldrec to finally tear his eyes from the maps. His eyes widened when he turned to look at Leif. Kalldrec's hands immediately went to the haft of his war ax, but he restrained himself from unsheathing it. Leif guessed that his eyes began to glow, and he fought to suppress the Berserker. He took a few more breaths, and he felt the anger recede. The two Svartalfar visibly relaxed, and Leif knew his eyes must have changed back to normal.

Leif said. "I am not some measly human who was out for a random adventure with my Ljosalfar friend. I may be one of the last living Berserker in existence, and this may sound arrogant, but right now I may be the only person who can prevent the war."

The two warriors exchanged looks and some short-clipped words before turning their attention back to Leif. "What do you know, Berserker?" Vestri asked in a suspicious tone.

"I don't know much, and I am unsure what I can reveal. But I do know I have some role to play in preventing Ragnorok, and whoever is trying to start it is trying hard to kill or capture me. I need your help to find the catacombs underneath Svartalfheim. After that, I will be out of your hair." Something Leif said must have struck a chord with Kalldrec because he leaned in and quietly addressed Vestri.

Whatever they discussed, Vestri wasn't too happy about it because she raised her voice a few times and slammed her hand down on the table. However, each time she did so, Kalldrec gave a terse response. Finally, Vestri let out a sigh of annoyance and turned back to Leif. "Fine. Kalldrec here will be your guide to the capital on Myrkheim. It seems he has a few ideas on who to contact that might be able to help you find your way to these catacombs. But know this. We have much to prepare for, and Kalldrec is the only general I have left, so I will not permit him to be gone long. If the ending battle is really coming, I don't intend to be caught without my ax, and if you keep Kalldrec away for too long, I will come to get him and abandon you." Vestri, resigned to this decision, took a deep breath, "You and Kalldrec will leave tomorrow morning at sunrise. Your friend's funeral will be tonight." She turned back to her maps.

One of the guards that had escorted Leif to the throne room tugged on his shoulder, pulling him out the door they came in. Leif let him, not feeling the need to put up a fight when he had just got what he wanted.

They led Leif back to Arias's room in silence. Leif watched as two Svartalfar women cleaned Arias's body and wrapped him in a white cloth. They both froze when Leif entered, but he sat down in a chair in the corner, leaving them to do their work. Letting his head roll back and rest against the cool stone, Leif pondered on the coming days and how he would pull this off without Arias's help.

CHAPTER 37

L eif jumped awake to the sound of the door opening. A burly Svartalfar in black robes and a white beard stepped in. Leif instinctively jumped up, unclipping both axes in one smooth movement. The robed figure smiled slightly, then said in heavily accented English, "I am sorry to disturb you. Vestri asked me to stop by and speak with you,"

"Ok," Leif said, a little suspicious. "Who are you?"

"Ah," the Svartalfar said, "I forget myself. You are the first Midgardian any of us have seen, and a Berserker at that. It has caused a bit of a stir amongst my people. I found myself nervous meeting you myself."

Leif raised an eyebrow. "I'm cool. I am under control. You just caught me off-guard. I was just thinking about what to do next." Leif inclined his head towards Arias's still form.

"Ah, yes. I am sorry to hear about your friend's death, but mourn not for the fallen. From what I heard, he suffered his wounds in battle and fought bravely against the Jontar. The gods surely would have opened the doors to Valhalla to such a courageous soul. As we speak, he is most likely eating and drinking in those storied halls, waiting for his chance to fight again."

Leif gave him a skeptical look, and the monk laughed.

"I see the way you look at me, Midgardian. From what I hear of your kind, I can understand your reluctance in believing in Valhalla. You must remember, unlike your kind, we have not been cut off from the Aesir. Though the Aesir have not chosen to step outside of their throne world of Asgard in many eons, the Svartalfar, just like Ljosalfar, are a long-lived race, and there are a few still around who remember when the Aesir took a more active role in the shape and flow of the nine realms. So be at peace. Your friend is in a much better place."

"Thanks," Leif mumbled. "Though I am very new to all of this, if what you say is true, it makes me feel a little better." Leif said.

"Good," the monk smiled. "It gladdens my heart to hear that. Now, it is time to pay your friend his final respects and give him the warrior funeral he deserves. If you will, please come with me." The monk stood and gestured for Leif to follow.

Leif followed the monk out of the room. Several Svartalfar garbed in ornate polished armor moved into the room after Leif, and with a grunt, picked up Arias's body, and walked out of the room and down the hall. Leif turned to the monk and asked where they were going. "Fear not my friend, they are merely taking him topside to the pyre."

"But why are you guys doing this for him?" Leif asked. "I mean, your people were attacked and massacred in the village because of us."

"Yes, the attack above was unfortunate. The reason for providing your friend with a proper burial is because many of the Svartalfar here are warriors and recognize the great courage both the Ljosalfar and yourself showed in staying and fighting the Jontar. Their ferocity in battle is widely known, and only the most skilled warriors outside of Thor himself would fight against the group that besieged our village above. Thus, the warriors of the underground city have decided to honor your friend and provide him with the warrior sendoff he deserves." The monk turned to follow the warriors. Leif shrugged and followed suit.

It took forever to make it to the surface, and Leif suspected the procession took a roundabout way to confuse Leif. All he wanted was to send Arias off and get to the bridge. Finally, they exited out of a hidden door in the mountainside. One of the warriors closed the door behind him. Leif turned to see the door was nearly invisible. If he hadn't just stepped out, there's no way he would have ever found it. Leif followed the procession to a small pyre stacked between the edge of the forest and the cliff face. The honor guards placed Arias's body on top of the pyre and stepped away. Leif noticed that as each one passed, giving a slight nod to Arias's body. Once the guards returned to the group, the monk approached Leif with a lit torch, and without another word held it out to him.

At first, Leif hesitated. Then, understanding blanketed his thoughts, and he took a firm grip of the torch. He slowly walked over to Arias's body and silently lit the pyre. Leif remained by the flaming pyre for a moment longer, unable to speak. Leif finally whispered, "Rest easy, friend. I will finish what we started." Leif returned to the ranks of Svartalfar.

Once the flames died down to smoldering embers, the procession turned away from the pyre and made their way back down into the underground city. Leif nodded one last time to his friend before turning to follow.

Leif stopped outside of Arias's room and the monk placed a tiny hand on Leif's arm, saying, "This will be your room for the night. Our leader has informed me of your plan to continue onto Myrkheim with Kalldrec. I don't mean to discourage you, but I feel I must warn you. Our kind has no love for Midgardians. Watch yourself over there. The Svartalfar in this city have lived here on Alfheim for many years and have shrugged off much of the animosity our kind still harbors towards outsiders. If you truly have a way to stop the upcoming war, I wish you the best of luck, and may the Aesir watch over you."

The Svartalfar held Leif's eyes, giving Leif the impression that Myrkheim was probably just as dangerous as he stated. He broke eye contact, nodded slightly, and left Leif to spend the night alone.

Leif went into his room, unclipped his axes, and checked to ensure the blades were still sharp. The Svartalfar had retrieved his pack and placed it in his room. He checked it to make sure he had enough supplies, and he repacked it. After he had done all he could, he laid down and was asleep within seconds.

Leif tossed and turned during the night. His dreams flashed from scene to scene like the colors changing in the ever-present veil above. In one dream he stood in front of a pyre, flames blazing so hot he had to look away. When he opened his eyes again, he noticed he wasn't on Alfheim anymore, but back in Los Angeles surrounded by thousands of funeral pyres. He saw row upon row of pyres lit with humans lying atop them. Leif looked closer and saw all the buildings were damaged and the sky above had taken on a strange red tint.

The dream fuzzed and flashed; Leif was back fighting the Jontar, but this time he defeated them all. Nonetheless, Arias still got injured and died in his arms. The dream flashed again, and he stood in a doorway staring out a grand balcony. Massive columns spread out in both directions, and the lone woman in the bright red dress stood with her back to him. Her long blonde hair flowing down behind her. The red dress was open in the back, revealing muscled yet feminine shoulders. The sky beyond was dark and starless, and there was a pale greenish light pulsing from somewhere down below. A creepy, ragged moaning sound could be heard somewhere in the distance.

The dream flashed and for the briefest of moments, Leif glimpsed three women standing in front of a simple wood cabin, each wearing a simple dress. The three women looked identical except for their eyes. They stared directly at Leif with bright glowing eyes of topaz, emerald, and sapphire. They stared unblinkingly back at him with such an intensity that even though Leif knew he was dreaming, the stares caused him to flinch. "Come find us," the trio whispered in unison.

The dream flashed again, and this time Leif found himself on his back, twin axes in hand, staring up at a monster Leif thought would only exist in a dream. It was a dragon. Leif spared a glance to either side, and he saw that he was now in a land full of dark gray and black rock. No grass or trees could be seen in either direction. The sky above was the same cloudy slate gray of the beast looming above him. The dragon's massively scaled neck arched down and its arrowhead-shaped head stared down at him. Its two massive gold eyes studied Leif. Leif knew somehow this monster was ancient and intelligent. The two slits the dragon had for a nose seeped out black smoke that curled up towards the sky. The dragon opened its maw and Leif gasped as he saw dagger-sharp teeth. It could easily swallow Leif whole if it wanted to. Leif willed his body to move, but he was so terrified that his body was no longer responding. The dragon arched back briefly, then lunged forward, too fast for Leif to follow.

There was a flash of bright light and a ringing so loud Leif clapped his hands over his ears. The vision fractured as he felt a strong hand clamp down on his arm, shaking him free of the nightmare.

CHAPTER 38

Leif was bathed in sweat. *The dream felt so real*, he thought. His heart was still racing when he found Kalldrec staring at him with his hand still clamped down on Leif's arm. "We go," he said in his heavy accent, gesturing with his thumb out the door.

"Ok, ok," Leif said, "Let me get dressed." *Luckily, I packed last night*, Leif thought. As he looked over at Kalldrec, who stared back at him with impatience. Leif noticed that Kalldrec had changed out of his armor and was now wearing a dark green shirt. Over the shirt he wore a series of small steel plates of armor sewn together to cover his chest, stomach, and shoulders. The stuff looked to be lightweight. He also wore tan pants that were tucked into heavy black boots. He wore his massive ax strapped onto his back. Over it, he wore a heavy traveling backpack.

Leif finished getting dressed, hooked his grandfather's axes to his belt, shouldered his travel pack, and gave the Svartalfar a thumbs up. Kalldrec reached into his pack and threw Leif a brown cloth bag. Leif almost dropped it because how heavy it was. Leif looked back at Kalldrec in surprise, raising an eyebrow in question.

Kalldrec shrugged, probably looking for the right words, "From Vestri. For travels. Wish good luck."

Leif nodded and opened the bag.

Inside there were a few strips of dried meat, a couple round objects that Leif guessed were fruit, and several gold coins. Reaching in, Leif pulled out one coin and inspected it. It was perfectly round, probably the size of a silver dollar. On one side there was a perfect rendition of a war hammer. The back side was covered in small Svata runes. Leif checked the others, and they all appeared to be identical. Leif marveled at the precision with which these coins were made, and he wondered how the Svartalfar created them without modern technology. He chalked it up to the legends about the Svartalfar being master craftsmen. Leif returned the gold back to the pouch, then stuffed it deep down into his backpack. He nodded to Kalldrec.

Out in the hall, Leif was surprised to see there was a pair of guards standing to either side of his room. Leif wondered whether they were there for his protection or to prevent him from sneaking out and exploring the underground city. Leif followed Kalldrec as they walked down several hallways in a forever attempt to keep Leif lost. Eventually, they turned down a dark hallway Leif hadn't seen before and entered a stairway. In the rest of the underground city Leif had been through, the walls, floors, and ceiling were all perfectly smooth and made of the same dark-colored stone. However, the walls of this hallway were a rusted dark red color and rougher. As they ascended the stairs, Leif ran his hand along the surface of the dark rock. It was jagged and porous to the touch, and it jutted out in odd angles as if the stairway was cut out, but unfinished in some way. They climbed and climbed. Leif felt a small amount of sweat break out on his forehead, and he called out to Kalldrec, "How much farther?"

He either didn't understand or chose not to answer.

Leif felt a pang of sadness as he thought about Arias and how he would have told Leif to "Quit his bitching" or something equally rude.

After losing count of how many stairs they had climbed, they finally emerged into an enormous chamber. It was dimly lit by two of the flame lanterns the Svartalfar were so fond of. Leif guessed the minimal light was on purpose. It cast the entire cavern in an eerie light that shifted across the room as the weird flames danced within their lanterns. The pressure in Leif's head was a clear indicator of the heavy flow of magic in the chamber. Either Leif was getting better at detecting magic or there was some next level magic going on in there. Kalldrec didn't care or didn't notice because he continued on through the middle of the chamber as if he didn't have a care in the world.

The dancing flames played havoc with Leif's night vision. Every time his eyes adjusted to the darkened room, the flame would shift closer to him, brightening his area and blinding him to everything but what was right in front of him. Luckily for Leif, they didn't have far to walk. They eventually passed out of the range of the dancing flames and Leif could make out two smaller, dimmer lanterns to either side of a gaping black hole. As they approached, two guards materialized out of the darkness and barked a challenge. Kalldrec responded without missing a beat, and the two guards melted back into the shadows. It was clear they had gone to great lengths to keep the bridge a secret. The more Leif thought about it, the more everything made sense. *Hell, even Arias had to track down Bargog back in Karcoa to get directions to this place, and even he wasn't one hundred percent forthcoming about it.* Leif was sure Arias would have told him about this underground city if he had known about it. Furthermore, the odd attempts to confuse Leif on the way here, the unnecessarily dark chamber, the hidden guards, and the bridge kept in darkness were all a precaution to confuse anyone who came looking for it. For all Leif knew, he was standing in a giant cavern, and without the help of his guards and Kalldrec, he would wander off in the darkness and get lost. Leif considered these precautions as brilliant.

Out of nowhere, two bright flames sprang into existence just a few feet from Leif, causing him to shield his eyes as they protested the sudden bright light. The guard to Leif's left lit two torches and was now holding them out for Leif and Kalldrec to take. Both Kalldrec and Leif took their respective torches, and the two guards nodded to them both before stepping back into the shadows. Leif looked to Kalldrec, eyebrow raised in an unasked question.

Again, Kalldrec neither knew what it meant or didn't care because he turned without saying a word and began walking through the inky blackness in front of them. Leif let out an exasperated sigh, shaking an angry fist to the sky above, muttering, "Arias is probably getting a kick out of this."

Nevertheless, Leif followed Kalldrec into the darkness. After a few minutes of walking through a large tunnel, Leif stopped to inspect the walls and found the same strange symbols cut into the stone walls as the bridge back on Midgard. Leif's vision fuzzed and his stomach turned in knots as he continued to stare at the symbols. Leif stood transfixed, staring at them until Kalldrec walked up and punched him on the arm... hard.

"Ow, fuck!" Leif yelled, rubbing his arm.

Kalldrec pointed the torch towards the carvings, "Dot star, not good for mind," he pointed to his head with his free hand when he said, "Mind. Curvoc not for Midgardian mind." He turned and continued down the tunnel.

Still rubbing his arm, Leif glared at the back of Kalldrec's head as he disappeared down the tunnel. *What a dick*, Leif thought as he picked up his torch and followed him.

Leif noticed the tunnel was slightly curved. He turned to look back, and he could no longer see the opening that they had walked through moments earlier. A soft light appeared ahead of them. By this time, Kalldrec had gotten ahead of him, so Leif jogged to catch up.

When Leif closed in on his angry little companion, the exit to the bridge came into view. When they got within fifteen feet of the exit, Kalldrec placed his hand on Leif's chest and slightly shoved, he then looked Leif in the eyes. Getting the point, Leif stopped. Kalldrec nodded and continued toward the exit. As he came within five feet of the exit, a bark of a command in Svata rang out from somewhere in the room beyond. The unmistakable kink-kink of armor accompanied the command. Kalldrec hooked his torch in a hole set into the tunnel to the side and spread his hands wide. He then responded in Svata. The unseen guard responded, and they conversed in a less hostile manner. At least that's what Leif thought because he didn't speak a lick of Svata. For all he knew, Kalldrec could tell them to skewer Leif the moment he walked through the bridge. *Nothing he could do about that now*, Leif thought. After a few more minutes of small talk, Kalldrec nodded and gestured for Leif to come forward. Leif cautiously walked up to Kalldrec, and they stepped through the bridge to Myrkheim together.

CHAPTER 39

The room beyond reminded Leif of the larger shadowed chamber they had entered by, except it was brightly lit. Leif wanted to ask Kalldrec why these rooms were so bare and unfinished, but he figured it probably wouldn't go over well, so he kept his mouth shut.

The two massive lanterns hung from the center of the small cavern, lighting the entire area. Six guards watched the exit, and all were in full battle armor with either a war hammer or double-bladed ax in their hands. A few had short swords strapped to their hips while a few others had small one-handed axes similar to Leif's. Their armor was polished to a bright steely sheen, but what really caught Leif's attention was that all the armor that they wore had an odd swirling pattern to it. Leif was no expert, but he thought he remembered seeing some expensive-looking knives back on Midgard that had a similar pattern to it. If he remembered correctly, it was called Damascus steel.

Leif surveyed the room and noticed the hostile glares that all six guards were directing at him. Kalldrec must have sensed the tension in the room because he placed a restraining hand on Leif's arm and stepped forward, shielding Leif. Well, at least Leif's torso and lower body. Kalldrec said something in a menacing tone, but the guards refused to relent. Kalldrec tried again, and this time Leif distinctly heard Kalldrec say "Berserker." That got their attention. None of them released their weapons, but their posture changed slightly. Leif met each guard's eyes, holding their gaze; he spotted an unfamiliar emotion hiding behind them: fear.

The Berserkers of the past must have been pretty badass if their reputation was still widely known., Leif thought. Kalldrec seemed satisfied with their change of attitude because he walked right up to the door at the end of the chamber, flung it open, and stepped through, motioning for Leif to follow.

Leif really didn't feel like getting jumped by the guards, but from the way Kalldrec nonchalantly exited the chamber, the matter of Leif moving on to the underground city must have been resolved. Shrugging, he reluctantly stepped forward, and when no one attacked, he kept on walking. The hairs on the back of his neck still stood on end as he passed the guards. An image of an ax smashing into Leif's unguarded back flashed through his mind, and he fought the urge to turn as he stepped through the door. Kalldrec slammed the door behind him, and Leif let out a breath he didn't know he was holding.

The hallway beyond was dimly lit, but Leif could tell, just like the hallways of the underground city, every surface was perfectly crafted. The walls on either side had a jagged pattern etched into them that careened into the shadows of the hall beyond. The ceiling was much lower than Leif was used to, causing Leif to hunch his shoulders. They were definitely not made with humans or Ljosalfar in mind. He also spotted the dancing flame lanterns hanging from the ceiling at equal intervals providing just enough light to see by. Kalldrec must have really wanted to get his tour guide gig over because the moment Leif stepped through the doorway, he was walking down the hallway. While Leif moved to follow, he noticed a soft hissing sound coming from down the corridor. The noise would come at regular intervals a few seconds apart, and it grew louder with each step. As they rounded a corner, Leif saw the exit, and a feeling of joy he wasn't expecting bloomed in his chest. *I am really tired of being ushered through cramped and dimly lit hallways and caverns.* Not wishing to repeat the standoff in the guard chamber, the moment he had stepped out of the hallway, Leif pulled the hood of his cloak up, hoping any pedestrians would assume he was just a traveling Ljosalfar.

When they reached the exit of the hallway, Leif stood dumbfounded. Never in his wildest dreams could he have thought up a landscape like this. True to their nature, the Svartalfar of Myrkheim lived underground, far from the surface of their world. The cavern was so expansive, it appeared to go on and on, without ending. He couldn't see any walls, no matter which direction he looked. Peering up, Leif could barely make out the ceiling to the cavern. After straining for a few moments, Leif could just barely make out several small points of light bouncing here and there off the ceiling. Leif wanted to ask what they were, but he held his questions for another time.

Looking out across the impressive expanse of the cavern, Leif took in the capital city of Svartalfheim. Stretching from floor to ceiling and evenly spaced as far as Leif could see were enormous pillar-like structures that Leif guessed helped keep the cavern from collapsing. These massive pillars looked to have windows and rooms carved into them, and Leif guessed these denoted different floors within the stone pillars, though, this was just a guess since the closest one looked to be a mile away. Stepping up to the railing, Leif peered over and had a momentary bout of vertigo when he saw how high they were. They were easily a thousand feet off the ground. Leif guessed he was standing on a balcony on one of the large pillars since all other buildings were far below him. Stepping away from the railing, Leif looked around at a small walkway that disappeared around the bend of the pillar. The walkway was inlaid with a beautiful carving of some intertwining pattern which also spread out in either direction, disappearing around the bend. A small railing was set at the edge of the walkway. The walkway wasn't packed, but it also wasn't empty. Every minute or so a group of Svartalfar would walk past them, deep in conversation with their fellows. They were so engulfed in their conversations they failed to notice the human staring wide-eyed at their majestic underground city.

The most impressive structures that Leif saw were two pyramids. One was built from the floor up, and the other ceiling down, like some massive hourglass. The points of each pyramid met in the middle. The structure was a sight to behold. The pyramids were gigantic even from few miles away. The two pyramids loomed over Leif and the rest of the city. *King Khufu would be very upset to know the Pyramids of Giza were outdone.*

Tearing his eyes away from the pyramids, Leif spied other weirdly shaped buildings, and even a few other pyramids poking up in the distance, but nothing so grand as the hourglass pyramid.

Kalldrec saw Leif staring and slapped Leif on the arm, pointing and saying, "King's house. We no go there."

Bummer, Leif thought. *It is good to be King.* Kalldrec made a motion for Leif to follow as he stepped out onto the walkway and disappeared around the corner.

Leif had to focus on not losing Kalldrec. Leif got a lot of attention from the passing Svartalfar, but thankfully none of them seemed to notice that he was human, and after a quick glance they mostly continued on with their own business. Leif again heard that weird hissing sound. Free of the hallway, it was much louder and actually caused Leif to jump when it sounded. A few passing Svartalfar turned to look at him, but he pulled his hood down farther and sped after Kalldrec. It was only a few moments later that Leif realized the sound was coming from an elevator that was cut into the pillar itself. Leif asked Kalldrec how the elevator worked, but Kalldrec remained silent. He nonchalantly stepped into the chamber, demonstrating it was safe-ish.

The elevator wasn't made of metal like the ones back on Midgard. Instead, it appeared to be made of the same stone as the pillar. Leif also noticed with a sinking sensation that there wasn't a door to the elevator. It was just the three walls, ceiling and floor. Leif really didn't want to step inside the box of death, but he had little choice. Another Svartalfar stood within to one side with a hand on a lever. After exchanging a few words with Kalldrec, he nodded and pulled the lever down. That same hissing sound came from just above Leif's head and the elevator dropped. A feeling similar to being in a car as it drives down a particularly steep hill fluttered through his stomach.

Several openings flashed past them as they descended, but the elevator conductor felt no compunction to slow or stop. Leif tried to count the number of openings they passed, but after the 200th he gave up. Eventually, he felt the falling sensation lessen and then stop altogether. Leif guessed the ground floor was coming into view. Another group of Svartalfar was waiting at the bottom floor and pushed themselves in at the exact moment the elevator stopped. Leif turned his head slightly to prevent anyone from noticing him and he and Kalldrec pushed their way out of the throng of Svartalfar. Once free, Leif turned to watch the elevator shoot upwards. Leif was amazed at the technology of the Svartalfar. He could see a pulley-like system with tubes going back and forth through the elevator chamber. He also saw a thick cloud of steam burst free of the chamber as the elevator disappeared. On the ground floor, Leif was flooded with relief at being free of the cramped stone elevator and turned to inspect his surroundings.

The cobblestone street was ten to fifteen feet wide and lined with shapes for as far as the eye could see. The buildings looked to be cut out of the very rock itself. Leif spotted a few Ljosalfar, Dokkalfar, and Orcs, along with a creature that looked to be made of stone, like a golem. The majority of beings clogging the streets were Svartalfar. If Kalldrec hadn't had his massive war hammer strapped to his back, Leif would have lost sight of him from the moment they excited the elevator. Every Svartalfar, be it male or female, carried some type of weapon, but none as distinctive as Kalldrec's. Many favored axes were similar to the ones Leif carried. Leif wondered if his grandfather had gotten his axes from a Svartalfar smith, which also made Leif wonder how his grandfather had visited Svartalfheim if they hated Midgardians so much. Just another question that Leif would never get answered. Shaking his head free from the thought, Leif again had to scan the crowd to find his guide. *The damn bastard was way out in front now. It's like he isn't even trying to wait for me,* Leif thought.

Leif set out at a brisk walk, slowly nudging Svartalfar and Ljosalfar out of the way in order to catch up to Kalldrec. As he walked, Leif watched as his annoying companion turned down an alleyway, disappearing from sight. Leif broke out in a run, which brought more attention to him, but not losing Kalldrec was his top priority. When Leif reached the alleyway, he swore under his breath. The alleyway was empty. Suddenly, a tiny hand reached out and pulled Leif into a small dark alcove just to the left of the empty street. Leif's left hand reached for his ax, but a hand clamped down on his wrist with a vice-like strength, stopping his hand, mere centimeters from the grip. Kalldrec emerged from the shadowed alcove and Leif relaxed. Kalldrec pulled him closer, and Leif let him. His heart was racing, and Leif bent down to ask what was going on, but Kalldrec held up his hand to silence him and point toward the busy street.

Leif saw nothing out of the ordinary at first, but as time passed, he picked up on the oddity that must have alerted Kalldrec. Four cloaked figures could be seen weaving in and out of the crowd. They passed back-and-forth right in front of the alleyway several times. If Leif hadn't been looking for something out of the ordinary, he would have missed it, but each time the cloaked figures walked past the alleyway, they would turn their hooded head ever so slightly to look down the empty street. After a few more passes, the hooded figures huddled together. With their hoods pulled up, Leif couldn't see who they were. They all wore the same dark brown cloak with a symbol of three parallel lines connected by three diagonal lines crisscrossing each other in gold stitched over their heart. After a few seconds, the group broke. One figure headed down the busy street, another went in the opposite direction, and the two remaining cloaked figures walked down the alleyway. Leif guessed the group saw him turn down the alleyway and were hoping to trap him.

The two figures pulled back their hoods. One was a Ljosalfar with the typical angular features and softly glowing eyes that seem to drink in the alleyway as he searched for his quarry. The other was a female Svartalfar, with a large nose and small beady eyes. Her hair was dark brown and tied in a tight braid that was wrapped around her head, making it look like she wore a crown. Neither had drawn a weapon, but their hands hung down by their sides, no doubt staying within reach of whatever weapon they hid underneath their cloaks. As the pair approached their hiding spot, Leif lowered his hand to unhook his axes, but a shake of Kalldrec's head drew him up short. Kalldrec silently shuffled closer to the edge of their alcove and drew twin daggers. The blades were made of a dark, almost midnight black metal. They were so dark that light refused to reflect off the blade. When their stalkers were within five feet of their hiding spot, Leif felt the pull of his Berserker calling for him. But Leif grit his teeth keeping it at bay, knowing an all-out fight could prove disastrous for him.

The Ljosalfar turned to his companion. "How could we lose the Berserker. The Nor…" Kalldrec unexpectedly burst from their hiding spot. He took three quick steps and launched himself at their pursuers. Within seconds the Ljosalfar and Svartalfar fell, a thick line cut across their throats. Their eyes were wide with panic, but it was too late. The Ljosalfar gurgled one last time before slumping to the floor. Without missing a beat, Kalldrec grabbed their two dead pursuers and pulled them into their shadowed alcove, hiding them from any curious passer-by. He grabbed Leif by the elbow and pulled him back into the open street. Kalldrec looked up at Leif and said in his deep accented voice, "Stay close, others." Leif nodded, still in shock at the swift brutality of what just occurred.

They walked for twenty more minutes, zig-zagging through Svartalfheim, eventually turning down a street that looked identical to all the others. Kalldrec walked up to an unmarked one-story building and knocked on the wooden door.

Wooden door, Leif thought. *Where the hell did they get the wood from? From the surface? Imported from another realm?*

After a few seconds, a voice called out from within the building in Svata. Kalldrec responded, and the door flung open. A figure resembling Kalldrec stepped out. The two clasped forearms and exchanged greetings before Kalldrec gestured toward Leif. Kalldrec's kin stiffened, and the jovial expression he held a moment earlier disappeared and was replaced with a violent glare. The Svartalfar balled his fist and took a small step forward, but before he could take another, Kalldrec reached out and pulled him back. He resisted for half a second before relenting and turning his attention back to Kalldrec.

A heated argument proceeded. The shouting match was quite spectacular, and at one point it got so loud that Leif feared their arguing would draw the attention of whoever was following them. Then all the sneaking around would have been for nothing, but thankfully no one came to investigate the commotion. After several tense minutes, Kalldrec convinced the other Svartalfar to let them in.

The Svartalfar turned and gestured for them to come in. Kalldrec and Leif followed, but before Leif could enter, Kalldrec touched Leif's arm to get his attention. Kalldrec motioned Leif to lean down and as he did, Kalldrec whispered in his ear, "No talk. My brother."

Leif nodded, thinking, *It's not like I could say anything to him even if I wanted to.* They stepped inside and closed the door behind them. Inside, the walls, floor, and ceiling were all the same brownish color. A small bed occupied one side of the room, and a small cook fire sat in the middle of the room with a cauldron hanging from a hook in the ceiling. On the walls near the bed, several tools hung from large hooks. Leif had no idea what their names were, but they all looked to be used for digging or excavation, and all appeared to be well used. A small stone table with two Svartalfar sized chairs sat up against one wall. Kalldrec's brother moved over to the cauldron and poured something inside. He then moved to the small table, gesturing for Kalldrec to follow. His brother took the seat across from them, immediately falling into a hushed conversation.

A few minutes passed, and a kettle whistled. Standing, Kalldrec's brother retrieved two clay cups and sat back down, pouring for himself and his brother.

Uncool, Leif thought.

The two conversed and drank, much to Leif's chagrin, for close to an hour. Leif, sitting on the hard-packed floor was seething by this time. Once they finished, Kalldrec spoke to Leif. He explained in a garbled mess that his brother was an excavator for the royal family, and that he knew the catacombs beneath Svartalfheim and would help them locate the tunnel.

CHAPTER 40

Leif woke the next morning, or he assumed it was morning, by a not-so-gentle slap to the face by Kalldrec. Leif automatically reached for his axes but settled back down once he saw it was Kalldrec.

Kalldrec's brother tended the fire and stirred something in the pot that smelled like rotten eggs. After seeing that Leif was awake, Kalldrec sat cross-legged by the fire and Leif joined him. Kalldrec's brother served up a bowl for himself and Kalldrec. Then, after a stern look from Kalldrec, he reached over and produced a third bowl. He poured a steaming ladle full of grayish slop and offered it to Leif. If it wasn't for the fact that Leif had barely eaten in the past few days, he would have passed on the gruel, but he didn't relish the idea of searching through the catacombs with his stomach's growl echoing through the tunnels. He plugged his nose and took a tentative taste. The gruel didn't taste great, but it also didn't taste bad. *It needed salt, pepper and a few green onions*, Leif thought. Once Leif got past the putrid smell, Leif gulped it down with gusto, and he even went back for seconds. With full bellies, the trio gathered their gear, and prepared for what Leif hoped to be his last leg on this long journey to find the Norns.

The catacombs were deep under the primary city, so it took the trio the better part of an hour to reach them. Leif had to keep his head down and hood pulled tight, lest some passerby notice him. It was all unlit corridors and musty, ill-used stairways leading down, always down. Eventually, Kalldrec's brother stopped the group just outside of what felt like the hundredth stairway. The tunnel beyond was as dark as a moonless night and Leif wasn't sure how, but a soft breeze could be felt ebbing and flowing through the tunnel as if they were deep in the lungs of some great leviathan. Kalldrec's brother pointed down the tunnel and said something in Svata. Kalldrec turned to Leif, gesturing down the tunnel. "Start search here," he said.

Leif nodded. A nervous excitement ebbed and flowed through him, just like the mystery breeze. That excitement quickly died down and was replaced with exhaustion and annoyance. Apparently, there were none of those fancy lanterns this deep under the city, and Leif's arm was tiring from carrying a torch.

The catacombs never seemed to end. It was just one endless dark hallway connecting to another endless hallway. How were they supposed to find a single doorway with a hammer carved into the side when there was a seemingly unlimited number of hallways?

They searched throughout the day and found nothing. Leif thought they should mark the tunnels they checked to ensure they don't repeat the same fruitless search repeatedly. So, they carved a diagonal line across the left side of each tunnel they searched. The rest of the day went on with a quick search, nothing, mark, and move on, and on and on until Kalldrec called an end to the search. Leif was exhausted from carrying his pack the entire time, and he was more than happy to call it quits.

The next day they chose a different tunnel and began the search anew. But again, after a long day of monotonously checking tunnel openings, Leif's nerves were frayed, and he was ready to leave the tunnel for the night.

They returned the third day and began their search down a new tunnel. As Leif had been doing with each tunnel he checked, he held up the torch, then searched from floor to ceiling for any distinctive marks cut into the stone and finally, there it was! It had faded over years, and if he hadn't had known what to look for, he probably would have missed it. But right there at shoulder height was a crude carving of a hammer scratched into the stone.

Once Leif realized he had found it, he called out for the others and they came running. All three had grown annoyed with each other over the long hours searching, so when they saw that they had found the entrance, they seemed excited. Kalldrec and his brother exchanged a few words before his brother turned and head back towards the entrance to the catacombs. "Wait, where is he going?" Leif asked.

"Entrance found. Job done," Kalldrec said with finality. Leif realized he was on his own now. Kalldrec had been sent to help Leif navigate the city and find the bridge to the Norns realm. It had been found, and he was done. No fond wishes or warm goodbyes, just time to go. Kalldrec held out his arm and Leif took it. With a single shake, the warrior turned and disappeared into the darkness of the tunnel. Leif turned back to the tunnel entrance, let out a nervous breath, and started down the dark tunnel.

As with every other tunnel Leif had checked over the past three days, this one was no different. There was the ever-present breeze wafting through the tunnel, causing his torch to snap and crackle. The walls, floor, and ceiling were all made of the same dark brown stone and all cut with a precision Leif could hardly believe possible without power tools. Leif cautiously moved through the dark corridor, not knowing what he would encounter. He walked for several minutes but encountered nothing to signify the corridor was any different than the hundreds of other hallways he had inspected. That's when the doubts began to creep into his mind. *Maybe this wasn't the right tunnel. Maybe the carving wasn't a carving after all. Maybe Grandpa hit his head and imagined the whole incident. But I can't stop now. Not when I am so close,* Leif thought. He rounded another bend in the tunnel and was confronted with a sight that sent his heart racing.

Fallen rocks blocked the end of the cave. There was nowhere to go; the way forward had been blocked by a cave-in some time ago. Leif ran up to the fallen rocks and boulders. "Fuck! This can't be happening! The universe must really hate me!" Leif yelled into the darkness.

Leif searched the rocks, looking for any way through. Beams of light spilled out between the fallen rocks and boulders of the cave in. Knowing he must be close, Leif wedged his torch between two larger boulders and then went to work moving as many of the rocks as he could, trying to form an opening large enough for him to fit through.

It was grueling work, and he cut his fingers and palms in several places as he strained to move the heavier rocks and boulders. After thirty minutes of intense labor, Leif cleared an opening large enough to fit through. Peering through, Leif spied a chamber lit by a single lantern hanging from the high stone ceiling. The light was bright enough to illuminate the entire room, which was circular in design with no visible doors leading into or out of the chamber. In the very center of the room, a skeleton lay on a raised dais. A spiked metal helmet sat on its bleached white skull but was otherwise armor-less. Its bony hands lay interlocked over the handle of a sword positioned over the skeleton's chest. Not knowing what to expect when he stepped into the room, Leif unhooked both axes then squeezed and squirmed his way through the hole and into the chamber beyond.

CHAPTER 41

After crawling through the pile of rocks, Leif quickly jumped to his feet, axes at the ready. Nothing jumped out at him. Nor did he see any signs of a bridge to another realm. "Fuck," Leif said to no one in particular.

Curious about the resident in the chamber, Leif stepped up to the skeleton and leaned over to take a closer look which was a mistake. As soon as he did so, there was an odd cracking sound that reverberated from the dais. Suddenly, the skeleton glowed with a soft golden light and two bright yellow pinpricks of light formed in the empty eye sockets. Fearful, Leif stumbled backward.

The skeleton's head turned, yellow eyes settled on Leif, and then it spoke. The skeletal sentry had a soft and willowy voice that sounded like the wind blowing through a densely packed forest. The words grated on Leif's ears, but unfortunately for Leif, he didn't understand a thing it said. What it did next made its intentions clear. The skeleton jumped off the dais with surprising grace and speed. Locking its hollow gaze on Leif, it shifted into a fighting stance, sword pointing at Leif's heart. The soft voice of the skeleton grated across Leif's ears once more, then it charged.

Shock and surprise flashed through Leif's mind as the

chamber guardian attacked. Leif drew on the panic that seized his heart to speed his Berserker transformation. As the power coursed through his veins, any fear Leif felt at the supernatural creature vanished and was replaced with a lust for battle.

The skeleton was fast, swinging the sword in a horizontal arc meant to take Leif's head off. Though the move was blindingly fast, it was fairly obvious to counter in his enhanced state. Leif raised both axes, blocking the skeleton's attack, grunting from the impact. It was immensely strong, and Leif's palms tingled from the impact. Not knowing if a skeleton could get tired, Leif pushed hard, forcing the skeleton and his sword momentarily back. Leif then ducked under the skeleton's counter strike, coming up inside the its guard. Leif swung his left ax in an attempt to take the skeleton's sword arm off at the elbow. However, he had gotten too close, and the skeleton lurched forward, head-butting Leif in the nose. CRACK! Blood gushing out as his nose broke.

Leif's eyes immediately watered as he fell onto his back. Luckily, he kept hold of his axes because the skeleton stepped up and with a two-handed grip, brought its sword down, intending to cut Leif open from collar to hip. Leif crossed his axes and blocked the downward strike, then pulled hard, catching the sword blade between his crossed axes. Yanking up and to the left in a quick movement Leif pulled the skeleton off balance.

The thing may be fast and strong, but it's still only a bag of bones, Leif encouraged himself. With the skeleton off balance, Leif uncrossed his axes and rolled to the right, scrambling to his feet, then lunged at the skeleton, slamming his ax in his right hand down to block a clumsy jab by the skeleton. Then Leif struck out with his other ax, hitting it in the chest. A resounding crack reverberated off the chamber walls as three of the skeleton's ribs cracked and fell to the ground with a hollow clunking sound. The skeleton, unperturbed, reached out and slugged Leif across the jaw. The hit stunned Leif.

The skeleton followed up with two quick shallow cuts to Leif's left thigh and forearm.

The fight was a blur of sword thrusts and ax slashes. The two danced back and forth across the chamber, exchanging a fury of blows. When they separated, Leif pulled away with a gash to his upper right arm.

Fearing the bony guard was going to just bleed Leif dry, Leif charged, dodging a sword thrust meant for Leif's heart, and tackled the skeleton to the floor. The skeleton dropped its sword as they fell, continuing to punch Leif repeatedly as they rolled around on the floor. Leif took several punishing hits to the gut and head before he was able to position himself on top of the thing. Finally, Leif grabbed hold of its bony wrist and pushed with all of his might, snapping the skeleton's wrist in half.

Throwing the now lifeless hand to the side, Leif wasted no time reaching for the skeleton's smooth white skull. The yellow eyes looked intently at Leif. Before it could stab Leif with the jagged stump it now had for an arm, Leif gave a quick twist and tug, ripping the skeleton's head off. The yellow eyes dimmed and went out as a soft whisper escaped from its lipless mouth.

Leif shakily got to his feet as the battle rush washed over him. Seeing no other threats, Leif concentrated on reigning in the Berserker. Bleeding and in more than a little pain, Leif bent down to retrieve his axes.

When he stood, Leif found himself standing on the edge of a grassy shore to an azure lake. Blinking a few times, Leif searched for the underground chamber with the angry skeleton, but it had disappeared. Somehow, he had been transported to this lush realm. He turned to take in his surroundings. The trunk of a gigantic tree stretched high into the distance, disappearing into a sky brimming with multicolored stars. Leif tracked the skyscraper-sized branches stretching out in all directions. Pulling his eyes away from the impossible tree, Leif spied a wooden cabin nestled against an enormous tree root off to his right. To the right of the cabin, a roaring waterfall cascaded down, feeding the unusually calm lake. Leif watched in awe as mist wafted off the falls, blowing this way and that on the cool breeze, while rainbows flashed and flickered in the ever-churning mist. The air was crisp, and Leif enjoyed the cool wind that blew off the lake. Taking a deep breath, Leif smiled as he filled his lungs, then sighed contently. It was a tremendous relief to be in the open, fresh air after spending so much time underground.

Not knowing what else to do, Leif set out towards the cabin. As his mind slowly recovered from the many strange and inexplicable events in rapid succession, a realization wormed its way into Leif's thoughts as he burst out in a carefree grin, yelling, "This is it! Holy shit, Arias! I found the Norns!" Then to himself he said, *That's got to be it.* Feeling hopeful as he walked but knowing danger could be lurking a step away, Leif dropped his hands down to his axes, ready to draw at a moment's notice.

Approaching with cautious steps, Leif spotted movement through a curtained window. Even though he could see no bright orb of sunlight burning in the sky above, light still permeated the verdant realm. When Leif got within twenty feet of the cabin, the door swung open and three beautiful women stepped out followed by a massive humanoid creature that set Leif's nerves on edge. The three women silently stopped a few yards from Leif and stared out at him with unblinking intensity. "Much of our sight has been blocked, Berserker, but it is clear to us who you are," the woman with jade colored eyes said.

"We tried to protect your bloodline until the time was right, but it seems we have failed. Hel gained wind of our designs and attacked before we could act," said the one with ice-blue eyes that bore into Leif.

"When our sight finally pierced the fog that had been inexplicably thrown over our eyes, we dispatched a few of our followers, but it was too late. Alexander and your Mother had been lost and we could find no trace of your sprit in the mortal realms," The one with golden yellow eyes said. It was hard to tell, but she at least sounded slightly mournful.

"With Alexander and your mother passed on to the storied halls and no sight of you, we feared your entire line had been wiped out, but it seems we were wrong," the jade-eyed women said.

"How did you come to find us, young Berserker? We sent out agents across the realms hoping to find one such as you, but none have returned," the blue-eyed Norn asked.

Taking a deep breath, Leif retold the events of the past few months. The entire time, the Norns and their bodyguard listened intently, unmoving and unblinking. When he finished, the three women shared a brief, knowing glance, then looked back at him.

The jade-eyed Norn spoke, "Those men your companion killed on Svartalfheim were our agents. Can you think of a reason Kalldrec would have killed them?"

"Wait," Leif was stunned. "They were with you? Why didn't they just come out and say it?" But he didn't need them to answer to know why. If they were with the Norns and knew what Leif was, they most likely didn't want to start a commotion right there on a busy street, revealing to the entire city that a Midgardian was within their mist. *But then why did Kalldrec kill them?* Leif wondered. It was then that Leif noticed the gold insignia sewn into the Norn's cloaks. It matched the symbols on the cloaks of the beings Kalldrec killed.

"It is no matter," The yellow-eyed Norn said. "You are here now and under our protection while we finish your training."

"What am I training for?" Leif asked. "For the past six months, my life has been flipped upside down, and I still don't even really know why."

"We understand your frustration, young Berserker," the jade-eyed Norn soothed. "We wish we could have reached out to you sooner, but with our sight blocked and the rumors of the Outsiders aiding Hel, there was little we could do."

"We can only push forward with your training now," The blue-eyed Norn said. "The Berserker is much more than the power you wield this day. It is not just a reservoir of strength and ferociousness to be relied upon in a time of need. You and your predecessors have only brought forth a fraction of the power Thor granted you, neither does Thor comprehend the full significance of granting such a boon."

Leif thought back to all the times he had berserked, and it was true. The Berserker was always there, silently waiting somewhere in his subconscious, waiting for a threat or challenge to rouse the sleeping beast.

Leif's head was hurting as the Norns once again switched speakers. The yellow-eyed Norn prompted, "But through our tutelage, you will no longer need to release or restrain the Berserker, but remain in your enhanced state perpetually, without the blind rage urging you to attack perceived threats. With our guidance, you will be able to remain in control with all its power at your fingertips. As a fully realized Berserker, you will have greater stores of strength and power than ever before."

Leif's eyes went wide at the revelation. He had already come to terms with the fact that he would need to maintain an iron-hard will over the Berserker for the rest of his life. *But if I could suppress it, gaining full control, I may have a chance of a semi-normal life once this is over. If I survive that is.* As Leif reflected on the possibilities, a sound like a bomb going off erupted somewhere behind him. BOOM!

"Um, what was that?" Leif yelled as he clamped his hands over his ears and turned to face the direction of noise. Seeing nothing, Leif looked back to the Norns. Each wore a unique expression on their face, fear, shock and confusion.

The one with ice-blue eyes turned to Leif, "You have been betrayed! Hel comes; get behind us." Leif ignored the command and unhooked his axes, using the sudden tension and palpable fear in the air to fuel the Berserker. *Like hell I am going to hide. Hel is the cause of all my pain and my family's suffering*. Leif thought as he readied himself to launch himself at the unseen enemy.

"No!" someone yelled from behind him. A hand materialized on Leif's shoulder, and he felt the red haze drain back down into his unconscious mind. "What are you doing?" Leif demanded. "I can fight; this is what my kind was created for!"

The yellow-eyed Norn locked gazes with Leif and shook her head. "Hel has chosen her battleground poorly," she said arrogantly. "This is our realm; our well of power comes from this very plane of existence. Now, stand aside."

She must have seen the skepticism flash across Leif's face because she gave him a wide smile, "Fear not, mortal. We are the Norns; we will not go down easily."

BOOM! BOOM! BOOM!

Leif's eyes were pulled away from the Norn as the very fabric of reality began to break. Red fracture lines sprang into existence at the very spot that Leif stood moments ago.

BOOM! The fractures grew. BOOM!

These fractures continued to grow and spread, reminding Leif of the time he cracked his windshield and neglected to fix it. Jagged red lines radiated out in all directions from the center. With a final bang and a rush of air, reality crumbled. It was one of the strangest and scariest sights Leif had ever witnessed. Where once a quiet grassy shore sat, there was now a gaping black hole. The fragments of reality that had been occupying that space fell to the ground and slowly dissolved, leaving a hole. Leif struggled to wrap his mind around what he just witnessed. Leif jumped as the warrior to his left let out a low growl that set his hair on end and stepped in front of the Norns, ready to defend them.

CHAPTER 42

"Is that any way to greet your kin?" a voice like honey said from with the inky tear in reality.

"How is this possible?" all three Norns whispered in unison.

"My dear cousins, you underestimate what an unrestrained Aesir can do. I am Hel, the daughter of Loki, granddaughter to the Allfather, Odin. I am ruler of Helheim, the realm of the dead and there is *nothing* I can't do," The woman announced as she stepped through the tear flanked by three larger than life Jontar.

"Unrestrained?" The Norn to Leif's left asked.

It's her, Leif thought. *The woman, no, the god, who invaded my dream.* But this time, instead of wearing a red dress, Hel was outfitted from head to toe in dark armor. Her white hair was tied back in an intricate braid that spilled down her back. She wore a small circlet on her brow of black metal that drank in the surrounding light. Her skin was pale, as if she hadn't seen the sun in years. Her oval face and sharp nose framed her eyes, which burned like an electrical storm. Her features were even more distinct and terrifying than the first time Leif saw her. She was the most beautiful and terrifying woman Leif had ever laid eyes on. Beneath her thigh and shin guards, she wore dark brown pants and calf-high leather boots. Her chest plate, greaves, thigh and shin guards were all the same black metal, which was an odd contrast to her glowing lightening blue eyes. A straight sword lay strapped to her back, with its handle jutting out over her right shoulder within easy reach.

She emanated the same overpowering strength that Leif felt from the Norns, but her energy felt wilder somehow, uncontrolled even. She reminded Leif of a tiger behind the bars at a zoo, pacing back and forth.

The god stepped closer to the group and everyone visibly tensed, which caused Hel to smile and spread her hands out wide, palms open as if to show she was unarmed and harmless. However, Leif knew she was anything but.

Movement behind the invaders caught Leif's eye. Peering past Hel and her guards, Leif spied a tiny figure peeking out through the rip. Leif immediately recognized the room beyond where he had fought the bridge guardian. Leif squinted and could just make out the features of a Svartalfar. It was Kalldrec! *That son of a bitch! He sold me out! Now I know why he stepped in and convinced Vestri to help me. He was working with Hel the whole time.*

"Please, cousins, you need not fear me," Hel purred. "It doesn't have to be this way. You don't know how it saddened me when you shut off access to The Well, our ancestral home. I have so many fond memories of our time together, walking the shore of The Well and debating the philosophies of our mantel and its place among the lesser races. Please, give up this folly and join me. You know my cause is righteous. Once father and the other Aesir are gone, I can ensure that peace is finally achieved throughout the realms and beyond. You three will no longer have to suffer the grim fate of watching the cruel and vile deeds done to righteous beings. I will see to that. Step aside and let me take the young Berserker back with me, please. No harm will come to him, I promise." Hel spoke with such passion that Leif almost believed her.

"Hel, cousin, you have fallen so far that you can't see how the Outsiders have poisoned you. You have abandoned your duties and now strive to start Ragnorok and usher in an age of darkness and despair. As it was set down eons ago, our kind was tasked with protecting the realms from the Outsiders, and here you are aligning with them. You have turned against those we are charged with protecting. We are sorry, but we will stand against you until the very end," the Norns spoke as one.

Leif had no idea what the Norns were talking about, but he was happy they weren't going to turn him over to Hel.

The smile vanished from Hel's face, and a look of grim determination took hold. "I am sorry. I take no pleasure in this." With an outstretched hand she softly said, "Kill them." She almost sounded remorseful.

The guardian let out a growl that Leif felt in his bones. It reached back with two meaty hands and unsheathed two short swords, similar to what gladiators used. The Jontar responded by drawing vicious single-blade war-axes from their belts and prowled forward to meet their foe. The two opposing forces paused momentarily to size each other up. Then, without uttering a word, the three Jontar attacked.

The guardian was corded with muscle and looked slow, but Leif was wrong. It was insanely fast. Leif could hardly believe his eyes. The Jontar had spread out, boxing the guardian in, but it didn't matter. It was like the guardian was everywhere at once. No matter what the Jontar tried, the guardian was there, blocking the Jontar with cold steel. He was a force of nature, a tornado of blades.

A snort of annoyance from Hel pulled Leif's attention back to her. She wasn't pleased with her opening salvo. With narrowed eyes, Hel moved to intervene, but suddenly froze. The air around Hel took on a fuzzy quality, like looking out into the distance on a summer day and seeing an odd distortion in the air. Her features swiftly changed, shock running plainly across her face before she furrowed her brows in concentration. Sweat quickly broke out across her forehead, but still she didn't move. She was trapped.

As the invisible struggle went on, it became clear to Leif that Hel was no match for the combined strength of the Norns. With visible effort, Hel changed tactics. Leif watched as she reached down and with a strained expression plain on her face, unsheathed a dagger at her belt. With a flick of the wrist so powerful that Leif felt a gust of wind brush across his face, Hel sent her knife flying. A moment later, there was a loud thwack and a bellow from the guardian. Trapped as she was, Hel still managed to hit the guardian above the knee in the small gap between his thigh guard and knee bracers. The knife sunk all the way to the handle.

To Leif's surprise, the knife at first didn't appear to faze the hulking warrior. That was, until he put his full weight on it. That's when his injured knee buckled, causing the guardian to lower his guard for a fraction of a second, which was all the Jontar needed. With a flash of steel and a thunk, the guardian's left hand fell to the ground, still clutching his sword. A heartbeat later, the guardian's headless body crumbled to the blood-soaked grass of the clearing.

As if they had felt the blow themselves, all three Norns shuddered upon seeing the death of their Guardian. With their adversary dead, the three Jontar turned and began stalking towards the unprotected Norns. The Norn to Leif's right pulled her gaze from Hel and raised her hand. Invisible bands of force lashing out to fend off the Jontar. Leif watched as all three Jontar suddenly froze in their tracks. Leif observed the same fuzzy distortion in the air that trapped Hel now also surrounded the Jontar.

A sigh of relief escaped Leif's lips. He had not wanted to face the Jontar so soon after his recent beat down. "You should have handed over the Midgardian when you had the chance," Hel said, pulling Leif's attention back to her. The strange distortion caused by the Norns' power still surrounded her, but it was less pronounced. "You three may be a match for me, but divided, I am stronger." With a grunt of effort, Hel balled her fist and punched out. There was a loud pop, and a sudden rush of air blew through the clearing. The Norns were flung back, landing in a heap of robes at Leif's feet. Leif was paralyzed with uncertainty. There was nowhere to run.

He was no match against Hel and a pack of Jontar, but he had little choice at this point. "I sure as hell will not go down without a fight," Leif growled at Hel.

She smiled in response. Suddenly a hand clamped down on Leif's ankle. "No!" The blue-eyed Norn yelled and Leif felt the Berserker retreat into his subconscious.

Back on her feet, the blue-eyed Norn turned to her kin. "Sisters, hold them as long as you can. I will prepare a bridge. We can't allow Hel to have him." She then grabbed Leif and pulled him away from the fight. Leif looked over his shoulder as he was dragged away. Hel appeared exhausted from her fight of wills against the Norns, but she flashed a triumphant smile as the three Norns split up. Hel again pulled a knife from her belt and sent it flying towards the Norn holding off the Jontar. The Norn easily deflected it, but the distraction cost her the battle. The slip in concentration freed the Jontar. They rushed towards the Norn and quickly cut her down. The two remaining Norns gasped as their sister was killed. One Norn stood resolute against Hel and her Jontar as Leif was dragged away by the other.

Leif stood helplessly. Tears streamed from the Norn's blue eyes and onto her porcelain face as she waved her hands in a complicated pattern.

"Hurry, sister!" The remaining Norn facing Hel yelled. A headache inducing pressure washed through Leif's brain as magic pulsed through the air. The feeling vanished as quickly as it came on, and the Norn turned her mournful eyes on Leif. She locked her gazes with Leif. "You aren't ready to face her. We are sorry. It wasn't supposed to be this way, but to prevent Ragnorok, we must stop Hel from taking you." She then pushed Leif, hard. He stumbled, and the ground beneath his feet vanished.

CHAPTER 43

Leif landed with an oof! Getting to his feet, he retrieved his two axes, which had slipped away during the fall. Leif could tell he was no longer on the realm with the Norns, but outside of that, he had no idea where he was.

The sky was a roiling mass of dark gray clouds and lightning flicking back and forth. He found himself again at the shore of some great lake. However, unlike the serene grassy realm of the Norns, the terrain Leif stood on now was covered in rocks with little to no vegetation. The lake itself bubbled and boiled as if there was some unseen monster just below the surface.

Then, as if summoned by his very thoughts, the lake surface rippled and shifted, creating enormous waves that radiated out from beneath the surface. An enormous scaled beast rose out of the water a several yards from where Leif stood. The monster's scaled neck swiveled in Leif's direction and a long arrow-shaped head looked down at Leif, studying him. Smoke curled into the sky out of two vertical slits that Leif guessed were the beast's nose. Just below its nose, Leif could see the tips of dagger sharp teeth the size of Leif's forearm poking out. The beast's two burning orange eyes stared directly at Leif and projected clear intelligence. The head and scaled neck of the beast rose thirty feet into the air; the rest of the beast remained hidden underneath the broiling lake. The scales of the monster were the same hue of gray as the clouds above. As the creature shifted, the scales perfectly mirrored the sky above, making it hard for Leif to truly grasp the size and shape of the monster. With a sound like thunder, the beast opened its massive maw and spoke.

The thunderclap of a voice sent vibrations through Leif's body from head to toe. "Who dares to enter my domain?"

The molten eyes dared Leif to respond.

"No matter," it said, with a quick shake of its massive head. "I am one of the great dragons of the realms. Whoever sent you here has sent you to your death."

Leif, rooted to his spot, shivered with dread. The magnificent dragon moved so fast he only saw a blur as it moved in for the kill. Instinct alone saved Leif as he dove to the side. Leif rolled as the dragon turned and lashed out again, attempting to bite him in half. Seeing it had missed for the second time, the dragon stopped and narrowed its eyes at Leif.

Leif knew his luck had run out. In his haste to jump away, Leif had inadvertently cornered himself against three boulders. Helplessly, Leif watched as the dragon reeled back. The dragon opened its massive mouth, displaying row upon row of pointed teeth. Unable to watch any longer, Leif shut his eyes and waited.

A second later there was a thunderous boom. And yet, Leif wasn't dead. Cracking one eye open, Leif was stunned to see Hel standing in front of him with her hand outstretched as if holding something off. Looking past Hel, Leif's eyes widened in shock at the sight of the dragon's head and neck unmoving, on the far side of the lake.

With the realization that he wasn't dead, Leif was suddenly assaulted with several aches and pains spanning the length of his body. *I must have gotten all cut up from dodging the dragon,* Leif thought as he felt a large gash across his head. Leif's hand came away bloody.

Hel looked down at Leif with a sad smile on her beautiful face. Leif tried to get up, but he must have hit his head harder than he thought because his arms merely wobbled, then collapsed. Leif's eyes locked on the fearsome goddess as he slowly sank into unconsciousness.

CHAPTER 44

L eif awoke to a splitting headache. His hand involuntarily went to his head, which to his surprise was wrapped in a bandage.

Leif then froze. The moment before he lost consciousness came screaming back to him in a flurry of blurred memories. *How the hell am I still alive?* He thought. *Where am I?* Opening his eyes, Leif looked around the room he found himself in. He appeared to be in some Victorian age bedroom. He was nestled into a massive four poster bed, which was as soft as any bed he had ever slept on back home. The bed was festooned with pillows on all sides. Checking under the sheets, Leif was surprised to find that he had been stripped down to his boxers. On a closer inspection, he saw his body was covered in bruises, but luckily no cuts or missing limbs. Sadly, his advanced healing did nothing for the soreness and stiffness that he felt resound through his entire body, which added to the pain radiating from his head.

Leif's shirt and pants were folded up on a plush, crimson sofa next to the bed. In front of the couch, Leif's axes and a large pitcher full of clear liquid lay patiently on a coffee table. Two equally plush red velvet chairs sat next to the table. A twisting metal chandelier hung from the ceiling. A raging fire crackled and popped in the fireplace, which when combined with the myriad of lit candles in the room gave off a gothic or medieval vibe.

Rolling out of the cloud soft bed, Leif tiptoed to the couch and put on his clothes, monitoring the only door leading into the room for intruders. Hooking his axes back onto his belt, Leif let out a sigh of relief. As he spent more and more time away from Midgard and its laws, he had increasingly found comfort knowing he was armed and could protect himself if need be. The twin axes at his belt had become a reassuring weight, and he felt naked without them. Once he was armed, he permitted himself to size up his surroundings.

The walls of the bedroom were hung with large murals running the length of the room. Leif approached one painting depicting a battle on a snowy landscape. The minute detail within the painting was astounding. It was like staring at a photograph. Leif had no trouble discerning small patterns on the warrior's armor, or clan symbols painted across the chest plates. The next painting also depicted a glorious battle. However, this painting showed a single warrior in full armor, and carrying a great sword, fighting off shadowy figures in a cavern. Turning away from the paintings, he took stock of the room.

Crossing the grand bedroom to the heavy oak doors, Leif slowly cracked them open, surprised that they weren't locked. Peering out, he saw the hallway beyond was empty. The floors were made of dark-colored marble, while the walls were made of the same black stone of the room he had just left. Another set of double doors lay at the far side of the hallway. To each side of the hallway, murals similar to the ones in the room ran the length of the hallway. As silently as he could, Leif stepped out and closed the door behind him. Leif was curious about the many murals that decorated the hall, but he pushed passed them in search of a way out.

Sadly, Leif couldn't hear a thing from the room beyond. Seeing no other way out, Leif cracked the door open an inch and peered through.

This looks familiar, Leif thought. The large fireplace had a roaring fire blazing in its hearth. Two sets of chairs and a small coffee table sat a few feet from the fire. A decanter filled with a dark brown liquid sat in the center of the table. Looking to his right, Leif saw a wooden table festooned with books, papers and miscellaneous items, and just beyond the table was a set of double doors leading out to a balcony where Leif knew Hel waited for him.

Knowing he didn't have any other option, Leif steeled himself for the coming fight. He unhooked one of his axes and slowly crept into the room. Leif silently scanned the area for enemies but found none. He made his way to the balcony and just like his dream, Hel was there waiting for him. She had exchanged her battle armor for a flawless red dress. Leif studied Hel for a moment, watching her as she leaned against the railing, surveying the landscape beyond. An odd greenish glow emanating up from the ground below silhouetted her. A ghostly moaning sound emanated from the distance, breaking the silence of the balcony.

His heart was racing, but Leif forced himself to slowly creep up behind his kidnapper. Mustering up the courage, Leif closed in on Hel. He raised his ax and asked, "Why am I not dead?"

Hel turned her lightning-blue eyes onto Leif, and with a lazy smile across her face, she took a small step forward.

Leif yelled, "Don't move!" He shook his raised ax menacingly.

Hel obeyed, stopping in her tracks. Still holding eye contact, Hel raised her hands, palms open. "Now is that any way to treat your savior?" In her honey-like voice she spoke to Leif like he was a child, "If it wasn't for me, you would have been devoured by Niohoggr. I am the one who saved you from that fate. A fate the Norns, the beings you fought so hard to find, consigned you to without a second thought." A vision of the three Norns flashed in Leif's mind at their mention.

"What... what did you do with them?" Leif asked. His voice cracked slightly.

"Don't worry about them. They were selfish creatures. They were too hung up on their notion of fate and the destiny of the nine realms. They wanted to keep things the way they are, and unfortunately, that belief stood in the way of what I am trying to create. Even though it saddened me, I killed them. No longer will we be slaves to the flow of fate. Once I rule, the beings of the nine realms will throw off the shackles of fate and be free."

Hoping to distract Hel, Leif asked, "What do you want with me?" But before giving Hel a chance to respond, Leif lashed out. However, even with surprise on his side, Leif wasn't fast enough. Without batting an eye, Hel reached up and caught the ax. Her hand tightened around the hilt, just above Leif's grip. Leif's eyes widened as she caught his attack. Hel stopped, the ax mere centimeters from her chest. Straining, Leif pushed with all his might, but it was useless without the Berserker aiding him. He just wasn't strong enough.

"If you would just listen to me, I think you would understand, little Berserker," Hel purred.

"Why would I listen to anything you have to say? You murdered my family and tried to kill me! Screw it," Leif snarled, releasing the Berserker, hoping he would be a match for her then.

However, Hel saw the change, let out a sigh and said, "Let's talk again when you have cooled off." She reversed her hold on the ax.

Suddenly Leif was pulled forward. He tried to catch himself, but it was too late. Hel punched Leif in the temple, knocking him out instantly.

CHAPTER 45

L eif woke with a start. He was draped across the sofa in
Hel's gothic mansion. His head was pounding, again. A
fire roared in the fireplace to his left, warming his sore
muscles. Sitting up, Leif nearly jumped out of his skin when he
saw that Hel was seated across from him, calmly studying him.
Leif's two axes rested on the small coffee table between them.
Leif wiped the drool off his chin, and he noticed Hel's toned leg
peeking out from the high slit in her dress. Looking up, Leif saw
that Hel had caught him eyeing her physique. Leif flushed, and
she smirked.

Reaching down between them, Hel picked up the decanter and
sloshed it around before pouring the golden liquid into the two
waiting glasses on the table. Setting the decanter down, she
picked up the glass and sat back. Leif watched as she brought the
glass up to her rose-red lips, sniffed the glass briefly, then took a
sip. With a contented sigh, Hel closed her eyes, enjoying the
liquor. "You really must try the drink, Leif. It's fermented water
berries from a small farm run by a family of Ljosalfar on Alfheim.
I have been buying their Afengi for thousands of years and they
never disappoint. I think the flavor comes from some unique
minerals only found in that part of the forest," Hel said.

Leif didn't respond.

Hel made a scoffing sound, "Leif, my dear, is this any way to treat your savior? This is my domain. There is no way out. You might as well relax and hear my proposition."

Leif, his mind racing, decided he would play nice for now. He picked up the glass and cupped it with both hands in his lap. Hel furrowed her brow slightly, shrugged, and took another sip from her cup. The two continued to stare at each other for another few seconds. The crackling fire and the creepy moaning sound from beyond the balcony accompanied their silent standoff.

With a sigh of annoyance, Hel set her glass down and leaned forward with her hands clasped in front of her. She didn't mind that this position gave Leif a direct line of sight down her low-cut dress. "Ok, Leif, I will level with you, I brought you here for a reason. I could have easily killed you back at the Well or let you be devoured by Niohoggr, or killed you anywhere along your long journey to the Norns, but no. I went through the effort to save you, even patched you up, and yet you still tried to kill me."

"You tried to kill me first!" Leif growled

"Listen well, little Berserker. I could have killed you at any time. Your entire quest was a series of tests. I was testing you to see if you were strong enough mentally and physically to fit into my plans. In the coming days I will need a strong Midgardian to be my liaison between your people and my new empire. But that's not all. Before I can create this empire, I need the Berserker's power. I couldn't use your grandfather. He had been a Berserker for too long and is predisposed to be prejudiced against me, even though he knows nothing about me outside false stories and myths the lesser beings tell. I couldn't use your mother. She was too old and wouldn't be strong enough. So, I chose you! You, to be the King of your world, bowing only to me as I rule the nine realms. I have given you a gift, you see!

"But all of those times you sent your minions to kill me?" Leif asked, confused.

"Ha! Mere tests. I sent those 'minions,' as you say, to see if you were worthy enough to stand beside me! And Leif, my boy, you passed with flying colors! You met each of my warriors in combat and survived! Not only that, with each fight you grew as a warrior! Learning with each fight!

"And If I hadn't defeated them?" Leif asked skeptically.

"They would have incapacitated you and brought you here to me. You see, in the end, all roads for you lead to me, Leif."

"What would you have done with me if I wasn't worthy?" Leif asked.

"You need not worry yourself about that," Hel said nonchalantly

"Bullshit! Be a king, you say! You killed my family. Your men killed Arias! You upended my life! We have unfinished business, bitch. One day you will find my ax buried deep in your chest as I watch your life seep away from you!" Leif was surprised by the rage that welled up inside him. He could feel the Berserker deep down, longing to be released. He wanted to grab the axes on the table and attack, but Leif's rational side knew now wasn't the time to act. Hel kept him alive for a reason, and Leif was determined to find out the actual reason.

Straightening up in his chair, Leif set the drink down, took a deep breath and looked Hel right in the eyes. "Fine, I'll bite. What do you possibly think I could do, that you, a freaking god, can't do? Why don't you enlighten me about why the hell I am here?"

Hel stood up and gestured out the open balcony and said, "First, let me welcome you to Helheim, though soon enough, I will be free of this forsaken place. Once I'm free of the duties my grandfather cursed me with, I will crush this realm until there is nothing left." Hel saw that Leif was giving her a perplexed look and laughed. "You must understand that I have been planning this for so long. You are the last key to my plan. I have spent a millennium planning with the Outsiders to overthrow Asgard and usher in Ragnorok. Once the dust has settled, I shall ascend to the throne and usher in a period of peace spanning the nine realms and beyond, just as it was in the beginning." She faced Leif with a manic grin on her face.

Leif thought to himself, *Wow! If I hadn't witnessed so much so far, I would have definitely checked myself into a mental hospital because this shit is insane. Just what the fuck have I gotten myself into?*

Hel moved back to her chair and sat down, looking at Leif expectantly.

Clearing his throat, all Leif could muster was, "Why?"

Hel was caught off guard by the simple question, and she stood still as a statue, then blinked a few times. Confusion was plastered on her face.

Leif tried again. "Why overthrow the Aesir? Why start Ragnorok? They had a reason to expel the Outsiders. Why do you want to end an entire galactic rule to let these Outsiders back in? Just so you can ascend to the throne? I see no reason I should help you and I still don't understand why you need me. I'm a bartender from Los Angeles. I only recently found out about my family and the Berserker power. Besides that, you're a freaking god. What can I possibly do to aid you? I doubt I would be a match against any Aesir in a fight."

Hel let out a sigh and looked at Leif like he was a child. "Ok, you need some convincing. That's fine. I can understand that."

Hel leaned towards Leif. Resting her elbows on her knees, she unclasped and re-clasped her hands, making a small clap noise. Leif thought it was a very human gesture. "I need your help to free my brother, Fenrir, the great wolf. You see long, long ago, the Norns read his fate and determined he alone had the power to kill Odin and would be the one to begin Ragnorok, the great war that kills the Aesir and ends their corrupt rule of the nine realms. Fearing Fenrir, Odin sealed him away deep under Asgard in a vault specifically designed to imprison a god. They bound him in chains of Drakenstein, a metal which was forged in Asgard's core and beset with an enchantment that allowed only one carrying the mantle of a god to unlock it." Hel said.

"So why don't you just free your brother yourself then?" Leif asked.

"I can't. I gave my word that I would do no such thing," Hel said.

"I don't understand," Leif said.

"Myself and all the other gods, even the Allfather himself are bound by ancient magic that has existed since the dawn of time. We are not all-powerful; we are governed by a strict set of ancient laws that prevent us from upending the natural order. Thus, when I gave my word to the Allfather, I was bound by that oath. However, that oath doesn't prevent me from sending my agents to free Fenrir in my stead."

"I still don't understand how freeing your brother has anything to do with me?" Leif said.

Puzzled, Hel looked at Leif. "Do you really not know what you are?" Hel demanded.

"I'm a Berserker. Thor bestowed my warrior ancestors with the power to help prevent Ragnorok."

"Yes, that is correct, but where do you think that power came from?" Hel asked.

"I don't know. I was very new to all of this when Arias told me that story. Besides, you guys are gods. I assumed you could just do things like that."

Hel laughed a deep, throaty laugh. "No, you foolish Midgardian. We can't just go around granting gifts of power to any being we see fit. Thor bestowed upon your kind a fraction of his own power. He gave the smallest amount he could, and even then your bodies struggled to survive it. It was foolish if you asked me, weakening himself like that, even if it was just an infinitesimal amount. I enjoyed watching many of the first Midgardians to receive the gift give into their bloodlust and wipe each other out. Many of the Berserker clans were wiped out within a few years of receiving the gift. Once the last living member of a Berserker family dies, that power then returns to Thor. I assumed all of your kind would be wiped out fairly quickly, but a few surprised me. It was then that the seeds of a plan germinated. None of the Aesir truly comprehended the significance of what Thor had done, but I did. By granting those warriors his strength, he also unknowingly bestowed upon them the mantle of a god. With a Berserker by my side, we can free Fenrir. Together we can overthrow Asgard, and I can get my revenge on Odin for banishing me down here."

"What's so wrong with being here?" Leif asked, side stepping the fact that Hel had just told him he was essentially a demigod.

"You just don't get it, little Berserker. I hear them all," Hel said, gesturing out over the balcony. "Do you hear that moaning? Of course, you do. Do you know what that is? Those are the cries of the dead. Oh yes, I hear them all. All those deemed not courageous enough to earn their rightful place in Valhalla come here. Do you have any idea how many innocent lives are taken across the nine realms? Those that were tortured, murdered, killed before their time? I hear them all. Over the eons, I have been tasked with overseeing those souls. They come with tales of cruelty, of pain, and being unjustly killed. And what do the Aesir do? Nothing, they sit in their plush realm and do nothing, while billions of beings are wiped out and they do NOTHING!"

The raw emotion startled Leif as he listened to Hel's plea. "I have heard their pleas, listened to their sorrows, and I concluded long ago that this injustice must stop! Back when the realms were young, the Aesir were seen as guardians, crossing from realm to realm, fighting evil wherever it sprouted up. During the early eons of Aesir control, the Outsiders attacked constantly, testing the Aesir's limits. They descended upon our realms, jealous of the Aesir, and they laid destruction and death across the realms. During that time, Odin himself would ride out from Asgard to stop the Outsider threat, to meet out justice.

"After several decades of bloody battle, the last of the Outsiders were banished from the nine realms. Once the threat of attack was eliminated, the Aesir grew lax, returning to their realm of milk and honey. For hundreds of years after the Outsiders' attack, the nine realms remained peaceful. The memory of the mighty forces Odin brought down against the Outsiders and their sympathizers kept everyone in check, but as years turned to decades then to millenniums, many of those battles moved from history to myths, or they were forgotten out right. And that's when evil began to seep back into the nine realms. Without the fear of Aesir justice or intervention, the beings of the nine realms showed their true colors again.

"You have no idea the mental anguish I have endured over the eons, hearing the pain and anguish of those lost souls in my domain. I. Have. Had. Enough!" Sorrow leaking into her voice. "My kind were supposed to protect the beings of the nine realms, and yet all the Aesir turn a blind eye to the realms, while billions of their charges suffer and die. So, I decided to step up for the good of the nine realms."

Leif was surprisingly transfixed by Hel's fervor. He leaned forward. "But how are you going to overthrow the Aesir? I mean, if I only have a fraction of Thor's power…"

Hel smiled. "Yes, my uncle is indeed powerful. In fact, he is the third most powerful being in the nine realms, only to be outshone by my brother Fenrir and the Allfather himself, but we need not worry about them. I have not been idle over the millennium. I have learned to cloak myself from the eyes of the Aesir and venture beyond the nine realms. Free from Odin's watchful eye, I contacted the Outsiders who are still itching for revenge against the Aesir. With them by my side, once I free Fenrir we will mount an all-out attack across the nine realms, forcing the Aesir out of their throne realm, spreading their forces thin. While fighting the Outsiders, they will be unprepared for an attack from Fenrir. We will kill Loki, Thor, and Odin. Once that is done, I will take the throne and usher in a new era of peace in the nine realms and beyond.

"Any who threatens that peace will receive swift justice. The Outsiders will have their revenge against the Allfather and free access to the nine realms. As long as they remain peaceful, I will allow them to move freely across the realms. They have guaranteed me that once we are successful, they will cease their attack and peace will finally reign throughout the realms. So, Berserker, I offer you a seat at my table. Join me and you will reign supreme on Midgard as my right hand," Hel said, extending her hand to Leif. "I began preparing a bridge to Fenrir's chamber the moment I brought you here. Please, Leif, if not for me, for all those innocent beings across the nine realms. You have the power to prevent their suffering."

Leif was deep in thought. *On one hand, she had a point. All across Midgard, men, women, and children are brutally murdered, tortured, or raped. The authorities back home do what they can, but there is just too much evil in the world to stop it all. And that is only in a single realm. If what Hel said is true, then these horrific acts are taking place all across the realms, and the beings that have the power to stop it are sitting back and doing nothing. If the Aesir really had returned and punished those wrong doers, it may actually scare others into submission. On the other hand, is war ever the right solution? Countless innocent beings will die. What gives her the confidence that the other beings will just allow her to rule? There will be more lives consigned to Helheim. I couldn't be a part of this asinine plan.*

In the end, there never was a question of what Leif would do. *Hel destroyed my life and killed my last two living family members. My grandfather may have been a warrior, but my mother wasn't! She was an innocent; she had no inkling of the other realms or Aesir politics. And Hel murdered her, just because she wasn't worthy enough in Hel's eyes. No! Hel must pay.*

Leif needed to escape, and fast. She had prepared the way to Fenrir's prison, so somewhere close there was a way into Asgard.

If he could get away from her, maybe he could warn the Aesir and they could stop her before it was too late. Deciding, Leif picked up his glass of Afengi and took a sip. It was smooth like honey with a hint something akin to strawberries to it; a slight burn chased the liquid down his throat. *Pretty good*, Leif thought. Leif looked up at Hel and smiled.

CHAPTER 46

L eif threw the glass at Hel, who swatted it away with a backhand flick. Hel reached out for Leif, her fanatical gaze transforming into a white-hot rage. Leif rolled forward, landing on the table that sat between them. Hel missed Leif's collar by mere inches. As Leif rolled over the table, he snatched up his twin axes. Leif tried to come up on his feet, but the chair Hel had been sitting on was too close and he ended up smashing into it. Using his forward momentum, he rolled up and over the chair, landing on his stomach on the floor behind the chair. *Damn*, Leif thought as the wind was knocked out of him. Not wanting to get caught, Leif rolled sideways to prevent Hel from grabbing him as he struggled for breath, but Hel hadn't moved from where she was standing. The rage she showed moments earlier had cooled to a contemptuous smile.

"Who do you think you are?" Hel demanded. "I am the god of death, and you refuse me? I will crush you and once I am done, I will send my forces to Midgard and make everyone you ever knew watch as I flay the skin from your bones. I will ensure that your death will be so painful that it will be all that you can remember once you are damned to Helheim."

"Wow," Leif said. "That's quite the threat from someone who

just spent the last ten minutes begging me to join her to cleanse the galaxy of suffering. You need me alive or your plan falls apart." At this point, the Berserker was raging to be freed, but he held it at bay, trying to stall and learn as much as he could before he needed to act.

"Yes, you are right. I need you alive, but not conscious." Hel said. "A few drops of your blood spread on Fenrir's locks should do the trick. It would have been nice to have you fight by my side, but if I kill you after Fenrir is freed, it's no great loss."

Knowing his time had run out, Leif allowed the red haze to fill the edges of his eyesight. Bloodlust and a desire to rip and rend Hel flooded through him. Hel blurred forward, producing a long, curved dagger from out of nowhere. Leif dodged, barely missing getting impaled through the stomach. With Hel only centimeters from Leif, he punched out with a left jab, slamming his fist into her face and sending her stumbling back. Hel tripped a little on her red dress but caught herself at the last moment.

Eyes like an electrical storm, Hel tore the lower half of her dress away, revealing her muscular legs. She kicked off her shoes and took a bladed fighting stance. With her dagger held in a reverse grip, she challenged, "Let's go, little Berserker."

Leif swung his right ax in a horizontal strike meant to take her in the shoulder. Simultaneously, he lashed out with a left hook. Hel never took her raged-filled eyes off of Leif. She blocked his ax strike with her dagger and caught his punch. She closed her left hand into a fist, and with a surge of strength, she attempted to shatter Leif's left fist, but the Berserker was stronger than she expected, and he withstood her assault. They struggled back and forth before Leif surged forward, head butting Hel in the face. She took the hit, not moving an inch. However, the attack had the desired effect on Hel. The head butt had surprised her enough to loosen her grip on Leif's fist. He pulled back and broke her grip.

Not wanting to lose his momentum, Leif swung his ax, slicing a line across Hel's thigh. A trickle of blood rolled down her leg.

Hel's eyes widened in surprise. She roared with a mixture of disbelief and anger before charging Leif. The pair moved through the room, exchanging a flurry of blows. Leif blocked many of the strikes; however, her dagger snaked through Leif's defenses, drawing a shallow cut on Leif's right forearm and leg. Leif feinted a killing strike and change directions, punching Hel in the face. With the wooden grip of his ax, he delivered a second blow in the gut, which momentarily sent Hel back a few steps.

Leif's raged filled mind kicked into overdrive after forcing Hel on the defensive, and he increased the intensity of his attack. He started taking more risks. Leif aimed his ax in a downward strike meant for Hel's right thigh, but she slapped the ax blade away with a flick of her dagger. She responded with a hard punch to Leif's ribs.

Leif fought Hel back into a corner. Thinking Hel was out of options, Leif feinted a quick kick to her injured leg but pulled back at the last moment. He then brought down both axes to bury one in her chest and the other in her neck, but faster than Leif thought was possible, Hel's hands caught both of Leif's forearms in a vice grip. Before he could react, Hel pulled him forward and kneed him in the stomach, doubling him over. She followed up with a knee to his face. Blood burst from Leif's nose and mouth as he fell back, but Hel wasn't finished. She followed Leif as he fell back, kicking him in the stomach. Leif flew backward. Sliding, then rolling, he eventually crumbled into a heap with his back braced against the balcony railing.

Blinking away the pain, Leif took a deep breath, feeling a sharp pain flare up in his ribs. Leif tried to take a deep breath again, but his lungs and aching ribs protested. Leif coughed and felt blood drip down the side of his lips. *Fuck*, Leif thought. *It was all going so well, too.*

Hel had a look of deep satisfaction on her face as she casually approached Leif. Leif was surprised to see that out of some crazy cosmic luck, both of his axes were within reach, and he could still feel the red haze of the Berserker boiling within, but the hit he had just taken quelled it somehow.

With a groan, Leif retrieved both axes, and shakily got to his feet. Pain exploded from everywhere. Hel stopped a few feet away, watching as Leif struggled to his feet and took up a fighting stance. "I have to give you credit," Hel purred. "Taking a hit like that and still kicking, you do your ancestors proud, Berserker, but it ends here."

Leif tried to respond, but he was in too much pain. He held out his axes, blades out.

Hel chuckled, then blurred into motion, not giving Leif a chance to respond. In a blink of an eye, Hel had Leif by the throat, and then to Leif's amazement, she lifted him until his feet dangled a few centimeters off the floor. Through his pain-rattled mind, Leif marveled at Hel's strength. Hel produced a small clear glass vile and held it up to Leif. She gently pressed it to the side of Leif's mouth and a trickle of blood dripped into the vile. Hel appeared satisfied, dropped Leif, and stoppered the bottle. Leif landed with a grunt and fell back onto the balcony. Hel pocketed the vile and looked down on Leif with pity in her eyes.

Snapping her fingers, two Dokkalfar warriors stepped out from a door to the side of the room. Hel said something in their singsong language and gestured towards Leif. The two Dokkalfar nodded once and took up position to either side of the door. Hel then crouched down, bringing her eyes level to his. "I'll be leaving you here for the moment. It's time to see my brother. I think a few millennia is way too long to ignore family, don't you? You and I have much to discuss once I am back." She winked and picked up his fallen axes. "I don't think you will need these anytime soon. Hmm," she murmured as she inspected the weapons. "You certainly have an eye for weapons, Midgardian. These are Svartalfar made battle axes of considerable quality. I have no idea where a Midgardian like yourself could have gotten your hands on such weapons. I will take these as a souvenir."

"You bitch! I will stop you," Leif slurred.

Hel looked down at Leif one last time, then with a swish of her torn dress she turned around and exited the room. Leif braced himself to stand up, but he slumped back down, wincing in pain before he slipped into unconsciousness.

CHAPTER 47

I t cost Leif an inordinate amount of energy to force his eyes to open. They felt like they had been shut for quite some time and wanted to remain that way. Exactly how long it had been since he had watched Hel walk away with his blood, Leif was unsure. Taking a few experimental breaths, Leif found he could breathe with only a small ache in his ribs. Slowly checking himself over, he found that several of the smaller cuts he suffered from Hel's dagger had already scabbed over. However, the deep cut he suffered to his arm still wept blood. His back and head hurt immensely, but it didn't appear that anything was broken. He had to hurry. The Aesir had no idea what was coming, and he was the only one who could stop Hel.

Leif got to his feet with a few grunts of pain. A pang of remorse shot through him at the memory of Hel's theft of his axes. Leif shook himself. *No time to dwell on it now.* Cracking his neck, he walked back through the still open balcony doors towards the two waiting Dokkalfar. Narrowing their eyes at Leif's approach, they shared a quick glance with each other and smoothly stepped forward, sliding into a defense position blocking the exit. Both Dokkalfar wore swords slung over their right shoulders. The dark handles stuck out within easy reach.

Hel must have warned them not to kill me, Leif thought. Neither guardsmen looked in a hurry to get this fight started, and Leif didn't really have the time to think of some plan, so he went for the straightforward approach. As Leif got within ten feet of the pair, he felt the familiar rush of fire as his Berserker half awoke. Many of his aches from the recent fight slipped away as strength flooded into him. The dreary Gothic room seemed to brighten slightly and to Leif's amusement, he saw for the briefest of moments a widening of the Dokkalfars' eyes as Leif embraced the red haze forming around the edges of his vision.

Leif feinted left, pulling the guard in, then instead of engaging, he sprang to the right, tackling the guard on the right, barring him to the floor. As they fell, Leif landed two solid jabs to the Dokkalfar's ribs. On the second punch, he felt a satisfying crunch as he broke several of the Dokkalfar's ribs. Leif landed on top of him and used the momentum of his tackle to roll up and over the fallen Dokkalfar. He got to his feet in a crouch. Spinning, he faced the enemies, he ducked as the other Dokkalfar rushed in close with a flurry of punches and kicks. He stayed in close, punching high, then low, each blow landing like a sledgehammer. However, after Leif's fight with Hel, the Dokkalfar's attack's felt slow. Leif could block many of their attacks, while redirecting others to less vital spots.

Leif let this go on for a few more seconds, then as the Dokkalfar struck out with a right hook, Leif stepped in, simultaneously grabbing the outstretched arm, pulling hard as he lowered his head, and he flipped the Dokkalfar up over himself, slamming him down. The air rushed out of the Dokkalfar's lungs with a painful wheeze. Not wanting to waste any more time, Leif held fast to the elf, pulling the arm taut then striking out with his other arm, breaking it at the elbow with a loud crack. Crying out, the Dokkalfar's eyes went wide.

Pain blossomed in the back of Leif's skull as the second guardsmen recovered and punched Leif from behind. Rolling with the blow, Leif came up in a guard, but it was useless. His other opponent took a page out of Leif's book and tackled him to the floor. The two rolled back and forth, struggling for control. The Dokkalfar proved far stronger than Leif would have thought. No matter what Leif did to break free, it was countered. The two struggled for a few more moments, then the Dokkalfar headbutted Leif, stunning him briefly. That moment of freedom gave the Dokkalfar all he needed. He wrapped his hands around Leif's neck and squeezed. The red haze faded to black as Leif slowly lost consciousness. Trying and failing to break the hold, Leif felt himself growing weaker. Panic and fear seeped its way into Leif's mind as he bucked and flailed uselessly. As he desperately fought to break free of the Dokkalfar's grip, Leif's hand struck something hard, and without thinking he grabbed it and brought it down into the side of his attacker's forehead, resulting in a loud crack as the hilt of the sword Leif held smashed into his attacker's temple.

Leif pulled himself away, gasping for breath as his freed lungs struggled for air. Holding out his newly acquired sword, he saw the Dokkalfar he had struck lay in a heap with a deep indent in his temple. Knowing Leif had little time, he picked up the dead Dokkalfar's sword and silently went to the door.

CHAPTER 48

L eif headed the opposite direction of Hel's room and found a wide staircase leading down. He hoped it led directly to the ground floor because he didn't have the time to look for an exit while who knows how many of Hel's underlings wandered around. The banister on each side of the staircase was made of a deep brown redwood that was polished to a sheen. Light from the candles hanging on each wall reflected off the railing as it led down the long corridor.

On silent feet, Leif peered down the staircase. At the base of the stairs, he spied another Dokkalfar guarding a large, ornate oak door.

The Dokkalfar was armored similarly to the two he had just killed. A single straight sword hung over one shoulder, which was accompanied by a small dagger shoved into his belt. Not wanting a prolonged fight with the guard, Leif walked around the edge of the railing and saw that if he could get the Dokkalfar to take a few steps away from the door he was guarding, Leif could jump down from the second-floor, landing on top of him. Not having anything but the two stolen swords, Leif walked around the edge of the stairwell until he was right where he wanted the guard to walk. He tossed one sword over the railing. It landed with a loud clang, which Leif hoped wouldn't draw any other guards to the noise. A silent moment passed, and Leif wondered if he had just made a colossal mistake. But then, slowly, Leif saw the Dokkalfar inching forward on wary feet, sword drawn. The moment the guard stepped into view, Leif jumped.

Whether it was luck or battle-hardened senses, the guard looked up the moment Leif jumped and had just enough time to roll slightly out of the way. Leif collided with the guard, face to face with the two going down in a heap. Both Leif and the guard's swords bounced off in opposite directions. Luckily for Leif, he still surprised the Dokkalfar. However, before Leif could wrap his hands around the downed guard, the Dokkalfar lashed out with a combo of punches that had Leif's head ringing. With the momentary reprieve, the Dokkalfar pressed his advantage and pushed Leif back. Leif landed hard on his back while the guardsmen scrambled to reach his fallen sword. On his back, Leif twisted and lashed out with one hand. He grabbed onto the guard's foot. and pulled the guard to the ground. Seizing the opportunity, Leif pulled himself on top of the guard.

Expecting another round of punches, Leif struck first, getting two hits to the side of the Dokkalfar's face before he brought his arm up to block. With one arm occupied with blocking Leif's onslaught of punches, the Dokkalfar reached down with his free hand, pulled the dagger free and swung up, attempting to plunge the knife into Leif's throat. Leif caught the Dokkalfar's wrist, and both struggled for control of the dagger. The guard's black eyes narrowed as Leif matched the Dokkalfar's strength. Feeling the strength of his Berserker aiding him, Leif pressed down harder, using his weight to push the dagger closer to the Dokkalfar.

A look of panic froze on the guard's face as Leif gave one last push, plunging the dagger deep into the elf's exposed throat. The Dokkalfar gasped once. Leif knew the sight of the guard's dead eyes staring up at him as he died would haunt his dreams for years to come. That was a thought for later. He didn't have the time to dwell on it ight now. Leif retrieved both swords and ran to the door.

Flinging the double doors wide open, Leif stepped onto the porch and stared out at an alien landscape straight out of George Lucas's mind. The ground beyond the porch was cracked and desert-like. Pulsing greenish light emanated from deep fissures in the ground, casting the land in a ghostly hue. No vegetation grew as far as Leif could tell. In some areas, there appeared to be small pools of water, shining with the same greenish light that escaped the fissures crisscrossing the landscape. Wraith-like beings ghosted across the terrain, causing chills to run up Leif's spine and his hands to shake. Everywhere he looked, figures wandered aimlessly. The beings seemed to congregate near the pools, but as they moved farther and farther away, they drifted apart from their fellows, choosing to walk the land alone. A few of the creatures drifted close to the house, and Leif examined them as they ghosted by. One was a Ljosalfar woman, with a gaping wound on her side. She was semi-translucent, but Leif could make out the woman's features, her clothes, and the gaping wound. A human male about ten feet from the Ljosalfar was missing an arm and a leg and sat on the ground staring into the distance. All around him Leif saw similar sights, including wounded Orcs, Jontar, and many other beings Leif had no names for. Were these the beings consigned to an eternity of pain and misery? Seeing that many of them suffering from grievous wounds, Leif could almost sympathize with Hel.

As Leif looked out over the hilly landscape, he spotted a raised platform built into the side of hill. Stairs led up to the platform that was crowned with an archway. Leif spotted three figures standing on the platform. Two of the figures stood ridged at the edge, Leif believed the third figure to be Hel. She stood directly in front of a stone archway. Hel was moving her hands and arms in a rhythmic pattern that reminded Leif of a choreographed dance. A slow breeze whistled across the landscape, increasing in intensity in rhythm with Hel's movements. Hel stamped her foot once, and the wind died suddenly. A torch-lit hallway materialized under the archway. *Huh,* Leif thought. *I guess the gods need not hunt down portals like us mortals do. That gift would have been handy a few months ago.*

Hel said something to the two guards, then disappeared through the portal. Knowing that she was mere minutes from freeing Fenrir, killing the Aesir, and starting Ragnorok, Leif sprang into action. He jumped off the front porch and began running towards the open bridge.

CHAPTER 49

As Leif ran, he tried to maintain as much distance from the wraiths as possible. For the moment, the phantoms seemed to pay the sprinting Leif no mind. As Leif got closer to the portal, the number of glowing green pools increased, and so did the number of wraiths milling around the pools. Leif dodged around numerous old, rusted pieces of armor that lay scattered across the landscape; a shield here, a helmet there, and even a few swords. One sword even still had a skeletal hand gripping the hilt. Leif wondered if they were the remains of other living beings who had stumbled upon this forsaken realm. *If these ghosts really are the forsaken spirits of living beings, they can't touch me, right?*

Leif dodged one wraith, and his foot slipped on a patch of loose gravel, causing him to stumble and fall through a Svartalfar warrior with a gaping wound to his throat and upper chest.

As Leif passed through the dead Svartalfar, a static shock-like sensation shuddered through his body. Leif came to a sliding halt a few feet past the wraith. He stopped next to a pair of intact skeletons, both clutching rusted axes. The wraith that Leif had plowed through stopped its aimless shuffling and turned to face him. The creature's placid features transformed into a mask of hate. Then it opened its mouth and a high-pitched keening sound escaped the dead Svartalfar's lips. In response to the scream, all the wraiths in the area looked up sharply and locked eyes on Leif. Their faces transformed to match the screaming wraiths. Adding to Leif's rising dread, the wraiths began shuffling, crawling, or clawing their way towards him. Not wanting to learn whether an incorporeal being can hurt him, Leif set off towards the bridge again.

As Leif ran, the wraiths continued to close in on him. Within moments, he had a veritable army of the dead hot on his heels. As Leif came within fifty yards of the archway, he could see the guards Hel posted at the top of the stairway looking down upon him with terror plastered on their faces. Leif guessed it was in response to the horde of vengeful spirits shambling their way toward them. The swell of wraiths grew so large that they effectively blocked Leif's path to the stairs. Sliding to a stop, Leif desperately looked for a way through the swarm, but all he could see was another set of old skeletons clutching rusted swords. Their toothy grins seemed to mock Leif's fate. Out of options, Leif did the only thing he could think off: he attacked. Ghostly green light reflected off the blades of his stolen swords as he lashed out at the closest wraith, but it had zero effect. The slow-moving wraith didn't so much as flinch as the sword passed through its translucent body.

The horde had begun to encircle Leif at this point, eyes full of hate and rage. The closest wraith burst into motion with surprising speed, clamping one transparent hand onto Leif's sword arm at the wrist. Searing pain radiated from the wraith's touch and Leif jerked back, grunting in pain. The pain immediately receded after Leif broke free of the spirit's grasp, but the memory of the pain was enough to forestall any rash action.

Leif continued to swing wildly at the wraiths, hoping he might hit some vital area or frighten them off, but it was no use. They showed no sign that they even registered the contact. Panic blossomed in Leif's chest as the horde continued to get closer.

A sudden motion caught Leif's attention out of the corner of his eye. At the outer edge of the ring of wraiths, a skeleton burst through the encircling wraiths. The skeleton was clad in torn and shredded leather armor. Two red-orange flames burned deep inside its eye sockets. The twin flames locked with Leif and the thing whispered in a language Leif didn't understand. For a moment, Leif assumed this was some new threat that was shambling over, but the skeleton surprised Leif by lifting a rusted battle ax gripped between bony fingers, and it cut the nearest wraith in two. There was a burst of wind and the wraith vanished.

It killed the wraith! Leif thought with a grin. The skeleton looked back at Leif and repeated what it said earlier, only more urgently. To help get its point across this time, it gestured for Leif to follow him. Not having any other options, Leif took cover behind the skeletal warrior as it hacked back and forth, cutting down any wraith that got too close. Free of the horde, his skeletal savior pointed towards the bridge, gesturing emphatically while the remaining wraiths continued their slow, deliberate gait after Leif.

"Yeah, I get it," Leif said. Leif guessed his new companion understood him because it turned back to the wraiths at their heels and charged headlong into the closest grouping, killing indiscriminately.

"Thank you!" Leif yelled as he sprinted towards the steps leading to the bridge. Taking steps three at a time, Leif was up the stairs in seconds.

The Dokkalfar posted to the left of the stairs was over-eager for a fight and sprinted forward. Leif dropped the sword in his right hand, spun past the Dokkalfar's wild stab, catching his wrist and using their combined momentum to hurl his attacker off the platform and into the roiling mass of wraiths below. The other guard, shock plain on his face, dropped his guard as he watched his companion fall from the platform. He paid for the distraction with a sword through the gut. The Dokkalfar Leif had thrown over the edge struck several wraiths on his way down, waking them to his presence. The few who weren't already climbing the stairs to get to Leif turned and converged on the Dokkalfar. Leif heard the poor souls screams as he rushed through the bridge, not risking a look back at his pursuers.

Once Leif passed through the bridge, he slowed to a walk, surveying his surroundings. He was in a stone chamber. Leif assumed it was some type of prison or vault on Asgard. The chamber was massive; it reminded him of a commercial airplane hangar back on Midgard. Leif stood on a thin concrete walkway about eight feet across. Leaning over the edge, he stared into an abyss. The walkway Leif stood on ran along the edge of the chamber. Directly in front of him there was a small bridge with no railing that reached out to connect to a massive stone cube that hung in the air at the very center of the large room. The room was illuminated by two large lanterns similar to the dancing flames Leif saw on Alfheim. Due to the sheer size of the chamber, the lanterns merely cast a low light over the entire area. The walkway led down fifty yards towards the only door Leif could see into the cubed structure. The door was open, but Leif couldn't see what was going on inside.

Leif heard the soft moaning of the wraiths through the portal behind him, and the hairs on the back of his neck stood on end. He rolled forward to put some distance between himself and the wraiths, twisting as he came to his feet, swords raised in a futile defensive position. The bridge Hel created cut right into the rock wall. To the left of the portal, Leif could see a stone double door carved with an intricate pattern and inlaid with a jet-black metal that seemed to drink in the light. Drawing his attention back to the bridge, Leif could see the wraiths were pushed right up against the opening; their translucent eyes were locked on Leif's, but they couldn't pass through it. "Thank the gods," Leif breathed. Turning, he ran down the walkway towards the open door.

CHAPTER 50

When Leif got within ten feet of the structure, he slowed. He quickly checked his swords, then he crept on silent feet towards the door. Peering in, Leif could see the building was about fifty by fifty feet inside. Four massive columns in a square pattern stood like silent guardians within the structure. All along the columns, Leif could see a swirling pattern etched into the rock, again inlaid with the odd light-drinking metal. Similarly, the patterns were on the walls of the prison cell. There were several odd etchings mixed in with massive glyphs. The glyphs were made of the black metal and ran from floor to ceiling in some areas. In the very center of the ceiling, a similar glyph was cut into the roof. Leif guessed these were part of some type of confinement magic the Aesir used to keep Fenrir imprisoned.

Fenrir was seated in the very center of the prison. Leif breathed a sigh of relief when he saw him. Instead of a massive, god-killing wolf, he was a mere man. About six feet tall, he had chin-length black hair hanging down in a wild mess around his head. He looked strikingly similar to Hel. However, while Hel's teardrop face conveyed a sense of overwhelming beauty, Fenrir's had a wild savagery to it. A scar ran from his forehead down his left eye, ending right above the edges of his mouth, which helped add to his wild countenance. Fenrir's eyes were the same lightning-blue of his sisters, which at the moment were glued to Hel.

Hel was at the edge of the boundary line of the four columns boxing in Fenrir and she had her hand outstretched, palm flat as if she was pushing against some invisible barrier. A look of excitement was spreading across Fenrir's face and Leif glimpsed sharp, fang-like teeth poking out over his lower lip. Hel looked triumphant, but profoundly exhausted. Forcing open a bridge to the prison must have been taxing on her.

Leif watched Hel's entire body tense for a split second. Then, as if with great effort, she pushed her palm forward, through whatever invisible barrier stood between her and Fenrir. A loud cracking noise spread out from where Hel stood, and for the briefest of seconds, a thousand tiny red colored cracks formed out of thin air, spreading from Hel to the open space set between the pillars. Just as fast as the cracks appeared, they vanished. Whatever barrier there had been, Hel must have destroyed it because she took a tentative step forward and nothing happened. Throwing her armored hands out wide, Hel laughed, "Brother, the time has finally come for me to free you and get revenge on those who unjustly imprisoned you. I waited and watched, and sure enough, the foolishness of our uncle opened the way to your freedom."

Gesturing to a leather pouch hung at her belt. "Today, we will begin Ragnorok, bringing Odin's reign to an end. The Aesir have grown lax in their time of peace. I have infiltrated this very prison under the nose of the Allfather, and once I free you, we will crush the Aesir together!" Fenrir gave a feral smile that sent chills down Leif's spine.

Fenrir's spoke with a rough and gravelly voice that sounded as if he hadn't used it in centuries, "Sister, I have waited for this day for a millennium, but how can we alone overthrow the Aesir?

Even with my prolonged confinement I know I can kill Odin or Thor in a one-on-one fight, but attacking them here in their seat of power with just the two of us… it would be suicide. We are outnumbered and would be quickly overrun. I do not wish to be returned to this infernal cell once I am freed, and I don't wish for you to suffer the same fate I have for the last millennium."

"Fear not, brother," Hel said. "I have made a deal with a group of Outsiders. Once you are free and attack the Aesir, I will signal for them to attack the great gates. The Allfather will not risk another invasion of the nine realms, and he will be forced to send Thor or Father to help repel their attack. With them distracted, you will be free to fulfill your destiny and kill Odin. With Odin gone, the rest of Asgard will surely fall, leaving the seat of power to the nine realms open. With you by my side, we will wipe clean the stain the Aesir left on the nine realms. We will purify the realms of evil and bring about a lasting peace, with the Outsiders on our side."

A snarl escaped from Fenrir's lips as he surged forward. He was roughly restrained by a black metal chain, fixed to a collar around his neck. "You have dealt with Outsiders?" He growled. "How can you make a deal with them? When they invaded the first time, they brought with them a war that touched all corners of the nine realms and left billions of dead. Sister, I wish for my freedom more than anything else, but aligning ourselves with those beings could spell disaster."

"Fear not," Hel said. "I have spoken with their leaders, and they do not wish to rule us like they did in the past. Now, they only wish to co-exist. They desire the freedom to travel between their realms and ours, and some have shown an interest in settling within the nine realms. And think, Fenrir, with the threat of the Outsiders gone, we will once again be free to push out past the nine realms and bring any who wish it into our kingdom. With your help, we could spell the end of the evils that Odin and his ilk have let fester within our realms. Brother, we cannot do this without the Outsiders' help. If they plan to double-cross us after Odin is dead, we will be ready for them and will fight side by side to exterminate them once and for all. So please, do not fear what hasn't come to pass yet. We must focus on the task before us."

Fenrir nodded, but he didn't look too happy. "So, how do you plan on freeing me then?" Fenrir asked.

In response, Hel reached down and with a sharp tug pulled the leather pouch free of her belt. Reaching inside, she removed the tiny vile of Leif's blood and held it up in the dim light. "The idiot Thor bestowed a fraction of his power to a group of war crazy Midgardians. Many of them, too drunk on their powers, killed themselves quickly, but a few bloodlines survived. I took this one from the last remaining member of one of those clans earlier today. With the power of Thor running through his blood, even a fraction of his blood should be enough to override the spellbinding and release you."

A wolfish grin spread across Fenrir's face, and he was visibly dancing foot to foot at the prospect of being freed. "Well, what are you waiting for? Bring it here and get this cursed chain off of me."

Hel unstopped the bottle.

CHAPTER 51

Leif knew he couldn't let Hel free Fenrir, and he felt that he had waited long enough. He burst into the room, yelling, "Hel!"

She turned at the sudden break in silence and locked eyes with Leif. The distraction worked. Leif had thrown his sword the moment he called out to Hel. So, she was caught off guard as the sword flew end over end, striking her hilt first in her outstretched arm. The vile tumbled to the chamber floor. Hel reached for the falling vile but was too slow. It hit the floor with a crack. Leif rushed in to engage Hel before she could smear the spilled blood on Fenrir's chains.

A roar ripped through the prison cell. The force of it stopped Leif in his tracks. Fenrir morphed into a gigantic grey and black wolf. The wolf had to be ten to fifteen feet from nose to tail, and Leif doubted his six-foot-one height would be any higher than the wolf's shoulders. The wolf, with its lightening blue eyes and scarred face, sent a chill down Leif's spine as it let loose a growl that would have caused an avalanche.

Leif knew that this was the time that Arias spoke about. He needed to allow the Berserker and himself to become one. He needed to trust himself and allow his power to extend his abilities rather than overtake him. He could no longer be Leif and the Berserker, but he had to become Leif the Berserker. Letting his resolve at stopping Hel wash over him, Leif opened himself fully to the Berserker. Fear, hesitation, and uncertainty all vanished at that moment and were replaced with rage. Rage at what Hel had done to his family. Rage at the death of Arias. Rage at her arrogance. The typical red haze solidified, casting the area with a red tinge. Leif knew it was now or never, so he slipped into a guard position. With his remaining sword held low, the blade's angle protected his torso.

"We end this here! Let's see if gods can die," Leif growled.

Behind Hel, Fenrir bared his dagger-sharp teeth at Leif and strained against his chains. Somewhere in the back of Leif's mind, he knew those chains had held for thousands, maybe millions of years, so as long as he stayed out of reach of Fenrir, he would be safe. Leif's words must have struck a nerve with Hel because her jubilance vanished.

Standing to her full height, Hel cracked her neck and reached down and unhooked a set of familiar looking axes. Twirling them slightly, Hel smiled as Leif recognized his grandfather's axes.

"You go too far, Midgardian. It really is a pity. Your kind are so weak and feeble-minded, but you had so much potential. Now, I may just give Midgard over to the Outsiders. Peace in eight realms will have to be enough. It's a shame that you won't be alive to see it."

Hel and Leif faced each other. Leif wanted Hel to move away from Fenrir, so he held himself back, forcing Hel to come to him. Leif noticed Hel was moving less gracefully than their last fight. Hel looked a little wild around the eyes, but she maintained a calm demeanor. Leif was a boiling ball of fury. The Berserker boiled and hissed inside, demanding justice for his family. He fought to keep it at bay, at least for a little while longer. The moment stretched out for a millennium, then they moved.

Leif, focusing all his pain and anger, pushed the Berserker to its limits as he moved to meet Hel. Steel flashed quicker than the human eye could follow. Hel had the advantage of speed and experience, but Leif noted that she wasn't as fast as she had been. The twin axes struck here and there, high then low, together and apart.

Leif focused solely on deflecting her strikes, pushing them aside or dodging. The two moved as dancers in a performance. Back and forth they fought across Fenrir's prison. Leif felt the slow burn of fatigue, and he worried he would slow, but he relied on the Berserker to keep him fighting. As Hel pushed Leif closer and closer to Fenrir, she slipped through Leif's defenses. A white-hot line of fire tore across Leif's cheek as the ax blade ripped a shallow cut along his face. Leif flung himself backward, knowing Hel's follow up would be seconds behind. But Leif took one step too far and Fenrir made him pay for it. A massive black paw flashed out and struck Leif in the side, sending him flying. Leif came down in a heap, rolling with the momentum of the strike. On the floor, Leif coughed, and blood splattered the ground. *Fuck, that hurt,* Leif thought.

The soft clicking sound of Hel's armor was the only warning of a follow up attack. Leif's body reacted on its own, reaching out to snatch up his fallen blade and bring it up in an overhead block. A second later, both of Leif's stolen axes clanged down. The two enemies glared at each other as they struggled for control. Leif was at a severe disadvantage on the floor, and Hel knew it. With a savage push, Leif got his feet back under him and pushed Hel away just for a moment, which was all he needed. Both of Hel's hands went wide, leaving her temporarily defenseless. Leif struck out with a horizontal strike that scored a deep cut across her armor. The force of the blow pushed her back a few steps, and Leif followed up with a solid right hook that connected with Hel's jaw, but she refused to fall. Not wanting to lose his momentum, Leif cut and slashed, hoping that one of his attacks would get through, but Hel's armor took each hit without breaking. Leif failed to draw blood, but he knew the force of the blows still had to hurt.

Hel regained her balance, and the two were once again moving back and forth across the prison chamber as their blades flashed between them. Hel landed a few more slashes, one to Leif's arm and another across his chest, but they were shallow.

After taking a hard kick to the shins, Hel was limping on one leg and blood dripped from her nose where Leif had punched her. As their duel dragged on, Leif could see Hel was growing frustrated. Her attacks became more frantic and less controlled.

Leif dodged another slice from his former axes. He noticed Hel's armor near her abdomen was thinner than the rest. He guessed that was to allow more freedom of movement. Leif knew if he could get in one good strike there, he could end the fight. He switched to a more defensive approach. His blood howled for him to press the attack, but he held strong. Leif knew he would need all the Berserker's strength to get past Hel's defenses and hopefully end the fight. Seeing the weakness in their foe's defenses was more than enough to quell the fanatical lust for carnage and move as synchronized berserked warrior, waiting for the perfect moment to strike.

Continuing to block and push aside Hel's attacks, Hel grew impatient and attempted to feign a charge. She followed it up with a horizontal attack. She attacked high then low, but Leif saw through it, and instead of reacting to the faint, he thrust forward with all his might and was rewarded with a gasp of pain from Hel. Leif's blade pierced Hel's armor below the chest plate and sunk deep into her abdomen.

The whole prison shook from the howl of rage that burst from Fenrir. Leif pulled the blade out and was satisfied to see deep crimson blood dripping from the blade. Hel dropped the stolen axes as her hands flew to her stomach, blood seeping between her clasped fingers.

Raising one blood-soaked hand to the sky, Hel said something in a language that Leif didn't understand. The words hung in the air longer than they should have. Leif felt the familiar tingle of magic. Not knowing what to expect, Leif stood his ground, but he was wary of his surroundings. Hel slammed her hand down, leaving a bloody handprint on the stone floor. The tingling sensation vanished, and a loud popping sound echoed from somewhere outside the prison cell. A few heartbeats later, the familiar moan of wraiths crept into the cell. Leif knew there was only one way in or out of Fenrir's prison, and Hel had just cut it off.

The flame lantern above shifted from the typical orange of a normal fire to a deep pulsing blue that sent the entirety of Fenrir's prison cell into a flickering chaos of light and darkness. Tearing his eyes away from the lantern, Leif looked back to where Hel had been kneeling. She was gone.

Leif was suddenly struck from the side and sent sprawling to the chamber floor. Leif felt a burning sensation as a hand pressed down on the cut to his cheek. Leif yelled as the pressure increased. He tried to rise, but excruciating pain bloomed in his right thigh. Leif stared into Hel's blazing eyes as she released the sword hilt.

She had somehow reappeared and had driven Leif's sword through his thigh and into the floor below, pinning Leif. Pulling her hand back from Leif's face, he could see blood smeared across her palm from his wounded cheek.

"Well, it looks like I won't get to prolong your death after all," Hel said as she stepped away and half stumbled towards Fenrir, who had changed back into his human form. "I am sad I won't get to see the wraiths tear your soul apart as you lay trapped." Turning to Fenrir, she continued, "I have alerted the Aesir to my presence and so we must flee before the Allfather sends reinforcements. Alas, brother, we will not be getting your promised revenge today, but with you free, it won't be long till we stand as rulers of the nine realms."

Hel limped to Fenrir, smeared Leif's blood across the collar, and the lock silently popped open, falling to the floor with a loud clang. Fenrir took a step towards Leif, but a restraining hand from Hel held him back.

"Brother, we don't have the time, the Aesir are most certainly on their way. I am injured, there is no way we can fight them off. We must flee now and regain our strength." Fenrir nodded silently.

Fenrir fixed Leif with a stare that caused him to shrink back. "You are lucky Midgardian, if it weren't for my sister staying my hand, I would tear you apart. Know this, if you survive this ordeal, one day I will come calling to settle this," Fenrir said. The pair then turned and sprinted through the open door.

CHAPTER 52

L eif slumped back. The pain in his leg was excruciating, but he didn't have the strength to pull the sword free of the stone floor. The moaning grew louder. The first of the wraiths reached the door and were creeping towards him. As they closed within twenty feet of Leif, a sound like thunder rumbled through the chamber, and then a bolt of lightning screamed down from the ceiling and struck the floor between Leif and the hungry wraiths.

A mountain of a man stood in the exact spot the lightning had struck. He wore chain and plate armor made from the same light-drinking metal of the glyphs on the walls of the prison chamber. The man wore no helm, and his golden blond hair fell in waves to his shoulders. The man held a hammer in his left hand. Both the head of the hammer and the handle were made of the same black material as the man's armor. Leif could see an angular pattern of bright silver etched into the head of the hammer that wound itself down the handle.

A moan sounded in front of Leif and his attention was drawn back to the swarm of wraiths that poured into Fenrir's empty prison cell. Leif wanted to shout a warning to the man, but he couldn't muster the strength. The prolonged fight with Hel and the sword rammed through his leg removed what strength he had left.

Leif watched as the man lifted the hammer high above his head and intoned in a voice like a thunderclap, "BE GONE, FOUL BEINGS!" Then a sound like crashing thunder and a blinding white flash filled the prison cell. A moment later, the wraiths were gone. With the threat dealt with, Leif's savior turned to him with a bright smile on his chiseled face. Leif tried to speak, but it was as if his tongue was made of lead. The man kneeled down and said, "Be at peace, friend. You have done well." Leif passed out from blood loss.

WHEN LEIF WOKE, he once again found himself in an unfamiliar bed. *I've really got to stop waking up like this*, Leif thought. Leif pulled the covers back, and pain burst all over his body. He noted he was covered in bandages. There wasn't one part of his body that didn't hurt. Pulling his eyes away from the blanket of bandages, he looked out over the unfamiliar room.

Soft golden light shone down from several dancing flame lanterns set high on the walls. Similar to Hel's mansion, the tapestries and murals around the room depicted glorious battles frozen in time. Peeling himself out of bed, Leif spotted his clothes and limped and shambled over to the chair they were dropped over. To Leif's relief, his grandfather's axes rested next to his clothes. Picking the garments up, Leif immediately knew they weren't his. Looking around, Leif didn't see any other clothes, so he decided to put them on. Pain shot across his body as he lifted his arms over his head to put on the white short-sleeve shirt. With each movement, the pain would steal his breath away. The pants were forest green and silky soft. After a few seconds to catch his breath, Leif pulled on his socks and his shoes. He clipped the twin axes back on to his belt and breathed a sigh of relief at the familiar weight.

With a slight limp and a lot of internal cursing, Leif shuffled to the heavy door set against one wall. An ornate tree intricately carved into the wood. Near the bottom of the door, he spotted a small waterfall flowing down into a lake. The sting of the Norns' fate flooded his mind.

Leif's head hurt as he thought back over all that had happened. He figured it was time to find out where he was, and if he was lucky, maybe find some Advil. Opening the fancy door, Leif was confronted with an armed guard.

The guard nodded to Leif. "Follow me," he said in a thick-accent. He then turned and walked down the ornate hallway at a fast march without waiting for Leif to respond.

Following the guard, Leif glimpsed the outside world through randomly spaced windows. The cloudless blue sky covered a sprawling city beyond, but it was unlike any city Leif had seen in his life. The entire landscape had a dreamlike quality to it, as if Leif had stepped into some futuristic science fiction world. The guard, who never once looked back to see if Leif was following, finally stopped at the door at the end of the hallway, waiting for Leif to catch up. Once Leif was within a few feet of him, the guard pulled the door open, gesturing Leif through.

Leif was ushered into a massive corridor. Immense statues lined each side. Each was so finely carved, Leif half expected one to step down and ask him for directions. Armed guards similar to Leif's escort lined the walls on either side. Their bodies were just as still as the statues above, but their eyes were in constant motion, scanning and tracking the myriad of beings that moved through the massive corridor. The beings all looked similar to humans or Ljosalfar, but there was also something very different about them that Leif couldn't pin down. Leif had slowed to gawk at all the people, but a gentle push from his escort got Leif moving again. The guard led Leif toward a set of double doors easily thirty feet tall at the end of the chamber.

The same carving of Yggdrasil was inlaid into these doors, only on a much grander scale. To either side of the door stood two guards similar to his escort, but instead of their armor being entirely black, theirs included a vibrant red stripe across their right breast plate. The armor looked truly amazing, and Leif guessed it was a designation of some kind, maybe royal guards. As Leif's escort stepped up to the door, the two royal guards pushed open the massive doors. The doors swung inward silently, and Leif was ushered in.

The guards quickly closed the door behind him. The room was circular. The central feature was a raised platform in the middle of the room. Two figures flanked a bearded man sitting on a high-backed throne. Behind the three figures a floor to ceiling window showed off the majesty of the realm beyond. Leif wanted to run to the window and drink in all that he could see, but he restrained himself. The thump of a gauntleted hand striking the armrest drew Leif's attention to the three figures. Leif was keenly aware at that moment that all three of the beings were staring at him. Their lightening blue eyes never wavered from his face.

Leif was still at the very edge of the room, so he stepped up to the imposing figures and met the gazes of the three figures. The figure on the left sneered, intoning, "You show such disrespect to the Aesir, Midgardian?" The man was tall, almost as tall as the mountain of the man standing to the right, which Leif recognized as the person who had saved him from the wraiths. The man who spoke wore the same armor as the two others, though Leif could tell he wasn't as comfortable in it as the other two. The speaker's hair was the same gold blond of the others, but his was cut much shorter and stylized. Leif would not have been surprised to see him in a modeling magazine back on Midgard.

"Be at peace, brother," the figure on the right soothed. He then continued. "This Midgardian quite possibly saved our lives by his brave deeds in the vaults below. If Hel had been free to release Fenrir and attack us, we may have passed on to the beyond, leaving the nine realms unprotected. Give him a little respect." Turning back to face Leif, the figure smiled then winked before resuming his stoic demeanor.

The figure on the left opened his mouth to respond, but a thump from the seated figure's gauntlet stopped him, drawing Leif's attention to him. His hair and beard were unlike the other two. It was white with age. The man looked to be in his sixties, with slight wrinkles around his eyes and mouth, but he wasn't weakened by age. He was built like a truck. Though he was covered in armor, the smoothness with which he moved gave Leif the impression that this was no retirement home elder, but a force to be reckoned with. The eye patch over his left eye didn't cover the entirety of a scar that peeked out from the bottom. The eyepatch tugged on Leif's little knowledge of the Allfather.

A loud ca-caw echoed from somewhere above. The sound was so unexpected, Leif nearly jumped. Two ravens flew down from the rafters and perched themselves on the high-backed chair. "Young Berserker, long ago, I advised against my son's desire to reward your ancient ancestors with the gift of power you now hold. And for the most part, I was right. The power gifted to those warriors drove them mad with rage and battle lust. Many perished after gaining the power. However, to my surprise, a few clans survived and mastered the Berserker within, eventually becoming formidable warriors. I was right to counsel against the gift, as we all can see now. With Fenrir on the loose because of an unforeseen loophole in the magic that bound him, the safety of the nine realms hangs in the balance. However, just as a trained wolf can bite the hand that feeds it, it can also protect its owner. And luckily for the nine realms, you redeemed my son's foolish actions by facing Hel, causing her to make a hasty mistake. And for that, I, Odin, the Allfather, protector of the nine realms, thank you. You have achieved a feat that no mortal in their wildest dreams could have hoped to accomplish, you have my gratitude and I wish you well. Now, be gone." Odin slammed his gauntlet hand down in two quick strokes. The booming sound resounded around the chamber, alerting the guards that the meeting was over. The doors opened up behind him.

That's it? Leif thought. *What about my murdered family?* Leif seethed. "Hel and Fenrir are still out there. They killed my family," Leif yelled. "Hel will be back; she is insane! They must be stopped." Leif hadn't meant to, but as he spoke, he had inadvertently taken a few steps closer to the three Aesir. Leif realized he had overstepped, but it was too late.

"Silence your tongue," the figure that Leif assumed was Loki hissed. "You dare show such insolence? You are lucky I don't flay the skin from your bones for what you did to my daughter. You should know better, mortal. Go back to Midgard and do not concern yourself with the happenings of the Aesir." Loki shook with rage, and Leif feared he might have pushed them a little too far.

Luckily, Thor stepped down and moved between himself and the angry Aesir. "Control yourself, Loki. This man fought bravely and saved us. Hel will recover, and when we find her, we will put an end to this minor rebellion she has started. Do not worry yourself."

Thor turned away from his seething brother and with a nod, gestured for Leif to follow him out of the throne room.

CHAPTER 53

F ollowing Thor through the exit, Leif noticed that every being they passed upon seeing Thor, would immediately stop what they were doing and bow. Thor for his part responded with a kind smile and a nod. The duo went down a few tapestry-filled hallways and up way too many stairs for Leif's liking, but they eventually stopped before a plain, unadorned wooden door. "I am proud of you, young Berserker. I, too, have shared my father's misgivings about the gift I bestowed upon your ancestors, but then you came along. You were thrown into the greater universe, and instead of running and hiding, you stepped up and fulfilled your kind's very purpose; to aid myself and the Aesir in Ragnorok. Now you must rest and recover because just as you said, Hel and Fenrir are still out there. I know my niece and nephew; they will not stop. A time may come when you are called upon to take up arms against those who wish to bring about the end of the peace that myself, Loki, and the Allfather have fought so hard to maintain."

Leif was so shocked at what Thor was saying that Leif took a few moments to respond. "Um, sir, so it's not over? I mean, you will go after Hel and Fenrir, right?" Leif asked.

"Of course," he said and clapped Leif on the shoulder. "It is our job, isn't it? I'm sure they are off hiding in some small corner of a realm nursing their wounds, but they will be back. But that's in the future, so don't worry too much. For now, it is time for you to return to your realm." Thor knocked on the door.

"Ok," Leif said, "But I have so many questions. There are things I need to know."

Thor smiled, "Ah, I had forgotten about your people's undying thirst for knowledge and understanding. Ok, Leif, I will answer one question before you go," Thor said.

A myriad of questions flew through Leif's mind. But in the end, he knew what he needed to ask. "My Mom and Grandfather, they aren't on Helheim suffering for all eternity, right?"

A wide grin spread across Thor's face. "Of course not," he boomed as he slapped Leif on the shoulder, nearly knocking him over. "Your grandfather lived a life of honor and made your ancestors proud at every turn. And in the end, he went down fighting like only a Berserker could. You should be proud to be his grandson and inheritor of the Berserker. And your mother, though she was never trained as a warrior, bravely fought Hel's minions. No, my friend. Be at peace knowing neither of your kin were banished to that cursed realm."

Leif breathed a sigh of relief at knowing his family's fate. But even knowing did little to alleviate the sadness their murders brought to his's heart. He can only hope that one day, if he was deemed worthy to walk through the gates of Valhalla, that he would get to see them again.

Just then, the door they were standing in front of opened and a tall woman stood in the doorway. She was over six feet tall, with brunette hair that disappeared down her back. She had a teardrop face similar to a Ljosalfar's and had the same lightning blue eyes of the other Aesir he had met. Her mouth was turned up in a smile as she regarded the two at the door. "Ah, I was wondering when you two would stop by." Her voice was soothing to Leif's ears. "This must be the Berserker everyone has been talking about." The woman turned her eyes towards Leif and looked him up and down. "So young for one to have defeated Hel. If it hasn't been said yet, we of Asgard thank you. I know your road was filled with death and dangers, but you should be proud. It is those same trials that shaped you into the warrior you are today." Then she bowed ever so slightly in Leif's direction.

"Well said, Heimdall," Thor said, clapping her on the shoulder before stepping into the room. Leif followed, but only after Heimdall inclined her head that it was ok.

Heimdall closed the door behind them and walked over to lean against the wall next to a roaring fire. Above the fireplace, there was a small horn hanging by its strap.

"Heimdall," Thor said, "I know it has been a while since we have deemed it necessary to open the Bifrost, but I believe our young friend here has earned his rest. We sealed it off at the end of the Outsider's war, but I believe dark times are coming, and we will need the Galajhorn once again. Sending Leif back using the Galajhorn can be a test run to ensure it hasn't lost its power. What do you think?" Thor asked.

It sounded like Thor was trying to send him home.

Heimdall had a pained expression on her face as she regarded Thor. "It was the Allfather himself who closed the Bifrost and retired the Galajhorn for times such as this," she gestured to the horn. "If it got into our enemies' hands, there isn't much we could do from stopping them from appearing anywhere in the nine realms and wreaking havoc."

Thor looked like he wanted to respond, but Heimdall held up her hand to forestall him. "But, after the events of the past few days and Hel's perplexing ability to force open a gateway into Asgard itself, I believe you are right. The Bifrost must be opened again, and Asgard must be ready to ride out to stop Hel and whoever is backing her." As Heimdall spoke, she unhooked the horn from the wall, and gestured for Leif to follow her to a door at the other side of the room.

Thor reached up and clasped Leif's shoulder. Then looked Leif right in the eyes, "Be proud Leif. You have been given a substantial gift. The power bestowed upon you is both a blessing and a curse. There is a reason many of your kind died out long ago or lived in isolation. The rage that pairs with the strength will always be there, inside you, clawing to get out. You have demonstrated an impressive ability to master it; continue your training lest you lose what control you have. Until next time, farewell. I hope you can return home and live a quiet life of Midgard, but I fear you will be pulled back into this war before you know it. So, rest, train, and be ready. Hel will not forget the slight you caused her."

Leif swallowed. "Wow, you really know how to make a guy feel good, don't you?" Leif said.

Thor smiled, "Ha! You are a warrior now. You are used to excitement and danger, and that is what the Berserker craves. Heed my words. The power you now wield is a tool of immeasurable power." Thor reached into a pouch at his waste and pulled out a small obsidian looking rock and handed it to Leif. Opening his palm, Leif could see the rock was as black as the sky on a starless night. It was carved like Thor's hammer. Leif looked up, a question on his lips.

"It is made of the same material as my hammer, Mjolnir. This will mark you as one of my chosen warriors. Press this against the Curvoc of a closed bridge and let a trickle of your Berserker out and it will open the bridge for you."

Leif's eyes widened as he digested what Thor had just said. *I can travel the realms?* "Thank you!"

Thor walked up to Hemidall, who was standing in front of the door. She reached up and grasped Leif on the shoulder, turned him towards the door and said, "Now picture the door that leads into your home. Once you have it fixed in your mind, nod your head."

Leif searched through his memories of life back on Midgard. It felt like another life now. He pictured the front door to his apartment. The number 117 on the outside, the slate gray of his apartment door, the brass doorknob and peephole. Once he had it, he nodded.

"Good," Heimdall said, then she brought the horn to her lips and blew. The tingle of magic pulsed at the base of Leif's skull as the sound reverberated out of the horn and into the distance. Leif could feel the magic of the horn stretch out past the door they stood in front of and into the abyss. A moment or two passed before Hemidall reached forward and opened the door. Shocked, Leif saw that the door had opened into his apartment.

Heimdall let go of Leif's shoulder and nodded towards him. "Farewell Leif. You have earned your rest." Leif stepped through and Heimdall closed the door behind him, cutting the link to the Bifrost.

Sighing, Leif unhooked his axes and set them down on his battered coffee table within easy reach of the couch. He then slumped down, resting his head on his couch's armrest with a groan and promptly went to sleep.

END

ACKNOWLEDGMENTS

I would like to thank Amy. Your constant love and encouragement over the course of writing this book was the fuel that kept me going, especially on those days when I questioned my writing abilities.

Natascha and Jessica my alpha readers, words cannot express how grateful I am to you two. You took time out of your busy schedules to wade through the disaster that was my early drafts. I laughed and cringed several times as I read through your comments and critiques.

Stacey, I am so thankful to have you as my editor. You took my manuscript and turned it into a story that I am proud to say is mine. Your guidance and mentoring during each step of the editing and publishing process was a godsend that made the process way smoother than I could have ever hoped! Thank you and I can't wait to work with you again on Accession!

ABOUT THE AUTHOR

Kevin D. Miller is an attorney in Southern California who spends two hours a day commuting to work while either listening to sci-fi/fantasy books or plotting out the storylines for the books he plans to write. When he isn't working, Kevin can be found spending time with his girlfriend, Amy, their two dogs, Pepper and Riley. He enjoys writing, playing video games, hiking and kayaking in Big Bear, and enjoying the ocean air in Newport Beach.

twitter.com/bifrost_books
instagram.com/bifrost_books

FROM KEVIN MILLER
AUTHOR OF THE AWAKENING

ACCENSSION

BOOK TWO IN THE
BERSERKER SERIES

COMING SOON

Made in the USA
Monee, IL
22 April 2021